EVELYN LOVED THEM WITH ALL THE FIRE OF HER HEART . . .

COUNT ALEXIS LEZENSKI: The dashing Polish aristocrat swept his child bride from London to the palaces of the czar—until revolution drove them to Shanghai, and desperation drove Evelyn into another man's arms . . .

DR. FISCHER: The mysterious Viennese expatriate commanded an empire in China—and a contraband network throughout the world. He would surround Evelyn with luxury, but his greatest gift would be knowledge: the secret of survival, and a black-market empire that would one day be her own . . .

MORGAN VALENTINE: Evelyn's wastrel brother, once *her* best and only friend. His looks were his fortune, until greed led him to plunder his sister's daughter, and her vast, seductive wealth . . .

VICTORIA LEZENSKI: Evelyn's lovely daughter harbored a lifelong resentment against the mother she barely knew. Morgan would give her more than she'd ever dreamed: a passion both fiery and forbidden, and the chance to confront her past . . .

MILES FOSTER: He made love with no apologies, war with no regrets—until Evelyn, the aging beauty he'd come to conquer, stole his calculating heart . . .

Most Pocket Books are available at special quantity discounts for bulk purchases for sales promotions, premiums or fund raising. Special books or book excerpts can also be created to fit specific needs.

For details write the office of the Vice President of Special Markets, Pocket Books, 1230 Avenue of the Americas, New York, New York 10020.

POCKET BOOKS

New York   London   Toronto   Sydney   Tokyo

This book is a work of fiction. Names, characters, places and incidents are either the product of the author's imagination or are used fictitiously. Any resemblance to actual events or locales or persons, living or dead, is entirely coincidental.

Another *Original* publication of POCKET BOOKS

POCKET BOOKS, a division of Simon & Schuster Inc.
1230 Avenue of the Americas, New York, N.Y. 10020

Copyright © 1988 by Evan Jeon and the estate of Stuart Buchan
Cover artwork copyright © 1988 Charles Gahms

All rights reserved, including the right to reproduce
this book or portions thereof in any form whatsoever.
For information address Pocket Books, 1230 Avenue
of the Americas, New York, N.Y. 10020

ISBN: 0-671-61970-5

First Pocket Books printing September 1988

10 9 8 7 6 5 4 3 2 1

POCKET and colophon are trademarks of
Simon & Schuster Inc.

Printed in the U.S.A.

For Evan Jeon

"O ghost, stay with me yet awhile, I must
Suffer before I join this Chinese dust:
Once more with face uplifted to the sky
Must call for bombs and fire to cool my blood."

—Emily Hahn, CHINA TO ME

Prologue

Peking, 1924

Evelyn Lezenski watched the line of mourners as they shuffled their way toward the Manchu tombs. The coffins of the Grand Duke Nicholas and his sister Grand Duchess Elizabeth, carried with the White armies across Russia and into China, rocked on the shoulders of their bearers. The setting sun hid the worst patches and stains on the clothes of all that was left of the court of St. Petersburg.

Evelyn stopped, holding onto the hand of Victoria, her eight-year-old daughter. The child was pale. The journey from Shanghai in the unheated carriage on hard seats had tired her; they had ridden in the train's third-class section with the Chinese peasants.

Ahead, Evelyn's husband, Count Alexis Lezenski, stopped and turned, looking back with a flash of his old imperious anger. His face was lined well beyond his forty-nine years, and his once thick gold hair had faded to white. He wore a dirty white tunic, the remains of the uniform of an officer in the czar's lost navy. "Hurry!" he called.

"Come," Evelyn whispered to Victoria, "it's not far now." At twenty-six, she was exhausted by the events that had overtaken the world and herself since her marriage to Alexis during the peaceful European summer of 1914. She could feel the smaller stones through the soles of her shoes and wondered if her daughter's shoes were sturdy enough for the climb up the last hundred yards to where the ruined Manchu tombs stood on the lower slopes of the western hills, waiting to offer temporary sanctuary to the bones of the imperial Russian dead.

Temporary. For a moment Evelyn was overwhelmed with despair. That was hunger, she told herself as she leaned down to pick up Victoria. The child was unnaturally light. She seldom had either enough food or fresh air in the dark, smoky room in the Chinese section of Shanghai where they now lived.

Temporary, her mind repeated as she stumbled after the winding line of shabby mourners, but she was unconvinced. She knew that the émigrés, led by Admiral Kowalski, had fought for this refuge for the grand duke and grand duchess, and that they were only reconciled to the resting place because they still believed that soon, soon they would all be going back to St. Petersburg.

Breathless, Evelyn stopped. The nearest tomb had been looted, she saw; that shouldn't have surprised her. The last of the Manchus had been deposed in 1911. There was a child emperor somewhere, locked away as a political pawn, but he had no power and never would.

The column was turning. The coffins slid back slightly on the shoulders of their bearers, and a rustle of confusion passed through the lines of mourners, their once-grand uniforms and dresses moving and shifting in a kaleidoscope of faded colors. The coffins moved ahead.

Evelyn stopped. Tears came to her eyes. The futility of it, she thought, the futility... The column moved across a ledge toward the tomb that had been prepared for its new occupants. The sun was sinking quickly now, red shadows racing across the hills. Evelyn looked back toward the distant sight of the Forbidden City, gold in the last of the afternoon's rays, and as the sun disappeared behind the hills the city faded from gold to brown and then was lost in the falling shadows.

As she turned back toward the funeral procession, the wind rose. The tattered double eagle of the imperial family's crest had been raised above the gates to the tomb. The black birds against their torn white silk background fluttered over the gathered mourners like vultures.

Alex beckoned angrily to Evelyn as she staggered forward with Victoria in her arms. She stumbled over the top of the ridge as the first of the Russian anthems, low and solemn, moaned in the gathering darkness. She put the frightened child on her feet and held her hand tightly, but before moving toward the wailing mourners she looked back once more toward the old capital of the Manchus. All she saw was darkness, a long plain of shadow, and, above, a sky pierced with the first light of new stars.

"I will get away," she vowed silently, holding her child's hand as the sad Russian hymn swelled to fill the night with heartbreak. "I will not die with them. I will live."

BOOK
ONE

1914

1

"Vulgar, isn't it?" Morgan Valentine said, looking down from his sister's bedroom window at the twin flags, Russian and British, hanging above the front door in the hot June afternoon.

"Don't, please, Morgan," Evelyn Valentine pleaded as she adjusted her wedding veil. Turning, she asked, "How will I look?" The sight of her seventeen-year-old brother leaning with his back against the window frame, one leg up on the sill, made her heart give a little stagger. She would miss Morgan, she realized all at once, more than she would miss anyone else when she left England tonight with her new husband.

Morgan turned his sulky, handsome face, eyes as bright as sapphires in the shadow of the bedroom, to stare at her. His blond hair fell over his brow and curled over his collar. "Ravishing," he murmured. "That old Russian will have his hands on you before the train has pulled out of Paddington."

"Morgan, *please!*" Evelyn exclaimed, the blood coloring her pale peaches-and-cream cheeks. Her mother had virtually forbidden her to go outside all spring and summer so she would look suitably fresh and pale for her wedding to Alex: during the best weather in a century, Evelyn had been forced to watch from the mullioned windows of the family's country house while her beloved brother rode, bathed in the lake, and played tennis. "And he's not old," she added.

"Thirty-nine is old," Morgan pronounced. He looked like an advertisement in his starched shirt and morning coat; like everything about Morgan, somehow his attire was exactly right yet completely unstudied. There was something common, Evelyn had heard her father say, about the way Morgan looked, a comment that in itself said all that needed to be said about the relationship between father and son. Morgan looked perfect, whereas Sir John's vices were apparent on his loose-skinned face and red-veined eyes for all to see. Yet they shared many common interests. They both liked women, drink, and gambling.

"Not for a man," Evelyn said. She stood up, pushing away the long Brussels lace veil held by a coronet of cabbage roses. "A man is only beginning his best years at forty," she said, echoing Alexis's mother's lectures.

"Does he kiss you?" Morgan asked suddenly.

His sister stopped, stooping once to get a closer look at her own face in the mirror. She knew the tone: he was angry. His rages, like their father's, could take the house apart in half an hour, but in half an hour he had to be at St. Margaret's for her wedding. "Yes," she said, but her voice was half a whisper.

"What's it like?" he asked her, still in the same half-repressed voice of fury.

Not much fun, was the answer she wanted to give, but a warning bell of caution deep inside her head stopped her. "Very nice," she said instead, standing quickly and throwing out her arms so he could see slim bridal gown, lace over antique satin, open very slightly at the throat and across the shoulders to show what her mother thought of as her best assets: her long, noble neck and very good bosoms.

"You look like a tart," Morgan said, but his voice was half-amused again. Evelyn wondered if he'd had a drink already.

"I do not!" she protested.

"It doesn't matter anyway," Morgan said, reaching into his breast pocket for his platinum cigarette case. It had materialized suddenly early this summer after he spent a week cruising with Lady Cavendish on the Cavendish yacht. "You'll be a countess in an hour, and there are separate rules for countesses." He was smiling by the time he finished speaking, looking at his sister appraisingly as he snapped a gold Dunhill lighter into flame and then drew in a long breath of tobacco smoke. He said, "You look beautiful, Evvy," in quite a different voice. Then, as the tears threatened to flood her gray eyes, he continued, "Are you sure you want to marry Alex?"

No. Yes. Not yet. But before she could answer, the door behind her opened, and their mother stood there, wrapped from head to toe in emerald satin, a statuesque hat of osprey feathers held by a diamond brooch perched on her head, tiny white kid shoes just visible under her long skirt. "What are you doing?" she said.

"Dressing," Evelyn told her, blinking back the tears.

"Morgan, what are you doing in here?" his mother demanded. "You're supposed to be on your way to St. Margaret's. You have to be there before the royals arrive."

Morgan sighed, blowing out a long plume of smoke. "Will they banish me if I'm late?" he asked. "Perhaps I could go off with Evvy. I wouldn't mind that." He looked out at the perfect weather; sunlight dappled the park in the center of the square. "Russia has to be more interesting than England just now."

"You don't know when you have it all right," his mother told him. Morgan's mouth tightened at the corners. "I suppose not," he said.

"Why aren't your bridesmaids here?" their mother asked, looking about the room.

"I told them to go to the church."

"Lady Anne, too?"

Evelyn looked with dislike at her mother. "Yes. You know I'd never met her before last week."

"She's your cousin," her mother told her.

"And the daughter of a duke," Morgan reminded his sister, smiling conspiratorially.

"And none of them ever wanted anything to do with us until Alex asked me to marry him."

"Alex!" her mother breathed with satisfaction.

"Count Alexis Lezenski," Morgan said, rolling out the title. "First naval attaché to His Imperial Majesty, Czar Nicholas of Russia's embassy to England."

"Did you see what the king and queen sent?" Lady Valentine asked.

"It was difficult to miss," Morgan said. "Sitting as it was all alone on a table among the gifts. I thought it a very modest little silver bowl. The queen probably pulled it from the attic at Buck House. 'Oh, here, look at this, they'll like this, won't they, if we polish it up?'" Morgan mocked in a high voice.

"Morgan!" said his mother, her royalty-worshipping soul deeply shocked. "You have to go. You'll make a scene."

"I shall protest," Morgan said, pulling himself to his full six feet one and yanking on his dove-gray vest. "When the archbishop says, 'Can anyone give cause . . .' I shall say, 'Yes. This young flower of English womanhood is being taken to Russia against her will, sold by her ruined family to pay their debts.'"

In the silence after he had spoken, Morgan looked at his feet and flushed with shame. "I'm sorry, Evvy," he said.

For a moment Evelyn couldn't bring herself to answer. "I do love him, you know," she said finally. "He's nice to me."

Her brother reached out his hand and took both of hers in his. "I want you to be happy, Evvy," he said.

"I will be," she said, but the tears suddenly returned.

"You're crying." For a second brother and sister were alone together again, as they had been all their lives, dreaming and talking of the future as they saw it. But they never saw a future that held a marriage that would separate them by a continent.

"No," Evelyn said, withdrawing her hand. As she did so she saw the pain in Morgan's eyes. "It's so far away, that's all. You have to promise me you'll visit."

"Yes," Morgan agreed, and his smile, like dawn breaking over a familiar landscape, flooded her with confidence, as it had all her life.

"Soon?" Evelyn asked.

"What could keep me?" he asked, sweeping his hand toward the sunlit window over Oxford Square. "Nothing's going to happen here. It's going to be one perfect day after another, one unchanging season of balls and shooting in August and Christmas parties exactly like last year's. If I want excitement, I'll have to come join the Cossacks."

"They don't have Cossacks anymore," Evelyn said, smiling. "Alex says they only have ceremonial Cossacks, like the Horse Guards, for show."

"Then we'll ride in sleds across Alex's estates, with furs over us and the wolves behind."

"I'll miss you, Morgan," Evelyn said softly.

Her brother was silent. He might have spoken, but their mother shifted uneasily in the shadows of the room, recalling both of them to the moment.

"You really must go down, darling," Lady Valentine said.

Morgan held his sister's eyes for a second longer, then a smile broke across his face again. He fumbled in the watch pocket of his waistcoat and produced a coin. "I couldn't think of a gift," he said, holding it out.

"Morgan!" his mother protested. "Really!"

Evelyn held her palm out, and Morgan dropped the coin into her hand. The gold shimmered in the light from the window. "A sovereign!" Evelyn exclaimed happily.

"I won it last night," Morgan admitted.

"Oh, Morgan," Evelyn said, standing on the toes of her oyster satin pumps to kiss his cheek. "I'll have it set in a bracelet so you'll always be near." When her lips touched his cheek, her brother put his hand on the back of her neck and kissed her on the cheek.

"Something reliable," he said when they broke, but his voice sounded strained. "Cash."

A sound from below took all their attention. Morgan waved once more and ran out of the room. Evelyn stood listening to his steps on the stairs, then to the muffled voices. She ran to the window and saw him stepping into a motorcar that left before the door was shut.

"I think that's in awfully bad taste," her mother said, looking at the sovereign.

"But definitely Morgan," Evelyn teased her. "I won't ever be able to look at it without calling him up like a genie."

"I hope you don't need genies like Morgan," her mother said, then sat down abruptly on the white cotton cover of the fourposter bed. "You are going to be happy, you know," she said earnestly.

Evelyn wished she believed it as fervently as her mother did. "I know," she said dutifully.

Evelyn couldn't help think that Morgan was right: Their mother, who tried so hard to fit in, stuck right out like some dressmaker's doll. Alex, Evelyn knew, would be mortified, but on the strength of that thought Evelyn crossed the room and hugged her mother. "I will be very happy," she promised.

"Money makes a difference," her mother said, clutching fiercely at the sleeve of Evelyn's dress. For a second Lady Valentine's own father, who had started behind a counter in a shop and risen until he could appoint the parson on his own estates, stood before her eyes. She had come to what many thought of as a romantic marriage with a dowry that was nearly exhausted. But her husband had other women, and his friends from years back had wives who ignored her.

"Alex is very kind," Evelyn said.

"Cynthia, are you coming down or not?" Sir John called irritably up the stairs.

Lady Valentine quickly rose to her feet, still, after all these years, dismayed at the thought of her husband's anger. "Yes, yes," she called.

As she left the room she turned and said, "You can come home again," but she didn't sound at all certain, and Evelyn felt an immediate twinge of fear. Her father called, "Cynthia. You will be the one who's late," and her mother ran from the room.

Esther was waiting outside the door to help her down the stairs. "You look lovely, miss," she murmured as she gathered up the train.

The house seemed unnaturally quiet as Evelyn came down the stairs; the rest of the servants had gone ahead to the church. Her father, smoking a long cheroot, was pacing the narrow hall. Both doors were open, and the shadows of the twin flags moved across the entrance. She stopped. "Will you come?" she asked Esther, ashamed that in all the preparations she had forgotten to think about the maid.

"Oh no, miss," Esther said, wiping her hands on her skirt. "I'm not changed. I'll change while you're at the church."

"Oh," said Evelyn. She heard some sounds from the back of the house. "The caterers are here, are they?"

"Oh, yes," said Esther happily. "And a splendid reception it will be. Quite royal, if you don't mind my saying so."

Alex had arranged most of the reception, sending cooks and waiters from the Russian embassy.

"Do come on, Evelyn," her father called up to her. "They'll think you've bolted if we don't get there soon."

Evelyn went down the rest of the way to the hall. "Nice," her father said, looking her over. He stubbed out his cigar in the blue and white Chinese export porcelain bowl on the table of the rented house. "All right, we're off," he called to Esther. "We'll be one step behind your mother. Why she couldn't have gone with Morgan, I don't know."

He held out his arm, and Evelyn threaded her gloved hand through it. As they stepped out of the house the sunlight blinded her for a second, and she panicked at the sound of the cheers from the people gathered on the sidewalk. When she opened her eyes she saw that the coachman had gotten down off the box of the carriage from the embassy. He held the door open, his black silk tailcoat gleaming in the heat, the scarlet breeches and gold stockings of his livery immaculate.

"Quite like an operetta," her father murmured, but he raised his top hat to the crowd as they walked among them to the door of the carriage. Seated inside, Evelyn looked out from what seemed an unnaturally high vantage point. The cheers continued until she realized that something was expected of her. She raised her hand and waved at just the moment the carriage lurched off, and the cheers rose higher, following them all the way around the square and out the side street.

"You'll get the hang of this quite easily," her father said

with satisfaction. He bowed to the crowds and, pleased with the result, bowed to the other side. "Quite a good show this, what? I expect it's like this all the time in Russia. They're very backward, from all I hear."

The carriage rolled through the streets, people turning to watch as the white horse clipped along. A ragged cheer here and there told her that she had been recognized. Her face had been all over the *Illustrated News*—PEER'S GRANDDAUGHTER TO MARRY RUSSIAN ARISTOCRAT—and in the *Tatler*, as well as in the yellow press. "Peer's granddaughter" sounded much more noble than she felt: she had met her grandfather only once before his death; her mother had been an outcast from the family until this match. Even now, as Evelyn rode to St. Margaret's beside her father, she couldn't believe that it was happening, that she would soon be a countess.

"Papa," she said, clutching his arm.

Ahead there was a loud, steady roar, muffled by the buildings between the carriage and the church. "What?" her father asked, placing his hand over hers.

"I'm scared, Papa."

Sir John was struck dumb for a fraction of a moment, as though his daughter had created a social gaffe such as her mother might have done. "Natural," he said, looking away from her out the window of the carriage. "A young girl . . . what?"

"Papa, I want to go home," Evelyn said desperately.

He wouldn't hear her. The carriage entered the square and slowed as it neared St. Margaret's. Her mother's car was just pulling away from the church door, and the bridesmaids, whom she barely knew, stood waiting.

Sir John drew a deep breath. "A title is useful" were his words when he faced his daughter. "I've always found mine so. You will find you'll never regret your marriage. It doesn't have to be . . ."

The carriage drew to a halt, and the cheers reached a nearly deafening crescendo. Evelyn thought her father said, "as stifling." The door by her side opened, the body of the glass carriage rocking very slightly with the movement. His last words trailed after her: ". . . as your mother has made it."

She reached the threshold of the church with her father at her side. She thought the pounding of her heart must be audible to everybody, but the organ pierced through the heat and the sound of the massed voices behind her. A thousand heads seemed to turn at once, and then she was moving forward, out of the sunlight into a darkness that was filled with music, the scent of flowers, and a hush above it all. When her eyesight cleared she was almost at the altar, and there was her distinguished bridegroom, Alexis Lezenski, in his white and gold uniform of the Russian Imperial Navy, his cocked hat under one arm and his eyes, as gold as Morgan's sovereign that she clutched under her bouquet, drawing her forward.

She remembered the first time she saw Alexis. He was standing across the paddock at Ascot, straight and handsome in his unfamiliar uniform.

"It's so boring," Morgan said moodily, distracting her briefly from her study.

"It's not for much longer," Evelyn consoled him. The sheer pleasure of having Morgan home from school made her feel lightheaded. This summer—glorious golden days one after the other, quite unlike England—had conspired to make her feel oddly emotional: sometimes weepy, sometimes so high-spirited that her mother sent her up to the low, narrow room under the eaves in their rented house near Windsor. The family had moved from the house in Plymouth, supposedly for the race season; but Evelyn knew and she supposed the servants did also that the rent on the Plymouth house hadn't been paid in six months. They'd probably leave this house one step ahead of the bailiff, too.

"A night flit," as Morgan liked to say, in his fake Cockney accent. None of the family's troubles ever bothered Morgan. He was like their father: debts were no more than minor inconveniences.

The man across the paddock turned and looked directly at

Evelyn as though he had felt her eyes on him. She blinked, felt herself blushing, and turned her back on him so rapidly that she trod on Morgan's new boots.

"Hey, Tuppence," he said, looking down. "These boots are barely worn yet."

"You'll get out of school next term," Evelyn said rapidly, half pulling Morgan away from the rail. "Then you'll be free. Men are so lucky."

"How?" Morgan asked, scanning the crowd for someone who might buy them a drink in the owners' tent.

"You can do anything you want. You can go into the city and loot and pillage, you could go out to . . . I don't know . . . Africa or somewhere and run a trading post . . . or further. China maybe . . . China seems interesting, don't you think?"

Morgan was only half listening. With the rest of his senses he was concentrating his considerable magnetism on a well-dressed woman of somewhere near forty who seemed struck to stone by the sight of him. At fifteen, Evelyn had noticed that her elder brother had this effect on many women lately. He had been her best friend all her life, her one strong rock in the turbulence of her parents' marriage and financial condition; but now she felt that somewhere in the last year they had reversed roles: she had become the rock, and he clung to her.

"Who is that?" he asked her. The woman wore a pale fawn coat and an ankle-length skirt that touched smooth calfskin boots. Her hat hid part of her face; Evelyn recognized her with surprise.

She laughed. "That's Dottie Cavendish."

"Who?"

"Mother's chum," Evelyn said, wondering if she might be abandoned. It had happened once in Bond Street. Morgan had almost walked right into a woman (not someone she knew), middle class but well dressed, and without her ever really understanding what had happened, Evelyn was on her way home alone.

"The rich one," Evelyn said maliciously, watching as Lady Cavendish made a little ceremony of tilting her parasol and looking out from under it with lowered eyes. Evelyn's sense of outrage at Lady Cavendish's behavior was as strong as her mother's might have been if another woman had done that to her father; she was almost old enough to be Morgan's mother, Evelyn calculated quickly.

"Rich?" said Morgan hopefully, letting a smile of his own answer the coquette across the lawn.

"Oh, Morgan, let's not stay here," Evelyn said impatiently. The handsome bearded stranger she had noticed across the paddock appeared suddenly in front of her, returning her scrutiny. "Who's that?" she asked, as much to distract Morgan as from a need for an answer, though the way the man stared at her made her blush. She held her head high, refusing to indulge in any of Lady Cavendish's tricks.

Morgan finally tore his gaze from Mrs. Cavendish. "Oh, Russian, I think." He looked at the way he was dressed with distaste. "They really don't know how to behave, do they? No one would wear a uniform to Ascot. It's a private function."

"I think he looks very . . ." She had been about to say "handsome," but added instead, ". . . dashing."

Morgan was searching for a cigarette. "Quite like the Middle Ages or something. They still don't bathe, from what I hear."

"Oh, Morgan, I'm sure that's not true!" Evelyn protested. She could feel a fit of giggles rising in her. Any second now she would behave as though she was back in the schoolroom and disgrace herself.

"They have huge palaces and no bathrooms." Morgan embellished the story. "The aristocracy bathe once a year, whether they need it or not."

Her giggles threatened to explode at any minute. To her horror, she saw that the Russian was moving across the distance between them with a look of amused determination on his face.

"How rich?" Morgan asked.

"What?" The confusion of the coming encounter seemed to have rooted Evelyn to the spot.

"Lady Cavendish," Morgan said, turning his heated gaze

on the lady, who was moving languidly along the line of the owners' tent. "How rich?" From inside came the sound of men laughing, of glasses touching, and, like a gunshot, the sound of a wine cork exploding, followed by muted cheering.

"Very," Evelyn said. "Mummy's people."

"Mummy's people" was a family code for the industrial middle class who were moving so relentlessly into the aristocracy, bringing with them much-needed cash to restore and maintain estates, country houses, and gambling habits.

"Ah," said Morgan with satisfaction, a new look smoothing out his symmetrical features. He brushed the hair that had gone the color of wheat in the summer sun out of his eyes and smiled directly at the lady.

Uncomfortable as she felt with Dottie Cavendish, Evelyn preferred her company to what seemed to be ahead. The Russian officer had stopped less than two feet away and stood with his hands neatly folded in front of him, waiting. Up close she saw he was older than she had thought, but still startlingly handsome, though in a thoroughly non-English way. He looked as though he rode bareback across the steppes, drank what he wanted, and lived by rules that, though she had no idea what they could be, wouldn't be at all like the English ones.

She found that she liked the way he was looking at her. She knew she should look away, that she was being bold and unladylike, but she found that she was almost imitating Morgan in the way she stood her ground and stared right back.

"May I ask you why you are laughing at me?" the Russian asked in perfect English. His voice was deep and solemn, but there was laughter in the gold-flecked eyes.

Morgan turned from his flirtation with Lady Cavendish and looked at the Russian officer. "I don't think we were aware of you, sir," he said insolently.

The blood rose swiftly in Evelyn's cheeks; she thought for a moment that the Russian might strike Morgan and create a scandal. She stepped away from her brother and toward the Russian, holding out her hand. *"I* was watching you," she admitted, the words out of her mouth before she had known what she was going to say.

He hesitated, visibly controlling himself, then relaxed. It was a movement that was animal in its sudden shifting of his whole body, as though he had shaken his anger away. He was powerfully built. His tunic pulled across his chest, and his legs were as sturdy as a farm worker's, pressing against the serge of his trousers as though he had outgrown his clothes. He laughed, showing strong, even white teeth.

"And why was an attractive young girl watching me?" he asked.

The sheer commonness of the remark—a remark that even Morgan wouldn't have directed to a young woman— made Evelyn smile. She could feel more than see that Morgan was about to intervene when a woman's voice said, "Aren't you Morgan Valentine?" and Lady Cavendish was upon her prey.

Evelyn turned to see Morgan preening. Dottie Cavendish met all the requirements for being "common" herself: overdressed, forward, and with an accent, for all the expensive schooling that had been forced upon her, that was ever so slightly off.

"Of course you are!" she exclaimed, holding the parasol so as to shade her face and hide the worst of the lines about her eyes and the corners of her mouth. She was undoubtedly an attractive woman, Evelyn thought. The same age as her own mother, but larger, brighter, obtrusive in a way that you either liked or detested.

Evelyn had never known whether she liked her or not until Lady Cavendish turned to the Russian and held out her hand. "Alex," she said, her smile that of a co-conspirator, "back again?"

At that moment she decided that she hated her mother's friend. She wondered later if she hadn't then become a woman, or learned some of the arts that her mother's set would have thought appropriate for a woman, for she sensed the competition without ever having to be told. She put her hand on the Russian's sleeve. "Have you been away?" she asked.

He smiled down at her. "For longer than I had expected," he said. "It's pleasant to be back."

"But very hot," Dottie Cavendish said. "One expires."

"Not a Russian," said Alex, still looking only into Evelyn's eyes. "And you are?"

"Oh." Lady Cavendish's sigh was one of such open relief that Evelyn thought she would laugh. She looked to Morgan to see if he shared the joke with her, but her brother had eyes only for the long string of dark gray pearls, each the size of a plover's egg, that bobbed and fell on Lady Cavendish's ample breast. "You don't know each other?"

"No," said Alex.

"Well," said Dottie Cavendish, taking over, "this is Evelyn Valentine, Cynthia's daughter, and this," she said, turning to Morgan with the full force of her charm, "is the surprise. The last time I saw you you were just a little boy."

"Then I must have grown up fast," Morgan said, bending very slightly at the waist, "for you, Lady Cavendish, are still exactly as I remember you."

The Russian's gold eyes danced merrily. "Since no one will introduce me," he said to Evelyn, "I am Alex Lezenski."

"Count Alex Lezenski," Dottie Cavendish corrected quickly.

"How do you do," Morgan said, dismissing Alex, but Evelyn said, "Are you here officially, Count Lezenski?"

"Yes," he said, "with the embassy."

"How fine for us."

The movement of the crowd around them signaled the arrival of royalty. The owners' tent emptied, well-dressed men moving toward the track, the women like birds of exotic plumage, a tapestry of color moving across the bright green lawns.

Morgan and his companion were swept along by the flow of people; Dottie Cavendish's enormous hat and parasol bobbed like markers ahead.

"Miss Valentine, will you accompany me?" Count Lezenski asked, offering her his arm.

Evelyn, who had felt abandoned, now enjoyed a rush of gratitude mixed with the feeling of being almost entirely grown up; she hoped someone she knew was watching. There was a sense of haste in the air, and ahead the open carriages of the royal family could be seen moving onto the track for their one circuit before they took their places in the royal enclosure.

She became aware of Count Lezenski's arm beneath her hand, and of the faint smell of tobacco such as her father had about him when she hugged him at night. She glanced sideways shyly and saw that the count was looking down at her, the same half smile on his face.

"Where were you going when I came upon you?" he asked.

"To watch the race," Evelyn said.

"I fear you've lost your brother," Lezenski said, peering over the heads of the crowd. He was much taller than most of the men, Evelyn noticed. "Shall I search for him?"

"If you would." The thought of being alone here with Morgan trailing after Lady Cavendish was too much for her. How would she get home?

"Or you could sit with me," the count proposed. "That would be very nice."

"You have a box?" she asked him, startled. Boxes, she thought, were reserved for friends of the king and others, passed down almost like the titles of those who used them. Her father's friends had boxes, but her mother was seldom asked, and Evelyn never.

"No, not quite."

Ahead of them was the enclosure. The count stood back, and Evelyn looked to see the queen, much taller than the little, stiff king, moving from their carriage toward the enclosure; then she felt Alex's hand on the small of her back. Before she could react to this indelicate behavior, she understood that he was pushing her very gently forward. The footman at the gate stood back, and to her amazement, she was within the royal enclosure.

"Are we . . . ?" she couldn't help but ask him. If, like some foreigners that her father spoke of, the count was pushing himself forward where he didn't belong, Evelyn wanted none of it.

"Trespassing? No," he said, his hand on the elbow of her new coat. "We're expected."

The king was coming forward through the small gathering of his relatives and close friends, nodding as he passed; the queen remained impassive. When he came to Alex, he stopped, looked at the uniform and said, "Ah," it was impossible to tell whether it was an expression of surprise, disapproval, or approval. His small eyes looked at Evelyn, who found she had dropped automatically into as deep a curtsy as she could to cover her confusion. As she rose she saw the king and queen had moved on.

"Can you make it?" Alex Lezenski was saying as she staggered very slightly.

"Yes. I can't believe I saw the king so close."

"And what did you think?"

"He was exactly as I thought he would be," Evelyn said, suddenly dizzy with the heat and excitement.

"Very tactful," Alex said. "Perhaps you should be the naval attaché. I think diplomatic appointments are wasted on men; women are so much better at diplomacy."

He was laughing at her, she knew, but she liked the way he referred to her as "a woman." She wished Morgan was here to see her. He was such a beast to run off with that awful Dottie Cavendish just because she ogled him and flaunted her pearls.

She must have smiled, for Alex said, "Much better. You looked pale for a moment."

"I don't get thrust in front of the king and queen every day," she heard herself say. It was a bold statement coming from someone who had never found herself alone with a man any older than her brother, if you could call being in the company of a thousand people at a race track being alone.

"I doubt his majesty gets to look at someone so lovely

every day either," Alex Lezenski said, and in spite of herself Evelyn gasped at what she thought was at the very least insolence, at the worst treason.

"Please . . ." she begged him, looking about in an agony of embarrassment. Foreigners really were different, she thought, exactly as people said.

"No worse than the Russian court," Alex went on smoothly. If I were king . . . or czar . . ." he said, teasing.

"Please, please, Count Lezenski," she begged him again. "Don't talk like this. It's . . ." She couldn't bring herself to say "bad manners."

"Rude?"

"No, no, no," she protested.

"Barbaric?" he suggested, and she thought she saw the laughter appear in his eyes.

"Of course not," she said.

"Worse?" He snapped his fingers. "Foreign!" he pronounced.

She liked him. She liked the way he was laughing at her without making her feel like a child, or stupid. "It's . . . unusual," she said carefully.

A hush passed over the crowd. The people around them stood at attention as the first strains of the national anthem rang out across the track.

When the crowd relaxed at the end of the anthem, Evelyn felt strangely close to Count Lezenski, as though they had shared a joke that wasn't quite in good taste but was very funny nonetheless. "Ah" he said, guiding her through the crowd to where they could see the jockeys attempting to bring the horses into line down the track. "You smiled," he teased her. "I saw you."

"Never," she said, watching the favorite, who wore the king's colors of maroon and gray.

The crowd stilled for the race. Evelyn leaned against the rail in front of her; the sun touched her face with its unseasonable warmth. She wondered if adult life was like this. She had been afraid nearly all her life—afraid of her mother's strange temperament that ricocheted from hysteria to collapse; of her father's unchecked temper, raging some days, so cheerful the next that it was almost as though he were a different man.

Morgan shared his moods. They were alike in many ways, she thought, catching a glimpse of Morgan down the track beyond the royal enclosure, his arm protectively shielding Lady Cavendish from the crowd. She concentrated, trying to make him turn and see her in the inner sanctum, but he was bent over Dottie Cavendish, his hair gleaming in the sunlight as he turned his full attention to her. Morgan had never been a child, she realized. He had always been Morgan, less powerfully male, but complete. He had had a presence as a child, a presence that grew and filled every corner of him as he became an adult.

Morgan wasn't afraid of anything, she thought, and he never would be—while she was afraid of almost every day. For Morgan every day was an adventure, whatever it brought; for Evelyn each day was filled with a sense of foreboding: bill collectors would be at the door, her mother would take to her bed, and her father would go shooting or fishing or just visit friends until it was all over. Whenever this chaos touched Morgan's life, he laughed, while Evelyn wanted to cringe and hide.

The shout at the start of the race startled her from her thoughts so abruptly that she reached out involuntarily and clasped Alex Lezenski's hand. Before she could draw back his strong bare fingers had closed over her glove. She tried for a fraction of a second to pull away, then left her hand in his grip. The horses pounded down the track toward them, and she moved back away from the rail. Count Lezenski was standing right behind her; she found herself pressed against him. She tried to move forward, but the crowd was pressing in around them. The feel of his body made her close her eyes quickly to stop herself from running away like a child. When she opened her eyes a moment later the horses were heading down the stretch past them and the king was on his feet, beaming as the horse that wore his colors fought for the lead.

The horses hurled themselves down the track and across the finish line. The king had lost.

"Not a very patriotic animal," Alex Lezenski whispered.

This time Evelyn found she could laugh openly. He had moved away from her as the crowd spread out around them, but she was still conscious of the warmth of his body pressed against hers. She looked down the rail for Morgan but found that he and Lady Cavendish had moved off through the crowd.

"Are you interested in racing?" Count Lezenski asked her.

"Of course," she began, then understood that she could tell him the truth. "No," she admitted. "My brother wanted to come."

"He bets," suggested Alex as they walked slowly toward the gate to the enclosure.

"Don't all men?"

He looked at her seriously. "No. Just bored men."

"And you're not bored?" She felt very bold challenging a man almost old enough to be her father. She was used to the gentle pursuit—and sometimes not-so-gentle pursuit—by her father's friends when they found her alone in the house or the garden. That was more like a ritual: the advance, the withdrawal. She thought sometimes that they forced themselves on her more from a sense of obligation than out of desire, to confirm that they were the men they thought they were. She suspected they were as relieved as she was when she rebuffed them and they could relax. She didn't feel that way at all about this Russian.

"I'm bored sometimes. But betting on horse races wouldn't cure it."

"What would?" she asked. He was leading them toward the refreshment tent that had been set up behind the stands.

"Going home," he told her, looking down at her with his tiger's eyes; they made her feel his foreigness more than the uniform or his manner could. His eyes seemed to see things in her she wasn't sure she understood herself and didn't want others to know about.

"You don't like England?" she asked. She knew she sounded angry and provincial.

"I like it very much," he said.

She looked at him, obviously showing her surprise, for he added, "Nothing bad could ever happen here, could it?" The way he turned and took in the race track and expensively dressed crowd, then looked beyond the spreading chestnut trees to where Windsor Castle was hidden in the distance, he included everything that was familiar to her.

"Surely peace is progress," she said, repeating the words that she had read in newspapers.

"Yes," he said, but there was doubt in his voice.

"What is Russia like?" she asked.

"I'm Polish."

"But I thought . . ."

He smiled, touching the small of her back again to push her through the opening of the green and white tent into shadow. "We were conquered a century ago," he said. "I have a commission in the czar's navy, but my title is Polish, and most of my family's land is in Poland. Some of it is in Russia. My sisters like Russia much better than Poland."

"Why?" she asked.

"Not so boring," he said. "Country life can be very boring. St. Petersburg is very . . ."

"Exciting?" Evelyn suggested when he stopped.

"Yes," he said. "Unexpected is what I might have suggested." This time it was he who looked as though he had said more than he intended.

"I saw the pictures in the *Illustrated News* of the czarina at her niece's wedding," Evelyn said. "Her jewels were extraordinary."

Though all talk of jewels or anything having to do with money or finances was considered "common" at home, Evelyn had noticed that even her father had stared at the pictures when she and her mother were exclaiming over them. There was something not quite right in the display of wealth that the czarina and her daughters showed at the wedding in Germany. Only the duchess of Edinburgh, herself a daughter of the last czar, though now married to a son of Queen Victoria, had been able to compete.

Alex offered her a smile that seemed to understand all the things she was thinking without her having to say them.

"The czarina has a remarkable collection of jewels" was all he said, but Evelyn didn't feel that she had been judged as gauche for mentioning them.

"I would like to see Russia some day," she said. Then she searched for something to add that would not make her words seem like an opening for an invitation. Her mother did that among her father's grander friends; sometimes the hoped-for invitation came, and sometimes it didn't. As often as not her father was invited alone to shoot or fish in Scotland. "It must be a fairytale world."

"Yes," the count agreed thoughtfully. "It is, of course." He looked toward the tables where the waiters were pouring champagne. "But European fairytale, not at all English."

"And what's the difference?" Evelyn asked as Alex gestured to a manservant for two glasses of champagne.

He didn't answer until the man had brought him their drinks. Evelyn was never even allowed wine at dinner, but now she felt that if she refused, she would be putting herself back into the schoolroom, reminding him he was old enough to be her father's friend, not hers.

She took the glass, feeling a thrill of guilt, and Alex said, "In English fairy tales there are a lot of very talkative animals who end up happily at the end of the garden. In European fairy tales there are dark woods, and witches and children get put into ovens."

"I think I like English fairy tales better," Evelyn said, raising the forbidden glass and feeling the bubbles tickle her nose. At her first sip she knew instantly she would love champagne for the rest of her life.

"You like it?" Alex asked, watching her.

"Oh, yes," she said. "It's wonderful."

He seemed so pleased at her happiness that she found she, too, was smiling. She didn't know the rules here, and yet she liked not knowing them. She sensed adventure and felt as though she finally understood something new about her brother. Morgan must feel like this every day, she thought, with a flush of happiness and resentment all mixed up together.

More people had begun to drift into the tent. As she

sipped her champagne Evelyn thought that perhaps grown-up life might not be so bad after all, but then Alex Lezenski said, "Are you out of the schoolroom?"

She choked, coughing up champagne all over the front of his uniform, and he slapped her on the back, exactly as someone would a child. Amused, people turned to watch. There were tears in her eyes, partially from choking and partially from humiliation. By the time she recovered she knew her face must look ugly—her piggy look, Morgan called it—the look of a stubborn little girl.

"I'm sorry." Lezenski didn't look it.

"I should find my brother," Evelyn said, trying to muster as much dignity as she could.

"And here he is," Alex said, waving his arm at Morgan and Lady Cavendish, who were standing in the opening of the tent.

Evelyn fought conflicting emotions: the wish to throw herself at Morgan and wail, "Take me home," and the desire to pull herself together quickly to try to save something of her triumph from the disaster. By the time Morgan and Dottie Cavendish had reached them, Evelyn had herself under control.

Morgan looked at the two empty champagne glasses in Alex Lezenski's hand. "I see," he said with a twinkle in his eyes. "Luring innocent young women . . ."

"Not at all," exclaimed Evelyn.

"Absolutely," said Alex Lezenski in the same breath.

Dottie Cavendish laughed. "You are a very bad man, Alex," she said, and Evelyn didn't at all like the personal and insinuating tone of Lady Cavendish's voice or the sudden rush of possessiveness she felt.

"We were in the royal enclosure," Evelyn announced.

Lady Cavendish's eyebrows rose with no pretense of anything but surprise. "Really?" She looked at Alex Lezenski as though this time perhaps she had made a mistake.

"My new appointment," he said quietly.

"Oh, yes," she said, ignoring Morgan, whose brows drew almost imperceptibly closer over the bridge of his statue-straight nose, the nostrils flaring like those of a spoiled horse who wanted his own way.

"The king spoke to us," Evelyn went on, enjoying herself thoroughly.

"He cleared his throat," Alex said gently.

Morgan said, "Dottie, would you like something to drink?"

The way Mrs. Cavendish froze at the use of her nickname made Evelyn want to clap her hands. She looked at Alex to see if he was enjoying the moment as much as she was, but the tiger eyes weren't sparkling with humor.

"Would *you* like something to drink, Miss Valentine?" he asked very formally.

"A little water, perhaps?" she asked.

His own eyebrows rose. "Of course. Some mineral water," he said to a passing manservant. Morgan took the chance to remove two glasses of champagne from the tray; his eyes moved resentfully over Count Lezenski's exotic uniform. When he offered the champagne to Lady Cavendish, she hesitated, then took it without thanks.

"Did you see the race?" Lady Cavendish asked Alex, ignoring both Morgan and Evelyn.

"The first one."

"The king lost. He looked very grumpy," she said spitefully.

"Not at all sporting?" Alex teased her.

"I say," said Morgan loudly; Evelyn noticed the change in the tone of his voice and wondered if perhaps he'd had a drink already. "I don't think that's quite the right way to talk about the king."

Evelyn knew her brother was spoiling for a fight. "Don't be an ass, Morgan," she murmured as quietly as she could. "He doesn't mean anything."

There was a long moment of silence, and Evelyn found herself mouthing a silent prayer until Morgan tipped back his glass and drank. He smiled, accepting his own childishness and demanding forgiveness by the sheer force of his charm. "We should go," he said, gripping Evelyn's elbow hard.

"Oh, must you?" said Dottie Cavendish, forgetting her own earlier indifference.

Morgan seized his advantage and backed away with Evelyn in his grip. "Yes, yes," he said. "So nice to see you. So nice to meet *you*, Count Lezenski."

Alex was close to openly laughing, Evelyn thought. Lady Cavendish lunged, her arm out as though she thought she could take hold of Morgan and drag him back. "You'll call?" she said, and her voice betrayed her naked interest.

"Yes, of course," Morgan said, and they were at the entrance to the tent.

The fresh air revived Evelyn as she stepped out of the tent, but she turned in an unladylike panic and looked back over her shoulder to where Lady Cavendish stood talking animatedly to someone nearby. Count Lezenski stood watching as though he had expected Evelyn to turn. She knew Morgan was impatiently waiting for her, yet she couldn't bring herself to step completely out of the tent; if she did, she felt that, like Alice leaving Wonderland, she might never come back, might think that the strange, unsettling happiness of the last hour had been a dream, imagined in the mind of an impressionable schoolgirl.

She wanted him to come across the short space to her. She couldn't go back to him—not without revealing herself the way Lady Cavendish had—and she vowed that she would never, never do that for any man.

At the last second, when she knew she had to follow Morgan, Alex moved. The world seemed to slow down, to go very still and quiet about her as he came across the short distance. "Goodbye, Miss Valentine," he murmured.

"Goodbye, Count Lezenski." The words tore at her as though she was leaving someone she had known for years and years. The confusion rose all about her again, threatening to allow her to make a fool of herself, reveal herself, to be a child, and she didn't want to be a child any longer. For the first time in her life she was happy, willing to leave childhood behind. She felt bold and elated, totally unlike her usual timid self.

"You didn't answer my question." He stood inches from her, his eyes locked with hers.

She couldn't think what his question had been. Her mind tumbled about as though she had been given an unexpected quiz. Then the joy flooded through her, making her absolutely certain that here was a friend such as she had never had before, and she laughed at him. "I am no longer in the schoolroom, Count Lezenski," she said, and she knew that she herself was flirting outrageously, uncaring of who might be watching.

Now he took her hand in his. She thought she would flame with embarrassment if he did something as foreign as kiss it, but he understood what she was feeling, as she should have known he would, and merely tightened his grip on her fingertips as he bowed very slightly, not letting his eyes leave her face. When he released her hand she stood as though under a spell until Morgan called her name impatiently from outside the tent.

"What was that about?" Morgan demanded as they walked away.

"The count wanted to say goodbye to me," she said, hoping Morgan would ask more, yet dreading his teasing.

"She has a yacht, did you know that?" he asked his sister. Evelyn relaxed as she saw that her brother was lost in his own complex designs. "She asked me if I would like to go to Monte Carlo with her."

"That's very generous," Evelyn said smoothly, but her irony was lost on Morgan. They walked on in silence to where they could get a car to take them to the station. It wasn't until they were riding through the sun-dappled lanes toward the town that he said abruptly, "Foreigners have such obvious habits, don't they? It must be awful to have to live abroad all the time."

When Alex's hand touched her face to lift her veil, Evelyn came out of what seemed a long dream. She was married. The fear that pulsed through her must have shown in her eyes.

"I love you, Evelyn," he said as he bent to touch her trembling lips with his own, on which she tasted brandy and cigar smoke.

She had rehearsed herself in her bedroom the night before to say "I love you," but what she said was "I'm afraid."

He held her face still for a long moment, gazing down into her eyes. "You mustn't be. I'll keep you safe."

As they turned from the altar Mendelssohn swelled from the organ. The aisle looked forbidding, a world waiting for her to take her place, framed by faces that she knew only from newspapers. She descended the two steps and felt her veil and train lifted by her attendants. Alex placed his hand over hers where it lay on his arm, and together they started forward. The music deafened Evelyn as she passed the beaming face of her mother, her father's skeptical look, and Morgan, suddenly sad, it seemed, for he looked at her, then down at the shining, polished toes of his shoes.

The bells in the tower began to peal as she neared the light of the doorway, and Evelyn unconsciously started to move faster. Alex held her back. "Shush, shush," he reassured. "The world will wait. We have our whole lives."

The momentousness of the decision struck her then, the irrevocability. No longer could she turn and run back down the aisle to her mother, to Morgan. She calmed herself and saw the light at the end of the carpet grow and fill the wide door of the church.

The cheers tumbling down on them from every side struck her like a blow when she stepped into the sunlight. They stood stock still for what seemed an endless time; then at last they were in the coach, moving away from the church, the bells still pealing for their happiness.

Evelyn looked back quickly once to see Morgan alone at the top of the steps, the other guests spread out like a multicolored lawn photograph. She turned to hold tight to her new husband's hand as they rode together into the future.

2

The rails clicked rhythmically under the sleeping coach as Evelyn lay in her bunk. Next door in the small compartment reserved as a drawing room she could hear Alex preparing for bed. She would fail him, she was sure of it. She thought of her mother's embarrassed murmurings the night before, so embarrassing for both of them that finally Evelyn had walked to the window and dismissed her with "Mummy, I want to sleep."

Morgan's voice mocked her. "And then," he had said while they were sitting about earlier in the day, enjoying a breakfast that for Evelyn was only toast and tea, "and then he'll pounce!" Wrapped in the expensive silk dressing gown that he had brought back from his cruise on the *Ionia*, the Cavendish yacht, Morgan had dropped the scone he was buttering and tickled her until she screamed for mercy.

The maid had opened the door. "You called, miss?" she asked.

Morgan fell back and reclaimed his scone. "Miss Evelyn had something lodged in her throat." Morgan bit into the fresh roll with his even teeth.

"Yes, sir," the maid said darkly, and she left.

"I don't approve of you," Evelyn told him.

"Not many people do," Morgan agreed smugly. "I'm a bad piece of work, it seems." He finished his scone, wiped his fingers on his napkin, and asked, "Did Mother tell you all about the dirty deed?"

"Please, Morgan," Evelyn begged, looking at the closed door. "Not now."

"Well, I expect you'll learn tonight, anyway," Morgan said. "You should have come with us on the yacht. Dottie could have—"

"Morgan!" Evelyn warned him.

But lying here listening to the rails under the train as it raced through the French countryside, she wished that she had listened to him. Alex was a man of the world, nearly forty. He would think her a childish little schoolgirl. She heard the door slide open and waited, her eyes closed, fingers crossed in some forgotten ritual against bad luck. She felt the cool air of the corridor on her cheek as he came in, then heard the door closing again.

"Are you awake?" he asked her in a low voice. He sounded almost uncertain.

"No," Evelyn said, finding that she could smile in the dark.

There was a silence, then she felt the mattress move as he sat down. "Talking in your sleep," he said beside her, and she smelled the familiar masculine smell of him. He touched her shoulder where the lace nightgown with the pink ribbon, chosen by her mother, revealed her skin. She felt his hand move over her skin, stop, and then more boldly move down into the nightgown.

She had prepared to tense herself, to endure what was ahead. Her mother clearly feared it, and Morgan made a joke of it, a man's joke. When he spoke as lightly as he did of his conquests, she felt a great revulsion.

But at the insistent touch of Alex's fingers moving over her bare breast she felt an unexpected response, powerful, deep, so complete that her body seemed to course with new blood in the darkness. Every inch of skin that his hand passed over—her breasts, her stomach, lower still until she gasped with a mingled shame and pleasure—came alive under his sure hand, making her arch her body. A new power had taken control of her, twisting her and finally making her cry out quite differently. She lifted her arms until she held onto his strong shoulders and pulled herself up to be kissed.

His mouth pressed against hers, opening her lips, exploring her as her hands held him tight against her. When he released her she fell back gasping, her sight blinded by the dark and the sense of blood pounding through her temples. With fingers rough from his horsemanship and time at sea, he pushed the lace of her nightgown over her shoulders and down about her waist. The mattress buckled as he stood up, and she heard his clothes dropping in the tightly closed compartment. Her breath was more even. She was glad the light was off so he couldn't see her confusion. She felt she was revealing herself to be less than she should, less than a lady, but her passion had hold of her like a drug coursing through her veins for the first time, taking her to heights of euphoria that brought with it both joy and fear.

Alex reached out and lifted the shade very slightly, bringing moonlight into the compartment. He looked enormous, broad of chest and shoulder, his hips solid from his horsemanship, thighs thick. She turned her face away, ashamed to feel her curiosity at the sight of the first naked man she had ever seen. She lay back, her own upper body exposed, and he touched her breasts again, the nipples responding as her throat seemed to close. Tears squeezed from her tightly closed eyes. His impatience grew as he pulled back the linen sheet, and then he pulled down her nightgown, leaning down and placing himself full-length beside her. She couldn't help herself; she clawed at his body, neck arched as his lips traced a path down her throat.

"Oh, God," she heard herself say in a voice she didn't recognize. And then a long groan as she heard the nightgown tearing. Their skins touched along the whole length of her body, Alex covering her. The heat in the small compartment threatened to choke her as she felt a dampness all over her. She was being carried forward on a wave of passion now, desperate until in a searing pain he entered her hard, stopped, and pulled back slightly.

"No, no," she cried, holding onto him, her legs about him, clinging to him shamelessly, and he entered her completely with a cry on both their parts. They began a rhythm, Alex plunging, Evelyn gasping until she thought that the pain and pleasure would kill her. She didn't care. She had one second of shock when she thought she would die, pierced with a pain that seemed to explode into light and softness, pleasure, a sense of belonging and rightness such as she had never known.

Her face was buried in Alex's shoulder. As the pleasure ebbed the fear came back: that he would despise her for her pleasure, for not being a lady. He rolled off her. She turned to the wall, bringing up the rags of the nightgown to cover her shame.

When he touched her on the shoulder, she tensed. He turned her firmly toward him, looking at her with his eyes like molten gold in the moonlight that came through the window. "Do you love me?" he whispered.

She did. The love forced out all other fears. "Yes," she managed to say, so softly she thought he might not have heard.

"Good," he said, looking at her so seriously she expected a rebuke. "We will be happy together, my little one," he said. "You will see that soon. Now," he said, wiping the damp threads of her hair from her forehead, "sleep for a while."

When she tried to cover herself better with the sheet, he took it from her gently. "No. I like to look at your body," he said. "You are very beautiful. Do you know that?"

She wasn't. Morgan was beautiful. Lady Cavendish, though older, was beautiful. She thought herself young, that was all; but the way her new husband uncovered her, making his own soft sounds of appreciation, made her feel that perhaps in some way she was beautiful tonight. She loved him all the more for thinking so. She placed her hands over herself, but he took those away also. "That is English," he joked with her, whispering the words. "You are not English anymore." He peered at her, his tiger eyes amused. "I think in your heart you were perhaps never English." And as she blushed, he kissed her on each cheek, on her eyelids, then on her mouth again.

The rocking coach lulled her to sleep in his arms, and when she awoke much later the moon was low on a flat countryside, the sky silver. Silhouettes of trees marched across the horizon, and a single farmhouse with a light burning toward dawn was the only dwelling. She was filled with a sense of happiness and looked at her sleeping husband's strong body without shame. She touched his chest, and his eyes opened. He reached for her, their lips opening before they met, and this time their lovemaking was bold, without apology, selfish, greedy, as they joined together with a hunger stoked by new familiarity.

They slept again, and when Evelyn awoke the second time morning was full on the land outside, where the train was climbing more slowly into unknown mountains. A stream gurgled below the carriage, and pine trees pierced the sky above shale mountains.

Alex stirred, opened his eyes, and stared at her, his expression blank for a second. The laughter came into his eyes slowly, and he relaxed like a large animal, reaching up to touch her face. She felt wanton, naked beside him, and when he touched her more suggestively, she found that small, half-formed sounds came from her throat, and soon they were making love again.

When Alex had left to wash and dress, she lay between the sheets watching the countryside pass by. The river widened and became darker, deeper. Among the trees she saw peasants in strange-looking clothes, and then suddenly a castle out of a picture book, spires and sheer rock faces, narrow windows and battlements.

Alex's valet's knock at the door interrupted her dreaming. "Would the countess like a bath drawn for her?"

She would only be a few days without a maid before they arrived, and Alex had assured her that at the estate in Poland there would be many, many people eager to help her. She would please them by putting herself into their hands, make them feel that Alex had not made such an unusual choice in his bride from England. Besides, Esther had blanched at the thought of leaving England. "Thank you," she called to the valet.

She stood up looking at herself in the reflection of the window, holding the torn lace of her nightgown against her skin, and she laughed. Her mother would be shocked, and surprised. She didn't feel in any way older or more mature, but rather filled with a secret happiness that would help her for the rest of her life. If only Morgan were here to share it with her.

She put on the matching silk peignoir, feeling like a slattern, and waited for another soft knock on the door.

Alex came in. "Dimitri has arranged a bath for you," he said.

"No easy task," Evelyn said, holding out her arms to steady herself as the train rounded a bend on the narrow gauge.

"No." He smiled at her. "Will you be long?"

"No." She wished she knew the right words to tell him her gratitude. "I love you" wouldn't come. It sounded unsatisfactory, even common.

"Shall I send you tea?" he asked.

"No. I'll be in the bath."

"We should have brought Esther," he acknowledged.

Evelyn looked down at the remains of her nightgown. "Esther would have been shocked," she said, and suddenly she giggled uncontrollably, dropping back onto the bed and holding her hands to her mouth. Alex watched her, smiling.

"You make me very happy," he said from his position against the door. He was dressed in a dark suit today, with a soft shirt and a cravat that Morgan would have envied for its opulent simplicity. This was a whole other side of Alex she didn't know: the country gentleman going back to his estates. All that she didn't know about him flooded over her, as it had when on the verge of her wedding she saw that she had agreed to a lifelong adventure with a man who was almost a stranger to her. "I want to be a good wife to you," she said, sobering. She was a child, she knew, and he would let her be for a little longer, but those waiting in Poland on the estates—Alex's mother, who had refused to travel, and perhaps his sister, if she came from St. Petersburg, the servants who had known Alex all his life—would be waiting to decide if she was worthy of him.

"Don't be like that."

"How?"

"Don't apologize," he told her. "I knew what I was doing. I love you as you are."

He came over to her, took her shoulders in his hands, and leaned down to kiss her. When he was gone, she sat for a little while thinking how lucky she had been, all doubts vanquished.

From outside the door Dimitri reported, "Countess, your bath is ready."

She heard the other door open and close and went out to find a small leather bath such as an officer might take on a campaign set in the middle of the compartment. The water, brought by pitcher, was lukewarm, but she dropped her clothes and lowered herself into the tight space, watching the water level rise and slop over onto the Oriental rug. The soap lathered into a fragrance of lavender. She lay back, the country beyond the sheer curtains of the parlor window a place of light and shadow. She felt as though she had been whisked in one magical wave of a hand from her old existence as a child into a new world of untold luxury and magic.

Dressing after her bath, she fumbled with buttons. She had never had to button herself. She uncertainly called Dimitri.

"Yes, madame."

"I'm ashamed to say I can't do this," she said, turning her back in the doorway to the sleeping compartment.

His hands at her back seemed as sexless as those of her nannies, as though she was just another charge like Alex.

"Thank you."

"The count is at breakfast," the old man said.

"Oh." She stood just inside the door that was held open for her. "Which way do I go?"

He gestured, stood back for her to pass, and bowed as she made her way down the rocking train. At each door between the coaches there seemed to be an attendant, and soon she passed into the brightly lit interior of the wagon-lit, where the table service was silver, the linen pure, and the crystal the match of anything in the Ritz-Carlton. Alex rose as she approached, holding herself erect, eyes directly ahead, wondering if people knew that this was her honeymoon. Fresh pink roses bobbed in their crystal vase in the center of the table.

"You look lovely," Alex said, seating her across from him.

"I'm very hungry," she said, surprised.

"And why wouldn't you be?" he teased her, sitting down. "Travel is meant to improve the appetite."

She looked at him, saw that he was laughing at her, and looked down at the gold rim on the plate. The waiter brought fresh tea, then an array of dishes for her to choose from. Passengers drifted in and out of the coach as the train pushed higher into the mountains through narrowed passes, the trees becoming at first denser, then abruptly thinner, spaced out in high alpine pastures where the late summer grass was still as fresh as pale, green silk, the flowers low to the earth and brightly colored.

Alex watched her with a small smile playing about his mouth. She found she was blushing, then suddenly giggling. "Don't do that," she whispered, looking at the toast on her plate. She glanced up, saw that he was trying to look innocent, and she started giggling again. Two mature women in dark traveling outfits at the next table glanced over, first at Evelyn, then at Alex, gave each other a significant look, and went back to their own meals with disapproval.

Evelyn felt like a schoolgirl. I am a married woman, she told herself severely. The giggles subsided and then bubbled up again until she truly felt she was making a fool of herself. "I'm sorry," she whispered.

Alex reached across the table and put his darkly tanned hand over hers. "Don't be," he said quietly. "I love you."

She should have been reassured, but instead she had a sudden rush of fright. I am a married woman, she repeated in her thoughts. My husband loves me. Everything she had ever read or heard told her that she should be very pleased, very happy; she had made a good match—a brilliant match, her mother insisted—and her wedding night had been a very happy occasion. Yet as she turned away to look out the window at the strange, forbidding scenery of the Tyrol her heart beat faster, as if it knew something her mind did not. She was very, very frightened.

England seemed a long way away.

3

"Our family," the dowager countess told Evelyn the first night at dinner, "predates the reign of Charlemagne."

"What my mother is saying," Alex said wistfully, "is that we are older than the Romanovs."

"Alex!"

He looked at his mother defiantly. "That is what you are saying, Mother."

The countess was the smallest woman Evelyn had ever seen, as small as a jockey, her skin as pale as a wraith. But the fire that shone in her eyes spoke of a bitterness that could never be extinguished. Now she looked with apprehension at the six footmen standing to the side of the tapestried dining room. "You must never speak like that," she muttered to the son who sat to her right.

On her left, Evelyn looked for help to Alex's elder sister. Natasha was tall like Alex, but without his gaiety and warm smile. Like her mother, she vibrated with bitterness. Mouthful after mouthful of meat, potatoes, and an unfamiliar noodle dish traveled from the table to her mouth, as though she expected not to eat again for some time.

"I am stating a simple fact, Mother," Alex said quietly. "This is not treason."

"You never know what will be treason at some other time." His mother reached out to touch her choker encrusted with rubies and diamonds, as though its presence reassured her. The servants, thick-bodied and in uniforms that looked as though they hadn't been cleaned in many years, stood stone-faced. Evelyn wanted to go to the long window at the end of the room, pull back the dusty draperies, and throw open the casements to let in some air.

"You have been too long in England," the dowager countess was saying when Evelyn turned back to the conversation between mother and son. Evelyn knew that she meant the marriage had been a mistake. The family, consisting of only the dowager countess and Natasha, had not attended, but sent word that the countess was too ill to travel.

As far as Evelyn could see, the countess showed no signs of illness at all. Instead, she possessed a meanness that in someone else would have seemed simple frugality. But in this huge castle, the meanness had transformed itself into filthy rooms, shabby furniture, poor food, and an atmosphere of deep resentment among the people who worked for her and were dependent on her for their lives.

"And you," Alex said, trying to lighten the oppressive atmosphere, "have been shut up here too long, Mother. You should come to St. Petersburg with us if we go."

The movement that the old woman made with her lips was one that might have ended with her spitting in her food. "A waste," was all she said.

"A life can be a waste," Alex told her, glancing at his sister, who looked up in the very act of putting more food into her mouth, her eyes filled with a pure hatred that took Evelyn's breath away.

"You know what I think of . . ." The countess left the rest of her accusation unspoken.

"And that is treason?" Alex said firmly, the laughter gone. "In the end, economies can cost more than expenditures. You cannot turn back the clock."

"This is more of the thinking you have heard in England," the countess said, her voice rising. "A bourgeois country, holding vipers to its breast, vipers that will turn on it one day. I warn you."

"A country moving into the twentieth century with confidence," Alex answered.

"You are infatuated!" his mother said with a hollow laugh. She looked at Evelyn. "We were kings once," she stated, as though Evelyn were personally responsible for their decline.

"We were not," Alex said flatly.

"The Lezenskis—" his mother shouted.

"Were very minor royalty, one branch of which were kings. We were not kings."

"You deny your heritage."

"On the contrary, I try to preserve it. This deception helps no one. We cannot live in the past, and if we romanticize it, we will not learn from the present and we will lose the future."

The meal was concluded to the sounds of Natasha's eating. Alex steadily served himself from the carafe before him, his mother's eyes watching the level of the wine fall. The servants cleared the table, and his mother left without a word before the fruit arrived.

Natasha, carving into an apple from their own orchards, said, "You should come home."

"Is that so?" her brother asked.

She shrugged. "She's old. She'll die one day. You'll have to come then anyway."

Alex stood without answering her. "Would you like to walk?" he asked Evelyn.

They went out through the dark hall, heraldic banners hanging in tatters from standards fixed to the beams high above. The light of a full moon, white as snow, covered the long slope of low fields that stretched away from behind the castle. The stones of the original defense had been added to haphazardly, so that the final result was like some child's construction, with meaning only to the person who built it.

Alex still had not spoken as they reached the wide river below the original keep.

"They hate me," Evelyn said.

"Yes," he admitted.

"Will we live here?" She heard her own fear.

"Someday," he said with a sigh, and she felt the tension in his arm. "Not yet." He looked back at the looming fortress. "It stifles me," he said, his voice choked. "I begged my

44

father to let me go to the university. I told him it would improve our position if I served in the czar's navy. He let me leave here for that reason only."

She laid her head against his sleeve. "What is St. Petersburg like?"

"Beautiful."

"More beautiful than London?"

He laughed, the tension draining from him, and placed his warm hand on her cheek. "London is not beautiful, my pet," he said. "You will see. Paris is beautiful, as are Venice, St. Petersburg. London is cozy. That is the word, isn't it? Cozy, like the royal family."

"The royal family isn't cozy," she protested.

"No? Perhaps not to an Englishman, but to a Russian or a Pole, they seem the very essence of the word."

"What is the Russian court like?" Evelyn asked, watching the way the stream gleamed in the moonlight, racing like quicksilver past their feet.

Alex seemed not to have heard her. His eyes traced a hawk as it drew a shadow across the face of the moon. "Extraordinary," he answered finally, "like a fairy tale. Like a fairy tale," he repeated.

"An English fairy tale or a European one?" Evelyn asked him, remembering the earlier conversation.

The hawk plunged, claws out, falling from the bright night sky like an assassin. When the screaming of its prey had echoed across the landscape and died into the gentle murmur of the stream, Alex answered, "A Russian one."

"Are they different?"

"They are darker."

The carriages moved along the Neva Prospect with their tops down, the parasols of the women shading them from the late afternoon sun and the braid and medals on military uniforms sparkling with flashes of light. "You were right," Evelyn called as she hung over the balcony of the hotel window. "It is like a fairy tale."

Alex, dressed in his official white naval officer's uniform

with its dark trousers and epaulets as new as freshly minted gold coins, came to stand beside her.

"Once upon a time," he murmured, leaning against the window.

"It looks . . . it looks so . . . old-fashioned," Evelyn said. She hugged Alex, her head on his chest where the tunic smelled freshly laundered. "Thank you for bringing me." The tears that seemed to brim up in her at any moment these days flooded her eyes.

He turned her face up towards his. "I could do no less," he said. "You endured like a soldier."

She blinked away the tears. "I don't know why I'm crying. I suppose they're tears of joy. You hear about that, but I've always shrieked with joy. Or I used to."

"When you were a child." She had to look up to find out if he was laughing at her. He was.

"I am a grown woman. I have a husband, and . . ." She still found it hard to say.

"And soon you will have a child," he prompted her.

"Not soon," she said, holding tight to him.

"Sooner than you think. Six months."

"I hope I'm not going to be sick the whole time," she said, moving away from him. The heat coming off the wide avenue beyond the window was suddenly stifling. She turned away into the wide, beautiful room, a room unlike anything she had known: French furniture, a rich blood-red carpet, gold drapes. It was a room that demanded things of its inhabitants.

"You're tired," Alex commented.

"A little."

"Rest while I report to the naval ministry. We'll go out to dinner later if you like, or take a ride through the park."

"The park!" Evelyn clapped her hands.

"Tomorrow perhaps we can go out to the summer palace," Alex promised. "It's Sunday. The czarina and the czar will be there with their children."

"Like Windsor," Evelyn remarked, allowing herself to be gently pushed toward the tall gilded doors to the bedroom.

"No, not at all like Windsor," Alex rebutted. "Like Versailles, perhaps, but nothing at all like that gloomy castle at Windsor."

"Very grand, I expect," Evelyn said as Alex pulled down the coverlet on the bed for her. She needed Esther more than ever now that she was to have a child. She felt ashamed but happy that her husband was willing to do such things to help her. His mother had suggested that she might like to take the servant girl who had attended her on the estate when they came to St. Petersburg, but Evelyn had already given up on her. "It's nothing," she'd said to Alex when he'd suggested replacing the girl. "We weren't nearly as grand as we tried to look when you were courting me. I looked after myself most of the time."

"Ah," he said. "I was lured forward, was I?"

"Shamelessly," she admitted.

The girl whom the dowager countess had assigned to her had thick fingers that broke fastenings, mirrors—in fact, anything she got her hands on. Finally Evelyn had gently ordered her to stand aside. They would be back in England in a month or two, as soon as Alex had made a dutiful journey to the court, spoken to the naval authorities about his new duties, and stopped at the Foreign Office.

The dowager countess would have been horrified to see her noble son turning back the sheets. After that single night on the estate neither had mentioned the court again, but hostility suffused all conversation about St. Petersburg. Alex had insisted Evelyn accompany him, and she was grateful; the old castle had been lonely enough with Alex there, and without him it would have been intolerable.

"We'll be back in England soon." Alex leaned down to kiss her forehead as though he had read her mind.

"Does it show so much?"

"A little." He sounded sad.

She reached for his hand. "I try," she said.

He sat down beside her on the mattress. "We will have to return here one day," he said quietly. "You know that, don't you? This is where I belong. My mother thinks I like

England for its ideas, but the truth is that when I am in England, I feel very Polish, very Russian. This is my land. Our land."

"Alex, I will love it like you do," Evelyn promised. "I will."

His face cleared, the gold and agate eyes filling with pleasure. "Of course you will. Even the czarina isn't really Russian. She's German."

"And the duchess of Edinburgh isn't English at all. She's Russian, the czar's sister."

"And the Queen of Denmark is English."

"The Queen of Romania was too."

"While the Queen of Spain is Romanian."

"And the Queen of Romania is Greek."

"While the Queen of Greece is Danish."

Evelyn laughed. She loved the way Alex could make a game of almost anything. It was almost like being with Morgan in the schoolroom years ago, when everything seemed much simpler.

"So one little countess," she said, "should be able to handle being English and married to a Russian count . . ."

"Who is actually Polish," Alex said. "It's very simple, you see, when you think about it."

"When you're here, it is."

"And I will always be here," he assured her, kissing her temple. "That's the nice part of marriage. It's forever."

"Yes." Evelyn drew in a deep breath.

"Now, you rest. Pull the cord if you need anything." He gestured at the long gold cord that hung by the bed. "A maid will come. The hotel has said they will find someone to assist you here. I'll ask again."

"Thank you."

When he was gone, Evelyn lay back in the shaded bedroom, fighting the waves of nausea that had suddenly swept over her. She clenched her teeth to hold back the moans, concentrating on having left the Bialystok estate. Even in the warmth of the hotel she found it hard to suppress a chill at the memory of the old, damp castle. The countess's implacable hatred had never changed, Natasha had ignored her, and the servants had moved silently through the halls as though they had had their tongues cut out.

Only outside, on the castle's land, had she been happy. The fields in daylight stretched away from the other side of the stream, shimmering in the unnatural heat of this summer of 1914, and as the crops ripened, the field workers burned tan as the darkest firewood, their sturdy bodies a shock of black against the fields that dried to the color of light cocoa, their hair as fair as the wheat. When the hay had been cut and sheaved, the castle looked like a military encampment, fawn-colored tents marching away as though the land had the castle under siege.

By then terrible thoughts plundered Evelyn's peace, fear of what her mother and father would say if she came home alone. Morgan would understand, but then Morgan was at the very least unconventional. Right now he was somewhere in the Mediterranean with Lady Cavendish, who, from all reports, had lost her head and was risking exile and worse for him.

Alex pleased Evelyn, and she knew he was pleased with her, too. Alone together, their happiness exploded in childish laughter. Evelyn remembered the day they rode across the fields toward the small distant hills where the forest grew low to the ground, into the depths of woods whose highest branches, locked together in some desperate embrace no more than twenty feet above the riders, shut out all light.

Looking at Alex, she knew he loved the lands about the estate, the tenants' farms. He was relaxed riding among them in plain breeches, a blue shirt open against the heat, and old riding boots. The first morning he'd come in to breakfast she'd laughed and put her hands to her mouth. He had left before she was up, and now here he was: a gypsy king, already lightly tanned along his neck and forearms. The extraordinary creature who had come through the door might have been a stranger.

"So," he said, holding out his arms for her to see him in all his glory, "what do you think?"

"I think you've deceived me," she answered. "You are not at all the man who married me."

Evelyn had done as much as she dared to make their rooms livable, banishing the worst of the furniture, scarred chests with heavy lids, horrible draperies about the bed that at night dropped evil insects onto their sleeping faces. When Evelyn suggested that something could be done with the large bedroom and two dressing rooms, the barren sitting room on the highest floor of the keep, Alex had shrugged and said, "If you wish," with an indifference to her enthusiasm that should have warned her.

When Evelyn had the private rooms cleared of the hideous furniture, her mother-in-law appeared like an avenging spirit in the door of the sitting room. "What are you doing?" she demanded, her small face twisted with accusation.

"I felt there was too much furniture here for Alex and myself. We would like—"

"My son has lived here nearly all his life." The dowager countess blocked the door. "I know what he likes."

"I asked him—" Evelyn said, her resolve already weakening.

"Ah, you," her mother-in-law retorted, turning away with contempt. "Do as you wish."

"Mother—" Evelyn called out.

She turned, as angry as Evelyn had ever seen her. "Who told you to call me that?" the countess demanded.

"I thought—"

"I do not want to be called Mother by anyone to whom I have not given birth," she was told, as though half-witted. "Can you understand that?"

"Yes. No. Yes, Countess."

The old woman looked at her from the end of the hall, the challenge bright in her eyes, then left. Natasha, who followed the argument between her mother and her brother's wife as though it were a sport, came out of the shadows.

"I don't mean to make her angry," Evelyn said helplessly.

Natasha shrugged her shoulders. "Why do you care? The castle belongs to Alex. Do as you wish. You can throw us out." The spite in Natasha's voice was general, directed both at Evelyn and her own mother.

"If you hate us, tell us to go. There are other houses."

"I don't hate you."

Natasha's silence was filled with disbelief. "I would make us leave," she offered, as though Evelyn had exposed a weakness in her own battle plan.

"Do you want to?" Evelyn was shocked at the challenge in her own voice. She could feel herself being drawn into this woman's battle against her will, feel it twisting her feelings about the estate and even her marriage. And for that she had begun to feel the first twisted stirrings of hatred within herself.

"What I want is unimportant." Natasha made no move to leave.

Wondering if she could help Natasha find some happiness of her own, she asked, "Can I help in any way, Natasha?"

Natasha looked stunned, as though Evelyn had put the sword to her own throat. Her laugh was a horrible sound steeped with incipient madness, and when she turned and ran, the echo of the laugh rang behind to mock Evelyn.

Evelyn had the worst of the furniture removed, but she held back on the rest, leaving the sofas and the draperies in the sitting room. She had intended to have them removed by the seamstresses in the castle, and have clean cotton draperies hung at the windows, new linens for their bed instead of the old, patched linens that they were given. Instead she rode out with Alex early and delayed her return until her back ached and the sun slanting across the fields had burned a pain into her brain.

"Stand up to Mother," Alex had said, but even he was only half-serious. He was careful with her himself, and at first Evelyn was dismayed, thinking that this was a moral failure. Finally she understood: He thought his mother mad, truly mad, and he was frightened for her, not of her.

"She has had a hard life," he suggested one afternoon when the sun was already low behind the distant hills.

"Was she like this when your father was alive?"

Alex turned away from her so one side of his face was gilded by the last rays of the setting sun that turned the other into a forbidding mask as unrelieved as a bronze statue. "No," he said, his eyes seeking the castle. "She was different then."

"She is lonely," Evelyn suggested.

He looked at her. "No," he said after a moment. "She hated him." The words were said flatly, with no emotion at all.

Not certain what was expected of her, Evelyn let her own glance wander across the fields to where a line of workers trudged home against the sunset. "I see," she said, though she didn't.

"I don't think so," Alex said, and when Evelyn made to spur her horse on, he put his hand out to hold the reins. When she looked back, his horse had shifted and the sunset blazed behind his head. "He captured her," Alex said, the words coming out of the darkness. "He brought her here from her home, and then he ignored and abandoned her."

The breeze sent a chill down Evelyn's spine, carrying voices in the twilight speaking a tongue she couldn't understand. "Could she have gone home?" She knew that they were both listening to the meaning beneath her words.

"He wouldn't let her."

The sun disappeared in one last angry breath, the heat filling the sudden dark before the breeze rose again more strongly, freshening the countryside.

"And so she slowly went mad," Alex said, but his voice had returned to normal.

"I won't," she told him boldly.

"I won't ignore you," Alex promised.

"Thank you." Not long before they had been close, friends riding home, a married couple, husband and wife happy in each other's company, and now she was thanking him like a stranger who had offered help.

He released her saddle and rode on ahead, spurring his horse to a gallop that led her into the darkness. She caught up with him as the lights came on in the lowest rooms of the castle, turning into the stables built where the walls had been allowed to fall into disrepair. Her own anger was hard in her, and it wasn't until after they had bathed and sat through another cheerless meal that she found the courage to ask the other question.

"What happened to your father?" She knew only that he had been dead for five years.

Alex was undressing. "He had a stroke," he said with his back turned, "I told you that." He threw his stiff collar on the table in the sitting room and growled, "This room is never warm."

"Shall I call for a fire?"

He was at the window, looking down on his lands. "When I was a child," he said, "I was never allowed a fire until October." He looked back at her. "My bones would ache."

"Your mother refused."

"My father. He thought of it as discipline. That and cleaning my own boots. I cleaned my own boots until I was fifteen. When I went away to the academy I learned for the first time that I had a position in the world. I was brought up like a peasant." He paused. "Perhaps that wasn't so bad. I lived in the fields, as my father did, and at night I came back here to the castle. I had a tutor, but he taught me nothing except how to read and write and some mathematics. That seemed enough. Then I went away to school, and there was a whole new world—literally. Russia." He seemed to relax for the first time in hours. "You will see. The grandeur. It cowed me at first. And the arrogance, quite different from what I had seen at home. My father was a strange man, unbending, unforgiving, proud, but he was never arrogant. He knew his place in this world and accepted it. He had no desire to leave here, none at all, and he walked his lands beside his people, a world unchanged in many ways for a hundred years— more perhaps."

Alex came back across the carpet to stand near Evelyn. "There was never a book in the whole house," he told her bemusedly. "Never. My schoolbooks, though those were simple. Then in St. Petersburg I discovered books, thought, art. It was a new world, overwhelming. But with it came the Russian court, where even the lowest of the pages, such as I was, had a title and his own servants. I felt that I had been thrown from high ramparts into a deep river, and I had to fight my way to the surface. When I got there, I was bursting with new ideas. I came back here and told my father what I had discovered." Alex stopped, looking down into Evelyn's eyes. "My father said," he continued, "that if I talked like that, he would bring me back. That had nothing to do with my life." He stopped again, as though Evelyn might not understand. "I was in despair, but I was quiet, for I knew he meant what he told me. I was at the court because I had been invited—a great honor—and I was expected to live at the academy until I could take a commission that would prepare me to fight for the czar should we ever go to war. These were perilous times. My father knew that, though he wanted to turn his back on them, and he knew that a voice at court could be useful, even essential someday.

"So I went back to St. Petersburg, but even there I couldn't talk about what I was thinking; the boys had been brought up with an imbued sense of their own importance. They couldn't conceive of any world except one in which they were superior. The only people who seemed to understand were the teachers, but they were frightened to speak out. They suggested books very quietly to me, and I read them. No discussion, just enough books to teach me that I was not alone in my thoughts. I served in the court, rose at the academy, became a naval ensign, and studied engineering, not because I was interested but because it was the only course of study my father would allow. He could see the use of it. After, I served in the navy until one night the news came that he had had a stroke."

Evelyn had to know. She said, "He died?"

He walked away again, poured himself a brandy at the table near the window, and held it up to her. She went to him and took it from his hand while he fought for time, deciding whether to continue. "No, he didn't die," he went on, finally, "not right away. I came back, and he was in his room. He couldn't speak. His face was frozen in a mask, twisted like a nurse's story that if a child didn't behave, the wind would change and his face freeze as it was."

The brandy warmed Evelyn. She sat as quietly as she could on the old sofa, hoping that he would tell her everything, remembering Alex's masklike countenance earlier that afternoon.

"And he had a nurse," Alex said softly. "My mother." He drained his glass. "She had her revenge. She waited on him herself, bringing in his food, feeding him like a child, wiping the spittle from his face, and all the time—she smiled."

Evelyn touched her husband's arm. "Alex," she whispered, "this doesn't matter now."

"The past always matters, Evvy," he said reflectively, the first time he had ever used Morgan's nickname for her. "That's what we bring to our judgments. I'm a product of all of this." He waved his hand about the dusty room.

"It will change when we live here," she assured him, but she heard her words as though they came from someone else's mouth. She had known, of course, that one day she would live here; already she had become accustomed to being addressed as "Countess" by the workers and the servants. At first she had found it uncomfortable, as though she were a little girl masquerading, but now she hardly heard the title. Still, the thought—spoken aloud—that she would spend the rest of her life here brought back all her troubled thoughts.

"It will be much better with you," Alex said seriously. At moments like that, when from within his great certainty and experience he treated her as an equal, she loved him with a strength she had never expected to find within herself.

"I love you," she said.

"A new world," he told her, holding her against him. "Built here on the foundation of the old."

"New curtains," Evelyn said, catching his spirit. "New furniture."

"So bourgeois," he said fondly, pressing the length of his body against hers, a body grown stronger, more demanding with the fresh air, the daily rides, the demands the estate had put on him while he was home.

"I'm English," she reminded him.

"No more," he said, leaning closer. He kissed the corner

of her mouth, ran his sun-streaked beard across the line of her chin so she had to raise it, kissed her where her throat touched her shoulders. A shudder ran through her.

"No," she murmured, "not English." She held tight to him, feeling the warmth spreading through her. She felt his fingers on the back of her gown, felt him pull at the fastenings impatiently. Her breasts came free of the brocade as a sense of abandon coursed through her that made her laugh deep within. "Not English," she repeated as his rough hands cupped them, squeezing gently as his tongue traced a path from her throat. He dropped to his knees, his lips closing over the nipple of one breast while his hands ran up under her skirts and along her thighs. She cried out with a joy that was almost childlike as the skirt fell, then her undergarments, and she was naked in front of him. His hands took hold of her buttocks, pulling her belly against his face, and her knees buckled slightly as he brought her down to him on the floor.

She lay among the ruins of her dress while he kissed her paler flesh with a hunger that made her go still beneath him. When he pulled off his shirt she could smell his own odor of sunshine and the faint sweat brought on by his lust. He took off the remainder of his clothes while his eyes held her transfixed, lying on her back, her arms wide beside her head, her legs pressed together. As he touched her gently a great languor went through her, and she stretched like a cat, secure in his passion, his need for her. His hands moved more surely over her flesh, finding the places that he had discovered most pleased her, probing, exploring until she cried out, arching her back, and reaching for him with a muffled plea.

His own body covered hers as she opened to receive him, taking him into her with gratitude, moving with him as he set their rhythm, the two of them alone in their passions, yet joined, rising to their mutual climax that exploded as she felt him pulsing into her. She clutched at him, the cries tearing unrestrained from within her.

They stayed locked together, damp with the exertions of their love, Evelyn's face pressed against Alex's neck as he drew deep breaths of the fragrance of her hair, the animal cries of the final moments of his passion becoming gentle murmurings. The pain and anger had left his tiger eyes, and Evelyn wanted to sleep there among the clothes. His lips touched hers gently, and then he crouched, lifted her in his arms, and carried her naked through the sitting room to the bedroom, where the moonlight falling through the open window imparted the beauty of a mountain cave to the big, ugly room. There he put her on the bed, straddling her so his heavy thighs lightly touched hers, and watched her silently until the sounds from beyond the window—a dog barking angrily somewhere on the castle grounds, a voice calling to it to be still—brought the present back.

She fell asleep in Alex's arms, safe among the odors of his body, the comfort of his strength, and she dreamed of an open countryside, broad, rich fields, flowing brooks, and soft green woods all empty save for themselves.

She awoke with terror coursing through her, sat up, and looked about. She was alone. The window was open, and the moon had journeyed over the roof of the castle so the world beyond was a black sky pierced with stars fading with the dawn.

Pulling a sheet about her, she went into the next room to see if he was there. His clothes remained tangled with hers on the floor, but the room was empty. The curtains moved in the dawn breeze. She went to close the window and saw there, far distant, a horse that she knew to be Alex's, the rider bent low over the saddle as the beast galloped across the fields toward the horizon. She held onto the windowsill, watching until the horse and rider were lost in the bleaching of the morning sky.

Hearing the grooms in the stables below, the maids moving through the halls, she gathered up the clothes and went back to bed. Alex, who had held her with such love the night before, had fled, driven by some demons of his own that found him even in his sleep.

Not English, she reminded herself when the maid brought her morning tea—weak, as unlike the tea at home as she was unlike the broad-cheeked peasant girl who placed the tea tray clumsily on the bedside table. This was her home now, she reminded herself when the girl was gone. She put the tea aside after one taste, deciding that perhaps she should give the morning coffee that the family drank another try. England was a long way off, and she was a fool to think that Alex's love for her and hers for him would be enough to make her feel at ease. She would have to work harder at becoming one with this place. But for a little while, just a little while, she wanted to remain English in some small corner of herself, listen to gentle rains, walk in a cooler landscape under a milder sun. They had the whole future together. To be English a little while longer would be permitted, she was sure.

Three weeks later, she knew she was pregnant.

Later in the day, Alex returned to the hotel room holding two red tickets in his hands.

"The theater?" Evelyn asked. She was spreading the dresses she owned on her bed—several as yet unworn, for in the castle she had learned that if she dressed well she risked disapproval for her extravagance—across the bed.

"Not just the theater," Alex said, coming closer to kiss her. "The ballet."

"Oh Alex, really?" Evelyn cried. For though she had been raised in a household where the only theater anyone ever attended was the Christmas pantomime, even she had heard of the fame of the Russian ballet.

"Ninskaya is dancing."

"Is she famous?"

"Better—she is notorious!" Alex said, looking down at the dresses on the bed. "Still, you may be the most beautiful woman there."

"No, I won't, Alex," Evelyn chided. "You mustn't say that. I will see that I'm not and be angry later."

"It's true," he said. "Except for the ladies on the stage, who are chosen for their legs as well as their dancing skills, the women at the theater will be like potato sacks emblazoned with jewels."

"Your mother's right," Evelyn declared, looking at the tickets. "One day you will be tried for treason."

"If I am, it will have to be in secret," Alex responded. "For if they tried me in public, I should simply tell the secrets everyone knows: The ballerinas are all fallen women, the nobles old lechers, and their wives filled with envy."

"It's not true, is it?"

"That the wives are filled with envy? Yes, absolutely, envy and potatoes."

"That the ballerinas are fallen women," Evelyn quizzed. "You know perfectly well what I am saying."

"Ninskaya started as a girl from a simple family in Georgia, and she now owns a very respectable collection of jewels, a townhouse that would suit an embassy, and a country estate that coincidentally is within riding distance of the Grand Duke Nicholas, the czar's uncle. Even the most thrifty of little dancers would have a hard time achieving that in five years."

"And she's going to dance tonight?" Evelyn asked, thrilled.

"Of course. The grand duke is in the city. They say he spent ten days talking to his nephew about the state of the army, gave up in despair because the czar kept advocating the values of a good home life and wouldn't listen, and fled back into the city to see his mistress dance."

Evelyn sat on the bed. "What will the czar do?"

"The czar, nothing. The czarina, however, will consider it a personal affront, which is probably what the grand duke intended. He hates her."

"Alex, please," Evelyn said, looking toward the door of the suite.

"You are becoming Russian," Alex said in wonder. "You're afraid."

"No, no, not afraid," Evelyn said, reaching out to touch the pale pink satin of the gown Alex had ordered for her from Paris. "But even in England no one would talk that way of the king."

"The king of England, like his cousin, the czar, lives a

blameless life," Alex pointed out, "unlike his father, however, who used to travel incognito through Europe tumbling women."

Evelyn was laughing. "I should wear these dresses anyway," she said, touching her stomach, where she could still not detect the child she was carrying. "Soon I expect I'll look like the other sacks of potatoes. It would be a waste not to wear them," she added wistfully.

"You will be the most beautiful potato sack," Alex assured her. "And afterwards you can buy new dresses."

"In Paris? These are the first French dresses I've even seen up close."

"Yes, of course in Paris. After the baby is born in London, you can go over to Paris with your mother. You can buy anything you want."

"Your mother will be very angry if I spend money like this."

"We don't want to make her too angry," Alex said. "Something terrible might happen to her, and we would have to return home before we were ready."

The thought of being recalled to the estates sobered Evelyn. "Why is the grand duke so upset about the army, anyway?" Evelyn asked. "There isn't going to be a war, is there?"

"There is always another war," Alex said quietly. "Eventually."

Evelyn looked toward the window where the northern sky was as pale as china, pink and the lightest blue. "Not soon, surely. Everything is so . . . peaceful."

"Yes," Alex agreed. "It is. I suggest the pink."

Evelyn stood and held it against her, looked in the long mirror, turning each way to examine herself. "Are you sure?" she asked doubtfully. "I don't want to stand out too much."

"Now there you speak again as an Englishwoman," Alex said. "A Russian noblewoman would insist on standing out. I'm afraid that even with your beauty and your new dress you will have some competition from the women's jewels," he said.

"I have the ruby necklace you gave me," Evelyn reminded him.

He shook his head. "It's nothing."

"Surely not."

"You will see," he warned her.

Later, dressed in the pink satin gown, her hair raised high above her head as she had seen pictures of women in Paris wearing their hair, she looked at herself in the mirror before joining Alex. The sight startled her: She was beautiful. The dress exposed her neck and shoulders, hinted cleverly at more bosom than she had, and fell snugly across her hips to flow around her ankles in a way she assumed only Paris dressmakers could achieve. When she walked, the dress moved subtly to show off her figure, parting very slightly at the ankle to reveal just a little of her white silk stockings.

Alex looked up as she came into the sitting room, stopped as he poured the champagne, and said, "It's true. Pregnancy does make a woman more beautiful, if that is possible."

"I can't believe it," Evelyn admitted, thrilled at the miracle that had been achieved.

"You must believe it," Alex said. "You will only get more beautiful."

"If you buy me dresses like this," Evelyn said, craning to see herself in the mirror over the mantel, "I shall feel shameless. I feel I want people to look at me."

"They shall," Alex promised her, pouring the champagne. He held out her glass to her. "To our future."

"Yes," she agreed. The excitement in her was that of a child faced with some unimaginable holiday, yet she felt more grown up than she ever had.

"You aren't wearing your necklace."

"I wanted you to fasten it for me," she explained. "I'm afraid it might drop off if I do it."

"Where is it?"

"On my table in the bedroom."

He came back dangling the ruby and diamond choker in his hands. "You should have more," he said. "You shall have more," he promised. She turned her back, and in the mirror she saw the rubies catch the reflection of the pink satin, bringing fire to her eyes, making her skin blush with health.

"You spoil me."

He kissed her shoulders, rubbing the palm of his hand toward her breasts.

"Please." She giggled. "Not now. I want to see the fallen lady."

"Risen, more like it." Alex laughed. "Risen quite beyond her wildest dreams, I should think."

"I don't know," Evelyn murmured, unable to take her eyes off her own reflection. She touched the diamonds and rubies with her fingertips. "I imagine a woman could dream extraordinary dreams if she was truly beautiful."

"I warn you," Alex joked. "If I so much as see you lower your eyes at the old goats who will be struck senseless by the sight of you, I shall ship you back to the estate."

Evelyn wrapped a silver silk stole that Alex had bought her at Worth's in Paris about her shoulders, and they descended to the lobby of the hotel. As the brass-caged elevator sank slowly into the two-storied lobby she saw that servants in the hotel, liveried as richly as though they worked for a private house, were watching for them. "You are the loveliest woman in St. Petersburg," Alex whispered to her. "People want to see you."

"If I am at all noticeable," Evelyn said as the glass and brass cage settled to a stop with a sigh, "it's because the real beauties are away for the summer."

"You are so modest."

The bellman opened the elevator cage, and as they stepped into the gold-carpeted reception hall Evelyn saw that people did indeed turn to look at the young bride and her handsome older husband. She felt a thrill as poignant as though she were doing something illicit, holding Alex's arm, head high as he had taught her, as they passed down the length of the imposing room with the management bowing, the lower servants keeping their eyes down and making their most obsequious bends. Above, a chandelier as large as some huts Evelyn had seen in the countryside shimmered in the early evening gloom, and as they approached the wide door the doormen threw both sides open so they could step directly into the evening without pause.

"I like being a countess," Evelyn sighed.

The carriage that Alex had ordered to take them to the theater was waiting.

"I wish we had one with the top down," she said.

"So you could flaunt yourself," Alex teased her as he settled beside her in the narrow interior.

"So I could see more," Evelyn insisted.

"You'll have plenty of time to see St. Petersburg," Alex said, taking her hand. "We won't live as my mother does. When we come back from England, we'll live part of each year on the estate and the rest at court."

"Could we?"

"I think it would be wise, if nothing else," Alex said as the carriage turned across the broad street so that they headed back toward the opera house. "These are going to be perilous years, and a wise man will have to watch his own interests."

Beyond the narrow window of the rocking carriage, the city lay bathed in a velvet night. The light standards on the bridges glowed like golden torches as the hooves of the horses clicked past them. "Everything looks so . . . so unchanging," Evelyn said, puzzled. "You speak as though there was trouble, but all of this is so much like a picture. I think I could live here forever."

"And forever it has been," Alex said quietly. "What you are seeing has nothing to do with Russia. This is St. Petersburg, a city meant to make all of us more European."

"It must be beautiful in the snow," Evelyn said as the great palaces of the highest nobles passed in review along the river bank.

"If you can imagine Venice with the canals frozen solid and the people wrapped to the eyes in coats against a cold so bitter you have never endured anything like it, yes," Alex agreed.

"Don't be angry with me, please," Evelyn said. "I don't want to make you angry. It's all so . . . so magical, that's all. Like a beautiful storybook."

"You are very intelligent, Evvy," Alex said. "Did you know that?"

"Morgan has the brains in the family."

Alex let several seconds pass before he answered her. "Morgan is very clever."

"You don't like him," Evelyn said, taking her eyes off the view outside the carriage that was now passing between two imposing buildings to enter the opera square.

"I like him," Alex said. "But sometimes clever people underestimate other people."

"Like Dottie Cavendish," Evelyn teased. She could see the opera house—as large as a palace, every window glowing from within with a light as golden as the moon that hung above the city.

"Not at all," Alex said. "Dottie Cavendish is much cleverer than Morgan, believe me. No, Morgan underestimates the people close to him."

"Me?" Evelyn said, surprised at her rising anger.

"Possibly. Me also. More important, he has a contempt for those in authority."

"As you do," Evelyn shot back at Alex. Her cheeks had heated for an argument.

Alex's face lost all expression. She saw a fire light in the depths of his eyes. "Don't you ever speak to me like that," he said coldly.

The carriage was coming to a halt at the end of a line of other carriages moving slowly toward the entrance of the opera house. The happiness of the afternoon seeped away. Evelyn knew she should apologize to Alex, but her throat had closed with the shock that she felt at the sudden change in his face, like a sky transformed by lightning, cold with dislike. For a second she thought he might strike her; then the muscles of his face relaxed. He drew a breath. "You are young," was all he said as their carriage reached the entrance to the theater.

If she had had the courage, Evelyn would have told the driver to return to the hotel, but the footman was already down from the box to open the door for her. She allowed herself to be helped out, the tears threatening to rise again into her eyes. Before her the broad steps into the opera house were filled with milling people, uniforms of such exotic richness that she might have been on the very stage itself, the women's gowns as they swept the steps shimmering with embroidery, cloaks of vivid red, gold, purple, emerald greens splashing the night with color.

She felt Alex take her arm. Without looking at each other they joined the throng moving toward the crystal doors at the head of the steps.

"Look," Alex whispered, "Grand Duchess Elizabeth." A tall, very thin woman dressed from head to toe in black satin and diamonds stood alone in a clearing on the steps while the theater managers bowed to greet her and her party, who stood two steps below her: an equerry, half a dozen courtiers, four ladies-in-waiting all encrusted with medals, pendants, tiaras.

"Why is she here?" Evelyn asked, leaning closer to Alex.

"Shush," he said gently as the imperial party moved forward through the tall, diamond-bright doors. The crowd behind flowed after them once more, pushing in on either side of Evelyn and Alex. "To give support," Alex murmured when they were within the dazzling interior of the hall. The walls glittered with gilt and framed scenes of women and men in pastoral settings, on swings, at rest by riverbanks, dancing in ways no peasant ever had.

"To whom?" Evelyn asked, her eyes darting to the double staircase that flowed out of the hall. On every second step a tailcoated footman in white brocade trimmed with gold stood at attention. As the grand duchess made her way up the left staircase, the footmen bowed at the waist like reeds in the wind.

"To the grand duke. She's his sister," Alex said, watching the thin black figure that stood out among all the varied colors reach the top of the stairs and disappear. "They all hate the czarina. The little dancer means nothing, but by appearing tonight after the scandal at the summer palace, she shows what the imperial family feels. It supports the Grand Duke Nicholas against his nephew."

"What will happen?" Evelyn asked. A tiny bell was

ringing through the hall as they followed the grand duchess's path up the stairs.

"What always happens," Alex replied. "Nothing, unless there is a catastrophe."

They had reached the first tier. Alex led them along the row of doors until he found the one he was looking for. A footman opened it for them, and they passed through into a small room, no larger than a closet and furnished with a sofa and some chairs. Beyond the drapes, which Alex held back, Evelyn saw four chairs with gold seats and slim backs set at the front of the box. Her heart did its own small dance as she stepped forward two more steps and the vista of the imperial theater lay before her, as rich and strange as the landscape from the castle window: the boxes on either side curving from the empty central box presided over by the imperial eagle and festooned with hanging roses; the pendulous chandeliers draped with crystals; the blue and pink ceiling where cupids chased an array of gods across the roof of the world; and, directly below, the stage with velvet forest-green curtains trimmed with silver.

As they took their seats in the front of the box they saw the grand duke come alone into his own box across the theatre. Tall, with a beard like Father Christmas, he looked to Evelyn like some kindly uncle who would dress up at Christmas to give presents to the children of an English estate. The grand duke seemed to feel her eyes on him and looked directly across the room to bow to her. Evelyn flushed in confusion.

Alex smiled. "You've made your first conquest," he told her.

The theater filled very quickly once the grand duke was seated, and then there was a long silence.

"What are we waiting for?" Evelyn whispered.

Alex sighed. "The grand duchess," he told her. "They play these little games. Tonight, as the czar's aunt she will sit in the imperial box, which will outrage the empress to a religious fury because of the lady on the stage. But even then, the grand duchess cannot sit with her brother, who, you see, is here as a 'sporting man,' as the English would say." Alex's eyes narrowed, watching the imperial box with all the other eyes. "So much energy," he said. "Such a waste."

As though called forward by his impatience, the imposing figure in black came through the curtains of the imperial box without looking to left or right. Her equerries arranged themselves with her ladies-in-waiting behind her, and the theater rose as one. The orchestra struck up the cacophonous Russian anthem, and they stood, men at attention and women absolutely still, until it had played through.

The theater went dark at the second the grand duchess sat, and then the performance began, with the dramatic stage lighting splashing on the curtain that rose on the elaborate set. Lost in the music, Evelyn drifted happily into a fantasy that seemed no more than part of the world she now moved in: the forest settings, the dancing sprites, the appearances of princes in hunting clothes, fairies dancing across the stage in flowing transparent skirts. All seemed an extension of the audience until, as the audience sighed with happiness, Ninskaya entered and stopped dead center, bowed formally to the stony-faced grand duchess, and then turned just the very slightest to give an almost imperceptible acknowledgment to her protector. The music struck up to cover the audience's appreciation of scandal, and the dance continued through pageantry, melodrama, and magic until the curtain came down at the intermission to thunderous applause led by the grand duke.

The imperial box was empty, Evelyn saw when she turned to say to Alex, "It's the most beautiful spectacle I've ever seen." She pointed. "Look, the grand duchess is gone."

"Assuredly," he said. "She left half an hour ago."

"Is she angry?"

"Not at all. She had done what she came to do. She didn't come to see her brother's mistress show her legs." He rose. "Come," he said, and he led her back to the small anteroom behind the box where mysteriously an ice cooler and a bottle of champagne, two glasses, and a silver tray sat ready.

But before they could pour the champagne there was a knock at the door. Alex, bottle poised, looked displeased, and at the sight of the military uniform, his face froze.

"His Imperial Highness, the Grand Duke Nicholas, requests that Count Lezenski and the countess join him in his box."

"Of course," said Alex shortly. "Come, Evelyn."

They followed the equerry along the corridor. Within the box the grand duke stood among several men and women, the men all in uniform, the women lavishly dressed and jeweled. Evelyn could feel Alex's anger as he held her elbow, his fingers pressing against her skin.

"Ah, Alex," said the grand duke, stepping forward. "I had heard you were married."

"May I present my wife," Alex said stiffly. "Evelyn, His Imperial Highness, the Grand Duke Nicholas."

The grand duke didn't take his eyes off Evelyn's face as he reached for her hand, bowed over it in the continental manner, and murmured, "Welcome to Russia, Countess Lezenski." His lips when he touched her fingers were fringed with his thick beard, which close up Evelyn saw was threaded with gray. And though his face looked old and weathered, he had the eyes of a young man.

"Thank you, Your Highness," she answered, withdrawing her hand carefully.

"And are you enjoying Russia?"

"I haven't seen much of it," Evelyn told him. "We have just arrived. What I have seen I find enchanting."

"Alex, you must be sure to show your wife only the best of Russia," the grand duke said, stepping back to slap Alex on the shoulder. "We must encourage beautiful women to love Russia."

As Evelyn blushed she saw women scrutinizing her from head to toe. She in turn looked over the extraordinary jewels: emeralds the size of stones in a stream, diamonds so large that in England they would have been dismissed as paste on anyone except the royal family, strings of pearls that were quail's eggs. A sudden feeling of claustrophobia overcame her. The very clothes about her, despite the summer heat, were made of material that would be fit for curtains, the uniforms of heavy serge. The room closed about her, and she held tight to Alex's arm.

He looked down at her. "Are you all right?"

She shook her head, dumbly.

"Your Highness, I must ask you to allow us to withdraw," Alex said. "The countess is unwell."

The grand duke disbelieved him for the briefest moment, his own expression changing from pleasure to petulance, but one look at Evelyn made it clear she truly was unsteady. "The excitement, I expect," he said, but he scrutinized her figure minutely, and a ripple of laughter went around the room.

Outside the box again, Evelyn could feel the tears rising. "I feel like such a fool," she said, holding her head high.

"We should leave," Alex told her, steering her toward the stairs while the crowd parted for them.

"Oh no, Alex, I don't want to spoil it for you."

Alex said nothing as he smiled their way through the crowd. In the fresh air outside the theater, Evelyn revived. "I think we could go back," she said.

Alex adjusted the silver shawl about her shoulders. "No, you have seen enough of the comedy for one night." Except for the theater servants, they were alone as the bell rang within the theater and the crowd drifted within for the second act.

In the carriage Evelyn sat in despairing silence until Alex took her hand. "Don't be sad," he reassured her. "There will be many, many other times, much nicer. I thought it would be amusing for you. When I am away, I forget how foolish it is."

"I didn't mean to make a fool of myself," she said in a tiny voice.

"Of course not, and you didn't. Among those people, how could you? They are playing out a grand comedy of their own."

"Is he really such a great general?"

"He could be," Alex said soberly, "if he were not reduced to playing little games such as you witnessed tonight." He looked at the passing parade of imposing palaces, their lights glowing brightly in the summer night. "It is a tragedy to have one's fate tied to such people."

Evelyn laid her head back on his shoulder. "It was a beautiful night anyway," she said. "Look, there is a private yacht!" A white-hulled vessel slipped slowly up the river past the marble-fronted palaces, another fantasy come to life.

"The czar's," Alex told her without moving his head. He watched until the yacht had passed them and was lost to sight.

"Was the imperial family on board?" Evelyn asked. The excitement of it all overwhelmed her—the pageantry, the jewels, the extravagance of everything, so unlike anything that could be seen in England.

"Perhaps," Alex murmured, lost in thought. "In summer they visit everywhere. The empress insists they go to Germany, where her family are."

"No matter what you say," Evelyn said with force, "I think it is all very, very beautiful." She kissed him on the cheek. "And I am very glad you asked me to marry you, because I shall love living here. I know it."

He smiled at her in the shadow of the carriage. "I shall be happy because you are here," he told her. He kissed her, and they were unaware that the carriage had stopped until the footman coughed discreetly at the open door.

Upstairs in their suite, Alex called for a light supper. Evelyn became lightheaded with more champagne. Before she undressed, she looked at herself one last time in the long mirror of the bedroom, still unable to reconcile the woman in the pink and silver dress with the gawky schoolgirl she still considered herself.

As Alex came up behind her to unfasten the necklace, she touched his hands. "I think I would almost like to sleep with it on," she giggled.

He undid the clasp and threw it on the table near the bed. "You will have many more much finer jewels," he promised. "A woman should be given jewels young, when she can still do them justice." The moonlight fell upon the carpet, and a breeze came from the river, as he held her in his arms before she slept. Later she would remember that for the first night as a married woman she had no dreams at all.

She slept deeply and soundly until Alex stirred suddenly and sat up. "What is it?" Evelyn asked, watching him with the sheets about his waist, his broad chest dark against the dawn's light.

"Listen," he hushed her.

Then she heard the bells pealing in the city, a relentless funeral dirge, calling from church to church, thunderous as their volume grew.

Alex dressed quickly, but before his boots were on there was a knock at the outer door. When he came back to where Evelyn cowered beneath the sheet he was as pale as the sky beyond the window. "The Austrian Archduke Ferdinand has been assassinated in Sarajevo," he whispered, sitting down on the edge of the bed.

"What does it mean?" Evelyn cried over the tolling bells that now seemed to fill the room with doom.

"It means," Alex said, turning wide, thoughtful eyes upon his young wife, "that what was a comedy last night is a tragedy today."

BOOK
TWO

China, 1924

4

Evelyn was already late for work as she hurried down the narrow staircase and into the rain. Beyond the door she could see the gutter running with filthy water, something gray and already formless decomposing, probably a dog. The Chinese family who owned the building and ground-floor herb store sat crouched around a brazier feeding their faces with chopsticks. They didn't look up as she pushed along the open corridor and into the narrow Shanghai street.

As she held her breath against the rank smell of the overflowing canal, hunger contracted her stomach. She wished she had the price of a rickshaw, but almost all their money had gone to the trip to Peking for the funeral of the grand duke and duchess. She was determined to speak to Mr. Sebowski today about an advance on her meager salary. But the thought of having to knock on his door and see him look up, his eyes as cold as the winter sky behind his small rimless glasses, made her grow cold. He would make her explain—beg, really—before he would call for the Chinese bookkeeper and arrange for the advance.

The bookkeeper, who always had money—like the rest of the Chinese who worked in the Russian-Asiatic Bank—would sniff his contempt for her as he counted out the money. There were some who said that the Chinese now owned the bank, that Mr. Sebowski was merely kept on because the foreign hongs preferred to deal with a Westerner—even a Westerner who, like Evelyn, had no country anymore. Mr. Sebowski, however, was still comfortable. He could buy another passport, if he hadn't already. Evelyn and the other Russian émigrés were stateless.

The small expanse of sky visible between the overhanging rooflines of the Chinese houses was black with rainclouds. Evelyn was exhausted from the nine-hour return journey from the Imperial City spent upright on the hardwood third-class seats, with Alex beside her, stony-faced in his grief, and his mother elbowing the Chinese in the compartment as viciously as though she were back on the estate. Only Natasha, the ever-present half smile playing about the corners of her broad mouth, seemed calm. There were times when Evelyn wondered if Natasha understood what had happened—an empire fallen, the imperial family murdered, the Lezenski estates lost—for in some strange manner Natasha had seemed to prosper in their exile. On their near-starvation diet she had grown fat, her bitterness turned to stubborness. Evelyn, with her meager education, had still been the only one of the family who could find work. Alex was too educated and too proud; Natasha simply refused.

Evelyn stepped quickly back onto the sidewalk to allow a palanquin to pass. The two coolies' feet splashed dirty water as the silk curtains of the carriage swayed to allow Evelyn a quick glimpse of a sing-song girl within, no more than fourteen years old but made up so elaborately as to appear a caricature. The bearers hurried on, anxious to get their mistress to her appointment before the worst of the rain began to fall.

Thunder rolled overhead, and Evelyn hurried faster toward the Bund. Alex's mother was meant to look after Victoria during the day, but Evelyn never left the three rooms where they all lived without fear for her daughter, who had been running a fever when they returned last night. The dowager countess made an attempt, she knew, to do what was right for the child, but her own children had been raised by servants. Most winter days she spent holding Victoria on her knee, talking to her of life on an estate that in memory became more magical, more poignant in loss than it had ever been. When the child cried, the old woman was helpless, leaving her alone on her narrow bed while the dowager countess paced the floor saying silent prayers for the family's return to Europe.

Natasha was stone-deaf when the child cried. She had never touched the baby, never helped in the long flight from Sevastopol, never spoke either to her or of her. Evelyn watched the child's food carefully to make sure she got her portion, as Natasha ate the scraps that the others left, her eyes as bright as those of the rats that lurked after dark at the stairs.

The smell of humanity crowded onto the little sampans that bobbed on the rising waters of Soochow Creek made Evelyn cover her mouth. Holding the oilskin umbrella lower over her head, she ran across the broad bridge and onto the Bund. There the avenue opened up as suddenly as though she were passing into a new country, long cars driven by uniformed chauffeurs stopping before tall European-style buildings. On the Yangtze side ocean liners moved very slightly on the current. Tenders pushed away from their gangplanks to bring passengers to the international settlement. On the other side of the river, cranes rose above the godowns and factories of the industrial section of the city.

The turbaned Sikh doormen turned their faces away at the sight of a European woman hurrying unattended through the rain, a curtain of slashing gray that obscured the ornate facade of the Palace Hotel as Evelyn turned into the side street and ran up the steps to the bank. The Chinese doorman in his black uniform with silver braid opened the tall gilt doors, and she passed into silence as another, louder roll of thunder warned the city. The lightning came in a flash, silvering the cold marble hall, the staircases to the right and left that rose to reveal the clerks' many cubicles.

"Good morning, Countess," Mr. Han Lee Cheong greeted her as she walked across the marble floor, leaving wet footprints behind.

"I'm sorry I'm late, Mr. Han," she apologized, closing the oilskin umbrella clumsily. A shower of raindrops fell on his face and the shoulders of his black morning coat, but he neither blinked nor moved.

"Mr. Sebowski wishes to speak to you, Countess."

Evelyn turned as cold as the marble underfoot. "Me?"

"Yes, Countess," Mr. Han said, the very faintest contempt in his voice, as his eyes swept the rows of clerks already bowed over their work.

"I went to the grand duke's funeral," she blurted out in a panic. "The train was very late."

Mr. Han said nothing, but his eyes revealed that he thought the funeral of a Russian grand duke of no importance whatsoever. He snapped his fingers at a passing Chinese clerk who hurried forward obsequiously. Mr. Han walked away, talking to the clerk.

Evelyn saw that she was being watched by the other clerks. She straightened her back and went toward the broad staircase to the second floor and into the disapproving gaze of Mr. Sebowski's secretary.

"Mr. Sebowski wants to see me?" she asked quietly.

The secretary, a Frenchwoman stranded in China by an unfaithful husband, instructed her to put down the dripping umbrella. "I'll tell him you're here." She rose, very thin, her hair crimped into the newest style that emphasized rather than denied her approaching middle age.

Evelyn put her umbrella against the chair leg in front of the desk.

"Not there!" the woman said. "You'll get the floor wet."

The sleepless night caught up with Evelyn, and defiance welled up. "You can call one of the boys to mop it up."

"They are not here to clean up after the clerks," the woman told her, one hand on the door to Sebowski's office.

Sitting down with her back to the woman, Evelyn heard the door shut sharply behind her. As she closed her eyes, images of the western hills bathed in the last of the afternoon's sun washed across her eyelids. As unbidden as a dream, St. Petersburg floated out of her subconscious—the Italianate buildings, the drive along the river, open carriages ... And then the dream shifted. The Bund's European buildings were shut to her, doormen standing guard as she hurried along the riverfront looking for shelter in a rain that fell with the fury of a rising storm.

"Madame Lezenski!"

Evelyn opened her eyes to see the Frenchwoman staring at her in outrage.

"Mr. Sebowski is waiting for you."

Evelyn jumped to her feet, straightening the white collar of her plain green dress. "I must have . . ." but the triumph in the woman's eyes stopped her. I am going to lose my position, she thought with a wave of despair.

"Come in, Countess," Mr. Sebowski said, rising unaccustomedly to his feet. Behind her Evelyn heard the Frenchwoman snicker, then cover her laugh with a cough. Evelyn went in. "Close the door," Sebowski said.

I am going to lose my position, Evelyn thought again.

"How was the funeral?" Mr. Sebowski asked, holding out a chair. He looked like a seal, Evelyn thought, with his thin black hair slicked down on his scalp, his face so smoothly shaved his skin shone. "Sit down, please."

"It was very . . . sad," was all she could think to say as she perched on the edge of the straight-backed chair. Now he'll think I'm stupid, she thought.

"I see," Mr. Sebowski murmured, his hands steepled in front of his face. He looked at her for a long moment. "You are not yourself Russian," he said finally.

"No," Evelyn admitted. He knew all this.

His stare was unbroken. "I see."

He's going to make me leave, Evelyn thought desperately, because I am not Russian. "My husband was an officer of the czar's," she informed him.

"Yes, of course," he said with what might have been a smile, turning to look at the rain beating against the high windows. "Countess . . ." he began.

"I prefer 'Madame,'" she heard herself say. Sebowski turned back, his eyes very still. "'Countess' seems so . . ." she couldn't think what she wanted to say.

"Sad?" he suggested quietly.

"Yes." He looked almost kindly for a moment. "I wasn't a countess for very long—not in Russia, I mean," she ended lamely.

"I see you are very realistic," he said. The distant thunder echoed through the room and obscured his soft words. After the next bolt of lightning had struck, he went on, "So many of our countrymen live in dreams."

Evelyn thought of Alex in his tattered uniform, of the gathering in the Orthodox church each Saturday night, of the long line of mourners like a childrens' pageant in their fading splendor. "They hope to return someday."

"Do not we all?" he asked her, but she knew he didn't expect an answer. You don't, she thought. You are happy as you are.

When neither of them had spoken for more than a minute, Evelyn said, "We are never going back." She had never dared speak the words aloud, nor barely admitted the thoughts to herself, but once it was out she took a deep breath and sat back in her chair. She crossed her legs and saw Sebowski's eyes on her wet skirt. She left it pulled up on her thighs, feeling giddy, as though her youth had been returned to her.

Sebowski shook his head. "I don't think anyone will be going back." He sat forward, his hands dropping from in front of his face. "There is a delicate matter I need handled, Countess . . . Madame Lezenski. You would be doing the bank a great favor if you could help us."

Evelyn was mystified.

"But I will have to ask for your complete discretion. May I?"

"Yes," she said uncertainly. The rain ceased as suddenly as it had begun, and the room seemed more silent than the tomb in which they had left the grand duke.

"This may involve some . . . how can I put this? . . . some divided loyalties," the banker went on.

"Just what are you asking, Mr. Sebowski?" Evelyn asked boldly.

He smiled, a smile startling in its venality, small teeth bared, the eyes bright with greed. "I am a good judge of character, am I not, madame?" He drew a breath, content, it seemed, with what he saw. "I have a transaction to make for the bank," he began. "For the bank, through a trustee. It involves a very, shall we say, disputed item. But the price is good, and we at the bank judge that the time is right. The trustee of this... item... doesn't disagree." He was watching Evelyn carefully for her reaction. "For reasons that will soon be clear to you, I need someone Russian but sensible to assist us. To travel, madame, with the item to assure that the transaction is made correctly. I think you are that person."

"You are going to sell the pearls."

The smile vanished, replaced by a hard stare. He will have me killed if I don't agree, Evelyn thought clearly. He could arrange that before the day was out.

"You speak, of course, of the grand duchess's pearls." His fingertips moved gently on the polished surface of the desk.

"They were meant to finance a campaign." Evelyn felt absolutely comfortable, almost amused.

"To retake the throne, yes," Sebowski said, allowing a small smile, his bright little eyes catching Evelyn's. "Neither you nor I think that the Russian throne will be retaken, do we?" he asked her. "And if it were, to whom would it go?" He opened his hands wide, as though presenting a reasonable problem to Evelyn. "You see the situation. There are valuable items here, items that will present problems in the future. A decision has been made to resolve those problems, a reasonable decision."

"What does the general say?"

Sebowski sighed. "The general is agreeable. So you see, there are no objections." Sebowski would open the vault for the pearls, and the general, who was the trustee for the émigrés, would not object.

"What will you do if someone wants to see them?" she asked.

Sebowski considered his answer. "Madame Lezenski, do you really want to know?" he asked solicitously. "Knowledge can be a burden."

Evelyn saw a spear of light pierce the clouds outside. "And for me?" she asked.

"This is for you," Sebowski repeated.

She faced him. "You understand, Mr. Sebowski, the position you are putting me in?"

"The opportunity, madame, that I am offering you."

"My husband is a Russian officer," she reminded him. "He expects one day to return to Russia. I am his wife; I owe his dreams allegiance."

"You have a child, I believe."

She waited.

"You owe her allegiance also, I should think." He left the rest unsaid.

She waited, letting the silence draw out as the room brightened.

"We are prepared to offer you ten thousand Shanghai dollars," Sebowski said.

A fortune, Evelyn thought, joy flooding through her, more money than they had seen in years. She kept her face impassive. "Twenty," she said.

"No," Sebowski said quietly. "Ten thousand Shanghai dollars."

As they sat the sounds of the storm, now far distant, came to them. The sky beyond the window brightened until it was as clear as fine export porcelain. "All right," Evelyn agreed.

"Very good, Madame Lezenski," Sebowski said, rising to offer his hand across the desk. His hand felt warm, and again he reminded her of a seal.

"When will this transaction happen?"

"Tomorrow." He was still standing. "I think in matters like this that speed is of the essence, don't you?"

"I have never dealt in matters like this," she reminded him.

"Perhaps, however, you will be able to help us again, Countess," he suggested quietly. The vaults were filled with small treasures, icons, jewels, coins. They intended to loot them, Evelyn realized.

"Will I have to leave the city?" she asked.

"Not far," he told her. "A day's journey. A car will be provided for you, and a guard for the items," he said very quietly, reminding her that she was merely the courier.

"I will arrange it."

"I am sure you will," he said, sitting down to show her that the interview was over.

As she reached the door he called across the room, "Countess?" She turned, her hand on the door. "Pearls die, did you know that? Left in the dark, they fade, like beauty. So you see, this transaction, it takes nothing away from the world. It preserves beauty. It would be many years, as you know, before they would be needed for the campaign, if at all, and then"—he opened his hand over the spotless desk—"dust."

"No." Alex shoveled a small amount of coal into the open stove.

"I shall make extra money."

"It's ridiculous," Alex said, closing the grate on the stove. He held his hands closer to the black body of the stove. "A woman. Why would they send a woman?"

"I just have to carry some documents, delicate affairs, to Wuhan. I wouldn't be gone more than a day and a night. I would be quite safe. Mr. Sebowski will be sending a guard with me."

"Why can't the guard carry the documents?" Alex's hands touched the yellowed maps of Siberia, tracing the lines of the imaginary campaign he and his friends discussed endlessly.

Evelyn shrugged. "I don't know." Sebowski had been right, she thought.

Late in the afternoon he had called for her again. "Everything is arranged," he told her. "You will be able to go?"

"Yes."

"Good." She knew that he had never had any doubt that she would. The money—ten thousand Shanghai dollars—would be a large bribe for anyone, but she was their best choice; she wasn't truly Russian, and she had a child.

At this meeting Sebowski seemed relaxed, almost jovial, as though they were conspirators. And, she supposed, they were. She quite liked the idea. Over the course of the morning she had thought about the fortune in pearls in the vault. The senior clerk who had once seen them often talked about their size. "Pigeon eggs," he would say, making an oval with his fingers. "Enormous." She was sure that he was right; she could remember the pearls the empress wore when she had come to Sevastopol during the war, strings and strings of them, all the size of very large buttons. Above them she had worn a choker of emeralds laid on scarlet velvet.

As the youngest bride in the port, Evelyn had been chosen to present a ceremonial bouquet, and she remembered thinking that it looked as if the empress had had her head chopped off and placed back on the trunk of her throat very carefully. Indeed, the way the czarina held her head so high and still, barely moving her hand to accept the small bouquet of out-of-season flowers, made her look bloodless and unreal.

The pearls were useless in the vaults; she agreed with Sebowski about that. As for the matter of whether he had the right to sell them in partnership with General Kornislov, well, she decided that was not her concern.

"Your husband," Sebowski said, broaching the subject that had consumed much of Evelyn's day.

"I'll have to tell him something."

"But not in detail," Sebowski said. He turned a silver and gold paper knife over and over in his small, fat fingers.

"He would go immediately to the authorities," Evelyn said, feeling a momentary loss of confidence.

Sebowski looked at her. "No doubt," he said. "Of course, that would result in nothing except a mild scandal. Someone would come to see the pearls, a delegation not unlike yesterday's, and of course they would still be there. But for you . . ." He didn't need to spell it out: loss of her position at the bank, discredit with Alex for starting a rumor, a loss of face for the Lezenskis among the émigrés.

"You may rely on me," she said. This time she sat down uninvited. Crossing her legs, she pulled up her skirt demurely, but not before she had seen Sebowski peering at her ankles.

"In cases like this," Sebowski said, "it is often best to tell as much of the truth as possible. I think you should tell the count"—he gave the title little weight—"that you will be carrying documents, important documents, to a lady who wishes to remain discreet."

"All right," Evelyn agreed.

Now, as Alex stood before her in their narrow room, she elaborated. "The documents are for a lady to sign. Sebowski thinks it will be more discreet if a woman goes."

Alex said nothing as his finger made a jagged line across the latest campaign map. "Why can't she come here?" he asked without turning.

"I don't know!" Evelyn shouted, the tears that she had kept back for years threatening to spill out. "In any event," she pointed out tonelessly, "I have to go, and we both know it. If I refuse, I lose my job, and we need the money." The color rose like flames out of the frayed collar of Alex's once-white uniform. He kept looking at the map, but his lips were pressed more tightly together, and his eyes bulged out very slightly. How old he looks, how tired, Evelyn thought with sadness.

Her own exhaustion diminished, as it had many times. She knew she had to be strong, for Alex, for Victoria, and for herself, even for the dowager countess and Natasha. In Sevastopol, until almost the end, there had seemed to be hope. In the flight, the terror had driven them all forward, made them cling to one another, be inventive. But in Harbin it had become deadeningly clear that the border was closed to them, and they had come south, first to Peking, then Shanghai, where the real shock had gradually sunk in. It had become as terrifying as Alex's report that night in Sevastopol that soldiers had seized the fleet and were wrapping chains about the officers' ankles and dropping them overboard.

The terror was that Alex, his mother, and his sister were helpless. Incapable of the simplest task. To shop for food, to find a place to live, to travel on trains, find an address by themselves—all of this had to be taught to them like children. Victoria, at two, had learned faster.

She stood up and put her arms about Alex. She held him, as she often did now, in the way he used to hold her, rocking him slightly, though he was taller—taller, but much, much thinner. He was ashamed to eat food that she had bought. Each mouthful was ashes on his tongue, and it broke her heart.

What had happened? she would wonder when her eyes snapped open of themselves in the darkest hours of the night. Alex would finally be asleep beside her, after hours of pacing in the other room. It was warmer there; the fire would die down slowly in the stove, casting a dark red light over the wide couch where the countess slept with the child and the narrow pallet that pulled out from below for Natasha. Natasha slept in her clothes, as though they were still fleeing, her few belongings in her hand under the pillow.

The other room was supposed to supply some privacy, but the marriage in that sense had withered with Alex's confidence. Despair made him turn his face to the wall.

Evelyn saw bustling Shanghai, the ships at anchor in the river, loading and unloading cargo, passengers, officials, and she realized the world had forgotten them. The world went about its business of making money, and Russia . . . There were times when she could hardly remember what Russia looked like, less real than England, though more recent. Russia seemed like a Christmas pantomime: rich, exotic, filled with unlikely events. At first she had half expected to come out into a fresh winter night and find the pantomime was over, that now they would go home to a warm house and a tree with candles and cotton wool on it. Instead, the days stretched out into months, months into years.

Sometimes Alex spoke out loud, words she seldom understood. But she remembered the tone: peremptory, confident. In his dreams he was back in Russia.

She rose and put her arms about Alex, laying her head against his back. "I will be back the day after tomorrow," she said.

The heat from his body warmed her cheek, as she listened to Alex's breathing. He didn't speak for several minutes. From the other room, Evelyn heard his mother talking quietly to Victoria. "Sometimes I no longer know whom to hate," Alex said in a constricted voice.

"Not me," Evelyn whispered. "Please, not me, Alex."

He turned to put his arms about her, looking down into her face with tired eyes. "Poor little one," he said quietly. He sighed. "I promised you so much."

"We will go back, Alex," she heard herself say, wondering that she could still lie so well. "Some day, you'll go back."

A light appeared deep in the faded eyes that for one moment reminded her of the blazing tiger eyes that she had married. "Yes," he repeated, "one day soon." But for the first time Evelyn thought she heard doubt in his voice. He knows, she thought with new pain.

5

The winter fields lay barren to either side of the tracks. Evelyn sat in the corner of the carriage, the old fur coat that she managed to bring with her from Russia wrapped about her, the collar turned up around her face. The guard that Mr. Sebowski had sent sat across from her in the first-class carriage, riding straight, his narrow eyes watching her every move.

She shifted the red leather valise on her lap, and she saw the eyes widen briefly until it was settled against the wall of the carriage. "I won't jump off the train," she said with a wry smile, but the guard's face was blank.

She sighed, turning back to watch the thin mist hover over the low rice paddies. In the distance the graceful rooflines of a small village seemed to float above the mist. She hadn't been alone for a long time, unaware how much she minded until the train had pulled out of the old North Station, Alex grim and thin standing beside Sebowski. Sebowski bowed to Alex as though they were both back in Russia, deferentially calling him "Count," but Evelyn wondered if Alex could detect contempt just below the surface.

The train had moved very slowly at first, almost imperceptibly pulling her away from Alex, and for a second she had wanted to thrust the leather case into Sebowski's hands and say, "I can't do this." But the train was slowly gathering momentum, the rails clicking faster underneath, and suddenly the lights went out, plunging the interior of the carriage into darkness thrown by the roof of the station. Before she could speak, she felt the guard moving, the seat beside her giving under the weight of his huge body, much larger than the average Chinese, and his thick hand closed over hers and the case.

As suddenly as the carriage had gone dark it was flooded by the daylight beyond the station. Releasing her, the guard got up, his back as wide as a door, and took his seat across from her again without a word. She massaged her wrist, thinking, with a new rage, that even he had contempt for her. When she pushed the valise onto the seat beside her, he leaned over, took the case, and held it out to her. She took it back, putting it on her lap among the folds of her coat.

As her anger dissipated a new feeling passed into her and then was finally identified: She was free. There was no one to rely on her, no one to complain or criticize. The unaccustomed luxury of the first-class carriage soothed her, and she sat back to watch the solid buildings of the international settlement drop behind as they moved through the more fanciful houses and public buildings of the French settlement, and in turn into the sprawl and disorder of the old Chinese city. Soon they were past the Nanking road and into the countryside.

"You understand what you are to do?" Sebowski had said at the bank, nervous now.

"Perfectly," she assured him.

He looked her over. "That is a nice fur," he commented, almost obsequious before the faded luxury of the sable that Alex had bought her the first winter in Sevastopol.

"A gift," she said.

Sebowski reached out and stroked the fur. "My father . . ." he began. To her surprise, Evelyn saw him blush. "My father was a fur merchant," he finished almost defiantly. "These are very good skins."

"I had never known a Russian winter," Evelyn explained, moving away very slightly. "My husband wanted me to be warm."

Sebowski smiled, the smooth, cold seal smile. "Ah," he murmured, as though mulling over a private joke, "the famous Russian winter." He stepped back. "You should sell those skins," he told her, the smile playing more openly in his eyes. "It will never get that cold in China."

"Life has taught me, Mr. Sebowski," Evelyn replied, "that one can never be sure of what one will need or won't."

He laughed. "Yes, of course, you are right." Turning to the red case that lay on his desk, he touched the leather where it was tearing at the corner. "There are so many surprises." His fingers plucked at the scar. "Would you like to see what you will be carrying?"

"Yes."

He undid the gold clasp, lifting it with the tips of his fingers. His eyes, still sparkling, found hers, and very slowly he lifted the lid.

She couldn't keep the sigh from escaping her lips. "My God."

"Beautiful, aren't they?" Sebowski watched her. His fingers had a life of their own, digging deep into the heap of pearls that were the color of day-old cream, glowing as though lit within by a low fire. He lifted his hand without taking his eyes off Evelyn, and the strings of pearls snaked out of the box, almost alive in the way they shone, dancing out of their dark gray velvet bed as though they, too, felt they were being freed.

"You see what I mean? Such things shouldn't be allowed to die, do you think?"

"No," she breathed, feeling foolish in the way her heart was beating more forcefully. She was looking at a piece of history, a tiny part of the imperial treasure that itself had miraculously escaped because the grand duchess had been allowed to wear the pearls one night. When the imperial family was imprisoned, she had fled with them sewn into the hems of her skirts.

"Would you like to wear them?" Sebowski was playing with her.

"No," she answered, excitement changing to a low dread. "No," she repeated, stepping back from the desk, "I don't think so."

Sebowski pulled them free of the box viciously, the ropes swinging low over the deep blue carpet. "You think there is a curse on them, Countess?" he asked, the light changing once again in his eyes, the pearls held out like a bribe. "A Russian curse?"

"Everybody who owned them is dead," she said, not wanting to admit her fear.

"Exactly," he said, his smile broadening, transforming itself into laughter. "Exactly." He dumped the pearls unceremoniously back into their box. "We owe allegiance only to the living," he said in a flat, businesslike voice, "to the future, to ourselves."

She knew he was speaking of Alex, the general, all the émigrés. "My husband will be taking me to the station," she said. "He'll recognize the box."

Irritation narrowed Sebowski's features. "Why?" he said, pressing harder on the box.

"He insisted," Evelyn told him. "It was . . . difficult to get him to agree."

Sebowski held his pugnacious stance, angry, facing her across the carpet, but then he burst into a merry, uncharacteristic laugh. Evelyn wondered if he might be slightly drunk, if not with wine or vodka, then with greed. "Jealousy!" he exclaimed, lifting his hands and almost clapping them in his joy. But at the last minute, he merely touched the palms together. "A beautiful young wife . . ." He left the rest unsaid but certainly implied.

"Mr. Sebowski," Evelyn interrupted, "please, could you put that box in something?"

He drew a breath. "Yes," he agreed, "but only until you are on the train."

"Why?"

"Because I am sending a guard with you," he said. He looked over his shoulder as he pressed the button on his desk. "I told you that."

Evelyn had forgotten. She had been awake part of the night with Victoria, who had refused to eat all day. The door behind her opened. "Madame Coutan, could you bring me a very large envelope?" Sebowski asked.

Behind Evelyn, the Frenchwoman said, "Would you like me to wrap something?"

"No!" Sebowski shouted. "Bring the envelope."

"Yes, Mr. Sebowski," the woman said in a thin voice. The door closed.

"Who will be the guard?"

"You shall see," Sebowski told her shortly, losing his interest in the game. "I shall come to the station with you also, in case your husband asks what's in the envelope."

"He won't."

Sebowski glanced up at her. "An officer's honor?" he asked flatly. "Russian aristocrats have no curiosity? They already know everything?"

"Not quite," Evelyn answered him, the fire rising in her. "He would think it none of his business."

"And what do you think?" Sebowski challenged her. Again the thought that he might be drunk rose in Evelyn's mind.

"I think I would like some assurance that I am going to get my money."

His laugh was high and genuine. "Ah, Countess," he said, opening the drawer of his desk, "I see I have made a good choice." He dropped the filthy Chinese bills on his desk. "All of it. You wish to count it?"

She looked at the paper, startled at the tears that stung her eyes. Money, so much of it that she had to control herself not to reach out and grasp it, take it quickly and hide it within her clothing, close to her skin, as she had the few gold coins they had when they crossed into China.

"No," she said, holding tight to her feelings. "I would like to open a deposit box, if you don't mind."

"You have not mentioned how much you are being paid," Sebowski guessed.

"I couldn't," she admitted. "It would have seemed too much for what I was being asked to do."

Sebowski nodded with what seemed admiration. "Wise," he agreed. "I will arrange for it immediately. You can stay here until the keys are brought." He was watching her closely again. "You are a clever woman, Countess," he said, more to himself than to her, she thought. "You will prosper, I think, if you allow your natural instincts to be free."

A knock followed by the soft opening of the door interrupted him. The Frenchwoman came in with her eyes low and handed the envelope to Sebowski. As she passed Evelyn on the way out she shot her a look of pure malice. "The guard has been told to keep his eyes on the case at all times," Sebowski said, his fingers neatly wrapping the thread around the clasp of the envelope. "Once the train pulls away, you must open the envelope and place the case where he can see it." He held out the case to Evelyn. It was much heavier than she had expected.

Sebowski chuckled. "They live, do they not?" he said. "You can feel them breathing inside."

Alex was waiting below when Sebowski and Evelyn came down the double staircase. Each acutely conscious of the change in their fortunes, the two men bowed to each other. On the ride Evelyn reached for Alex's hand, aware of how the long-unaccustomed interior of an expensive car was affecting him by the way he sat so straight beside her, his eyes, unseeing, focused on the thick neck of the guard who rode beside the driver. On the platform, Sebowski had said, "You will remember my exact instructions, Countess, will you not?"

By the time the city was lost in the winter mist, the leather of the case, wedged beside her between her thigh and the wall of the compartment, had become familiar, comforting. She threw back her coat, breathing in the smell of the velvet curtains by her face, clean, mixed with the polish of the woodwork. Memory played its tricks on her, bringing back the long train journey through Europe when she had gone to the estates. If she closed her eyes, everything that had happened in the last eight years might have been a dream, terrible, a reminder that all she enjoyed—the touch of the seat beside her, the soft brush of the sable by her shoulder, the comfort, the security of the first-class compartment—was part of a life of privilege.

I shall deliver these pearls, she thought, her fingers clasping the leather as though the pearls might push the case open in their desire to be free, and then I shall return to Shanghai. With that thought came images, complete with odors, of the two rooms above the Chinese herbal medicine shop, rich and foreign spices of the East pushing up through the boards of the floor to impregnate her hair, her skin, her very clothes.

Automatically she lifted the collar of her coat again and held it near her face to see if she could smell the spices. No, she realized, with a relief out of proportion to the gesture. All she could smell was lavender from the sachet she had managed to buy for the box under the bed where her clothes were stored. "A waste," the dowager countess had sniffed when she had come home with the lavender, but Evelyn had insisted.

She held the box, closing her eyes on a weariness that descended upon her as the train left the plain and began to climb very slowly toward the mountains. Despair came to greet her like an old acquaintance, like one of the many, many Russians she had known in the years of exile, all characters in some vast play that, once begun, had to be played to the end. The luxury of the carriage and the new-found sense of freedom mocked her. Oh God, oh God, oh God rang silently in her mind—not blasphemy, not a prayer, but some heartfelt cry.

She slept, opening her eyes to mountains that seemed older than anything she had seen before, each crevice cunningly carved, each tree artfully placed against a sky of deep blue, a landscape like a scroll revealed mile by mile as they journeyed north.

The guard said, "You eat."

"What?"

He made a mimicking gesture with his hand, lifting imaginary chopsticks to his mouth.

"Yes," she said, conscious that she had been hungry, it seemed, for years. But this hunger was different—not pain, but a hollowness, a child's hunger. She rose, holding the case. "Yes, let's have a meal."

The guard raised his hand, and she thought he would push her back into her seat. "No," he said, filling the space between her and the door, "you wait."

Dim lights glowed in a distant village. Evelyn pressed her

fingers against the cold glass of the window, while the guard stood in the corridor. After some minutes a waiter arrived, placing a tray on the small table that folded out by the window. Under the cover was a cold chicken, asparagus, and thinly sliced cucumber. Two hard rolls and fresh butter looked as appetizing as the pearls.

The guard sat back with his hands folded in his lap.

"Are you going to eat?" Evelyn asked him, her mouth watering at the thought of the food. She wanted to touch the small glass by the carafe of wine, lift the silverware, fondle the white lace cloth.

"You eat," he told her, watching her with the same impassive eyes.

She tried to take small bites, to fight the desire to pick up the chicken in her hands, tear the rolls apart, fill her mouth to overflowing. The wine soothed her, lifting her into a lassitude where the dreams of an hour ago blended with the rhythmic clicking of the rails and the pinprick lights of the countryside that had flattened out into a high plateau. When she had finished, she sat back with a sigh. She felt guilty eating in front of the guard, but her eyes scanned the plate looking for scraps.

"More?" he said.

"No, thank you," she answered him, but she wanted to cry out "Yes!"

"You want tea?" he asked. "You can have tea."

Evelyn looked at the wine in the bottom of her glass. "Is there coffee?" she asked boldly.

He made a face, stood up, and took the tray away from her. Her hand twitched with the desire to take the last of the wine off the tray; she knew he had seen, but she didn't care. She sat back, her face against the velvet of the seat. The white curtains swayed with the movement of the carriage. She heard the guard talking in the corridor, and soon he came back with a silver coffee pot on a smaller tray, a white porcelain cup with a rim of gold, sugar and cream. The cream poured richly into the dark coffee, tinting it the color of the Soochow creek, she thought, suppressing a giggle. The smell was more intoxicating than the wine. She drank the coffee, allowing the thoughts of England, of other meals, coffee, train rides through the soft English landscape; meals with her mother, who wrote occasionally, and with Morgan, who had gone to Africa with the John Hall Trading Company. There were times when she longed for Morgan's company, his voice and laughter, for anything but the unrestrained drabness of her life.

Far off across the plateau a denser grouping of lights shimmered in the dark. "Wukan," she said to the guard, touching the wet glass of the window.

He craned to look. "Soon." His eyes searched for the red leather case she had pushed into the folds of her abandoned coat.

She needed to go to the commode. She wondered how to raise the subject. The food and wine, the rich, strong coffee had made her another person—not new, but someone she used to know. She stood up without apology and said, "I have to find a ladies' room."

"You stay," he told her, not moving.

"No," she said, shaking her head determinedly and reaching for the case. "You come with me."

"No," he said, blocking her passage with his arm.

She picked up her coat, handed it to him, and said, "You come," her voice ringing with an authority that she had forgotten.

She saw the wavering doubt in his eyes before his arm dropped away. He took the coat from her and pushed open the door.

"I wait," he said to her outside the door marked "Ladies."

"Yes." She smiled at him, but he turned his wide back.

In the narrow mirror above the washbasin, she peered forward, looking at the new flush in her cheeks. "I'm pretty," she observed, seeing that the thinness of her cheeks gave her a new allure. After washing and powdering her face, on impulse she pushed her long hair behind her ears. With satisfaction she realized she was almost beautiful, her eyes larger in the narrower face, her mouth still ripe despite the years of hardship. She picked her hair back at her neck, made up her mouth more boldly, stood and surveyed the change.

The black dress with the severe white collar made her look like a clerk. She tore off the collar and the dress became elegant.

When she came out of the ladies' room, the guard looked at her silently, eyes coming to rest on the red leather case. On the way back to the carriage, she stopped at a tray left outside another compartment to pluck a tiger orchid from the cloth. In the carriage, she took a safety pin from her handbag and pinned the flower at the nape of her neck. Her reflection gave her a joy that had been lost for years.

Lights outside multiplied, spreading like a stain across the night, and in the corridor were noise and movement. The train slowed passing through squalid suburbs that the night invested with the mystery she had hoped to find in the East: moon gates, lanterns hung on poles, rooflines silhouetted against a flat black sky where a sickle moon seemed to vibrate with golden light.

As the train pulled into the station Evelyn rose and threw the fur carelessly over her shoulders. "All right," she said, her voice still strong.

The guard led her into the chill winter night, peering over the milling crowd. His large hand closed about her arm next to the case.

"Countess Lezenski?" General Kornislov stood to one side of the platform, a very large doll in his double-braided black overcoat, no signs of the uniform he sported on his visits to Shanghai. His almost Oriental features, evidence of his Mongolian blood, blended smoothly in the dust cloud in the station. He smiled at the red leather case but made no move to take it from her. The guard dropped his grasp.

"Shall we?" The general offered his arm. She put her hand very lightly on his, and he led them through the teeming station, where coolies pushed their wheelbarrows piled high with luggage, stately Europeans looming like cranes over the mass of poor Chinese. The crowd parted for an elegant mandarin in his long robe and black hat, his eyes staring directly ahead as he made his way toward a train.

Frost iced the ground outside, where the general raised his hand. A dark sedan honked its way through the rickshaws until it nosed against the curb. General Kornislov stood back to let Evelyn step into the interior.

"How is Alex?" the general asked as he settled beside her, the car gliding away from the curb.

"He knows nothing about this." Evelyn looked into his small eyes with a challenge.

"No, of course not." Kornislov's eyes were curious. "He wouldn't approve at all. Do you?"

"I have no opinion." Evelyn disliked his stare.

"You look different," he offered admiringly.

Evelyn closed her coat with her fingers. "Will I be able to return tonight? Alex will be waiting for me."

"Surely you told him that you might be gone longer."

"Yes," she admitted, "but . . ."

He rested his hand on her coat where it covered her knee. "Evelyn. May I call you that?"

She nodded.

"Evelyn, you understand, do you not, that what you see is nothing very terrible?"

She looked out at the quiet, empty city streets, the hurly-burly of the station far behind. "I haven't thought about it," she lied.

"That may be best for you," he suggested, "but, believe me, I have thought about this. We are not going back."

The car pushed into the hills behind the city, slowing in front of several low buildings softly lit from within.

"A temple," the general said in the darkness beside her. "Curious, is it not?"

Surprised, Evelyn peered forward to examine the buildings in more detail: A large central structure of one story with swooping eaves was surrounded by unplanned outbuildings that sprawled in all directions. Behind the temple, against the night sky, she could make out other buildings set unevenly along the steep hillside. "There are monks here?" She was thinking of the long string of Buddhists coming from the Manchu tombs what seemed like a lifetime ago.

Kornislov laughed. "No," he said. "Our . . . purchaser

lives part of the year here. A conceit, I expect. The wicked at rest where the pure used to struggle with their humanity."

"Oh." Evelyn sat back as the car came to a stop before a long wall that shut out all other views.

"The visitors take the spoils," Kornislov said. "The architecture of a regime outlives rulers. I understand that the peasants use the buildings we left behind in St. Petersburg as though they had used them all their lives. It is easy to become used to comfort, I suppose."

"Easier than to become accustomed to poverty."

Kornislov laughed, a harsh, thin sound that made her skin contract at the nape of her neck. The butcher of Siberia, they had called him.

An opened gate threw a coffin of light on the bare ground. She knew just from watching the European as he came toward the car that he was not the man they had come to meet. He walked with his shoulders hunched against the bitter cold, and his face, when he pressed it against the back window, was narrow and sour. "He is waiting for you," he said when Kornislov rolled down the window, letting a cloud of frosty air into the interior.

Kornislov's breath plumed out into the air. "The courier is with me."

"Just you," the man said, turning back to the house.

"Come," Kornislov said. For the first time he took the leather case from Evelyn.

She stepped out of the car after him, the chill night air bringing tears to her eyes.

"Not her," the man called from the gate. "Just you."

Kornislov put his hand under Evelyn's arm and moved forward with his back as rigid as though he were reviewing his Cossacks. As they passed through the gate, the man shrugged and closed it behind them. "He will not be pleased," was all he said.

Evelyn stopped, startled by the rows of lanterns reflecting in pools where carp rose to snatch at tricks of light. From the steps to the main building she could see the sloping hillside drop to reveal an immense plateau on which the city glinted, as small as a child's plaything in the far distance.

A narrow door opened onto a long room, its bare floor polished to a high gloss. The European furniture was sparse, a single long settee faced by two chairs. On a table before the settee a fine celadon bowl shone green in the light of the smaller lanterns hung from the beams.

A man in full evening dress stood with his back to them. He finished pouring himself a drink at the table in the corner and turned, his eyes taking in Kornislov and the European who now melted away, and coming to rest on Evelyn. He was stocky and of medium height, with startling white hair. But the hair fell over his brow, and when he lifted his hand to push it back, it was the sharp gesture of a younger man. His eyes, bright as gas flames, were clear and alert as he came forward.

"You are here," was his only greeting to Kornislov. He held out his hand to Evelyn. "Dr. Fischer."

His hand, when she offered hers, closed over her own cold hand with a warmth that was almost like a fever.

"Countess Evelyn Lezenski," Kornislov was saying. Evelyn could hear the tension in his voice.

"Not 'Countess,'" Evelyn murmured.

"Alas, you are right," Fischer said, fixing her with his blue gaze. "The time of honors is past, I fear."

"There will be new honors." Kornislov tried to make it sound brave and amusing, but it sounded vulgar, ringing against the celadon bowl in the stark room.

Fischer smiled. Still holding Evelyn's hand, he spoke to Kornislov. "New masters," he suggested, and he turned his attention back to her. "Madame Lezenski, may I pour you a drink?"

She nodded. The feeling of comfort and warmth she had enjoyed in the train swept over her again as she took a seat.

"Whiskey?" he suggested. "I have some good whiskey. I wasn't expecting company." The implication was clear: Kornislov was here on business.

Either ignoring the insult or not understanding its subtlety in English, Kornislov asked greedily, "English whiskey?"

"Irish," Fischer said, bending over the tray. "But it will do the job, I assure you, General."

Again the high, harsh laugh echoed among the beams of the temple as Kornislov opened his coat. "You know how to take care of yourself, Fischer."

Fischer's face tightened very slightly as he looked across at Evelyn. "Neat?"

"Yes, please."

He brought it to her in a heavy crystal glass. "Are you cold?" he asked her. "I can have a fire lit."

Evelyn looked about for a fireplace. There was none.

Fischer touched her fingers as he handed her the glass. "The servants bring in braziers and place them in the center of the room in the Japanese style."

"The monks didn't need fires, eh, Fischer?" Kornislov said.

"The monks didn't entertain ladies." Fischer smiled as he turned away.

"Who knows what the monks did, Fischer? In Russia the monks did everything except support their children."

Evelyn could feel herself blushing under Fischer's silent glance.

"In any case, the monks are gone." Kornislov gulped his drink.

"In any case this was not a religious order," Fischer murmured. "They were scholars, not fanatics."

"Scholars are the worst," Kornislov pronounced. "They make men think who do not have the capacity to do so. Fanatics understand the sword soon enough and stop, but with thinkers . . ." He shook his head as though it was still a puzzle to him. "They burn, they burn with hatred. Such men are dangerous."

"Where are those the pearls?"

Fischer stood while Kornislov snapped open the locks of the case. He threw back the lid dramatically to reveal the rolling coils of pearls that in the lantern light seemed to move of their own accord. Kornislov watched Fischer closely.

"Yes," Fischer said quietly, "yes." Evelyn rose, suddenly flushed, perhaps by the unaccustomed warmth of the whiskey. "Would you mind if I went outside?" she asked.

Fischer looked at her with open concern for a long moment, but the pearls drew his attention again. "There is a garden, but you have to be careful, as the path is steep. There are lights, but I can call servants, if you wish, to show you the way."

"That won't be necessary," she apologized. "I just need some air."

In front of the temple the terraces looked over to where the horizon paled with a slim band of light, the city. Finding the path, she walked carefully through the twisted shapes of low pines laced against the starlit sky until she came across a stone bench. She sat with her coat open until her breathing was normal once more.

The sight of the pearls had upset her. Alex would never forgive her. Poor Alex, she thought, this time her pity objective. It was several minutes—minutes spent looking at the many shadowed blacks and grays of the plateau where she could now make out what must be a river snaking towards Wuhan from the craggy shapes of the mountains—before she understood what was different: She didn't feel connected to the tragedy that had befallen her husband.

"Are you feeling better, Countess?" Fischer spoke from the path above her, looming against the night sky.

Evelyn jumped to her feet. "You startled me," she said to cover her confusion.

"I'm sorry," he said flatly. "Have you eaten?"

"Yes, yes," she said impatiently, hungry for solitude. There was always someone: the family in the two rooms, the Chinese below, the bank workers, so here the sense of freedom and space was more intoxicating than the whiskey.

"The general has left."

Her heart froze as still as the trees framed against the night. "When?" she demanded.

"A few moments ago," Fischer said, coming toward her against the starlit backdrop.

"I have to go with him," Evelyn said in panic, pushing past Fischer on the narrow path. Stepping back, he stumbled, his whole body in jeopardy of falling to the path below before Evelyn reached out and took hold of his lapels, pulling him toward her. His body fell against hers, pinning her against the cliff face for a few seconds, his face close to hers. Then he recovered himself, brushing off the sleeve of his coat.

"That was unnecessary," he said with anger.

"I'm sorry," she said, embarrassed.

He didn't reply. Together they heard the car start up somewhere above them and drive off, leaving the silence of the night behind. "You'll have to stay until the morning now, in any case," Fischer informed her, the displeasure clear in his voice. "My own car won't be here until then. I thought you understood that."

"I was to take the train back tonight."

"Russians are such fools!" Fischer exploded with a violence that made Evelyn step back. "He's left you here as . . ."

As a whore, Evelyn thought. Russian women were the whores of the Orient now, less exotic even than the Chinese dance hall girls available for the price of a meal or a drink. She apologized again, though her own feelings were in turmoil. "I'm sorry, I shouldn't have left the house. He probably thought . . ." He probably thought, she realized as the flush of shame rose up the column of her neck, that she had wanted him to leave her behind in this unaccustomed luxury.

"We will have to make the best of it," Fischer said grudgingly, his good manners gone. "I was going to have a meal. You might as well join me."

"I'm not hungry."

"Oh, don't be a fool," he said irritably as he turned back up the narrow path along the cliff face. "Of course you're hungry. Come up here. It's not safe on the paths at night. The monks knew every step; each rock had its own story. I have better things to do than memorize a landscape."

He left her and disappeared onto the terrace above. Brushing her coat off, she followed him carefully. As she topped the path she saw the house had been transformed, glowing with light from end to end. Servants moved through the rooms, and from one wing she heard music.

The lit windows revealed several bedrooms, some with handsome fourposter beds, others more simple; a dining room with a delicate beechwood table where a servant was setting another place; a study with a heavy carved Chinese desk and glass-fronted cases displaying small jade statues; and finally a long living room absolutely different from the spartan room where Fischer had received General Kornislov. Here there were low divans covered in yellow silk, red lacquered tables trimmed with gold leaf, a larger and more delicate celadon bowl, the glass almost as translucent as the leaves of the lilies that floated in it. The music came from a hand-wound Victrola on a high black lacquered table behind the divans.

Fischer stood looking through records. "Do you like dance music?" he asked, his manner abruptly changing again.

"I used to."

"Take off your coat," he told her, pulling a disk from its jacket.

She thought to object, as much to his tone as to the suggestion, but she obeyed, dropping the coat on one of the yellow silk divans. Fischer made no pretense of disguising his interest as he looked her over.

"You are a beautiful woman," he said simply, winding the Victrola.

Evelyn said, "Hunger does make one thin." He looked up, surprised, and she was pleased to have caught him off guard.

"Where is your husband?" he asked thoughtfully.

"In Shanghai." She sat down on the divan and held out her hands for the warmth of the braziers.

"Where did you escape from?" Fischer asked, the Victrola arm poised above the record.

"Sevastopol. My husband is—was—a naval officer."

"And you came through Siberia," he guessed, his gaze serious.

"Not all the way. We fled when the fleet mutinied, and we took a ship from Vladivostok."

"You and your husband?"

"His mother was with us, and his sister." She paused. "I have a child," she added, looking directly at Fischer.

"I see." He lowered the needle, which cast a tiny spear of candlelight onto the record. Music shrilled out into the room.

Fischer put his hands in the pockets of his well-cut evening jacket. He rocked back very slightly on his heels, his head cocked as he listened. "Do you like it?"

"I don't know it."

"It's called a tango. It's all the rage in Europe."

"I saw some people dancing something called a Charleston," she offered, "in a nightclub along the Nanking road. I thought it barbaric." She had gone there with Alex to take a message to another of the Russian plotters, another former military officer now working as a waiter. The men and women had leapt about the floor in such contortions that she had at first thought they were all suffering from some public madness. Between songs the women stood looking bored with the men who were paying for their company, while the men talked to one another.

"Barbaric times," Fischer said, "call for barbaric relaxations."

As the tango filled the room, Fischer surveyed the woman in front of him. "Would you like another drink, Countess?" he said.

"Please call me Evelyn."

"Evelyn." He tasted the word on his tongue, his fingers tapping on the red lacquer table. "English?"

"Yes."

"The Russians admire the English." Fischer opened a cabinet and took out a decanter. "The king, Queen Victoria, your splendid fleet. They never could quite imitate England, though." He poured two glasses of whiskey. "The Russian landscape hardly resembles a small wet island."

"I liked Russia," Evelyn told him. His fingertips were dry and warm as she accepted the whiskey. "I thought St. Petersburg beautiful."

"A folly, of course," Fischer stated as the record wound

down. "Another attempt to become European, if not English."

"I've never thought of England as European." The whiskey burned through Evelyn, and she sat back on the couch. Touching its yellow silk was like running her fingers over fresh butter.

"A sign that you are a true Englishwoman," Fischer agreed. "Europe thinks of England as part of it, but England doesn't think of Europe at all."

"I wouldn't quite say that," Evelyn rebuffed. His profile as he rewound the Victrola was sharply handsome. It had been a long time since she had sat and flirted like this with a man. "Some Englishmen love Europe, like the old king did. My brother told me that when he was in the south of France he saw a whole boulevard named after him. They still spoke of him as the Prince of Wales, though he had since become king and then died."

"The wicked prince," Fischer said, clearly enjoying himself. Evelyn wondered if his mood could be attributed to the pearls, or if it was her presence, a thought that made her shiver, then smile. "Why the smile?" Fischer asked as another unfamiliar song filled the night.

"I can't tell you." She sipped her whiskey demurely.

"Every time a woman has said that to me, it has meant that nothing could keep her from telling me."

"I was thinking," she said, dropping her pretense, "that I haven't enjoyed myself in a long time. I had almost forgotten how simple pleasures could make you happy."

Fischer blinked, astonished, and looked about his lavish room. "Simple pleasures?"

"You have a very beautiful house," Evelyn apologized. "I didn't mean it quite as it came out."

"What was your house in Russia like?" His mood had dropped a notch or two.

"Terrible," she admitted. "Enormous and cold. And it wasn't in Russia, it was in Poland."

It was Fischer's turn to shiver. "God." He sighed, raised his glass, and offered, "Not to the past, to the future."

Already slightly dizzy from the whiskey, Evelyn felt

obliged to drink to that. But the future seemed as perilous as the narrow path down the hillside. She made a play of touching the lip of the glass to hers. "I used to think I knew the future," she said as Fischer came across the room to sit facing her. "Now . . ." She looked at the flames and saw the fires that had burned the night they had fled Sevastopol. "Now it terrifies me."

"Don't!" Fischer murmured as she grew reflective. He reached across and placed his hand on hers where it lay on her knee. "You are a young woman," he told her when she glanced up at him. His eyes were warm; the heat and the whiskey made her suddenly tearful. She blinked, more scared of yielding to a moment of weakness than of him. To cry now would be to admit all the fears that she had been pushing away for years.

She put her glass down and stood up. "You must find me some transportation. I must go back tonight."

"You are truly frightened, aren't you?" he said without moving.

She nodded, reaching down for her coat. The little orchid that she had fixed to the collar had withered, miserable testimony to a moment of weakness.

"You don't have to be afraid of me."

"You?" The whiskey took its toll, and she laughed out loud. "What could you do to me?" But her defiance faded as fury drained the color from his face. His answer was to stand and lift the arm of the Victrola viciously from the record so the music died with a thin cry.

"I can't oblige you, madam," he said in a tight whisper. "There is no transportation until tomorrow. In any case, the train will have left for Shanghai." New dislike shone in his eyes. "I would have thought experience might have taught you to make the best of your situation. I can offer you the hospitality of the house and transportation tomorrow, nothing else. Now, if you will excuse me, I have some work to do." He went out without a word, leaving her standing, holding her coat.

She heard him shouting to the servants as he passed from room to room, and sat down, clutching her coat. Her hands trembled, and to still them, she lifted the whiskey glass again and took a deep draught.

"Miss?" a voice whispered at her shoulder. She started, dropping the glass and staining the yellow silk of the couch with whiskey. She looked about her frantically for something to wipe it up, but the servant impassively knelt by her feet, dabbing at the whiskey as it soaked into the cloth.

"Is it ruined?"

He nodded, his eyes flat and accusing. He stood up. "Master say I show you room," he told her.

With a last glance at the stained couch, she followed the white coat and black silk trousers out into a corridor, and then, unexpectedly, into the central courtyard of the temple. Here the lines of the building became clear: four square walls around the moonlit central court where a gong hung from a carved beam. As she followed the boy she saw Fischer across the courtyard at his desk, his head low. The boy stood indicating that she should go before him.

The room held a narrow bed set against one wall, a white coverlet dropping to the floor in a wide skirt. There was a dressing table with a vanity mirror against another wall with two silver-backed hairbrushes and a matching mirror lying on it. Candlelight flickered gently on the stone walls, and another porcelain brazier fought the chill.

Curious, she picked up the soft camel's hair brushes, observing blank spaces where the monograms might have been. He brings his women here, she thought, looking in the mirror at her image, burnished by the flickering candlelight. Loosening her hair, she remembered other times at her vanity in England when Morgan had come in to brush her hair and talk.

For a second she thought the force of memory had actually conjured Morgan up. But the second image in the mirror was Fischer's. She stopped brushing her hair, carefully replacing the brush on the mirrored top of the vanity.

"I came to tell you that I am going to eat now. If you wish to join me, please do so." He looked almost apologetic, facing her from a distance in the mirror, eyes downcast. "I have been hungry myself many times. Whatever you think of me, you should understand that you do not know much about my life."

When he looked up she was still watching him in the reflection of the mirror. "I spilled whiskey on your couch," she told him. "Did the boy tell you?"

"It's nothing," he said, the shoulders of his dinner jacket lifting in a shrug. "We shouldn't become attached to those things." His eyes sought hers in the glass. "Are you ready for dinner?"

"Yes," she said, turning. "Thank you."

"You should wear your hair loose," he told her. "It becomes you."

She touched her hair where it fell in soft waves past her face. "I used to when I was a girl," she said.

"You are still a girl." He offered his hand. "Come, let us have our dinner."

Fires burned in open braziers in the courtyard. The gong loomed against the starlit night sky. Fischer led Evelyn into the dining room, where two places had been set at the bent willow table. She noticed champagne in a silver bucket, and orchids in small silver vases by each place.

"You live well," she admitted grudgingly.

"One never knows how long one will be fortunate."

The waiter brought a clear, warm soup with a blossom floating in it.

"You don't mind Chinese cuisine?" Fischer queried.

"No."

"One adapts," he said, smiling at her over the rim of his porcelain spoon. "That is the trick, is it not?"

She didn't answer. Alex and his family thought all the local food unfit for Europeans, but the soup was delicious. For a few minutes the only sounds were the gentle clinks of the spoons against the translucent bowls.

"You do drink champagne?" Fischer asked, reaching for the silver cooler.

"No," she said with a smile, "but I would like to." She felt giddy and warm.

He poured the champagne into her tall glass. "I imagine life has not treated you very well, has it?"

Why did her eyes sting so quickly? She turned her head away. "No worse than other people," she answered him harshly. But from where she sat with her head averted, all she could see was the beautiful courtyard with the fires glowing like rubies in the cool night. She heard him say, "I did not always live this well."

The Chinese servants came to clear the soup bowls and bring the next course of very thinly sliced pork. "Would you like chopsticks?" Fischer asked.

"I don't know how to use them."

"Would you like to try?" His voice had an edge, and he signaled to the waiter to bring the chopsticks. "Watch," he instructed, holding his pair to the light. "Thus."

She tried to imitate him, but the ivory sticks flew across the table, knocking over the orchids by her plate. He rose to stand behind her, and she could smell the fresh soap and a cologne of musk—very faint, but as opulent as the champagne and food. He put one hand on her shoulder and with the other took her right hand. Guiding her fingers, he helped her to pick up a slice of pork. He raised her hand to her mouth and fed her like a mother bird its young.

A kaleidoscope of sensations coursed through her: his touch and aroma, the tang of the meat, the sense of helplessness. She felt herself yielding part of herself as he watched with his bright blue eyes, his hawk nose very slightly narrowed, as though he, too, was feeling some heightened sensation. Releasing her hand, he flashed a smile and stood back. "Again."

As the candlelight flickered across his face she wanted his arms about her again, willed him to lean over and make her do what he wanted. She tried again and succeeded in a clumsy manner.

"You will find it easier very soon, my dear." He went back to the end of the table and he ate his own meal swiftly, putting his chopsticks down neatly at the edge of the plate. Evelyn felt awkward struggling with her own.

"Forgive me." He sighed. "I eat like a barbarian. It comes of having been hungry for a long time." He sipped his wine. "Enjoy yourself," he told her. "There is nothing that will shock or outrage me. If I could tell you what my life has been like, you would never speak to me again."

"I doubt that." She was getting better, but her impatience grew. She put the chopsticks down.

"Fear and hunger will make a man do almost anything," Fischer said thoughtfully. "All the rest"—he waved his hand about the beautiful proportions of his mountain temple—"this is a luxury, a choice. All books, philosophies, morals, principles—all of it is mere words. Thought means nothing in the face of action." He looked over at the chopsticks at the side of her plate. "You aren't hungry?"

"Very," she said, picking up a piece of pork in her fingers and feeding herself. "I shall learn to eat with chopsticks another time. For the moment, I'll take your advice: action." She took another piece of the thin pork in the sweet sauce and put it in her mouth.

Fischer laughed. He watched, delighted, while she finished the pork, then wiped her fingers on the delicate lace serviette.

They ate quietly, their eyes every now and then seeking each other down the length of the table. When Fischer stopped pouring the champagne she had thought it a politeness, perhaps even a flirtation, but now he seemed to will the servant back into the room at the right intervals: to pour the wine, to change the dishes. They ate fish wrapped in bamboo shoots, two rice dishes, each perfectly spiced, a dish of large, limp dark brown mushrooms, shrimp in batter, and finally fresh litchi nuts, as sweet and delicate as anything Evelyn had ever enjoyed.

At the end she said, "I know why they need sedan bearers."

"You liked the food."

"I have never liked food more," she admitted.

Fischer stood. "Would you join me in the living room, or are you tired?"

She was beautifully tired, in the way of a child. She had traveled a long day, met a man who brought out conflicting emotions in her, eaten and drunk well. In the single bed in the room across the courtyard, she would slip into a sleep untroubled by dreams of flight or cries that woke her to pad into the other room and hold Victoria until she slept again.

Out of politeness, she said, "For a few minutes, perhaps." The lovely room with the white willow table and the plain porcelain plates tugged at her as nothing had when she fled Russia. She had thought then, of course, that she would be back one day, while this room, she knew, she would see only once.

In the living room, she looked guiltily at the stain on the yellow silk couch. "I am terribly sorry about that."

Fischer shrugged. "Brandy?"

"I'll be very drunk," she said. "I don't think I should."

Fischer's bright, wise eyes held her as he set the two glasses side by side. "You will be quite safe, my dear," he assured her.

She blushed. "I wasn't thinking that."

He smiled, bringing the glass over. "You should have been. You are a lovely woman."

Evelyn looked out over the terraced garden. A mist had risen to fill the whole valley below with a fine gray fog, and the distant city was lost. Evelyn felt as though she were floating on some mysterious island above all the turbulence of the world below. "You are very lucky."

"But it wasn't always so." He stood well back from her, playing with a gold lighter and a cigar. He had a small device, also of gold, that clipped off the end. She thought of all the baubles that she and Alex had once owned: watches, rings, riding crops, and silver handles. Some of them had been left behind, a few brought along and sold long ago. She had no desire to have them back. The gold cigar cutter looked foolish, offensive.

Her thoughts must have shown. "A ridiculous object," Fischer acknowledged. "You are thinking that I indulge myself when others are hungry."

"No," she said. "I was thinking of all the similar things I once owned. I miss many things, but not those. I miss the money," she said, thinking that the champagne and brandy must have made her mad.

Fischer bit on his cigar, so it rose like a wand in his

mouth. He took it out. "Bravo!" he said. "Finally a sensible refugee. I had begun to despair. Kornislov and all his type . . ." He dismissed them as he put the cigar into a crystal ashtray.

"The general seems to be thinking of himself very well," Evelyn retorted, thinking of the sale of the pearls.

Fischer waved the brandy glass. "That money will be gone within a few years. There are essential lessons that are learned young or never. The general is too old and too greedy to learn any of them."

"Such as?" Evelyn asked. She found that the alcohol was making his smugness intolerable.

"Are you really interested?"

"Maybe." Surprised to find her glass empty, she poured herself more, sat down on the couch, and on impulse reached behind and took a cigarette from the silver box behind the couch. As Fischer leaned forward she snatched up the lighter from beside the silver box, leaving his gesture incomplete. She lit her cigarette without looking at him and repeated, "Such as?"

She could see him reassessing her. Did he know that she was playacting?

"Money is only security if you put it to work for you," Fischer began.

"Everyone understands that," Evelyn said dismissively. She hadn't smoked since she was a young girl, in the garden, where Morgan had taught her how to draw the smoke into her lungs.

"Of course," Fischer said quietly. "But you must understand also that money itself has no value at all. Rubles, Shanghai dollars, pounds sterling, American dollars"—he cast them figuratively at her feet—"useless."

"Not entirely," she countered. "Pounds sterling still seem very good things to have."

"For now," Fischer said. "Who can tell you what will happen tomorrow or the next day?"

"England—" Evelyn began.

He stopped her, mocking her tone. "Russia, China . . ." He looked toward the valley, now even deeper in the fog.

"Down there there are Russian nobles, Chinese nobles. Ten, twenty, fifty years ago all of them thought that they were secure in putting their fortunes in their land, their country's currency." He breathed out the words on a cloud of cigar smoke. "Completely secure."

"But if nothing is secure . . ." she said uncertainly.

"I didn't say that," he said, relaxing in his role of teacher, "I said that the old assets are not secure. Land can be taken away, can it not?"

"Yes."

"Money can become worthless in a moment, is that not so?"

"Yes." The Chinese currency issued by the central bank was worthless before it could be taken to the market. In Europe she had heard that the German marks dropped in value from one hour to the next.

"So, what have you left?" he asked her, master to pupil.

"Pearls?" she asked.

"Certainly," he said, but he hadn't coaxed out the answer he wanted. "But those are insurance, nothing more."

She reassessed this small man with his white hair and the young man's eyes in his unlined face. He must be very rich. "What would you say has value," she asked, "enduring value?"

"Nothing," he countered, rocking back on his heels with a smile of satisfaction on his smooth face.

The fury that coursed through her was out of proportion to the moment. She felt teased, as though knowledge that could help her had been snatched away at the last moment.

"I have to sleep," she said flatly, crushing her cigarette in the ashtray.

He let her play out the game of putting down her glass, standing up, and preparing herself to bid him good night before he said sharply, "Sit down."

She subsided onto the couch. She watched him sullenly while he lit himself another cigar very deliberately. "Nothing," he repeated, like a sulky child. And again, "Nothing."

She drew a breath, thinking for the first time of Alex. Alex had liked to act as a teacher when they were first married, taking her through different stages of perception. He had shown her how to look at art, buildings particularly, for he could make dead stones come alive with stories of how they had come to be arranged in just such a way. Later, as the war continued, he explained politics, which had become an obsession. Many of his statements veered close to treason, but by that time the whole navy, as far as Evelyn could see from her limited vantage point of a young naval wife in Sevastopol, was waiting for some change.

The news from the capital was that the czar had retreated to his country estate, running the war through his wife and her priest. When the revolution came, however, it took such an unexpected form that Alex and his contemporaries had themselves been stunned, casting about frantically for some legitimate government that would allow them to remain in their own positions. Later, he had simply stopped talking, as though his own words had betrayed them all. For a long time Evelyn had lived in a state of suspended animation, unwilling to admit that Alex and his émigré friends who met each week in the Cathedrale were as outdated as some Ruritanian operetta.

Now she said, "I am very tired; I apologize." She could learn from this man, if he would teach her, yet it seemed ironic to change from one lecturer to another. Men created this terrible confusion, then other men came along to try to solve it. No one asked what a woman thought.

"Knowledge," Fischer said shortly.

She looked at him uncertainly.

"Everything any of us has ever known is gone, or changed at the very least." he spoke in a normal voice, all theatrics abandoned. "China is changing, Russia is dust." He ground it into the floor with his polished evening shoes. "England"—he shrugged—"even England will one day have to change. Germany, France . . ." He reeled off the names of countries as though they alone were the evidence. When he had stopped he stood in front of her so she had to peer up into a face more serious, less kind. But he looked strong, too, and she had missed that in a man since Alex's defeat by the realization that he, too, would have to take flight. "There can never be any more security." Fischer spoke so she had to crane back to look at him. "Even gold is heavy in any great quantity." He stepped away again, and she was ashamed by her audible sigh of relief. "But knowledge," he said over his shoulder, "will always be of use. Information."

"Spying," she supplied, trying to mask her disappointment with contempt.

"No," he said, and she saw he was disappointed. He looked as though he might stop speaking, and she was afraid that he would dismiss her, let her leave here tomorrow with nothing more than some money.

"I'm sorry. I am very stupid."

"Of course you're not," he retorted. "Knowledge, information as to what is likely to happen, is useful. You can make plans on that—never completely safe plans, but as close to security as anyone can get anymore."

"A fortune," she suggested.

"That, too, but that isn't the important part, is it?"

"It would be nice."

"Nothing anyone does for money alone is ever successful in the long term," he went on. "Goals—ideals, if you wish—whatever it is that deludes a man or woman into pushing forward, that is what makes for success. Hatred, fear, revenge . . ."

"Greed?"

He smiled. "Greed. All the dark little secrets. And of them all, fear is the best, the fear within each of us. Even for our souls." He seemed to find that funny, smiling broadly.

"What do you fear?" she asked.

"I fear being trapped."

The long windows rattled slightly, making her shiver. "I feel trapped all the time," she admitted. Then, blinking because she was suddenly very tired and thought she might do something foolish like cry, she added, "Sometimes I think that all I want is some time to make decisions, to think . . . and sometimes that seems to be all I do. Think, that is."

He was watching her with concern. He put his cigar in an

ashtray, crossed to her, and touched her forehead. "You have a fever," he diagnosed.

"Now I must sleep," she said.

"I'll have the boy draw a hot bath for you," he told her. "You'll sleep well."

She didn't have the will to resist. He took her silence for assent and was gone for some minutes. She sat with her knees pressed together, her shoulders hunched in her black dress, her glass of whiskey held before her with both hands.

"I'm getting drunk," she admitted when he came back.

He took the glass out of her hand like a disappointed nanny. "That's enough. Now come with me." He drew her to her feet and took her back out into the courtyard.

The temperature had dropped sharply. Her breath plumed out before her against the night sky that was brittle with stars. A Chinese woman was waiting in her room. The woman was ageless, her skin smooth and gold, her hair thick, black, parted in the middle and caught at her neck with two gold pins. Her savings, carried on her body. Evelyn wondered how many servants were in the house to fill its various needs.

"Lye Choy will help you." Lye Choy smiled a golden smile—more savings—and took Evelyn from Fischer's care. Before Evelyn could thank Fischer he was gone, his heels clicking over the courtyard where snowflakes now drifted from the night sky.

The Chinese woman undressed her with soft gestures and led her naked and shivering into a room where a bath like an old-time military campaign bath had been set up. The small interior room was filled with the steam from the hot water. Evelyn let herself be put in the bath, then sat back feeling the deepest luxury soak into her. The woman brought bath salts, and Evelyn had a moment when she wondered why Fischer had bath salts that smelled of gardenias. Then she remembered why she was there, and was offended for a fraction of a second. She forgot it though all in the time it took to clear a hair from her forehead. She soaked while Lye Choy washed her, then allowed herself to be dried with a large towel while she stood obediently in the center of the room.

The Chinese woman helped her, drowsy and happy, into bed. "Thank you," she started to murmur, but she was asleep before she finished the phrase.

For the first time in years she slept without dreaming. In the middle of the night, she awoke suddenly to the glow of the coals in the brazier. She thought she saw a shadow at the door to the courtyard, then she felt the weight on her bed, ran her hand down, and found that someone had covered her with her sable coat. The Chinese woman was asleep under a pile of covers on a pallet in the corner. Until the courtyard began to pale with the dawn's light, she lay awake, watching the large gong change from a shadowed form to a thing of sharp angles, green with tarnish. She slept again.

6

When she awoke the Chinese woman was gone. The fire was glowing healthily once again, and outside a new snowfall glistened. Her spirits soared. She had forgotten what happiness felt like, forgotten without knowing that she had. She stretched languidly. But at the thought of her return, her mood evaporated. As she sat up, swinging her legs out of bed, the door to the courtyard opened, and the Chinese woman came in with tea on a red lacquer tray. "No get up," she said firmly.

"I have to," Evelyn said, rising, but her legs betrayed her, buckling under, and she hit the side of the bed as she slipped to the floor. The Chinese woman put the tray down quickly and ran to her. She felt sick, very sick, and closed her eyes at the comfort of the Chinese woman's hands as the covers were tucked under her.

The tea smelled of jasmine. She opened her eyes again. The Chinese woman brought her a bedjacket in the Chinese style, heavy silk, padded within. She put it on, wondering who had worn this before. After she had sipped her tea, she asked. "Mr. Fischer. Is he having breakfast?"

"Gone," said the Chinese woman.

"Where?" Evelyn said wildly.

"Write letter," the woman told her, and she went out into the courtyard. A breath of cool winter air flurried the coals. Dropping back against the pillows, Evelyn drank the tea. When the Chinese woman came back she was holding pieces of paper.

"Madame Lezenski," Fischer had written, "I have to

leave early this morning. I came to your room to ask if I could take you into Wuhan, but it was clear that you are in no condition to travel. Therefore I have arranged for the bank to contact your family, assuring them that you are still on bank business but unwell. I know that this will not please you, and I apologize, but I really must leave immediately on urgent business. A day of rest will no doubt restore you. A car will arrive tomorrow to take you into Wuhan.

"I wish I could say my farewells to you myself. Forgive my rudeness. Last night's company at dinner and the conversation, if you will allow me to say so, were most pleasant."

He signed himself Leonard James Fischer.

Evelyn dropped the sheets of paper on the bedclothes. She felt a disappointment, then great anxiety. Alex would be furious, she thought. But then she imagined Sebowski in his office at the bank, smooth and assured, and her fears subsided. Sebowski would think of something.

The Chinese woman came back and bustled about the bed, arranging the bedclothes. "You want books?"

"Books?"

"Master have many books," she said with the satisfaction of a loyal servant announcing a cultured master. "Many, many books."

"Yes, thank you."

"I get," the woman said.

The room shadowed as fresh snow clouds passed over the temple. Evelyn watched the first flakes fall lazily past her window, working to keep her mind blank. If she liked this too much, the pain of returning to her own life tomorrow would be too great. There had been no relief before, no moment for luxurious contemplation, only terror and survival.

"Books," said the Chinese woman, opening the door and closing it against the snowfall that seemed from the bed to be made up of large individual flakes, enormous, as though they were magnified by the glass.

There was something by Tolstoy in Russian that Evelyn thought might be *Anna Karenina, Madame Bovary* in

French, and in English a volume of Wordsworth. She was amused; imagine a sentimentalist beneath all that worldly advice.

"Thank you." She placed them beside her. "Do you live here?" she asked.

For the first time the Chinese woman looked at her with suspicion. She noticed the change in her black eyes; the friendliness disappeared the way the flakes of snow did upon hitting the glass, there one moment, a glaze of moisture the next. "Yes," she said, turning away.

"For a long time?" Evelyn asked.

When she looked back after straightening the items on the dressing table, the hostility of her gaze was unmistakable. "Long time now."

Evelyn watched the snow fall while she listened to the soft sounds of the woman moving about in the next room. The world had comfortably shrunk to this single room, the one next door, the temple about them. Beyond was a world that could be ignored with safety for a few hours, hidden by the snow.

"You want food?" the woman offered, friendly again, as she came in.

"I want to get up."

"Master say stay in bed."

"I must be up soon," Evelyn told her. "Where are my clothes?"

"I wash," the woman said, looking at Evelyn reproachfully. "Not clean."

Evelyn felt herself blushing. No, her dress wasn't very clean, she thought, a detail that would once have obsessed her. "When will it be dry?" she asked humbly.

"Later," the woman said. Without looking at Evelyn, she announced, "Many clothes here. You want clothes, I get."

"Women's clothes?" Evelyn asked.

"Many women's clothes."

"They probably wouldn't fit me," Evelyn said quietly.

"Plenty different clothes, all sizes," the woman said.

Evelyn blinked. "Oh," she said. She shouldn't have been

so shocked, she thought; he was a single man. It was the planning that shocked her; it seemed cold-blooded. Her fingers touched the book of poetry absently. "Could I have some slippers?" she asked. She stuck a foot out from under the covers, gesturing at the Chinese woman's shoes. "Slippers," she repeated.

The woman was gone for a few minutes. She returned with satin slippers lined in soft, dark fur. Evelyn wiggled her toes as she slipped them on. The woman giggled, establishing a bond of friendship again between them. Evelyn dropped the padded bedjacket and threw her sable coat over her shoulders. She walked toward the window.

"No, no, men," the woman said.

Evelyn assured her with a gesture. She opened the door to the biting cold, looked doubtfully at the satin slippers, then stepped boldly out into the snow that was already inches deep. Fischer could afford more slippers, she thought recklessly. He must have brought many women here.

I am living like a tart, she thought, amused and offended as she entered the rooms on the other side of the courtyard. She had a desire to go into Fischer's room to see his private things. The Wordsworth hinted at Germanic sentiment. She giggled at the thought of Fischer weeping as Wagner blared through his exquisite temple, but the image wouldn't take hold; she could see him crying, but not as a pathetic character. For a small man, he loomed large in her memory.

And anyway, she thought as she went into the cold main room where the brazier was empty and clean, he probably didn't leave anything of himself about the house. Where did he live? she wondered. A dozen different possible worlds pressed against one another. Not Peking, she was sure, and not Wuhan. Shanghai seemed right. He could be anyone he wanted in Shanghai, and no one would care.

The snow fell in sheets, drifting on the unseen wind from the valley. Even the crippled shapes of the trees pleased her. Her feeling of well-being left her, leaving deep loneliness. Not the loneliness of lying beside Alex in the middle of the night, but the loneliness of reflection. She could have cried, but these tears were what the nanny who had cared for Morgan and herself would have called them: crocodile tears of self-pity.

Warm from the fever, she opened her coat, leaning against the glass of the windows. The snow fell quickly, the house as silent as it must have been when monks worshipped there. They had chosen their place well, she reflected. The view demanded introspection.

Hearing a sound behind her, she saw the boy from last night watching her silently from the door into the dining room. "Hello," she said, but he vanished as though her word had broken a spell.

She went back to her bedroom, passing across the snow-filled courtyard, and kicked off her wet slippers, guiltily propping them near the brazier to dry. She climbed into bed, picked up the books, and opened them each to the fly page. There in a bold script was Fischer's signature. She was surprised at the way it made her feel: personal, secret, as though she was a girl again. She touched the small, strong letters with her fingertips as though they could tell her more about him.

Madame Bovary and *Anna Karenina,* cheap novels about cheap women, she thought, then reproached herself. Her mother had thought like that, and Evelyn had seen far too much to make those judgments anymore. Still, she wondered if Fischer or one of his women had bought the books. Fischer, she decided. He wasn't the type of man to keep books he didn't read, certainly not to claim them with his name.

So Fischer read books about great romances. Yes, she thought, settling back amid her pillows. That and Wordsworth. A man who believed in love, or had. She had, also. The sort her mother had wanted for her—a good marriage, security, safety . . . money. Then Fischer's words came back: There's no security, not anymore.

"Knowledge," he had said to her, and like a fool she had wanted to laugh. Now she took the word like a talisman and turned it over and over in her mind. The word was a gift like those fairies bestowed in old wives' tales, with a legend to be deciphered. If she could decipher it, perhaps it would keep her safe. The terrible feeling of continued loss, the feeling that life was too large, too fierce, that had been growing in her day by day, month by month, seemed to ebb at the mere thought.

She opened the Wordsworth but after a few moments put it down; dells, daffodils, soft English fields seemed to dance off the pages to taunt her. She closed her eyes and slept, and when she awoke the room was dark, the brazier glowing like a ruby in the corner. The snow had increased a hundredfold, wrapping the temple with a soft gray curtain, and she was frightened that the servants had gone, abandoning her to this desecrated temple with its ghosts. In the damp slippers she ran out into the cold. She threw open the doors, calling out, "Hello, hello," running from room to room until she reached the entrance hall where she had come in the night before with Kornislov.

He seemed to materialize before her as the servant had vanished earlier, a specter out of a dream that darkened, became real, and moved toward her, and she screamed.

He caught her at the entrance to the living room, taking hold of her by the shoulders. She shrugged out of the coat, ran forward, tripped on her nightgown, and rolled on her back, screaming out the years of terror. Until the blow hit her hard on the forehead, she struggled like an animal. Her mind went dark, and she fell away to the edge of the garden beyond this room, about to fall over. She felt the ground giving way under her, then nothing for one long moment until she felt herself grasped roughly and lifted.

There was shouting nearby, a man, then other voices making explanations. She felt a rough cloth under her cheek, smelled cologne, and opened her eyes to light that made her blink.

"I didn't think of you as a hysteric." Fischer sounded furious.

"You came back," Evelyn said. He was holding her uncertainly as servants rushed about, lighting the rooms.

"The snow stopped me," he explained. "Can you walk?"

Her legs buckled under her again, so he carried her through the dark house. Seeing the Chinese woman bent over the brazier, Fischer erupted with a torrent of angry Chinese. Head bent, the woman kept pushing coal into the brazier.

As he lifted her onto her bed Evelyn was surprised to feel that she was no weight at all for him. "I feel like a complete fool," she said.

"You should," he agreed.

The Chinese woman rose without raising her eyes and hurried out into the snow.

Fischer said, "They miscalculated, that's all." He said it in a bored, almost amused manner.

"How? They thought you weren't coming back."

He turned to look at her, searching in the pocket of his dark blue overcoat for his cigarette case. "That, of course. But they thought you were a fallen woman, shall we say."

Evelyn flushed. "I can see where they might get that impression."

Fischer stood with his coat on, watching her as she pulled the covers over her. "We may be here some time," he told her, ignoring her barb.

"I can't be," Evelyn said, panic rising at the thought of Alex in Shanghai. She felt the way she used to as a child when she had been sent to bed by her nanny: at first deliciously indulged, then increasingly fretful.

"If you wish to walk down the mountain, go ahead," Fischer offered, rocking on his heels, his coat open over a handsome double-breasted gray suit.

"My husband . . ." But behind Fischer the snow was lit by the glowing rooms around the courtyard, and Evelyn realized that she felt increasingly happy and had for some moments. Fischer made her feel young again.

"I think you should get out of bed," he said, exactly as her nanny had. No nonsense.

"All right."

His smile broadened. "I'll meet you in the living room in

half an hour." He turned. "Do you want the woman back? She'll hide now, afraid that I'll get angry with her."

"I would like a bath," Evelyn admitted.

"I'll send her."

"As a child," Fischer said, leaning back against the cushions of the yellow silk couch, "I was indulged."

"You were rich?" Evelyn asked. Feeling the effect of the dinner wine, she warmed her brandy glass in both hands. The fire blazed high in the small stove, and the snow fell as heavily as it had in St. Petersburg.

"Oh, yes." Fischer was a different man tonight, less guarded, more playful. The sense of isolation they felt in the house had reminded him of his own childhood in Austria. "Rich Jews from Vienna. My father was a banker, a very private banker."

"I see," she said, reassessing him. He seemed to change before her like a chameleon.

"You thought I was poor and angry, grubbing for money so that I would never be hungry?"

"Something like that," she admitted. She picked her feet off the ground and curled them under her on the sofa without thinking. The Chinese woman had brought back her black dress, washed and ironed. She could smell the fresh soap, though she felt plain in her simple dress. The closet in the room had revealed a dozen different dresses, and the Chinese woman had offered to bring more. Touching the silk—jade green, pale yellow, pink—Evelyn had been tempted. She knew many Russian women who were now dance hall girls in Shanghai, available for the night for the price of a meal, a few dollars, some champagne. Alex and his friends despised them, but to Evelyn, who had seen them drop away from the Russian community one by one, they were merely victims.

She, however, was a married woman who knew her place in the world. She would refuse him, but the flirtation was more intoxicating than the brandy.

"No, no," Fischer said, laughing. "No, my father was rich.

He lent money to his betters—aristocrats, army officers, all of them. None of them had any money beyond their positions, but he accepted that."

"What about their estates?"

Fischer shrugged, sipped his brandy, and said, "Certainly. But how would a Jew attach their estates? Go to the emperor? I think not. No, there was no recourse in the courts if they defaulted. He knew that."

"Then why did he lend them money?"

"For information," Fischer said.

"Information?"

"Yes. My father's fortune was based on information, like the Rothschilds'. The money he lent was an investment. He knew that at any time he could have been accused of treason, tried, executed, that no one would have cared. But he relied on people's greed. That is a constant."

"How cynical you are."

"Not at all," Fischer said, and Evelyn thought of the Wordsworth, the Flaubert. "But I understand that the source of all trouble is human nature. If you consider that in all your transactions and rely on people to follow their own interest, you are seldom wrong."

"As opposed to what?"

"As opposed to countries, flags, political beliefs."

"You don't believe in those?"

"I believe those are mere passports to power, laissez-passer," Fischer said. "Men mouth slogans to justify their power. But power is what interests them. The Russian aristocracy evolved out of brutal landowners holding onto their power. The czar made them too weak to threaten his; the Bolsheviks used Marx to attain power but now will abandon him except in speeches. Here in China one dynasty has fallen, and there will be a struggle to see who rules for the next century."

"Sun Yat-sen," Evelyn said, mouthing a name she had heard spoken around Shanghai.

Fischer raised his eyebrows. "Where did you hear that?"

"People talk."

"I wouldn't have thought you'd know about him."

"What do you think of me?" She knew she was flirting.

"I think of you as a captive," Fischer said with a smile, "but perhaps not such a willing one. I think perhaps you will break out."

As soon as he said it she knew in her heart that that was what she wanted: to live, to breathe, to be able to talk freely again.

"But it won't be Sun Yat-sen." Fischer took her half-finished brandy glass away without asking, to refill it. He looked moody suddenly, as though recalled to worries. "There will be a struggle," he said, resting his shoe on the brazier. "The warlords will fight it out; the great Chinese merchants will struggle to push the Europeans away so they can grab the spoils of the old empire for themselves. It will be a time of alliances, shifting every moment until some great cataclysm puts one or another segment in power." He looked at her directly. "Then they will kill millions," he said flatly. "And whoever wins will only hold onto their power for fifty or perhaps a hundred years. Telephones, wireless, the speed of communication has made time move faster, and with it history will be transformed."

"So what can one do?" Evelyn wanted to learn everything this man could tell her.

"One can enjoy one's life." He smiled over his shoulder, and as she had the night before, she felt a rising sense of fury, as though he had offered her a gift and snatched it away.

"Well," she said flatly, putting the brandy on the lacquer table before her, "you obviously enjoy yours."

"I try to." He faced her across the room. "I was a spoiled young man, and then abruptly I was destitute. My father's business failed, and he committed suicide. The details do not matter, but I have known fear such as you have known, hunger, all of it. Now I enjoy my life again, but I am changed."

She faced him. "My brother believes in enjoying his life."

"And you don't?"

She reflected, feeling her answer might turn out to be important. "I used to," she said. "I have a child now. Children change things."

"I know that."

She looked at him more quickly than she intended. "You have children?"

"Two daughters." He paused. "And a wife," he added.

She was shocked by her extraordinary sense of pain. "In Shanghai?"

"No," he said, looking into his glass. He spoke softly, making up his mind. "In Vienna," he said. "My wife and my daughters live in Vienna."

"Oh, I see."

"Perhaps not. Jews are great snobs, did you know that?"

In spite of herself, she laughed. Then she was mortified by the way he flushed, pushing the door of the brazier with the toe of his shoe so it clanged loudly in the room. A servant ran in, and Evelyn realized that everything they said here, everything that transpired between them, was being watched, listened to. Fischer wouldn't care. These people were hired, trained to watch out for his every need. He waved the boy away, and when the servant was gone Fischer had himself under control. Evelyn had a shameful sense of satisfaction at having finally reached him the way he had reached her.

Still, she apologized. "That was rude of me."

He shrugged indifferently. "That's what most people think."

"Tell me about your . . ." She almost said "wife" but caught herself at the last moment. "Family."

"My wife is an Austrian Jew of a good family, as I was . . . am," he corrected himself. "She despises Polish Jews, Russian Jews . . . Zionists. In Vienna she can maintain her own view of herself, so she refuses to come out here."

"But you did."

"Yes," he said, once more looking at her directly, as though to underscore his point. "I came out here in nineteen

129

nineteen, and I knew from the first moment the ship turned into the Yangtze that I would stay."

"Why?"

"You won't laugh?" But clearly he didn't care if she did, because he was laughing.

"I'll try not to."

"Because I liked the way it smelled."

She laughed.

"You see," he teased her, "you don't keep your word."

"Shanghai smells terrible," she pointed out.

"Ripe," he insisted.

"Fine, ripe. The Soochow Creek smells of . . ." She wanted to say death.

"Humanity," he suggested.

Evelyn could remember her own first sight of Shanghai: of the Whanpoo industrial area across the river, low godowns, coolies sweating in the midday sun, and Alex trying to stand tall in his old uniform while Evelyn bargained with a rickshaw driver. To her surprise, she saw that she had then been hopeful for the first time in months. They were by the sea again, or near enough, for there were the ships in the river, pockmarked with rust, sleek-hulled liners, the tiny sampans of the river people skimming the dirty yellow surface. They had to stop and make some type of stand, for there was nowhere else to go.

"I think I can understand that," she agreed. "When we reached Shanghai I was tired, mostly. I wanted to sleep."

"I went back after six months and asked my wife to come out," he told her.

"And she refused?"

"No, she came out after the war. When the ship docked and I saw she was alone, I knew she wouldn't stay. She stayed six weeks and went back. We never fought."

"You never thought of going with her?"

"To Europe?" He was surprised this time. "Not for a moment."

"What about your family?" she pressed.

"They are taken care of," he said. His tone told her that

the subject was closed. The images of the books that the Chinese woman had brought her came back again.

"You didn't love her," she said simply.

He said nothing. "I don't remember," he said finally. He looked over at Evelyn. "Do you love your husband?" he asked her.

"Yes, of course," she said too fast.

"There isn't any sin," he said. "If you don't, there isn't any sin. Life is more complicated than we know when we are young."

"I love my husband," she repeated.

"I may have loved my wife," he said thoughtfully. Evelyn thought Fischer might be getting drunk. He was lost in some distant place of his own. "All that seems like a very long time ago, another life. Surely you must understand that."

He had no right to speak to her like that. "We can't abandon people just because the circumstances of our lives change," she said angrily.

"I haven't abandoned them," he replied.

She couldn't think what she would shout, but she wanted to raise her voice to him.

"I was happy when my wife went home," he said defiantly, "and so was she, I think. We didn't speak of it. She just left, saying she had to think about the effect this place would have on our daughters. We never referred to it again, in letters or anywhere else."

"So you see them?"

"When I am in Europe, yes."

"What do your daughters think?"

"That I am a sinner," he said, and he laughed. "To have a father who is a sinner can be very satisfying. They are both old as you, so it wasn't as though I walked out on them when they were children."

"I think I shall go to bed now," Evelyn said, rising. The memory of arriving in Shanghai, how tired she had been then, made her realize she was stronger now.

"I'll see you across the courtyard," he offered.

"That isn't necessary." He didn't push her. His eyes

followed her as she walked out into the courtyard, and she heard him pouring more brandy, a sound of crystal against crystal.

In her room, the fire was lit, the bed turned back, and the Chinese woman was waiting by her pallet. Evelyn felt a twinge of disappointment that she was honest enough to admit was due to Fischer's letting her go so easily. She must look like a very small conquest, she decided, looking at her face in the mirror.

Her face was solemn, more oval than round now, and her hair, though unfashionably long, gave her a gravity that became her. Another disappointment waited for her as she realized that at some point her very face had altered, the old outlines there like faint lines in a map of a well-known country, but as though someone had changed the landscape while she had been gone.

She was a new person in some fundamental way. But no one would ever know it. Her life stretched on, day after day ahead of her, a long journey that suddenly seemed impossible. She sat down facing her reflection.

"Mem wants?" the Chinese woman whispered. She still wouldn't meet Evelyn's eyes.

Evelyn felt sorry for the woman. It helped, she realized, to feel sorry for someone else. There were times when Alex and his friends were so contemptuous of others as poor as themselves that she wanted to scream. But now she saw she pitied them. Their fear made them wall themselves in with their own prejudices, hatred, rituals.

"You don't have to stay," Evelyn said quietly. The woman looked at her for the first time in hours. "I will be all right."

"I help mem."

"No," Evelyn insisted. "I'm used to helping myself. I can do it." She reached out and took the woman's wrist where it came out of the dark blue padded jacket. The skin was rough, like old paper. "Thank you," she said, holding onto the woman's wrist. "You've been kind."

"I bad woman," the Chinese woman said in shame, looking at where Evelyn held her wrist. "Master right."

"Of course you're not," Evelyn said sharply. "You've been very good to me."

"I not understand," the woman said.

"Not understand what?" Evelyn asked, but she was afraid of what she would hear. The woman made a move to take her hand back. Evelyn held on. "What?" she insisted.

But the woman shook her head.

So Evelyn said what she suspected was closest to the truth. "Does he bring many women here?"

She was loyal. "He good man" was all she said.

"Good and lusty," Evelyn murmured. She had a sudden sensation of how it would feel to be touched by Fischer. She shivered violently, and the Chinese woman looked at her with concern.

"I help you," she insisted, taking her wrist away. She lifted Evelyn's hair at the neck, undoing the combs that held it. She undid the buttons on the dress, opened it to expose Evelyn's back, and massaged a tension that had grown in the last hour. Evelyn's head dropped forward, her mind lost in reverie. Her body was waiting for its cue, flaming into a passion she had thought lost to her. The Chinese woman slipped off the black dress so her shoulders were bare. She felt her fingers undoing the cotton brassiere and reached up, crossing her arms over her breasts. "Please," she said in a voice she hardly recognized. "Leave me."

Evelyn couldn't let the images form, but she sat until she heard the door open again, the cool breath of the snow-filled wind on her back. She couldn't look in the mirror, either, but when he came up behind her and put his hands on her shoulders her whole body shuddered.

As he undid the brassiere, his hands sliding under the folds to take her breasts from behind, she looked up at their reflection. The sight stoked her growing fire. She arched her neck against the rough feel of his dinner jacket. His face was hidden from her by the low mirror, but his hands, now familiar, strong, and as hot as her skin, moved boldly over her, her neck, her shoulders, down to her breasts again.

She groaned, turning to him. From below he looked

solemn, his eyes alight with discovery but careful. He's had many women here, she thought, but she wanted to be one of them, to be led back into the ranks of living women. She clutched at the opening of his jacket, but he took her wrists in his strong fingers. "No" was all he said.

He took her by the hand like a child and led her to the narrow bed. "Undress."

He watched her take off her dress, her stockings, and her undergarments. For a moment she thought he might reject her as she sat there naked before him. But at once he tore off his jacket as though his own passion had caught up with him, then his shirt, and he pulled her against him hungrily, his hands rougher against her skin. His eyes, close to hers, glowed with knowledge. She could smell his cigar smoke, a smell of yeast. Softer than Alex's, his body was that of a man who indulged himself, but his touch brought her to new heights of desire. He laid her down, leaning over her, his lips kissing her throat, her breast, moving over her, drawing her essence to him as his mouth worked across her skin and his hands smoothed her flesh until she cried out, "Please, please . . ."

He pulled off the rest of his clothes quickly while she lay sprawled across the bed, and then he was beside her, his shoulders surprisingly strong and broad. She felt an abandon that told her this man above her could understand everything she thought or felt, and as he forced her legs apart to lock about his heavy waist, his belly against hers, she shocked herself by crying out, "Take me, take me, please. . . ." He thrust at her roughly, and she was lost, the passion rising like a tide to whip her until she clawed at his back, low sounds breaking from her, closing her eyes against the glowing fire of his eyes. Her passion broke with a terrible urgency, and she cried out again and again as he held her down, forcing his own passion on and on until the warmth and pleasure that had made her cry out was lost to a pain that made her cry out again in another voice. He ignored her, pressing his lips against hers, and when she turned her face he forced her mouth open. Her protest was lost as his own passion erupted in her, and she felt another release that made her go limp throughout her whole body.

And then she cried.

He got out of the bed and left her alone with her tears. Like her passion, they welled up now from long-dammed springs. She lay amid her bedclothes crying fiercely, more fiercely than when they had made love, still damp from the sweat of their passion. She pressed her face into the pillows, crying bitterly, crying for the past, for dreams, for what she had done, for Alex, for her child. But mostly she cried for herself.

"Have you finished?" Fischer asked coldly when he came back into the room.

She wiped her eyes on the sheet. Fischer, she saw, was dressed in a long robe.

"Come to my room."

"No."

"Don't be a fool," he said, holding out her coat.

"I'll stay here." She pulled the sheets about her. He sat on the edge of her bed, put his hand on her shoulder. She made to pull away, but his touch comforted, and she relaxed. "All right," she whispered. "I would like to sleep with you tonight." He laid her head against his chest, and she could hear his breathing as he stroked her hair.

"Come," he whispered. He held her coat to her again. She found her stained slippers beneath the bed. The sight of herself, dimly caught in the mirror, made her giggle. She looked like an overdressed schoolgirl.

Beside her, Fischer, looking not at all romantic but rather pompous and somehow smaller, more round, smiled. "Much better."

"We look ridiculous," she said.

"Physical love is ridiculous."

Love with Alex wasn't. But neither had she ever felt Alex knew her as this man did, knew every secret thought.

"I don't think I would want to be a monk," she said, shivering from crossing the snowy courtyard.

"I don't think there's any danger of that," Fischer said, and she realized his levity was far better than sentiment. She would judge herself later, soon, but not tonight.

In his room, he helped her into the tall red lacquer bed with the gold trim and lit a lantern. He dropped his robe by the bed, but not before she saw that he wasn't at all the shape that a girl would imagine in her dreams. Yet when his skin pressed against hers, her own flesh responded with another wave of desire.

He knew what she wanted, and he leaned over her, kissing her more tenderly. But she held him against her, his chest and the full weight of his body on hers, so she felt smothered, lost, desire making her shameless. She opened her mouth to be kissed more forcefully, arching up under him. Her one moment of reserve was lost in a fraction of a second; her own desires, undammed at last, swept through her. "Again," she moaned, "please."

He took her more slowly, holding back while her own passion screamed. Slowly he allowed his desires to make demands. When she parted from him, he refused silently, pulling back, and then he began to murmur commands, very softly, suggestively in her ear. She followed them, uncertain at first, then repulsed, but then curious as her mind freed her body. He took her high with his care, mistreating her gently, making her cry out in small ectasies, each throbbing deeper, more suggestively, stripping her of what few defenses she had left until the room blurred in movement and sensation as they rose together to a final climax.

This time there were no tears. Sleep washed in, cleansing the last of the passion. She lay against his chest, her leg thrown over his.

She awoke to a dawn as soft as the gray sheen of the pearls that he had bought. Fischer held her close, and she lay awake against his even breathing. When she awoke the second time, sunlight sparkled on the snow, and Fischer was sitting at a desk across the room in a quilted robe of maroon velvet. A fire was burning, and someone had brought tea.

He looked up at her after a few moments and went back to

his work. Finally he put the black and gold pen on the paper. "The snow has stopped."

"Yes."

"I will be driving to Shanghai today."

She felt a chill, colder than the night wind in the courtyard.

"Would you like to come with me?"

Her dreamless sleep had left her refreshed; the lovemaking had awakened her like the fairytale princess who slumbered amid the thorn-covered vines; but now she felt the exhaustion of the last years moving toward her again like a tide.

She thought of her child. "I can't," she said.

She wanted him to force her to go with him, stay with him, but all he did was pick up his pen again. "I'll make arrangements for you to travel home."

"Thank you."

He left the room, and the impassive Chinese woman came in. Evelyn turned her face away so she didn't have to look at her. Now she knows she was right before, Evelyn thought. I'm like all of Fischer's women. To her surprise, she felt freer.

"I would like a bath," she said aloud.

"Master has bath," the woman said, pointing.

"Could I have it in the other room?" Evelyn asked quietly.

Afterwards she dressed herself carefully in the black dress and her own shoes, crossed again to the dining room, and saw that Fischer, too, was dressed, this time in a navy blue suit with a white shirt and discreet tie. He looked like a voluptuary nonetheless, sated, she thought.

"Ah," he said, looking up from his breakfast. "There will be a train at midday. If you leave in half an hour, the car will drop you before I continue on."

"Thank you."

He smiled at her. Please don't make any remark about last night, she begged silently.

When the servant came, Fischer waited for her by the front door, leading her out like an honored guest. He was treating her as he would a lady, and she was furious about it. It meant nothing to him, she concluded with sudden shock. I was just another woman.

As they rode down the winding curves of the hillside the valley looked as beautiful as a print. Admiring the line of the river and the city perfectly situated at the other end of the valley, she turned to find Fischer watching her thoughtfully.

"It's lovely," she said, wishing she could peer up the mountain to where the temple stood facing out on all this perfection. She knew that within the distant city walls there was poverty and despair, but from here everything looked exactly right. And then she was reminded of the view from Alex's castle, the fields glowing in the late summer sun, and the same feeling that everything was as it should be and would be forever.

"Yes," he agreed, not taking his eyes off her face. "Beauty is very cheap in China."

She felt the flush of shame; he might as well have struck her. "But underneath," she said angrily, "it's sordid."

"If you look at it that way."

"How else would you look at it?" They were almost at the bottom of the mountain, where frozen fields draped in the deceptive purity of the snow stretched away in every direction.

"I would say that in China the necessities of life are bare to the sight; there is less deception."

"Yes," she said weakly, "all right."

He reached out with his gloved hand and took hers.

"Don't do that, please," she whispered, and he released her.

They rode silently until peasant villages surrounded them. The wealthier houses were compounds like the temple; square courtyards for the first wife, second wife, concubines, were set one beside the other; life was ordered as it had been for a thousand years. Soon they were among the outskirts of the city, passing under the gates where two bloody heads, the eyes pecked out by carrion eaters, were set on bloody stakes for all to view.

As they came up to the station Fischer said, "I want to give you this."

She thought he was offering her the train tickets but turned to see a small velvet box.

"No." If he had the box here in the car, he had had it in the house, ready for her or some other woman.

"Open it," he said, "please."

"I don't want it."

"This is very foolish, my dear," he said, his face softened in the expensive gray plush interior of his car to express a paternal concern. "We are not children, either of us. I will think none the less of you for taking this, and I hope you are old enough to think no less of me for offering it."

Her anger seeped away. "Please don't think me ungrateful," she said quietly, "but I would rather not."

He continued to watch her, then shook his head slowly. "You are still so young," he said wonderingly, "younger than I had thought. Perhaps that is good." When she didn't reply, he said, "My dear, listen to me very carefully, will you?"

Evelyn nodded. The car had stopped, but she had no desire to get out.

"I am happy for you that you are still so trusting, but remember please what I said to you last night: The world is changing. People like you and me, for reasons we perhaps will never know, will always find ourselves in the very center of this chaos. For us, to see and understand the truth is vital . . . vital," he said, grasping her hand in what she thought was an unconscious gesture, his grip hard and painful. "People will lie to you, will not want you to succeed, survive. But you have a good mind, and if you trust in it, you will know the truth, and it will keep you safe. Not happy, perhaps, but safe. Do you understand me?"

"I think so," Evelyn said. Then in a flash of recognition, she said, "The emperor is naked."

And Fischer smiled, a smile of delight. He released her hand. "Yes, yes," he said, sitting back to look at her with pleasure. "But most of the people must believe that he is clothed. People will not like you for telling them that the emperor is naked, but you must believe your eyes and follow what you see."

"Yes," Evelyn said. She leaned across and kissed his smooth cheek.

"You won't take this small gift?"

"No."

He put it in his pocket. "Would you like me to walk you to your train?"

"No." She signaled to the driver, who opened the door. "But thank you for asking."

"Goodbye, Evelyn," he said.

"Goodbye, Dr. Fischer."

She strode through the station, feeling more confident than on the outbound journey. She settled in a corner of a carriage, watching the hawkers on the platform carrying their trays of food from window to window until the train began to move. When she reached for her ticket she found a thousand Shanghai dollars and a note: "Perhaps you would prefer to choose your own gift." He had signed with a small neat *F*, the way he had signed the books in his house.

Not until the train had passed through the city walls did it occur to her that he had anticipated her rejection of the gift in the car. She laughed. Perhaps the box was empty. Perhaps he hadn't even intended to leave yesterday, had come down to the city and returned, knowing she would be there for the taking. The long snow-lit plain darkened into a Chinese twilight of purple mountains under a gray and pink winter sky before she realized she didn't care.

Alex, Shanghai, and her child seemed a long way off; an effort of will was required to remind her what drew closer with every click of the rails. She ate and drank wine as night hid the country, wondering what he had done with the pearls. He had had them with him, she decided, somewhere in the car.

She fell asleep marveling at the last few days' flow of money around her: the pearls, the ten thousand dollars in the bank, Fischer's gift. She reflected on the possibility that she could be rich again, but her chest constricted at the thought.

When she awoke fear struck, noise and light assailing her on every side.

The attendant opened the carriage door. "Shanghai," he announced.

7

She hurried past the coffin maker's shop, holding her coat closed at the throat. She was careful where she stepped in her new fleeced-lined boots, but no more careful than she had had to be in explaining how she could afford them. She had a new position at the bank—Mr. Sebowski had beamed with pleasure at her return—which brought in more money; not much, but enough to justify the small extravagances, such as firewood to keep the fire burning all day, coal, a few delicacies from the Russian Market. Natasha watched her with suspicion, but now spent all her days at the church. Evelyn's suspicions were that the religion gave Alex's slovenly sister an excuse not to work, but Alex and his mother spoke of her piety with reverence.

The prospect of their two cheerless rooms waiting for her kept her working late many nights, a fact that didn't elude Mr. Sebowski. He stopped by her new desk from time to time to see what she was doing.

"You are very thorough, Madame Lebowski," he remarked late one night when the city outside the bank had gone through the transformation from a bustling commercial center to an exotic place of fast-moving cars, women entering hotels on the arms of rich men, Chinese cowering in the shadows.

"It pleases me to see the columns come out even," she explained with a smile. When she had come back two days late, she had feared mockery or contempt, but on the contrary, they had become almost like old friends. Conspiracy must be like that: the actual deed almost forgotten, but the feeling of complicity blending smoothly into something near to friendship.

"You have a good mind," he said, touching the ledgers. His eyes looked into hers. "And you are loyal, a rare quality."

His words confused her. She wasn't loyal at all; she had betrayed Alex and his cause, though she had done Sebowski's bidding.

The return from Wuhan had been difficult, though life had indeed resumed, unchanged. The rooms were waiting for her, Alex, her child, who now made her feel so guilty. Victoria, however, seldom paid any attention to her mother. Her grandmother was her life, and indeed the old woman had imperceptibly aged into an accepting attitude toward the new circumstances of their life. Unlike Alex, who talked constantly of the return, and Natasha, who became more mystical each day, the dowager countess had turned her entire attention over to the granddaughter she adored. The child did not lack love, Evelyn realized, as though something important had been taken from her.

Of course, she had the money, too. Sebowski eventually asked her what she intended to do with it.

"Nothing," she told him. She couldn't touch it. Alex would know. But just knowing it was there made her feel free in a new way. It was her security.

"You should do something with it," Sebowski counseled. "Money left in a box could become worthless overnight." She lay awake all that night, terrified at the thought.

She had thought of Fischer many times, ached sometimes for his gentle lovemaking, but now she recalled his advice, trying to fit it to her circumstances. But how? She had knowledge of a few large accounts at the bank, which were now her exclusive province. She totaled the profits from them—the shipping merchants, the trading kings—at the end of each day and reported to Sebowski. But she would never dare use that knowledge. She would lose her position at the first breach of trust, and Evelyn knew that that was not what Fischer meant by knowledge.

She thought now of so many questions for him, the first of which was what she should do with her own small capital. He wouldn't think that money at all, she supposed, but to her it was still a fortune, the difference between walking through the streets feeling like a beggar and walking through them looking for her opportunity.

"You should invest," Sebowski advised.

"In what?" she asked doubtfully.

"Anything," he said, waving generally at the Bund beyond the bank doors. "Everything is for sale out there. Choose something that will retain its worth—gold, perhaps."

So despite the dangers, she had taken to walking home on nights when the Shanghai winter was not too cold. The richest man in the Orient, Sir Victor Sassoon, lived in splendor in the entire top floor of the Palace Hotel. She'd heard that he had once delayed an ocean liner for six hours so he could see his horse run in the Shanghai stakes. She knew why she always chose the route past the Palace Hotel. She had learned that Fischer lived there. But she never saw him.

She liked the French quarter's small rococo houses, houses such as she imagined were to be found in small French towns or even in New Orleans. The French colonial presence was less imposing and self-absorbed than the British, the heat and the cold seeming to have undone the French in ways that the British would never allow. The French were amused, less concerned with making vast sums of money, it seemed, than with maintaining a certain style. But the Americans were almost like the Chinese, interested primarily in trade, in money, without the British insistence that profit be accompanied by good works, such as bringing law to the heathen.

She had found the boots in the French concession. The small shops there carried items that Evelyn thought the very height of sophistication. For the next few days after she spied them, the boots were a symbol of all that she longed for now that she was open to possibilities other than the return to Russia.

A few days later, running from the bank on her lunch hour

and indulging in the unheard-of luxury of a taxi, she arrived at the shop in a feverish excitement. Taking in the good fur coat and her worn dress, the old saleslady in her practical French way had immediately assessed the situation. "Mademoiselle deserves these boots," she said in a kindly voice. The price had astonished Evelyn. She hadn't thought anything could be that expensive.

"Madame," Evelyn muttered automatically.

The Frenchwoman looked for Evelyn's wedding ring, but that had been sold long ago. Alex refused to allow her to wear a simple band, insisting that he would replace the ring soon. The English accent was more confusing than a Russian one would have been. "Perhaps a small adjustment in the price," she murmured.

Evelyn, grown used to haggling these last years, would have scrubbed the floor, although she did have enough money in her handbag. But now she smelled a negotiation, and a softened sensual feeling passed through her. "So very much, madame," she answered respectfully, touching the leather that seemed more alluring than any dresses of her youth, or gifts from Alex. They would transform her in some way she didn't understand but knew was real.

"Worth every penny," the woman said.

"Of course," Evelyn said sadly. She turned to the door. "Another day . . ."

"Madame!" the woman said as she opened the door.

Evelyn turned, her expression appropriately arranged into heartbreak. "I am sorry to have troubled you, madame," she apologized, casting one last longing look at the fur lining and cuffs. "You are right, they are beautiful."

"I would like you to have these boots, madame," the Frenchwoman said with decision. "What will you pay for them?"

Evelyn blushed, partially as artifice, but partly at finding herself engaged in such an underhanded performance. "I would be ashamed to tell you what I can afford," she said. She thought from the way the Frenchwoman's eyes narrowed for a moment that perhaps she had overbid her hand.

But the woman made her decision. "I will sell you them for one quarter less than the price," she said. "Take it or leave it, madame."

"I'll take it," Evelyn said, both of them dropping the pretense of negotiation.

Alex had been less enthusiastic. Evelyn was certain he had no idea of the cost of things, but Natasha looked at them carefully. "Fur," she said, touching the boots. Evelyn picked them up and took them into the second room. Behind her she heard Natasha say, "I have only thin leather."

Later Alex said, "I think Natasha needs new boots."

Evelyn retorted, "To pray in?"

The sharpness of her words took Alex by surprise. He looked at his wife as though he didn't know her, at something new in her stance as she faced him in her plain white nightgown. "She is very religious," he murmured, averting his eyes.

"Very," Evelyn agreed, not trying to hide her disdain. The subject was not raised again, but she saw Natasha eyeing her boots with a look as filled with envy and hatred as the first night Alex had brought his bride home.

The street stall proprietors, wrapped in rags, stoked the fires for the noodles and scraps of meat they would sell. Hammering reverberated as she left the narrow street with relief; the coffin makers would do a good business this week. They said this was the coldest winter in a hundred years. The corpses of the faceless poor being thrown on the cart, however, would be burned in the fields beyond the Nanking Road. She shuddered, unable to forget that only her job kept her family from joining them.

Running up the steps to the bank, she thought again of the house in the French quarter. Set back from the street behind a small wall, the house had a wide veranda running along both stories. An estate agent had been showing people out as she had passed the night before.

In her mind she had pictured the interior: square, well-shaped rooms, cooled by ceiling fans, a garden behind, perhaps with a spreading banyan tree. She longed to go inside. She had watched the grim estate agent drive off with his prospects, a bovine woman and a small, irritable man in a dark suit, who despised the house, it was evident. They wanted something larger, she was sure, more in keeping with their imagined station in life. At home they had probably lived in a cramped, ill-furnished house. But out here they were now part of the ruling class, set apart from even the rich Chinese, and a small house like the blue one that they had been shown was contemptible.

"Ah, Madame Lezenski." Mr. Sebowski came forward to greet her at the top of the stairs. "I have been waiting for you."

"Am I late?" she asked in panic.

"No, no, you are never late," he said, taking her by the elbow. "Come with me."

Her heart fluttered with fear, but the image of the eleven thousand Shanghai dollars lying in the box when she returned the money she hadn't needed for the boots calmed her. She allowed Sebowski to draw her forward as the tugs drew the liners forward in the river.

When Evelyn returned from Wuhan Mr. Sebowski's secretary's desk was empty.

"Is anything wrong?" Evelyn asked anxiously as she undid her coat.

"Wrong?" said Sebowski, startled. "I have discharged my secretary," he said, gesturing toward the empty desk.

"Discharged her?" Evelyn repeated stupidly.

"She is a fool. She treats the Chinese like coolies." Sebowski sat behind his desk, wiping his brow. "Madame Lezenski, times are changing, changing, changing." He stuffed his handkerchief back into his breast pocket, where it lay as limp with perspiration as a lily out of water. "We have to accommodate ourselves. Do you understand?"

"Yes, I think so."

"Why are you standing?" he demanded. She always stood. "Sit down. Sit down."

She did as she was told. Sebowski was almost in a panic. "Do you know who the Chinese Tu is?"

"Big-Eared Tu?"

Sebowski blinked. "Yes," he said. "Such a stupid name, Big-Eared Tu." He giggled as though he had lost control of himself, stopped, and cleared his throat. "A very prominent local businessman." Sebowski sighed with relief when she didn't comment. "I can rely on your discretion, Madame Lezenski, can I not?"

"Yes, Mr. Sebowski."

Sebowski reached for his handkerchief again, stopped himself, and placed both hands carefully on the desk before him. "Mr. Tu was here."

"Here?" said Evelyn without meaning to. The thought of Tu, leader of the Green gang, who controlled the waterfront, nightclubs, prostitution, was startling. She knew of Tu because many of the girls who danced in his nightclubs were Russian. Alex and his friends despised the girls and hated Tu.

"Not during the day," Sebowski explained. "He came by private arrangement, later. That stupid woman," he said, waving at the closed door, "refused him entry." He slapped his desk, swallowed, and contained himself with an effort. "Mr. Tu wished to deposit money in the bank. He doesn't trust . . ." Sebowski corrected himself. "He is more comfortable dealing with this bank than one of the Chinese. . . ." The Chinese banks, particularly the Bank of China, run by T. V. Soong, Evelyn thought, would track Tu's money. He was wise to come to a European bank, and wiser still to have chosen the Russian bank, where control was much looser than in one of the big English banks.

Sebowski was frightened, terrified. He said, "I wish you to take over from that stupid woman, to become my secretary."

Evelyn couldn't think of anything to say. It was a large promotion.

"You agree?" he said, almost as though, like the woman in the store, she was negotiating. "Of course, your salary will increase with your duties."

"When shall I begin?"

"Immediately," Sebowski said, rising. "Mr. Tu will be arranging for a transfer of . . . of gold," he said, as though the word itself could only be whispered, "later today. I want you to stay tonight to help me."

"I'll have to make arrangements to let my family know," she said.

"Of course, of course." He waved the objection away. "Now, please move your desk. Now."

Evelyn looked at the desk outside Sebowski's office and imagined how she herself had stood before it under scrutiny. Opening a drawer, she saw that the interior was a chaos of pencils, pieces of paper, rubber bands. She sat down guiltily, still in her coat, feeling as though at any moment the other woman would turn up and send her packing.

Sebowski opened the door. "Get me the chief clerk," he ordered. "Go down yourself and bring him up."

"Yes, Mr. Sebowski." Evelyn hung her coat up in the closet she found by the door to the outer office. She changed out of her boots, left them with her coat and umbrella and ran quickly down the double staircase to find Mr. Chua. Chua followed her back up the stairs silently.

When Evelyn and the chief clerk returned, the former secretary was searching in the closet for her belongings. She looked with shock at Evelyn, then grabbed up her umbrella and left, slamming the door behind her.

Shaken, Evelyn knocked on Sebowski's door. "Mr. Chua is here."

"What was that sound?" he asked her, looking up from the papers on his desk.

"Nothing," she stammered. "The wind."

She stood back, and the chief clerk went into Sebowski's office. Hands damp with nervousness, Evelyn braced herself, opened the rest of the drawers, and emptied them into a wastebasket.

When Chua came out of the office, he passed her with a small, polite bow, his Oriental face impassive. Sebowski buzzed for her, and she went in. "If you need time to tell your husband you will be late, you can take it at your lunch hour," he told her.

"How late will I be?"

"I don't know," Sebowski said. "The bank will send you

home in a car. Mr. Tu will be here after closing. Do you understand?"

"Perfectly." She couldn't face the scene there would be at home. "In fact, I won't need extra time," she said, "if you will allow me to send a bank messenger instead."

"Certainly," Sebowski said, evidently relieved. As she left he called, "Countess . . ."

She turned to protest the use of her now-meaningless title.

"There will be room for great advancement here, if you do your duties satisfactorily," he said.

"Thank you," she said for the third time in less than an hour. Sitting uncertainly at her new desk, she wrote a note to Alex and sent it off with a messenger. Then she sat calmly, reflecting; all that came to mind was a small blue house with wide balconies, a garden in the back, and a banyan tree for shade in the summer.

The day passed. She lunched alone in an inexpensive restaurant near the Select Department Store. She watched how the Chinese lined up in the cold for careful scrutiny while the Europeans swept in with assurance, and her thoughts went to Big-Eared Tu, a notorious killer.

When the rest of the staff had gone, she waited in the dark, empty bank. When the guard at the front door rang, she went into Sebowski's office where he waited with Chua, the chief clerk. "He's here."

Sweat broke out in a line along Sebowski's brow, and his hands shook. The chief clerk watched impassively. "Come," Sebowski said, hurrying forward.

Uncertain if he meant her also, Evelyn trailed behind, staying at the top of the stairs. The guards held the double-thickness brass panels open for the broad figure flanked by two henchmen.

From where she stood, their voices were merely a murmur. She saw Tu's eyes sweep over the hall, look intently up at her. Once his overcoat had been removed by one of his own men, Evelyn saw that he was enormously fat, with a neck that rose in folds of flesh to a flat face and totally bald skull. He wore a dark European suit.

Sebowski led the party toward the vaults. Evelyn waited at the head of the stairs until they had gone, then she went down slowly to wait by the guards.

The two henchmen came back first. They gestured for the doors to be opened. The guards refused, looking for Sebowski. The two Chinese began to shout, gesturing frantically at the doors.

Evelyn stepped forward. "What is it you want?" she asked calmly, trying to appear confident.

"Open door," the first Chinese commanded. He was half the size of Tu, with a scar down one whole side of his face. Execution in China was still by decapitation, usually in a public place, and Evelyn wondered if he had once been the victim of a botched execution.

"No one can open the doors without Mr. Sebowski's permission," she explained. The guards looked at her gratefully.

The thin Chinese reached in his coat and took out a revolver. "Open door," he said menacingly.

"No," she said, clasping her hands together to stop their trembling. The hoodlum's moment of doubt lent her the authority she needed, and she moved toward the vault. "Wait here," she said. "I will get permission. Don't open the doors," she instructed the guards.

Once out of sight, she ran. Sebowski was glistening with sweat as he showed Tu the vaults that had been left open for his deposit.

"Mr. Sebowski," Evelyn said, slowing down, "can I talk to you?"

"Not now, Madame Lezenski," he told her irritably. The Chinese clerk stood by, his hands folded behind the shining fabric of his cheap dark suit.

"I must speak to you."

Tu was looking at her intently. His eyes had a slim band of yellow across the whites. He licked his lips with a thick tongue, turned his back, and spoke in Chinese to the clerk.

"What is it, madame?" Sebowski asked her irritably as he took her aside.

"They want the doors opened."

"So?"

"The vault is still open," she pointed out, looking past him.

Suspicion rose in Sebowski's mind like a mist from the Soochow Creek. If he had the doors opened, there was nothing to stop Tu and his men from taking what they wished. If he refused, there was Tu to deal with. "Dear God," he whispered.

Tu spoke in rapid Chinese. Mr. Chua looked apologetic, his eyes on the tips of his shoes, and translated. "Mr. Tu wishes to know why there is a delay."

Sebowski looked desperately from the vault, standing open, to Tu. He was choked for words.

Evelyn spoke up loudly. "Tell Mr. Tu that we cannot open the doors again as long as the vault is still open. We can close it and open it again for his deposit once the main door is locked. In the future, such procedures would be for his own protection, so we must insist on it now."

Sebowski had gone as still as death. As the clerk translated meekly, Tu kept his eyes on Evelyn, then looked at Sebowski, who moved very slightly, as though he feared being struck.

Tu laughed, a high cackle. He slapped his palms together, and his head rose, pulling the folds of flesh tight, then collapsing them again like the neck of an ancient tortoise. He bowed to Evelyn, laughing and laughing. When he spoke, Mr. Chua tittered nervously. "He agrees."

Sebowski's relief came in the form of a gasp. "Close the vault," he said primly when he had recovered.

Tu stood chuckling, looking from time to time at Evelyn as both Sebowski and the chief clerk spun their combinations. Then Mr. Chua led Tu back into the hall. Sebowski looked sick while he waited for the front doors to be unlocked.

"Could I get you some water?" Evelyn offered.

"No," he said irritably, wiping his brow with his wet handkerchief. "I just want this over with."

Presently they heard the procession. In two trips Tu's men brought four chests.

"Would you like us to open them for inventory?" Mr. Sebowski asked.

When translated, Tu started to laugh again.

"Mr. Tu prefers that the chests remain as they are," the chief clerk said. "He wishes them locked in private storage." Private storage was the part of the vault where large items could be locked away as securely as though they were in a safe deposit box.

"Certainly," said Sebowski, his skin as yellow as his clerk's as he waited for Tu's men to leave. Once the vault was reopened, they called the men back to load the chests into the deepest recesses. Tu showed no interest in going into the vault, merely smiling until the deed was done.

Tu allowed himself to be helped into his black overcoat and went out into the night laughing.

The silence he left behind echoed with Sebowski's fear.

"You may leave now, Mr. Chua," Sebowski said, and the clerk bowed and left.

"There are one or two small points, Madame Lezenski," Sebowski said. "Would you come back to the office?"

They went up into the darkness, down the dim hall, and into the outer office, where Evelyn had left the lights blazing. Sebowski slumped into the first chair within the door. He leaned forward, his head in his hands. "They could have taken everything," he whispered in an anguished voice.

"But they didn't," Evelyn reminded him.

She went into his office where he kept his liquor and came back with a glass of brandy. "Try this," she said, touching his shoulder. Sebowski trembled as he gulped the brandy. "Killing one person is nothing to him," Sebowski said, but he was speaking to himself.

"They wouldn't have killed us," Evelyn said briskly.

Sebowski's eyes had lost confidence. "No," he murmured. "They wouldn't have to."

"Where would that have left him to put his own riches?" Evelyn asked.

Sebowski didn't seem to follow the argument. "You don't understand," he said. "That man is the government of the city."

"One government," Evelyn said. "Not all of it."

"No, no," Sebowski said to himself. "You are right, of course." He paused, "For a moment, I thought . . ."

Evelyn knew what he had thought: that Tu was going to double-cross him. It would have been simple. But that wasn't the lesson. The lesson was how fragile the rule of law. Tu wasn't the law, whatever Sebowski said, but he bent the laws because he was powerful.

Powerful, Evelyn thought, thinking of Fischer's words about security. Not rich. Powerful.

"You may leave now, Madame Lezenski," Sebowski said, getting unsteadily to his feet. "You have been of great assistance. I have arranged for a car to take you home."

"Whore!" The first blow broke her lip. Evelyn stumbled to her knees. Alex grabbed her by her woolen scarf, whipping her head back to face him. "Prostitute," he said, slapping her across the eyes.

Blindly she covered her face as the child began to scream, but the blows rained down on her shoulders. He had lapsed into Russian, screaming as he beat her. She heard another voice raised, his mother's, then Natasha's, triumphant as she shouted at the dowager countess. As he dragged her across the bare wood floor she could taste the blood in her mouth, feel the warm trickle from where the skin had broken above her eyebrow.

He dropped her. His mother's voice was screaming hysterically. Evelyn scrambled away blindly until her hands touched the wall, cowering there until he dragged her back. Her voice erupted into a scream of pain and outrage as he struck her again, her eyes clearing to see Natasha smiling from the door, Victoria at her knees. Alex was trying to shake off the dowager countess.

"You defile our name!" he shouted at his wife, his face transformed by hatred. He raised his fist, and as the blow struck her shoulder she heard the break as clearly as a

154

gunshot. She screamed, and the pain throbbed in waves until she lost consciousness.

She floated to the surface of the pain a moment later, wave upon wave breaking over her. The child was crying from the second room. "Go, go," the dowager countess begged her, lifting her to her feet.

Alex pushed his mother out of the way. She fell across the cot, crying, "Alex, Alex, no . . ."

"Alex, please," Evelyn begged, holding her hands before her face.

Her dress ripped down the front. He tore the fabric of the bodice so her breasts came free. "I heard what you have done!" he shouted at her. "You are no longer part of my family!"

"What have I done?" she cried defiantly.

He hit her again, throwing her back against the wall. "Whore," he repeated venomously, "English whore."

"My child," she stammered, stepping toward Victoria in the doorway.

"You have no child," Alex told her. He took her neck in his hand, and threw her against the wall. "Get out!" he said.

"No!"

"Get out!" Her heel caught on the stairs as he pushed her. She fell past the Chinese family gathered on the landing below.

"Alex, Alex, please," his mother cried. "Do not demean yourself. You are a nobleman."

Alex's eyes closed and his hands clenched. His mother gently pushed him into the room. Turning, she hissed, "Go, go!"

Evelyn tried to pull her dress across her chest. "What has happened?" she appealed.

"You know what has happened," the countess rebuked her angrily. "The woman from the bank was here. She told us what you have done to get her position. You are a peasant, a child of the fields. Go."

When the door closed hard behind her, Evelyn heard only the murmur of angry voices. The Chinese children giggled nervously and were summoned into their room.

She was alone, too terrified even to retrieve her handbag. Her coat would keep her warm. Outside, the babble of the crowds pushing past the noodle stalls with their lanterns and their fires hid her shame.

People stared at her, and after a while she paused to catch her reflection in a car window: her eyes were swollen, her lip broken, and a line of blood ran down her cheek.

She moved toward Soochow Creek, coming out onto the broad avenue where the sampans of the river people were moored tightly together for the night. Kneeling, she tore off the hem of her dress, dipped it in the filthy water, and sponged off her face. She didn't care who saw her.

She had to find a place for the night. Tomorrow, she reasoned as her heart calmed down, she would be all right. She would go to the bank, get her money, find an inexpensive hotel, buy some new clothes, have some time to think. At the thought of Victoria her mind reeled, for if she had a child, she would have to have someone to look after her. And a place to live.

She crossed the bridge over Soochow Creek to the French concession. She heard music, then laughter, and stopped in the shadow of a wall; the pain that pierced her heart in her loneliness was worse than anything that Alex had done to her.

She went into the church without thinking. A priest turned from the altar as she made her obedience, watched while she sank into a pew. She leaned forward, praying, "Father, forgive me . . ." Not raised Catholic, she couldn't remember the rest. She had promised Alex she would convert to Russian Orthodoxy, but there had never been time. The tears flowed through her fingers, falling on the floor beneath the pew.

"Madame . . ." the young priest said at the side of the pew.

"I'm sorry." Evelyn gathered herself to leave.

"No, no," he said. "You can stay." He sat beside her in the pew. "Could I help you?"

"I am not a Catholic, Father," she said.

"This is God's house, you are welcome here." He looked at her face. "Let me clean that for you," he offered.

"No," she said. "I will be all right, if I can just rest awhile."

He rose. "Stay as long as you wish. The door will be locked to keep the beggars out," he said, looking in shame at her feet. "But you . . ." He turned to approach the altar, bowed, and disappeared behind it.

Evelyn bowed her own head and tried to pray. "Father, forgive me, for I have sinned. . . ." But she could get no further. The tears were gone; the pain all that was left. She sat still, her head raised so she could see the tortured figure on the cross.

Later the lights were dimmed, and she saw the young priest peer through the gloom at her. The sounds of the night outside died down, followed by a long silence that at first frightened, then soothed. Finally the windows began to pale with light.

She heard the priest coming down the aisle, the doors being unlocked. He came back and might have spoken, but she turned her face away.

When the church glowed with the dawn, she made her way to the door. It was a gray winter day; the carts were already moving through the streets to gather the frozen dead. She saw the car without comprehension.

The driver opened the door. "Get in," Fischer said. "I have been waiting."

BOOK
THREE

San Francisco, 1930

8

From the deck of the ship, she tried to pick out Morgan in the crowd.

"Prepare your documents for disembarkation," called the ship's boys as they patrolled the decks behind the passengers. Below, the gap between the white hull of the liner and the crowded deck closed inch by inch as the tugs pulled the great ship into her berth. Holding Vicky's hand as she looked across the pretty, pastel houses that climbed up the low, rolling hills of San Francisco, Evelyn had the strangest feeling: everything looked foreign.

"Will Uncle Morgan be waiting for us?" Victoria asked.

"Yes. He sent us a wire, remember?"

Morgan would be thirty-two, she thought as she adjusted the white collar on the navy blue coat she'd had tailored for Vicky in the Nanking Road. She had to prepare herself that he would be changed. Automatically, she raised her head very slightly to smooth out the almost imperceptible pouch under her chin.

She found herself standing halfway down the gangplank while the dozen photographers pressed forward. Her small hand wet in her mother's, Victoria pressed her face against Evelyn's coat.

"Enough, enough." She knew with a thrill that the voice was Morgan's, ringing at her across the sixteen years as it once had from her dreams.

His bright sapphire eyes mocking her from beneath a fall of blond hair, he appeared amid the photographers and then was gone. The shock was that except for his tan, he looked exactly as he had during their farewell in London. When she blinked his face reappeared closer, lips parted against white, white teeth.

She waved. "Morgan! Morgan!" She happily abandoned her hard-won self-possession. The years were racing backwards, and she was a child in the country. She had one glimpse of Victoria's astonished face looking up, and then she was in his arms. He was laughing as he hugged her, and she kissed his neck, oblivious now to the photographers, who were taking more pictures.

"Countess Lezenski!" he whispered, just loud enough for her to hear, holding her away from him.

"I *am* a countess," she insisted with a giggle.

"And much, much more," he said, looking into her eyes. Up close she saw the small lines that had appeared beside his eyes, making him even more handsome, filled with the high spirits that had preceded the malaise of the last summer they had spent together.

"And this," Morgan said, sweeping his arms open, "is Victoria."

Victoria looked suspicious.

"I'm Morgan." He crouched. Evelyn reached down to part the shimmering strands of his sun-bleached hair. He looked up. "I've missed you," he said.

"Morgan," she said, holding the skein of gold that was his hair in her fingers, finally admitting that she had never expected to see him again.

He stood up, his carelessly wrinkled white linen suit falling elegantly about his tall frame, setting him apart from the grimy newsmen. "Who are you?" they called out. "Are you anybody?"

"No," he replied, looking at Evelyn. "I'm nobody."

Evelyn threaded her arm through his. "He's my brother," she said. Her carefully made-up face felt as though it would crack with the strain of smiling, but she couldn't stop.

"Do you live here?" someone called.

"I live in Hollywood," he said over his shoulder.

"You're an actor?"

"Yes, yes." He laughed in Evelyn's face. "Why not?" he whispered.

By now they were away from the gangplank and into the shed where the luggage was being unloaded. "I don't have to clear customs," she informed him.

"Of course you don't." He stopped dead as they walked toward the sunlight at the other end of the shed. "My God, you're beautiful," he told her. "What happened?"

"I grew up."

They seemed to be enveloped in a quietness of their own for a long time. She saw something new in his eyes, something that might be remembered pain or sorrow, but it was gone as swiftly as it had appeared. "Don't I look wonderful?" Mischief danced in his eyes.

"Yes," she admitted. "Are you an actor?"

"I might be soon," he said. "I've met Chaplin."

"The comedian?"

"Yes. Little fellow. He makes incredible amounts of money for doing a sort of pantomime."

"I've seen them," she said.

"In *Shanghai?*"

"Snob," she needled him. The light as they approached the door revealed subtle lines in his forehead, and his jaw muscles now tensed as he spoke. Their father had accused Morgan of being slack-jawed, too lazy to close his mouth.

"Have you seen them talk?"

"Talk?"

"They're talking now. You'll see when we go to Los Angeles. Everyone's in a spin about it."

"How odd," Evelyn said. "Talking pictures. I can't imagine. It would be like seeing real people, except they would only be a quarter of an inch thick."

"Chaplin thinks I could be a film actor."

"Like Douglas Fairbanks?"

"I suppose so," Morgan said, and in a flash she saw the boy he had been, who lost interest from one moment to another. "There's the car," he said, pointing to a long cream automobile with its top lowered.

163

"Oh, it's beautiful. Is it yours?"

"Sort of," Morgan said evasively. He looked about. "Is your luggage coming off the ship?"

"I told them you'd arrange it," Evelyn said cavalierly. "I'm not sure it'll all go into that automobile."

Morgan's mood was suddenly upon him. "You brought a lot, I suppose," he said, in the same sulky voice he'd used as a boy to accuse her of crossing him.

"Yes," she said. "I'm meeting Fischer." Morgan stared at her, and she felt herself blushing. "I wrote you about him," she said, and then, as though in his silence he was accusing her, she added, "I know I did."

"Your friend," Morgan said cryptically.

"Yes," Evelyn said. She stroked the cream enamel. "Whose car is this, then, if it's not yours?" she asked, eager to change the subject.

"My friend's," he said harshly, and she was taken aback by the anger in his voice, but suddenly his mood changed again. "I'll go back into the shed," he said with a smile. "They arrange the luggage under the passengers' initials. What are yours?"

He was teasing her, a boy again. "L, I suppose," she said, letting him have his game.

"Not C, for Countess?" he suggested.

"Don't," she begged. "I'll explain later."

"I understand," he told her. "Hollywood is full of nobility. If I had a title, I could be a rich man."

"You look as though you're doing all right," she returned. For a moment his mood wavered, then held steady. "I'll check Y, for Your Highness, too," he said, smiling, "and perhaps D, for Deposed Aristocracy."

"And if you don't come back, I'll send someone to look for you under B, for incorrigible Brats," she said.

They looked at each other for another searching moment. "I really am terribly glad to see you," he told her. "There's so much I have to tell you."

"And me."

He looked at the small diamond necklace Fischer had

given her and the large double diamond clasp that held the scarf at her throat. "Yes," he said. "I can see that."

"Beast."

Morgan disappeared into the shadow of the building. "Uncle Morgan will be back soon," Evelyn said to Victoria. The child was watching her with the stillness that troubled her mother. Sometimes, watching Victoria, Evelyn had the disturbing sensation she was looking into Alex's tiger-colored eyes. She knew that her guilt was largely imagined, but she often wondered how much Victoria had understood of the last years.

Alex's sister still came to the house each month for the money that allowed Alex and his family to live, but Evelyn contrived to miss her visits. She had once asked if she couldn't open an account, had spoken to Sebowski at the bank about it, but Natasha insisted on coming to the house. She sat in the hall, refusing either food or drink, but if Evelyn happened to pass through, she stared at her with eyes that mocked her as a whore.

"Even a whore's money is good," Evelyn murmured to herself, opening the door of the car. "Would you like to sit with Mommy?" she asked Victoria.

Victoria shook her head, waiting for the rear door to be opened. There were times when Evelyn still felt like a commoner around the child's natural assurance that other people were her inferiors. Evelyn felt her heart contract, as it often did when Victoria turned a cold face to her. She closed her own door very carefully and sat with her face to the northern California sun.

The tension drained slowly out of her. Busy with a new business matter, Fischer hadn't written for the ten days before she had left Shanghai. She had seen the change in him. One day he'd been talking of buying land in Northern China, the game they played about how they would wish to end their days—both knowing that any such talk could only be a dream—and then he had been called to Japan on business.

When he returned, something within him had undergone

a sea change. He stopped talking about China and started talking about the possible course of events in Europe, a topic they usually scrupulously avoided.

Suddenly Fischer was obsessed, reading every foreign language newspaper, working late after dinner in the small study he had furnished for himself in her house. He still lived in his own suite at the Palace Hotel, but now he had started bringing his business meetings into the house in the French section. Surprisingly, most were with Japanese.

At first she had been pleased at his use of the house as more than a retreat, which made her feel like the kept woman that the European community considered her. At night, in the nightclubs on the Nanking Road where the White Russian girls were paid for their time, she was in a no-man's-land, but in the day in the Select Department Store, in Fouquets Tea Room, or out at the race course, the women allowed themselves the luxury of showing their contempt. The men looked appreciative, but they made no attempt to disguise the nature of their interest.

"I hate it," she had said, stripping her gloves off as she came through the door. Lye Choy was waiting for her and took the snakeskin handbag, retrieved the shoes that Evelyn kicked off on the way to the long living room. The white willow chairs had come from a noble's house in Peking with the red lacquer table and cabinets.

She poured herself a stiff brandy. "I won't go there anymore."

"Yes, you will." Fischer took off his own gray doeskin gloves very carefully. Evelyn had gone to look out into the shadowed garden where the fire trees were flaming with blossoms. "You can't lock yourself up here."

"They might just as well say I am a whore."

Fischer said nothing, pouring himself a drink.

"I am a whore," she said.

"Yes," he agreed.

Shocked, she had spun on him, ready to throw the drink at him, but his cold gaze stopped her. "You are," he said, "but that is only one way to define a relationship like ours. You are not a sing-song girl, nor are you what they imply. I know that, and so do you. Nothing we could do would change their attitude, and if you fight them, they will have the added satisfaction of rejecting you."

When she was calm, she asked, "What should I do, then?"

He raised his shoulders in a shrug as he sipped his drink. "Be beautiful," he suggested. "Look happy. You will make them insane with bitterness. Do you think they are happy locked away amid their prejudices?"

She loved him. The thought had come to her quite clearly one night when his soft hand touched her on the thigh beneath her nightdress and she had shuddered. He could speak to her and raise her to the brink of a climax as Alex's rough lovemaking had never been able to. She became impatient as Fischer took his time, but the climax was like a series of detonations that literally made her mind reel and her senses spin. He took her out of herself.

"Don't you mind," she asked, looking at him across the dim room, "when those women look at me like that?"

"No," he said, coming up in front of her. Without her shoes they were eye to eye. He put his hand into the bodice of her dress, boldly taking hold of her. "It excites me," he murmured. "I like to think that they know what you and I do for each other." He kissed her then, showing her what the other men were thinking.

There was something shameful and exciting in their lovemaking, as though his friends were there in the room watching. They heard Lye Choy close the door, and she was grateful that the other servants were shut away in the back part of the house. Later, naked on the floor beneath the window, she started to laugh. "I feel naughty."

Fischer, who after lovemaking quite resembled a well-stuffed plush toy, moved over her and traced the line of her jaw. "You should," he smiled. "You are a wicked woman."

"Seduced."

"Any of those women out there would love to be seduced," he said, "but they don't dare. That's why they hate you so."

"I have nothing to lose," she said.

"Me," he said.

The fear, always present just beneath the surface, flowed through her. She closed her eyes and turned her face away so he wouldn't see. He was the cleverest person she had ever met, so he had to know, but they never discussed it.

"Later," he said, in a tone that told her he was ashamed of his cruelty, "if you are rich enough, it won't make any difference how you became so. They will merely be old and married."

"I'll be old, too."

"Old rich is quite different from old poor," Fischer said, stroking her breasts. She opened her eyes. "And you won't be burdened with an old, demanding husband."

"I might like a young one," she said, teasing him.

"Several," he recommended, "one after the other."

"Gigolos," she said. She could feel her body responding again to his touch, and his, too. He was never beyond making love.

"I'll treat them very well," she said as his hand slipped lower.

"Never treat your lovers too well. It lulls them into false security."

"Ohhh," she said as his strong fingers caressed her. "I'll want them to love me."

"Admire you," he suggested, leaning down to kiss her neck where the pulse was beating more strongly.

"Love," she insisted.

"No, no," he murmured. "You mustn't confuse sentiment with your self-interest." He was kissing the nape of her neck. Her body arched as his hand probed her, and then his mouth found hers and conversation stopped until they had made love, slowly at first, less insistently than before, then building to a climax that left them damp and drained.

In the darkness that had overtaken the room while they made love, she said, "I would want anyone whom I loved to love me back."

"But the young are different," Fischer murmured, also serious now that they were done. "Remember that, if you ever love one of them."

"Do you remember that with me?" She searched his face in the dark. She could feel the draft from the door behind them.

"You are unusual," Fischer said. He touched her face gently, lovingly, and for a moment she felt secure in his care for her. "Don't assume others are like you. You'll be hurt."

"I don't ever want to be with anyone but you," she said fiercely. "I love you."

His silence was gratitude, but he couldn't bring himself to break his own code. "Be careful, Evvy," he said, a name he seldom used. "The world is unkind, and the young the unkindest of all."

Thinking of Fischer's words, Evelyn craned to look at her daughter in the California sunlight. "Isn't this a beautiful place?" She often felt as though she was attempting to make conversation with a stranger.

Victoria turned her attention away from the distant hills. She didn't answer.

"You'll like it here," her mother said.

Victoria let her eyes flick toward Evelyn with a light that might have been dislike, then back to the pretty houses so unlike the chaos of Shanghai.

Morgan came out of the shed and waved. "Madame, your luggage will be forwarded to your hotel," he said. "Anything can be arranged for the right price." He laughed as he got behind the wheel. "Where to?" he asked. "The hotel, or a drive around?"

"A drive," Victoria said from the back seat in a voice that was startlingly old for her age. Morgan turned to look at her, surprised.

"As my lady wishes," he said seriously. To Evelyn he said, "I'm practicing my Fairbanks imitation."

"You'll swing on ropes," she said as he started forward smoothly, the car rushing down the street as though he was just barely in control.

"Save women in distress," he went on.

"You'll be famous," she agreed.

"And rich." The way he added "rich" was not unlike the sudden change in Victoria's voice, as though he had for one second revealed what he was truly thinking.

"All of this," he said some blocks further on, "isn't at all like the rest of California. This is much, much more genteel."

"I think it's very beautiful," Evelyn told him, and she did. She hadn't realized how much she had missed cleanliness. It was as though in sailing out of the Yangtze River they had left behind corruption, dankness, the constant rotting smell of humanity and vegetation. The world smelled different. She drew a deep breath. "God, that's nice."

"What?" Morgan asked her. Across the bay she could see rolling hills furred with low vegetation, almost gray in the watery sunlight.

"No pong."

He looked at her and laughed. "Does Shanghai stink?"

"A constant pong," she told him, reverting quickly to the language of their childhood. "All of China has it. They say we smell peculiar, but I don't know how they can tell."

Morgan drove more slowly through Golden Gate Park, pointing out the Palace of Fine Arts, a baroque white building rising beside a reflecting pond. Evelyn had trouble believing that the whole edifice was made of papier-mâché. "No," she said. "It's not possible."

"This is a land of illusion," he assured her. "You won't believe what they do in Hollywood."

"It must be beautiful," Evelyn agreed.

"No," he said. "It's not wonderful. It's an enormous children's party for grown-ups."

"Well, I think that would be wonderful," Evelyn said.

"Except you keep waiting for the nannies to come to take everyone home. But it just gets later and later, and the party goes on and on. Finally you get . . . I don't know . . . it just doesn't seem as much fun."

Evelyn watched him, the jaw tensing again. Her heart went out to him. He had never been happy, except for brief moments when they were children.

He looked over as though he understood what she was

thinking. "I'm glad you're here," he said again. "I've missed you."

"I want to talk about Mother," she said.

He nodded, but instead started to talk to Victoria, who laughed at his fantasy that the whole city was made of papier-mâché and would melt if it rained. "So you see," he said as they topped a hill rolling back toward the center, "we have to hope that it doesn't rain, or you may wake up and find that the walls are going soft around you, and the floor is buckling, and if you're on the third or fourth floor, who knows what could happen?"

"No!" shrieked Victoria. Evelyn was delighted by the joy in her voice. She put her head back on the headrest, turning from one to the other.

As they drew up at the hotel a black doorman came forward. "Can I take your car, sir?" he asked.

"No, but you can put it somewhere until I need it again," Morgan said, and the man laughed. People like him, Evelyn thought. They like him immediately.

"Yes, sir." The doorman saluted as they passed up the steps.

Here at the Palace Hotel an attempt had been made to bring everything down to a human scale—luxurious, but elegant in a way that China could never be. They were swept through the lobby and up in the brass elevator with the glass sides to a suite. The room was filled with flowers. "You shouldn't have," Evelyn said.

"I didn't."

"Oh!" She took the card from the first basket of overflowing white roses and read, "Fischer." How like him, she thought, to announce himself so economically. Tears came to her eyes, however, which surprised her and then Morgan.

"Tears?"

"It's nothing."

"It's about five hundred dollars' worth," Morgan said, taking in the stands of roses, the draping honeysuckle, the orchids.

"You'll like him," she said hopefully.

Morgan picked a tiger orchid out of a wicker basket and

put it in his button hole. "I expect I will," he said thoughtfully. "This is some room," he said, pulling back the curtains to look out across the rooftops to the bay and the bridge.

She blushed. "Darling, would you like to wash your hands?" she said to Victoria, who was standing in the center of the carpet as though waiting for directions.

Victoria headed for the bedroom, its open doors revealing more flowers. Evelyn watched her disappear around the corner, and Morgan must have seen the worry on her face.

"How is Alex?" he asked.

"I don't see him," Evelyn admitted. She was washing one dry hand with the other before she saw Morgan watching her and stopped. "It's been very difficult." She looked at the open door, walked over, and closed it. "She worries me. That's why I brought her here, for school."

"She'll be a long way away from you." Morgan dropped onto the damask couch, crossing his legs carefully. Evelyn had an impression of how he would look on a screen: a powerful male presence. He looked like an animal that had been too long in the wild in a very rough season. His movements were still sleek, but he looked hungry, too.

"I'd be grateful if you'd watch her."

He didn't answer her until his mood had shifted. "I'll do what I can," he said sulkily. "I'm not reliable, you know."

"I don't expect that anymore," she admitted. "Of anyone, even myself." As though afraid he would pursue it, she asked, "Would you like a drink?"

"All right."

After she had ordered, she didn't know what to do with herself. She was nervous, pacing up and down the carpet, looking at each arrangement of flowers as though it mattered.

"I can't get used to you as a woman of the world," Morgan said.

Suddenly very weary, she sat down on an armchair and asked, "Tell me about Father's death."

"Mother wrote you."

"A few words, that's all."

Morgan brought out a cigarette case, snapping it shut before he thought to offer one to Evelyn. She stood up to get one and leaned down to have Morgan light it. She had learned to identify essential commodities like gold and diamonds on sight, and the lighter was solid gold. He snapped the flame off but was silent until she was seated. "He died in great pain," he said.

"You weren't there?"

"Not until too late," he said. He wouldn't look at her. Evelyn felt that this was a new Morgan, one she hadn't known before. "They cabled me in Africa. I went as quickly as I could, but . . ." He blew out a cloud of smoke, waved it away, and said, "You didn't go."

"I didn't have any money," she said. She could feel the anger rising.

"You seem to have plenty now."

"Yes," she admitted. The gulf between them was growing.

After a minute or two, Morgan said, "Mother closed the house. He left a lot of debts, very little money. She has enough to live in a grubby sort of way. She's gone very peculiar." If he expected her to ask questions, he was disappointed, so he continued. "She's religious. Goes to church almost every day. She talks of converting to Rome."

"No."

"Anyway," he said with a sigh that seemed to drain the tension from him, "I didn't go back to Africa. There didn't seem any point. After I had been in London, the thought of returning to that miserable hellhole up the river was more than I wanted to face."

"It was bad."

"It was absurd," he said. He looked at her. "It's over, all of that white man's burden stuff, except they don't know it. I was sent out there after an earnest little talk from a tiny, badly shaved man who told me all about free enterprise and 'making my packet,' as though I was some hungry little schoolboy from the Midlands. When I got there it was fun for a while; the hut was just like a Conrad book, a long shack on the river. Inside I had a store like the High Street gone native. Palms and pythons outside, a long counter inside with shelves behind it. I had two boys to help me, but mostly it was me. The black ladies came in wagging their behinds, feet bare on the boards, and I sold them what I'd been sent from London. I sold them corsets once, all of them, and they wore them over their dresses to Sunday services. The missionaries wanted to feed me to the crocodiles. They wrote in protest to the local commissioner, but as I had the only gun in that part of the river, they decided they'd better be my friends, since their flock might at any point decide to eat them."

Evelyn was laughing.

"It's all true," Morgan said, smiling ruefully. "I tried, honestly I did." But he began laughing, too. "After the war was over . . ." But that brought other thoughts, and he took his time stubbing out his cigarette and lighting another.

It was a cue for Evelyn. She said, "Our war seemed to go for much longer. Alex is still fighting it. He expects to go back."

"Sad," Morgan said.

"No," she said, fiercely angry in a flash, "it was cruel. Cruel to me and to Victoria."

She could tell by the way his lips twitched that he didn't have much sympathy. "Lots of people lost more than you did."

"I didn't give a damn for what was lost," she said. "I wanted us to live, and he wanted to stay with his memories."

"And you left," Morgan said.

"Not quite," she admitted.

"Tell me about this new chap." Morgan smiled to show that they were friends again, the way they had been on the dock, children at play in a large world.

"Fischer."

"A Jew."

"Jews aren't like Papa used to think," she said, and she was blushing as she spoke.

"No," Morgan said, swinging his legs over the arms of the sofa. "In America they're much richer." He seemed to think that funny. "What's he like?"

"He has a remarkable mind," she said carefully.

"Every time a woman has told me that a man has a remarkable mind," Morgan said, "she was apologizing for his body or his pocketbook."

"He's not poor," Evelyn said. She shouldn't laugh, she knew, but she was going to.

"So he's"—Morgan made a face—"an ogre."

Evelyn had a quick flash of the feel of Fischer's body against hers, of his hands on her thighs. She was short of breath for a second and recognized that she hadn't allowed herself to think how much she missed him, and she turned her head to hide. Morgan was smiling when she turned to face him again, a small, teasing smile through the smoke that curled up from the forgotten cigarette burning near the carpet.

Evelyn got up and stubbed it out in an ashtray. "You'll set fire to the hotel."

"You haven't answered me," Morgan said, reaching out to take her wrist. He tightened his grip, and her mind went back to their days in the garden of the London house when he would say, "I'll burn your wrist," twisting until she cried out. She pulled her hand away.

"He's a good man," she said, thinking that the words were inadequate, perhaps even a lie. But what would Morgan say if she said, "He makes love to me as no one ever has." Or more the truth, "I feel safe with Fischer."

She tried that. "He makes me feel safe."

"Married?" he asked behind her.

"Yes," she admitted.

"All is clear."

Nothing was clear, but she felt it would be impossible to explain, so she changed the subject. "So you came to America."

"Not immediately. There were some . . . difficulties," Morgan said. He looked angry, the same look he had as a child when caught out.

"How serious?"

"They could have been very serious."

175

"The police?"

"No, not in the end. I left," he scoffed, "before I could assist them with their inquiries, as it were."

"Mother must have found that difficult."

"I don't know if she knew." He scanned the room. "Anything to drink in this rain forest?" he asked. "She probably found out, but I'm not sure she would have understood anyway. Anything not related to the question of the virgin birth isn't important to her. It was the Cavendish woman."

"Dottie!"

"Yes." His eyes flashed with the memory. "She had her own reasons for making trouble for me."

"You dumped her."

"Not exactly. Well, something like that."

"Oh, Morgan," Evelyn said, relieved. She had had visions of something much more sinister. Life with Fischer—life in Shanghai—had inured her to the small problems of love and betrayal. Trouble in Shanghai, particularly if it got so far as to involve the authorities, would have meant murder at the least. A broken heart, a betrayed woman's revenge, were children's games compared to those that Big-Eared Tu or the Green Gang—foolish names for deadly friends and associates of Fischer—engaged in.

She walked across the room and ruffled her brother's hair. "Women," she said. "They'll ruin you."

He took her hand more gently in his. "I'm on the lam, as they say here."

"Don't worry," she said. "I'll look after you."

He turned her hand over and kissed her palm. She felt his tongue, shuddered, and took it away. She wondered what he would say if she told him what she had seen in the Whangpoo garden, how she had been there in Nagpoo the next day when the body floated by garlanded with paper flowers.

She picked up the telephone. "I'll find out what's holding up your drink."

He wouldn't believe her, she decided as she listened to the ringing of the telephone in the bowels of the hotel. Evil, as

Fischer said, was as relative as virtue. She was glad to know that, as she was glad for everything that Fischer had taught her. All her knowledge helped her, protected her, but as the phone rang unanswered elsewhere in the hotel she felt burdened by the knowledge that Fischer had given her, as he had given her her clothes, the food she ate, jewels, the house in the French settlement.

9

Evelyn craned to look back toward the convent. The mother superior had rested her hand on Victoria's shoulder. The girl faced the long driveway without expression, her neat navy blue coat and white straw hat reminding her mother of formal photographs of the young grand duchesses on the imperial yacht.

How Russian she looks, Evelyn thought. The child stood with a straight back and unblinking eyes, watching her mother and uncle drive away.

"I hate leaving her," Evelyn murmured.

"That's what you brought her to America for, isn't it?" Morgan reminded her. He slowed the car at the end of the long avenue of plane trees. Dust rose from beneath the wheels to settle on Evelyn's demure gray dress as she raised her hand in farewell. The mother superior, a figure out of a chess game in her long black robe, bent slightly to speak to Victoria. Victoria turned her back and walked into the red stone convent. The nun watched the driveway and the car as it passed behind the stone gateposts; then she, too, turned to walk into the building.

The sun was much warmer today than it had been in the week since their arrival. Evelyn undid the small white collar of her dress and fanned her throat with her gloves.

"You'll like the coastline," Morgan assured her. "It's like Cornwall in a way. Rugged, wild."

Evelyn tried to remember what Cornwall looked like. Talking to Morgan, she had discovered that her England was frozen into a series of picture-book illustrations. For a long time she had thought that one day when she had enough money she would go back there. Victoria would grow up, Fischer would . . . but she never allowed herself to think about what might happen with Fischer. When she had first been married, Alex had made so many promises, sketched so many dreams. None of it had occurred, and what had taken its place had not been imaginable even as a terrible story. But in the very distant future, a future far enough away to hold no disappointment, no surprises, she was living again in England, quietly, secretly, with her own knowledge of the world safe in her memories. Victoria was grown and . . . but she stopped at that point. It was the transitions that she hated. She could dream dreams, but she knew too much to try to make the small essential bridges from one moment to the next. You had to allow fate to take care of that, and fate, though relentless, was unreliable and cursed with a twisted sense of humor.

This last week, however, she had felt the first uneasiness about her dream of eventual return. The England Morgan spoke of was not so unlike Shanghai—parties and nightclubs, all sorts of changing morals that wouldn't have gone unremarked on the Nanking Road. Unable to say "Stop," she still resented his stories.

"And you'll find Hollywood terribly funny," Morgan said, but his eyes narrowed in memory. He didn't look particularly amused.

"Fischer will be arriving in ten days," Evelyn said. "I have to be back here by then."

Morgan looked at her as he pressed the accelerator to the floor, leaving the last of the houses behind. He looked angry, as he often did when she talked of Fischer, as though he had come to represent to Morgan what her lost dreams of England meant to Evelyn. And so she had stopped talking about Fischer entirely.

The sun warmed her face, and she closed her eyes, opening another button on her dress. Morgan drove very fast along the almost deserted road. Twisted oak trees rose up on all sides, and the hills rolled away like overturned brushes, the grass swept by the wind, all of it painted in colors of yellow and green and red.

"There's a train from Union Station in Los Angeles," Morgan said. "You can get back here overnight."

"How long will it take us to drive down?" Evelyn asked.

"Three days. It's eight hundred miles."

"And we can drive all the way?"

"Of course," Morgan said. "This is America. The roads aren't all good, but we can make it. Trust me."

Trust me. She had trusted him all her life, and nothing in the last week had made her excitement at their reunion diminish. But the moody boy had become an angry man. The charm was there, but he delighted less in it. He had a contempt for other people's gullibility and something close to a fury at himself.

As though he could read her mind, Morgan said, "That old battle-ax will be good for Vicky."

Evelyn opened her eyes and sat up. She reached for the crocodile handbag that had slid off the seat onto the floor. "I just want her to feel happy," she said.

She knew that he would mock her. "No, you don't," he said. "Nobody's happy, not like you're talking about. You know that by now."

She did, but she meant something different. "Happy as a child should be," she said. "We were."

He looked at her, his eyes filled with the peculiar smokiness he got when they talked about their childhood. "We were, weren't we?"

"Except that you were a beast," Evelyn said.

"You were so trusting," he said, laughing. "I wasn't nearly as beastly as I wanted to be. You just were such an easy victim."

"I was smart enough not to let you know, that's all," Evelyn said. "I knew I could keep your beastliness down to mere torture if I appealed to your huge male vanity to protect me. Female wiles," she said, taking out a new silver cigarette box that Morgan had presented her with yesterday. She rarely smoked, but the beaten silver "To Countess Lezenski from a commoner" and Morgan's scrawl reproduced in the silver had seemed to demand it. Now she tapped the short American cigarette hard on the cover to shake loose the poorly packed tobacco, put it in her lips, and turned to the gold lighter already held out.

"She won't ever be like other children," Morgan told her, snapping the lighter shut. "You can't unremember things."

"But she can still be happy," Evelyn insisted.

They drove south through the warm afternoon. Evelyn fell asleep, and when she woke the entire landscape seemed to have fallen under a spell. Pastel shading raced across long, rolling valleys. The sea was on the right, a sea very much indeed like Cornwall, with steeply dropping cliffs, rocks like rough jewels thrown among the spray. And far off, birds flew across the face of a sinking sun. The long, flat plain beyond the shore turned for one astonishing moment entirely gold, then navy blue, and finally silver as a new moon rose.

When she saw that the night was upon them, she found her heart was beating with a strange new excitement. Anything was possible in the dream landscape through which they were passing, heading down toward the shore itself where tiny lights had sprung up like diamonds.

Morgan stopped the car at a lodge above the sea where they seemed to know him. He booked them two rooms, elaborately introducing his sister as a countess. The woman at the desk became flustered, bowing her head and bobbing into a curtsy.

"That wasn't nice," Evelyn said, taking Morgan's arm as the woman's husband carried their bags down a long, plain corridor on the second floor.

Morgan said, "It's astonishing how much they like all that. I mean it. In Hollywood they behave as though they were in one of their own films when a title appears. You could never do that in England."

"Because in England they would know exactly what my title was worth."

"No," said Morgan as the man stopped down the hall to unlock and push open the door for Evelyn. "It's because they want to believe. If you find out what it is that people want to believe, you can make them do almost anything."

"How cynical," Evelyn said in wonder. She could see in a flash that Morgan and Fischer would detest each other.

People who believed the same thing often did. Maybe it was because they had once wanted to believe otherwise, but experience hadn't allowed it.

"Do you want a meal?" Morgan asked.

"I want a bath," Evelyn said. The woman's husband had laid her twin pigskin suitcases on the bed. Looking at his patched trousers and faded shirt, she wondered if he'd known the locks were gold. Morgan had. He'd snapped them open and closed for a good quarter hour, finally turning to face her silently, as though to reassess her.

"The bath's through the door and down the hall," the man told her. He wouldn't look at her but kept stumbling over his words.

"Like English hotels," Evelyn said.

"Like English houses," Morgan reminded her. He said, "I'll come for you in an hour."

"Where are you going?" she called after him, but he was already at the stairs.

The man left her, refusing a tip, then accepting it as he blushed crimson. In the oval mirror on the scarred maple dresser she saw a reflection covered in dust, her face burned a new color from the long drive, a dusky brown. She liked what she saw, turning about to see herself more clearly. But when she undressed she was dismayed to see that the drive had tanned her arms only as far as the three-quarter sleeves of the gray dress. Her head and neck looked as though they had been stuck onto someone else's white body.

In the bath she rubbed at the color on her skin as though she could scrape it off. Finally she sat back in the deep water and threw the sponge at her feet.

When she opened her door, Morgan laughed. "A peasant," he said.

"So much for a title." She had chosen a cream cotton dress, beautifully tailored but simple enough to blend in with the rustic atmosphere of the inn. She hadn't wanted to leave her jewelry behind in the unlocked room, so what she couldn't hold in her handbag, she was wearing: an emerald and diamond bracelet that she knew was shamelessly expensive, the five-carat diamond that Fischer had first bought her that she always wore, and a string of pearls that could have bought the small hotel.

"Come on, Marie Antoinette."

She felt stung but laughed. He was right. They went down the stairs to a large room overlooking the cliffs. Below the sea was dark but loud, a thunder that never stopped. There were two tables set. They walked past a wide fireplace where another couple, older, sat holding hands.

"Hi," Morgan said, the American greeting sounding strange and foreign in his English accent, holding out his hand. "I'm Morgan Valentine," he said. "My sister"—his eyes teased Evelyn—"Evelyn Lezenski."

The man and woman were both small and sturdily built; the man, dressed fastidiously in gabardine trousers, boots, and a shirt of navy flannel buttoned to the throat, was darkly burned, with bright eyes. The woman wore a plain brown dress buttoned to the neck. Her ankles were crossed over what in Europe would have been called sensible shoes.

"Gatti," the man said in English with an accent from the continent. "Carlos. And my wife Sofia." The woman offered a welcoming smile, but didn't speak.

"She speak little English," the man said.

The woman looked at Evelyn's jewels with the curiosity of a child. She smiled again, raising her eyebrows and pointing to the bracelet.

Evelyn put her hand over it to hide it, realized she might appear rude, and held it out to the woman to look at more closely. The firelight set fire to the emeralds. The woman touched it gently, shaking her head, made a remark in Italian to her husband, and laughed.

Mr. Gatti said, "My wife thinks I should buy her such a jewel." He touched her hand again, and Evelyn had the impression of very young children.

Morgan went to get cocktails for himself and Evelyn. The man smiled at Evelyn, holding his wife's hand. The firelight was kind to both of them, smoothing away the wrinkles that might have come from a lifetime working in the sun.

The woman who ran the inn appeared suddenly from the kitchen. Evelyn saw how the small Italian woman blinked several times and looked at her own plain dress. The innkeeper had changed, Evelyn saw, into a remarkable confection, part late afternoon dress, part something that one might expect to see on the stage at Christmas, a dress for a pantomime fairy.

"Countess," the woman said, curtsying slightly, "dinner will be served soon."

"Oh, thank you," Evelyn said, embarrassed.

When the woman left she didn't know what to say, where to look. Mr. Gatti, his own eyes twinkling, said, "You are royalty?"

"No, no," Evelyn said, shaking her head as though she had been accused of some deception.

"But she called you by a title."

"I used to be a countess," Evelyn said, frantically looking about for Morgan. "A long time ago in another country."

The man translated her words for his wife, who nodded at Evelyn as though to reassure her. Her husband said, "Everyone comes from another country. It is nice, no?"

Evelyn liked him. "Very nice," she said. "Everyone starts again." She realized that that was how she felt. Everyone had started again at some not-so-distant point.

"Yes, yes," he said excitedly, telling his wife what Evelyn had said.

The woman answered quickly, and the man looked shocked. She giggled.

"Tell me what your wife said," Evelyn asked him.

He shook his head. "My wife is a very bad woman," he said, not at all upset. He shook his head at his wife.

"No, no, you must tell me," Evelyn begged. She reached out and took hold of his wife's wrist gently. Her skin felt like dry parchment. "Make him tell me," she said to the woman who was shaking her head.

The man, blushing, said, "My wife thinks you have very beautiful jewels. She thinks that if we all start again, as you say, you run—how do you say it?—the race much faster."

The woman was giggling and rocking herself. For a flash of a second Evelyn didn't know whether to be shocked or outraged, but then, looking at the woman's lowered, dancing eyes, she burst into laughter. "Tell your wife," Evelyn said to Mr. Gatti, who was watching uncertainly, "that she is right, and I thank God every morning that I can run that fast."

It was Gatti's turn to look shocked. He repeated Evelyn's words to his wife, who rocked faster and laughed more openly at Evelyn. When she stopped she was wiping tears from her eyes. She spoke to her husband, who said, "My wife says that if she wasn't so fat, she might learn to run faster, too." He shook his head. "She is a very bad woman," he said, but he held more tightly to her hand.

Morgan brought Evelyn a drink. "What's the joke?" he asked.

Mr. Gatti shook his head, embarrassed to repeat it. "I'm a fallen woman," Evelyn said, feeling lighthearted. She thought she could live happily here in this hotel for the rest of her life. She began to sort out her feelings about America. In San Francisco the images had come too fast, all wrapped up with her feelings about seeing Morgan again after so many years and parting with Victoria.

"Well . . ." said Morgan uncertainly. He sipped his drink. "Do you live here in California?" he asked Mr. Gatti.

"Yes, yes," Gatti said, squeezing his wife's hand. "We live in the north."

"And you do . . . ?" Morgan asked him.

Evelyn was startled to hear Morgan ask such a direct question. In England or even some parts of China that would have been considered the height of rudeness. But then her encounter with Gatti and his wife had had a refreshing directness also.

"We have land," Gatti said with pride. "Not so much, but good. Good for grapes."

"Grapes?" asked Morgan.

"For wine."

"From California?" Morgan sounded skeptical.

Gatti shook his finger at Morgan. "You will see. One day there will be wine from California."

"If you say so," Morgan said. He looked with amusement at Evelyn. "I suppose anything is possible."

The woman from the hotel came back to lead Evelyn and Morgan to their table near the window, overlooking the cliffs. When she had gone to settle the Gattis across the room, Evelyn said, "I like America."

Morgan nodded thoughtfully. "I can see that."

"And you don't?"

He moved his glass in a wet circle on the red and white tablecloth. "I don't know," he said irritably. "I don't feel I belong."

"But you do!" Evelyn said quickly. "You fit in wonderfully."

"No," Morgan said with another of his mood shifts. "I still feel like an outsider."

"Maybe after a while . . ." Evelyn suggested.

"Yes," Morgan said shortly. "I expect so." The anger was still there, and Evelyn picked up the short menu that lay beside her plate to allow him time to calm down.

The hotel woman served a magnificent meal, a beef stew with fresh vegetables such as Evelyn hadn't known she'd missed. The potatoes tasted different from anything she'd had in China, and the string beans served with bacon brought back more memories of home than had anything so far.

Her mind wandered as Morgan drank the wine with a determination that made her nervous. Watching his handsome face go slack with alcohol, she felt pity, but also contempt. Alex, at least, would never give up. Her guilt transformed itself in the only way possible: sentiment rose up and became love. She loved Morgan. He had been her favorite person when she was a child, and now she knew that, in some mysterious way, she was now older than he.

She reached out and covered his hand before he could lift his glass again. "Do you have to do that?" she asked.

"What?" he asked dangerously.

She wouldn't answer him directly. "I'd like to walk along the cliffs," she said.

"And you think I'll be too drunk," he said. The scene could go either way now. He could make light of it or brood and erupt.

"Well, I can't drive," she said, trying for a joke. "If you fall into the ocean, I'll be stuck here until I'm an old woman."

He hesitated, then laughed. He pushed the glass away, but his eyes followed it. "Let's walk," he said, getting up abruptly.

Evelyn found him at the edge of the cliff looking down at the spume the ocean tossed into the air where the water hit the rocks. She put her arm through his and laid her head on his shoulder. "Don't be sad," she said, the words coming out of the far distant past. She had been a very young child, three or four, and he had been beaten for something long forgotten. When he was crying at the bottom of the garden she had come out, distraught to see her favorite person crying; she had put her arms about him and whispered those words. They had become a talisman all through their childhood. They had each other, the words said, and as long as they did, the sun would rise again to play in other gardens.

He turned his head, kissed her hair, and said, "I've missed you."

"So much has happened," she said, moving along the narrow cliff path, arm in arm with Morgan. "Do you remember when I went off to Russia, how we used to dream that you'd come to the pages' school, then become an officer of the czars. . . ."

"I never really wanted that," he said quietly. "You knew that, didn't you?"

"You wanted to wear the uniform with all its gold and white. I knew that. Alex could have fixed it," she said, and her voice faded in wonder, scenes of the past floating out of her memory to taunt her.

"A brilliant marriage," Morgan said, making a fair imitation of their mother.

Evelyn laughed, but the laugh died. "Alex has had a terrible time," she said.

"Everyone has," Morgan told her harshly. "Everyone except the profiteers." She thought he might mean Fischer, though they hadn't discussed Fischer's business. They walked on a few steps, listening to the wind in the stunted pine trees that clung to the cliff face below them. "In the next war," Morgan said, "I'm going to be a profiteer."

She didn't know why, but she was shocked. There had to be something you believed in. Or didn't there? She wouldn't think about what Fischer would say to that. She asked, "Do you think there'll be another war?"

"There's always another war," Morgan said.

"In Europe?" The word sounded as though she was speaking of some magic, distant place, part myth.

"Everywhere," Morgan said. "That's what I think."

"Not in China," Evelyn said. She tried to think of Tu involved in a war. He would be a profiteer, of course, and get richer. China was always involved in one type of war or another these days. Since the fall of the monarchy, the warlords ruled their own kingdoms, waging incessant, minor war on each other. Sun Yat-Sen's central government was more honored in the breach than in fact. Only T. V. Soong's Bank of China really had any authority.

Looked at from this California cliff, the sea silver to the horizon and the moon a diamond crescent low in a black velvet sky, it all seemed like a long novel. You became used to it. The thought of a larger, more serious war in which people you knew died or lost everything, as they had in the Great War, made Evelyn shiver violently. Sheer terror seemed to rise out of the abyss at her feet. She had a desire to turn and run back to the inn, a need to do something so that history wouldn't repeat itself for her. She didn't want ever again to feel that she couldn't control at least some part of her life.

And there was Victoria in the convent school outside of San Francisco. Victoria had only now been returned to her. She had vowed she would keep the child safe.

"You frighten me," Evelyn whispered.

"Everyone should be frightened," Morgan said. "Everyone who can see what's going to happen."

"What's the point of thinking like this if we can't do anything about it?" Evelyn asked, her voice rising with frustration.

"You have to think about it," Morgan said, looking down at the darkness below them. "That's the point, don't you see? You can't stop thinking about it when you know what's coming. It's always there. It changes everything."

They walked back through a night with the wind rising off the ocean.

Evelyn said, "I'm tired." She kissed Morgan, smelling the sweat of the day, sunshine, and dust. "Go to sleep," she advised. "It doesn't do to think about the future. I don't believe in it anymore, not like I used to. The trick is to live in the present."

"I'm going to have one more drink."

Evelyn watched him go into the main room and push at the embers with a charred stick. She felt sad, but very tired. In her bedroom she heard the wind rising higher, crying out around the inn, and the loneliness she had sometimes felt in the house in the French section returned to wrap itself around her. She had meant it when she said she tried to live in the present, but the truth was that in her heart she found it almost impossible to convince herself that she could ever be safe.

She awoke to darkness and the certainty that someone was in the room. For a long moment she couldn't remember where she was. She thought she was in China, and that the stranger might be here to rob or kill her. She lay very still, then knew with a rush that she was on the California coast.

"Evvy?" It was Morgan's voice, very drunk now, coming out of the dark.

"What is it?" she whispered.

"Hold me."

She felt him reach the bed, touch it with his hand, then crawl onto the covers. He curled up like a child beside her, and she put her arms about him, touching his hair where it was matted on his forehead. He didn't say another word, dropping like a child into a deep, immediate sleep, but when she tried to take her arms away from him he clutched at her in the dark, and she settled back to hold him while he slept.

In the morning he was gone.

10

Chaplin sat with a teenage twin on each knee. His smile—the smile of the little tramp—seemed, in the smoke-dimmed light of the roadhouse, half-witted.

"God knows what that's going to cost him," said Morgan, watching from the bar. Then, directing his attention to Evelyn, he said, "All this must look very foolish to you."

"Not at all," Evelyn said, thinking of the roadhouses out on the Nanking Road that Sebowski owned. "I've seen worse."

The roadhouse, Morgan had explained to Evelyn when they'd arrived earlier that day, belonged to Thelma Dorsey, a fading Hollywood star, and as far as Evelyn could tell, a close friend of Morgan's. It had opened as a bar years ago, and now was the hottest thing on Malibu beach, boasting blackjack tables, a roulette wheel, and rooms to rent.

By midnight the room had begun to fill, the roadsters and limousines of the film colony lurching out of the coastal fog, lights yellow in the gloom, to disgorge a drunken horde of the most beautiful people she had ever seen. Evelyn missed Fischer, and wondered what he would think of this. This was their first extended parting in years.

Thinking of Fischer, she found not only that she missed him, but that she was afraid. When he had said, "Would you like to take the child to America?" tears had come to her eyes.

She knew by then that under Natasha's tutelage Victoria was coming to hate her. The old countess, who could have been relied on to insist that a child honor her mother, was dead.

"Alex wouldn't allow it," she said.

"It might be arranged," Fischer had murmured. "Most men can be bargained with."

"No," Evelyn had said, discouraged. Alex would never agree to her having the child. Natasha got fatter and fatter, more slovenly every year. The child went to the convent school that Evelyn paid for, but Alex and Natasha lived in the same two rooms.

"I was thinking," Fischer said, "that he might agree for a sum of money, perhaps a larger sum, if he thought that the child would be put in another school, away from you."

"You mean leave her in California?" Evelyn exclaimed.

"In another school, with more nuns," Fischer said, smiling his smile of gentle disdain for religious education. "It might in any case be the wisest course for her to be away from China at some later point." His eyes shadowed then as they had more frequently of late. "America would be a safe choice."

So it had been arranged. Evelyn bargained with Natasha, meeting her in a tea shop in the French quarter. Evelyn had dressed as carefully as she could, leaving her jewels at home, choosing a simple gray suit, a cloth coat. But she had ridden there in Fischer's Packard with the Romanian chauffeur he had hired. Natasha, sullen and unbathed from her sleep, stared about the room with its polished floor, small marble-topped tables, and wicker chairs with blue velvet cushions. Evelyn saw the resentment in the small eyes that were sinking deeper into fat with each succeeding year, and realized she should have chosen some bare place where Natasha's envy would have nothing to fix upon.

She came across the room to Evelyn, swaying her broad hips in their dirty maroon skirts, ready to insult her, but then she saw the cakes, sandwiches, cold meats, and her anger faded before her gluttony.

The bargain had been surprisingly easy to strike. Fischer had set a sum, and he had been right. Later, Evelyn saw that Natasha must have been fearful that the child, now almost grown, would leave and take with her what security Natasha had. So she had sold her.

For the weeks of preparation, Evelyn had been happier than she could remember being. The fear had come later, when she understood that Fischer wouldn't accompany her to California directly.

They were sitting in the small willow wood dining room, the red lacquer chest displaying her small but excellent celadon porcelain collection. The lights of the candles floating amid the pink and white lotus blossoms in the green glass bowl made the dull gold of the wallpaper warm and close. "It is better this way," Fischer told her gently. He had put on more weight, looked almost Oriental with his round face and smoothly tailored suits, tonight a gray worsted made in Hong Kong. He looked sleek and attractive despite his growing bulk. He looked powerful, his eyes shining with secret knowledge. "You will have time to learn to know each other again on the crossing."

Except for small visits in places chosen by Alex or Natasha, Evelyn had not spent any time with her child. She went to the convent occasionally, but their conversation, supervised by a disapproving nun in the corner of the room, was stilted.

"You'll go to Europe, then," she said. They both knew what she was leaving unsaid.

"Yes," he said gently. They never spoke of his own family. She knew he was in correspondence with his wife, but she never saw the letters. In the day, Fischer still conducted business in his suite of rooms at the Palace Hotel, and she supposed he must receive his mail there.

"I must," he said. Fischer owed her no explanation.

She was grateful, therefore, for his offer of even those two words and struggled to keep her own concern hidden. "Yes, of course you must," she said, as calmly as she could.

"I have to see for myself what I am hearing from Europe."

She looked down the table at him. "Is it that bad, do you think?"

"Definitely."

Out here, most particularly in Shanghai, the world seemed insulated against the Depression, the result of the war. Except for the detritus of the revolution—people like

Alex, Sebowski, herself—they saw nothing. The East was a rich marketplace where great fortunes were being made in almost every way. The streets were paved with gold if you could reach past the starving and the dead to pick it up.

Fischer roared out of the harbor on the Pan American Clipper whose propellers churned up the water beneath the pontoons of the plane, rising awkwardly and then more surely, flying out of the city that he loved. She watched that morning until the plane was lost in the dirty air above the docks, and it occurred to her that she might never see him again.

Fischer was a strange man, with no scruples, no morals, no allegiances but himself, his fortune, and those he chose to take care of. But his word was ironclad, and he had said he would meet her in San Francisco, where he had more mysterious business—this business that was making deep circles even in Fischer's smooth face as he sat up nights alone in the study in the blue house—that had to be conducted on his way east again.

Natasha brought Victoria to the docks. The American liner sat in the river waiting for the tenders that pushed back and forth through the garbage-strewn waters, taking on passengers and luggage, bringing back visitors half-drunk from their farewells, giddy with the thrill of departure. This time Evelyn had dressed as she wished. Though she wasn't sure she could rely on Natasha, Fischer had refused to allow the payment to be made until the child was actually on board the ship.

"She's your child," he pointed out. "She's on your passport." He had arranged that, too.

She saw the way Natasha eyed her sealskin coat with the monkey fur collar, the small, dark gray cloche hat. Victoria had the blank look that worried Evelyn. When her eyes swept over her mother, the fire was there; but when she looked away, she seemed to be elsewhere. She stood silently in the navy coat and black shoes that Evelyn had sent over days before. The rest of the clothes that she had had made for Victoria were already on board, packed in with Evelyn's clothes in the twelve Vuitton suitcases bought in Saigon the month before.

"Here," said Natasha, pushing Victoria.

The hatred that flared in the child's eyes encouraged Evelyn. She had thought that Victoria herself might object. She was a strange child, observant. Twice when she had dined in public restaurants with Fischer and her mother, Evelyn had seen how she looked at Fischer—with fascination, as though she had to memorize everything about him. "She's strong," had been Fischer's assessment, "which is good." He liked her; this made Evelyn's love for him, which grew at unexpected but quite identifiable moments, increase. There were times when she would think how much she owed him, how much she respected him, then suddenly, at moments such as the one when he had offered to send Victoria to California to finish her schooling, Evelyn would abruptly be moved to tears with gratitude. He seemed to love her in his own way. He was gentle, thoughtful, inquired after her opinion, listened, and made love to her and no one else, which in Shanghai, for a man of his position, astonished her. She had been prepared for other things, but then, after some years, she saw that for Fischer, sexual fidelity was a question of taste. It was in bad taste to be unfaithful; it was untidy. She was a fortunate woman.

Evelyn had the draft ready. "Are you ready?" she asked Victoria.

Her child looked at her. "Yes," she said, and she moved away toward where the last of the passengers were being checked by the steward against the manifesto. The last of the visitors had already left the ship.

Evelyn took out the draft from her bugle-bead handbag, handed the envelope to Natasha. "It's what we agreed," Evelyn said. "Mr. Fischer had it drawn." She thought that Natasha would have some spiteful last remark to hurl at her in front of the child, and she braced herself. But all Natasha did was take the draft and turn without a word.

She hadn't even said goodbye to the child. Evelyn searched for what excuses she could make to Victoria, but when she looked for her she found that the child had already embarked on the tender. She sat very still in the stern, her hands crossed over her knees, her face turned away from the city. She, too, it seemed, had no words of farewell.

11

Across the room Morgan was steadily getting drunk on champagne, carrying bottles as he moved among the crowd. Right now he was stopping to talk to Mary Pickford, who had arrived with a group of people made up as though they had come from the set of a film: The women's makeup was broad, extreme, their eyes as bright as though they were drugged.

"She doesn't look as though she's enjoying herself," Evelyn said to herself. Miss Pickford's famous nose was narrowed to twin tunnels with disdain as Morgan leaned over her to breathe boozily in her face.

The room was warmer now. Smoke pressed down from the ceiling, and the laughter became manic. She thought of Sebowski's discreet nightclubs out on the Nanking Road where the hostesses wore imitations of European gowns copied from out-of-date fashion magazines. The girls out there had a pride that these women lacked.

"Dance with me," Morgan said as he came up beside her, wearing the same white trousers he had worn earlier, stained and bagged at the knees. His dirty white shirt was open three buttons to show his chest.

"You're drunk," Evelyn said, trying not to make it an accusation.

"Thankfully," he told her, pulling her against him as they walked to the dance floor. He held her with his surprising strength, and she was aware of him down the length of her pale blue gown. "Why aren't you, sis?" he asked, looking down.

She wanted to be with Fischer. There was a danger here among these people that Evelyn had forgotten, the same danger she had felt when she had had no money, no papers, little hope. No one had cared what happened to her then, and the same was true here. They didn't like one another. Morgan danced well, and she allowed herself to relax, swaying with him to the music.

"You miss your lover," he said near her ear.

"Fischer," she corrected him.

"Fischer." He made it sound distasteful. She looked up at him and was afraid of the strange light in his eyes; they looked as though they were fading like some movie special effect, the blues going pale while the whites got china-shell white.

"He's a good man," she said, stung.

"And good men are hard to find," he said, making it an accusation of himself.

"I don't think so," Evelyn said. They had talked for hours in the last days, yet the conversations had always been oblique. Morgan had to win points. That was what had changed. Before, he had been mischievous; now, he was bitter.

"Alex was a good man," Morgan said. He was taunting her.

"Yes," she agreed. "He was. He is," she corrected herself, but she was too late. She saw the triumph in his eyes.

"But poor now, and broken."

It was her turn to be angry. "Why do you mock others?" she asked. "You're better than that."

She might have slapped him, he was so surprised. Then he was happy, and she knew she was in danger. He laughed, stood back, knocking other dancers aside. "Silence," he shouted.

"Morgan, don't," she begged him, though she didn't know what he would do.

The room became quiet, as though all the actors recognized a cue. A laugh rose from the back and was stilled.

"Morgan . . ." Evelyn pleaded.

"May I introduce my sister," Morgan said, looking about

the room. He turned to Evelyn, bowed. "Countess Lezenski," he said.

Evelyn tried to pull away, but he held her wrist tight. The next laugh was more nervous but more general.

"We don't meet many *ladies,*" Morgan said, turning with wide, mocking eyes to the room. "We play many here, don't we, dears? But we don't *meet* many."

Evelyn saw with the corner of her eyes that Mary Pickford was leaving and wondered if it was because of Morgan or because she judged it a good time to beat the check.

"And those we do meet seldom have their own jewels," Morgan said, looking at Evelyn's wide emerald bracelet.

Evelyn pulled harder, broke his hold, and stood uncertainly. She tried to smile to defuse the moment, saw the pity and the scorn about her, and pressed her lips together.

"But then, husbands don't give jewels, do they?" Morgan asked the room at large. "Lovers do. Isn't that right, Countess?" He turned to face her, and she saw pure hatred in his eyes.

She turned quickly now and ran for the door. The laughter was uncertain at first. Then much, much louder.

"Shut up," a woman shouted as Evelyn reached the door. "You bastard," was the last she heard before she ran into the night, narrowly missing being struck by Pickford's Pierce-Arrow pulling out into the fog. She ran onto the sand, and the tears began. She ran until she stumbled, left her shoes where they were, and ran some more. The night was very cold. She felt the water beneath her feet and walked parallel to that until she came to a pier. Here she huddled, crying, until she vomited into the sand at her feet.

"Fischer, Fischer," she whispered to the surf. "Fischer."

She stayed beneath the pier until her tears had stopped. The dawn was not far behind. Quiet now, she moved further up the beach to where it was dry and watched the sky pale to gray. The years with Fischer had lulled her, but now she was awake again.

She walked back through the dawn to see Morgan slumped with his head in his hands and anticipated his remorse. As she came up to him he said, "I'm sorry."

She had no words. She didn't know him anymore. She lived somewhere else, not just in another country, but among people of different ways.

"You'll leave," he said as a statement.

"Yes."

"I'll miss you."

"No, you won't. You've never missed anybody."

"I'll miss *you*," he repeated.

"You haven't asked me one thing about myself," she said flatly.

He looked stunned.

"You haven't even asked me if I'm happy," she said. As a child she had listened to his schemes, his dreams, his stories, his adventures. She had stories of her own now, but he hadn't thought to ask her about them except in the broadest detail.

His eyes narrowed with his own pain, and she came close to pity, but then he shrugged. "I'm ugly now, aren't I?" he asked. She knew the abrupt shift of focus was a trick, perhaps not even a conscious one.

Fischer would be in San Francisco soon. She would go there immediately and wait.

He wiped his face with his hand as if he could scrape it off. "No," she said. "You're not ugly, Morgan."

"Yes, I am," he said, and he sighed. "I know it. I can't seem to stop it."

The sun was rising somewhere; the sky was pink. Nothing bad could ever happen here, the palm trees above the roadhouse seemed to promise. But like Morgan, so fine outside, she knew better.

"Try to take care of yourself," she said. She wanted to touch him but was afraid if she did, he would plead with her, and that she wouldn't be able to leave him here as she must. She had herself to save, and Victoria.

She began to walk away.

"Evelyn . . ."

She turned. He was so handsome, she thought. He would survive. There were separate rules for the beautiful, and Morgan had always known what they were.

"I'll visit Victoria if you want."

Her heart turned as cold as ice, filled with foreboding. "I don't think she's allowed visitors," she said very carefully.

"She will be able to if you arrange it. See me, that is. You'll be a long way away."

"Perhaps," was all she could manage, the single word, and she thought that he must have smelled her dread.

Her heart was racing as she steadied herself to walk in her torn stockings across the road. A truck came shaking down the road, passed with a smell of cattle and fear. She went into the darkness of the dirty bar where the air was redolent of spilled liquor and dead cigarettes.

She would tell the nuns that Victoria was specifically not to see her uncle.

12

Fischer said softly, "I have missed you."

Evelyn spun from the window where she had been watching for his arrival. "Fischer!"

He came forward, smaller than she remembered him, but familiar and dear to her. Seeing him walk toward her across the pale yellow carpet, stout as before but his face more drawn, the lines deeper about the eyes, her heart went out to him with an emotion stronger than love—longing, gratitude. Fischer was back. She ran past the bellboys carrying his suitcases and threw herself into his arms.

They clung to each other like children until the bellboys coughed and Fischer gently disengaged himself to tip them.

"How did you get in?" Evelyn asked as the door closed. "I can see every arrival from here." She pointed to the long windows that faced on Union Square.

"I came in the side entrance," Fischer said. "Agnelli sent a car to the airport for me. They have a special entrance for important people." He smiled bashfully.

"Oh." She wanted to memorize every detail of him again: his ruddy skin, the bright gray eyes, the way his heavy body moved smoothly as he undid the jacket of his double-breasted gray suit. (New, she registered, bought in London, probably. She was proud of Fischer's clothes, almost as proud as she was of her own.) There was more gray in his beard than when she had seen him off on the Clipper, but it became him. Fischer was a man who as he aged was visibly becoming the man that destiny had intended him to be. Unlike Morgan, who was visibly failing his early promise.

"You look . . ." Fischer stood back, watching her. "Radiant," he decided. Radiant was a word quite unlike Fischer. He knew it, seemed slightly embarrassed. "America becomes you."

"America is very strange," Evelyn said.

"California."

"Yes, perhaps that's it."

"This is pleasant," Fischer said, looking about the suite. Fischer was not a man for small talk, and the first pang of concern entered Evelyn's mind.

"I thought you would want a suite," she said. "And I wanted to be in the front where I could watch for you. I've been here ten days," she said vaguely, thinking of her flight from Los Angeles.

Neither of them spoke for a moment or two, and Evelyn thought perhaps they had become strangers.

Fischer looked at her. His eyes were indeed more tired than she had ever seen them. The long journey from Europe to New York, then on by train, must have tired him. The idea of Fischer, who had more energy than any man she had ever known, being tired was alarming.

"I have missed you, my dear," he said. The emotion seemed to trouble him. She had known for some years that he cared deeply for her, but Fischer was a man who had his emotions as closely analyzed as his business dealings.

"Oh, Fischer."

He laughed. "We've become accustomed to each other."

"Old shoes." She was blushing.

"No, please, not that." He sat down suddenly in a chair, and her concern for him rose again.

"Are you all right?" she asked, coming to him.

"A glass of water. No, wine, please. That's it."

She ran to the telephone to call for the wine. "What? What?" she shouted at the man on the other end of the line, unable to make sense of his words. "Oh." She turned to Fischer. "What wine?"

"Champagne seems appropriate," he said, smiling. His color was better. "Yes, champagne. And none of this terrible California wine I've been reading of." He shuddered.

"Champagne," she said. "Veuve Cliquot '27, if you have it."

They seemed offended she would ask, taking offense with the pride of the newly sophisticated.

She went and sat near Fischer while they waited like children. He looked quite recovered. "How was your journey?" she asked carefully. She mustn't pry into his time with his family.

He waved the question away. "We'll talk about that later. Let me kiss you."

She folded against him, inhaling his rich smell, and her heart opened as though she had returned from a journey of her own. She sat on his lap like a chorus girl, and they held each other, savoring their kisses until she felt his body responding. His hand was in her dress when there was a knock on the door, and before they could answer or move apart, the door opened.

The waiter looked astonished. He blushed crimson while Evelyn jumped off Fischer's lap to rearrange her clothing.

Fischer rose, attended to the waiter, then opened the champagne himself. At the explosion of the cork, Evelyn clapped her hands. She felt lighthearted. "I could dance," she said, realizing that she hadn't danced since Fischer left Shanghai. There, dancing was a ritual, and she had learned to take their late evenings at the New World Dance Hall, or at Sebowski's several nightclubs, or even at the roof garden of the Palace Hotel, for granted. She had almost become bored with their routine. Afraid of Victoria's disapproving glance, she hadn't danced on the ship at all, though many of the bachelors returning home had asked her.

Fischer brought a glass over to her, holding her glance. "Together," he said, clinking the glasses.

It was almost obscene to watch Fischer as giddy as herself like this, but she loved him for it. Except for the exhaustion in his eyes, she was seeing him as he must have been as a young man.

She drank the champagne, tipping the glass back, then spat it out, choking. Fischer laughed. She looked into the glass and saw the diamond butterfly pin.

"Take it out," Fischer said.

The champagne was cold and sticky on her fingers as she pulled out the pin. The wings of the butterfly were two and a half inches across, pavé with diamonds, and the body was two rows of diamond baguettes. Delicate silver antennae quivered with more diamonds. Fischer took it from her fingers. "It breaks apart," he said, demonstrating. The butterfly divided into two equal clips, each as beautiful as the larger pin. "You can pin it on your dress collar."

"Oh, Fischer," she said as he reached to pin the brooch on her. "It's so beautiful. It must have cost you the earth."

"I saw it in Cartier in Paris. There's only one. I wanted you to have it."

"Thank you, Fischer," she said, laying her palms over the brooch. She felt the rough touch of the diamonds beneath her hand. "Thank you. I only needed you."

"I knew that," he said, looking at her. "That's why I wanted you to have something else."

They sat down on the long sofa, Evelyn leaning back against Fischer. "Did you see your brother?" he asked.

"Yes." She made no elaboration, and Fischer requested none.

"And Victoria?" he asked quietly.

"She's in the convent. I saw her yesterday." She didn't add that she had gone each day to the school, calling for a car and chauffeur, riding out across the beautiful bridge that spanned the bay and through the oak-covered California hills with her heart telling her she was as frightened as the night she had left Russia. Each day the nuns brought Victoria to her, and each day Evelyn asked her simple questions and was answered in monosyllables while Alex's eyes stared at her accusingly.

"There were no problems with her aunt?"

"None."

"The child will be safe here," Fischer said with a deep intake of breath.

Evelyn craned to look up at him. "What's wrong?"

He didn't answer immediately. "There's going to be a war, my dear."

"Where? In Europe?"

"Perhaps everywhere," he murmured.

"Again?" She sat up.

"Worse," Fischer said, "much worse." The fatigue in his eyes had turned to sorrow.

Evelyn stood up, walked to the window. She didn't want to believe him. They had called the last one the war to end all wars. For a few years the memories had faded, but meeting Morgan again had recalled the terrible cost that went beyond the dead, the loss of empires. In the square below the flower carts were splashes of vivid color, the sunlight as innocent as childhood. "Can't it be stopped?"

"I doubt it," Fischer said.

"Germany again?"

"This fellow Hitler." Fischer sighed. "And Mussolini, too. We mustn't mention any of this to Agnelli tonight." They were to meet with Guido Agnelli, the California banker who had sent the car for Fischer. "That's business." With Fischer, business was a matter apart from politics.

"What will happen in China?"

Fischer walked over to pour himself more wine, which in itself was unusual. "China will be the rehearsal."

"For whom?" she asked, uncomprehending.

"For Japan. Japan will go to war to win the East."

She was so shocked, she touched the wood of the windowsill. "No," she said, though she knew Fischer was seldom wrong. "England would never allow it, nor France."

"It will be a world war, my dear," Fischer said. "A *world* war."

What was he saying? The last one had been a world war, but the East had been separate, safe. "What are you saying?" she asked, as though Fischer was talking in a foreign tongue.

"I'm saying the weapons will be much worse, the distances greater. This time it will engulf everyone."

"Not *here?*" she asked, thinking of Victoria in the cool walls of the convent across the bay. Involuntarily she looked that way.

"No, probably not, not at first, anyway. It's too far."

She came away from the window, sat down, and began to

cry. The tears must have been there just below the surface. The long absence from Fischer, the child, Morgan. She hadn't known she was going to cry, and she hadn't cried in a long time, so she cried hard, like a child. And when Fischer let her cry by herself, she wept all the harder because she felt she was letting him down.

When she finally stopped, he was watching her. The room had filled with the late afternoon light. "We must be strong, Evelyn," he said to her, like a lesson.

"I'm sorry," she said, looking for her handkerchief in her sleeve.

"My love." He had never called her that before. She looked up quickly to see him watching her, and she touched the butterfly wings again to reassure herself. He went on, "We are both experienced people of the world. You can cry now, if you have to, but you must listen and you mustn't cry. You can be afraid, if you wish, because I am." Fischer, afraid? "But there will be no time for tears later, none at all. We must save ourselves and those we love. You understand that, don't you? You and I, we're strong, and they'll rely on us."

His words soothed her. If Fischer was with her, it would be all right, no matter what happened. She stood up, excused herself, and went through the bedroom to the bathroom, where she bathed her face. Her eyes were red from crying. When she came back Fischer had poured more wine. She took it and put her cheek against his. She was quite steady when she asked, "Are you leaving me?"

"No, my dear," he said, shaking his head, "no."

The relief was as great as the grief that had overwhelmed her. "Then I'm not afraid."

Fischer took her then, caressing her face, then her breasts while they stood facing each other as though demonstrating to each other that they would not bend. She shuddered when his hand reached her nipple, turned to strip off her dress, and stepped out of her undergarments, and soon they were on the floor among the rumpled clothing. The feel of the hair on his body against her own soft skin roused her, inflamed memory so that she had no shame, and Fischer had an appetite that he had not had before. He savaged her, and she cried out, but when he withdrew she cried, "No! No! No!" Fischer made love the best way, selfishly—used her for his own pleasure and left her satiated.

The room was dark with twilight when they were spent, damp with sweat, love, their secrets. Lying apart on the hard floor was shameless, stripped them of all privacy.

"I love you, Fischer," Evelyn managed to say, not caring if he wanted to hear it. It was against the rules of their life together.

"I know," he said. "I'm grateful."

"I'm going to tell you everything," he said after the moment for his reply had passed.

As they lay in each other's arms in the darkened bedroom, Fischer sketched a picture in which Europe would be aflame, Asia lost, America at bay. His calm made it worse.

"And in the end?" Evelyn asked when he had stopped. The curtains were still open to reveal bright stars in a soft black night.

"I think America will win."

"Surely there's no doubt."

"There's timing," Fischer said. "It won't be easy to bring America into the war. Europe could be gone by then; Asia, too. In any case, the old empires will be gone."

She wanted to cry. She had lost one world already, made her concessions, and now another was to vanish. "When?"

Fischer moved away from her. She heard him sigh and could imagine his expression. "When Germany is strong enough. It will be a delicate calculation. England will have to rearm, and she'll have to do it quietly to keep the pacifists from marching. One day they'll have to bring Churchill back." He sat up impatiently, as though if he could take charge he would sort all this out immediately, without the troubles others would have. "It's all so unnecessary," he commented. "It could have been arranged at the conference table in 1918."

"Why wasn't it?"

"Idealism," Fischer said, and for once she heard not the

calm observation of human foible, but bitterness. "Between Europe's feuds and America's idealism we've created another war. And if America wins . . ." He shrugged his heavy shoulders.

"But surely she has to. She *must,*" Evelyn said desperately. *"We* must."

"I suppose." He was weary of even his own cleverness.

"So what happens now?"

He moved away, his voice coming from the shadows. "Any number of events can happen now, none more than a prologue. The question is, what can one person do?"

"To stop it?"

He laughed, a terrible, sarcastic laugh. "Oh, my dear, have you learned nothing? We can only protect ourselves."

She thought for a moment and found that she didn't care if there was nothing she could do to stop whatever was coming. She didn't have the passionate belief in a country that she had had as a child. She wasn't English, except by passport—a paper document, no more. She had never felt Russian.

Fischer came back from the shadows. "Evelyn," he said, sitting on the bed in a blue silk dressing robe from Charvet, ravishingly expensive and reassuring after his words of disaster. He lit a cigarette, snapped the onyx and diamond lighter shut, and said, "I'm not a young man. There are things I must do to keep my family"—he saw her pain, for he took her hand in his warm grasp—"and you safe. You may not agree with them, but I may need your assistance, so I am going to tell you of my business dealings." He paused, drew on the cigarette. The dark Russian tobacco, again rich and reassuring, filled the room with smoke. "These dealings will make us very rich."

She registered the "us." Fischer had never spoken of his finances before, and she had no idea how rich he was.

"How?" she asked.

"Where money is always made before a war." His voice showed little pleasure. "In the rearmament."

"Of Germany?"

"No, no," he said, shaking his head. "A Jew? It's too late for Jews to make money there. The Germans themselves—von Thiessen, Krupp—are already making more fortunes. They created the little devil Hitler for that purpose, among others. No, in Asia. Japan."

"You'll go to Japan to help them?" She couldn't help the shock that filled her voice. He dropped her hand, and she quickly took his back. "I'm sorry, I don't understand."

"You *must*," he said forcefully. He was seldom angry with her, but now he was that and more—impatient. She saw he was stretched thin. She wanted to ask if there wasn't some other place they could go to hide. But he had said it would engulf everyone, even the degenerates and debauchers of Hollywood, which seemed the more obscene for playing against such a backdrop.

"Tell me, Fischer," she said. "I'll help you." Their roles were changing, and that scared her, too.

He turned to put out the cigarette with his free hand but left his wrist in her grasp. "Metal," he said. "Japan needs metal to build the ships and planes, guns." He might have been talking about a shopping list. "I've been there to talk to them several times, as you know. Britain won't sell to them, nor will America . . . legally."

"So where will they get this metal?" she asked, hope flaring up. If they couldn't arm, then they couldn't go to war.

"Here."

"But you said . . ."

"I said legally," Fischer said in the same flat voice. "The metal can be bought here as scrap—cars, old ships, anything—it doesn't matter what it once was, as long as it's purchased by an American and shipped to another American port. There it can be unloaded and shipped on to Japan as long as it's purchased in the second port by a national of a neutral country and shipped through another neutral port."

"So complicated."

"For perhaps a hundred million dollars," Fischer said dryly, "a little complication is to be expected."

The magnitude of the profit stunned her. "My God."

"It's very large, isn't it?" Fischer said, exhaling. "A hundred million dollars, even divided a few times, could provide security in whatever world we have some years from now."

Evelyn took her hand away from his skin. She lay back among the soft pillows. Her mind refused to take in the scope of the fortune. "How will it be done?" she asked.

Fischer laughed very softly. "Quietly," he said. "And respectably, the way all really great fortunes are made. Tonight at dinner you'll see one of the partners."

"Who?"

"Agnelli himself. Who else? He can't sell to the Japanese directly, but his allegiances are, shall we say, divided. He's Italian. He sees a greater Europe, with Italy as . . . as who knows what? Men dream out of their own inadequacies, their frustrations, and Agnelli came here forty years ago as a poor child and was called names, but now he owns one of the greatest private banks in California. He'll buy the metal to arm Japan because he thinks that Italy may benefit if England, France, Holland are stripped of their colonies, or at least kept busy in the East while Germany and Italy take Europe. It's a fallacy, but one which, by coincidence, will make Agnelli richer by light-years than he already is. He will buy the metal here. And I will arrange the shipment to Manila—the Philippines are a United States protectorate, so theoretically that is still an American port—and there you—"

"Me?"

"You have a British passport." And she had thought he arranged the passport for her and the child. Now she was saddened, but he was still speaking, and she had to listen, to understand every word, because if she failed him, he might not offer her this chance again. "You will take delivery as a British subject in Manila and ship the metal on to Japan, through some Chinese port—Shanghai or Canton. It may not be necessary to touch it there at all. If not, then Tu—"

"Big-Eared Tu?" She began to see the form of the thing.

"Tu will arrange for us to pass through China without

formality. He wants the Japanese to attack, believes that when the European powers are gone, the spoils will be his, not Japan's. Another fallacy. The metal then will go to Yokohama."

Neither of them asked what would become of it then. It would be made into weapons, which would come back to kill thousands, millions.

Evelyn walked to the bathroom and stood naked, looking at herself in the mirror. She was thirty and perhaps more beautiful than as a child because she had lost the smooth puppy fat of youth; her breasts were good, firm and large, and her complexion was still miraculously that of a woman raised in the damp English climate. But she was too old to endure the destitution that she had withstood as a younger woman. She had a child to take care of. But she could if she had to, she thought. People could do remarkable things.

She was weak, she thought, looking into her own violet eyes. She bathed her face carefully and went back into the bedroom. Fischer was smoking in the dark, the Balkan Sobranie tobacco filling the room. "Is there nothing that can be done?" she asked.

"I don't think so," he said from the armchair. "I thought perhaps there would be, but in Europe . . . You don't need to be involved," he said.

"Of course I'll do it," she said angrily.

Fischer smoked for a little longer. "My wife," he said abruptly from the darkness, "refuses to believe me."

She registered that he had probably had this conversation with his wife first. Perhaps he had wanted her to fulfill Evelyn's role. And for a split second she was enraged.

"She thinks I am a fool. She doesn't care for me anyway. We have been apart too long. My daughters are married, have solid bourgeois husbands in the Jewish community in Vienna. Rich, of course," he added almost to himself. "They don't believe that this man Hitler will destroy them. They think he's a German first, and all the rest . . . Anyway, they won't leave, not one of them, not even for England."

"It's not that bad," Evelyn said.

"For a Jew," Fischer said thoughtfully, "it's mortal danger. Yet they seem blind, almost as though they've imagined Hitler. Curious."

Evelyn had seen men and women like that in Russia, their worlds so secure, they couldn't conceive of threat. The czar, the czarina had committed national suicide believing that way.

"There's a stench to this," Fischer continued. "I understand that. There's a strange perfection to it also," he said with a small laugh. "None of us can do it alone—not the Japanese who came to me, not Agnelli, not myself, nor you. There's more agreement among different nationals over this—this barbaric opportunity than there could be among the nations we represent. Curious."

Evelyn sat down on his lap, and put her arms about his neck. They didn't speak any more of the metal.

Guido Agnelli could have been cast from one of the films that Evelyn had learned about from Morgan. He was tall and powerfully built; he dwarfed Fischer. She thought he was in his late sixties, but he looked perhaps forty, with tightly curled gray hair, dark eyes, a prominent nose. He was male, and she was aware of it, withdrawing from his handshake quickly.

"Welcome," he said, his voice booming through the baronial hall. They had crossed the bridge in the car he sent for them, the span strung like Evelyn's necklaces—a long-ago gift from Fischer—of single diamonds strung along a platinum thread. She wore the two butterfly pins also, on her shoes this time. Fischer had been amused to see her snip the black satin bows off with a nail scissors and clip on the diamonds.

"Yes," Fischer said, smiling. His superbly cut British evening clothes made his figure look solid rather than heavy. His dinner jacket was double breasted, his tie flaring with small dark butterfly wings of its own. He was the Fischer she loved: luxurious, like his tobacco.

"No one will believe they are diamonds," she said, smiling at him. It was the type of joke Fischer liked: to make people reach for the counterfeit while the genuine eluded them. He always told Evelyn that he had chosen her because he understood quality, and though she knew she should have been insulted by the comparison with a good rug, fine porcelain, diamonds, vintage wine, she was secretly very pleased. The genuine item, bought at a decent price, could protect you later when you sold it. She had sometimes wondered if Fischer had assigned her a resale value, because he reminded her frequently that all possessions were to be thought of as impermanent. One bought. One sold. One didn't accumulate because then possessions became a burden.

"The English rich will understand that one day," Fischer had said. "They've accumulated for generations, and now they will divest themselves. It's the same principle, only over a longer period of time. We have no time, so we must be fluid."

But who would buy her? The time had come to take Fischer's lessons to heart.

Agnelli moved just enough to allow his hooded eyes a thorough look at her breasts, which were exposed in the loose drapings of her bugle-beaded gown. Evelyn looked into Agnelli's eyes, thinking he would be embarrassed, but instead he raised his eyebrows in silent appreciation.

Fischer said, "Countess Lezenski has put her daughter in school nearby."

The house was on the same side of the peninsula as the convent. Evelyn said, "Yes, the nuns of the Holy Cross."

Agnelli lost a moment while he reassessed her, then said, "An excellent education for a young woman. I have a granddaughter there. She goes by day."

"My daughter will stay here when I return to the East."

"Of course. Sad, but necessary to insure the proper upbringing." They were moving through the enormous yellow stone hall with the red and yellow staircase that wound toward a minstrels' gallery above. They passed through a lower hall carpeted with rich green and red Orientals, then down more steps into a room two stories high with a large hooded fireplace that rose to a point where a crucifix held a tortured Christ. There were two green velvet sofas beside the fire, many tables holding lamps, crystal ashtrays, dishes, and everywhere religious art: paintings, scrolls, illuminated manuscripts behind glass.

A short woman rose from the sofa at their entrance. "My wife," Agnelli said, and there was a change in his voice. He's afraid of her, Evelyn thought as Mrs. Agnelli looked at her, then Fischer, then her husband. Evelyn saw the flash of warning in the lady's eyes and thought: She knows he's a womanizer, and she knows how to deal with it.

Fischer approached, took her offered hand, and bent over it. And vain, too, Evelyn thought as the woman raised her head to preen as Fischer brushed the air near her hand with his lips.

"A very beautiful house, signora," Fischer murmured.

Signora Agnelli smiled more broadly. She was about to comment when her husband said, "We bought it and had it brought over stone by stone from the village where we were born." The fury that passed across his wife's face left him unperturbed. They don't like each other, Evelyn thought. They've built all this together, and they don't like each other anymore.

"Roberto, call the servants," Signora Agnelli said, sitting down.

"Your pictures are magnificent," Fischer said smoothly. Agnelli cast a sly look at Evelyn.

"I bought them on the advice of the cardinal," Signora Agnelli said in a disinterested tone.

Evelyn carefully chose a chair far away from Signora Agnelli's husband, and when the servant arrived to offer drinks she requested mineral water. Fischer looked at her in surprise, then took a glass of wine. Agnelli drank scotch and his wife nothing, not even water.

"You are here for a holiday?" she asked Evelyn with the flat hostility of a plain woman for an attractive one.

"Countess Lezenski has brought her daughter to the Convent of the Holy Cross."

"Here?" The surprise was rude.

215

"Yes," said Evelyn evenly, "here."

Signora Agnelli raised her heavy shoulders in a shrug. Her silence said more than words.

They talked then of Europe, and when the lady understood that Evelyn had not accompanied him, she flowered again, ignoring Evelyn while she and Fischer spoke of Rome, of Florence, of Naples, where it was understood the Agnellis had the use of the king's villa whenever they wanted.

Agnelli, bored, came to stand near Evelyn's chair. "I have never been to Shanghai," he said.

"It might suit you," Evelyn said to him. He moved closer to her chair than was comfortable, bullying as Fischer would never have.

"I've always thought so. Perhaps I'll go out there."

"We'd be happy to entertain you."

"Where?" demanded Signora Agnelli, cutting off Fischer's smooth flow of talk.

"The Far East."

She made a scoffing sound. "Dirt," she said. It was left to the listeners to decide whether it was them or the actual place to which she referred. Evelyn wondered how Agnelli had managed to have herself invited tonight. She could imagine what the lady would have to say about her after the evening was over. Then she understood that though he might be afraid of his wife at one level, it was Agnelli who decided who came to the house where business was concerned, and his wife's greed forced her to go along.

"And disease," Agnelli said cheerfully. "Like Naples," he added mischievously.

His wife shot off the sofa as though bitten. "Dinner will be ready soon," she said. "I will check on the kitchen," and she was gone without a backward look.

Agnelli cocked his head, smiled. "I apologize," he said.

Neither Fischer nor Evelyn said anything.

"So," Agnelli said looking at Evelyn, "we are to be partners." Fischer, Evelyn saw, was watching detachedly.

"Fischer has said I may be needed." She wanted Agnelli to be clear where her allegiance lay.

"Yes," Agnelli said, looking at Fischer. "Of course."

Fischer's look at Evelyn was one of understanding. Agnelli might be richer, but Fischer was the more experienced. "I have told Countess Lezenski the details in outline."

Agnelli drank deeply on his scotch and soda. "The money is arranged," he said. "We can conclude everything tomorrow if you want to come to my office at the bank."

"Good," Fischer said. "We sail on Friday."

"So soon?"

"We've been away from Shanghai for three months," Fischer said. "There are matters that I have to attend to. And I want to see Samoa."

Agnelli laughed. "Samoa?"

"Yes," Fischer said. "I've had a curiosity to see Samoa."

"Then we shall have to arrange everything so you can leave with your mind at rest."

13

Mop-headed palms waved from the corniche beyond the beach as the steamer passed through the narrow entrance to Moorea Bay. Papeete lay sleepily in the morning sun. Metal roofs patchworked toward the slope of the mountains that rose in shades of pale to deepest green. Fischer said, "Except for the town, this must have been exactly as Cook first saw it." He leaned on the rail in his cream linen suit, his eyes fixed on the line of surf that rolled in across the reef.

The Matson Line ship cut engines, and the anchor dropped with a shriek into the clear blue water. Canoes pushed toward the liner through the surf, and the fresh breeze brought music to the passengers lined up along the rail.

Evelyn put her arm through Fischer's. "We could stay here," she said, leaning her head against his shoulder.

Fischer smiled. He had become almost a different man on the journey from San Francisco. Always thoughtful, he now seemed lost in his own thoughts. At Honolulu they'd gone ashore, but Fischer had asked to return to the ship within the hour. "And you could wear a grass skirt," he suggested.

"You would go out on the reef to fish for our dinner."

The canoes were directly below the ship. Looking down at natives offering up necklaces and woven mats, Fischer said, "We would starve."

"You'd learn," Evelyn said.

A passenger threw a silver dollar that spun over and over to drop into the still water. A dozen dark-skinned boys dived after it. Fischer sighed. "Money," he said.

Evelyn thought Fischer might refuse to go ashore. She said quietly, "It's no different from coconuts."

Fischer put his hand over hers as he led her away from the rail and over the lintel into the dining room, where a long buffet was set out for breakfast. "You can eat a coconut." Evelyn followed Fischer, wondering if his mood would lift soon. The final arrangements had been made with Agnelli for the loan. The metal would be accumulated from all over America, from junkyards and scrap dealers, and shipped to Seattle, San Francisco, Long Beach, and San Diego for shipment on. Fischer seemed to have a need to explain each detail of the deal, though clearly it gave him no pleasure. Still, the precision and scope of the operation enthralled her.

Fischer took his food to a small table for two. On the first leg of the journey out of San Francisco they had sat at the captain's table, courtesy of Agnelli, but after Honolulu, Fischer had asked for a table to themselves.

"Do you mind?" he'd asked her. "The holiday spirit aggravates me."

"Of course not," Evelyn replied, though she had hoped for a small holiday, perhaps to dance, walk the decks in the moonlight. They had passed through some important moments while they were apart, and she had found herself thinking they were on a type of honeymoon, though Fischer's melancholy belied her fantasy.

"I'm not very amusing, am I, my dear?"

"Fischer, what's wrong? Is it this . . . arrangement . . ."

He looked shocked. "You?"

For a brief moment she was struck with sheer terror. Perhaps she had misjudged Fischer's mood entirely. Perhaps he was bored with her, with their life. "You can speak honestly with me," she said, though each word seemed to catch in her throat.

He held both her hands in his. "I love you, my dear. You must know that by now."

Then she did cry.

Today, watching Fischer pick at his food, her growing

concern for him rose up to make her say, "Fischer, your suit is getting too large."

He looked at her. "No, I am getting too small. My suit is not growing." He seemed amused by the idea.

"You must eat more," Evelyn said gently, for he had left most of the food he had chosen untouched.

"You have been chiding me to lose some weight for six years," he said, still smiling.

"I've changed my mind," she said. Then, after a pause, "could we go ashore?"

"Yes indeed," Fischer said. "I want to see the island as Cook saw it." He looked through the nearby porthole at the wide sweep of the bay. The island of Moorea rose like crumpled paper in a thousand different shapes of green and blue until its highest peaks were hidden by the mist, a golden sun shining through like a picture postcard. "Man hasn't spoiled it," Fischer commented. "I wonder if we could go out there. When Cook arrived, a religious sect that specialized in sexual acts lived over there. At certain times of the year they came over to the main island to put on displays. It was innocent enough, a celebration of plenty, giving thanks to the gods for the many things, including physical love. But of course the missionaries stopped all that, along with the other simple pleasures of going naked, playing in the sea."

The launch crossed the silver-green water where blue and yellow and red fish darted across the yellow sand bottom. Two canoes now followed the launch, dark-skinned native boys, some as old as their late twenties, laughing and paddling with their heavy, muscled arm to keep up with the heavily laden launch.

On the pier, Fischer said, "I would like to see Gauguin's house." They found a Renault Deux Chevaux, rust-stained and windowless. The driver, a mixed-blood Tahitian who stood shorter than Fischer, but very wide, offered to drive them down the coast. Evelyn wondered what Fischer was thinking as they climbed into the tiny car. Native women, barefooted, with baskets on their heads, their wide hips swinging in their long flower-print dresses, swayed by the roadside as the driver, laughing and calling to each of them, pushed his little car to the limits. Ganguin had left a wife and children, fled here to paint. Did Fischer contemplate a similar flight, not necessarily to here, but anywhere that no one could hold him to account? She couldn't imagine Fischer in a short lava lava like men pulling on the fishing nets along the beaches they were passing. Fischer indolent. The Fischer laughing as the driver described the women they were passing with good-humored appreciation—*"Une jolie fille, n'est-ce pas?"*—was not the Fischer she knew.

They left the sweep of the bay and were on a dirt road passing under the coconut palms. The driver said, "You know Gauguin?"

"I know his work," Fischer replied.

"A difficult man," the driver said. He laughed as though that was a compliment. "Always with the wine."

"And the paints," Fischer said.

The driver laughed harder, as though that was more absurd than being difficult. "A man comes here six, seven, maybe more years . . . you know him. Mr. Maugham."

"The writer," Fischer said.

"He came here. He buy a window," the driver said, coming to a division in the road that seemed to take him by surprise, for he threw the small vehicle into a sharp right-hand turn that rocked them all dangerously back and forth. Fischer laughed. "He sees a window that Gauguin paints. On glass," the driver said, slowing as the road narrowed even more. "He buy from the house." The idea of someone paying for window glass, handpainted or not, astonished the driver, who showed his appreciation for life's unexpected absurdities by pressing his foot to the floor. The car shot out of the palm-fringed path and into hot sunlight. "There!" shouted the driver, "just there."

The house was a shack, unpainted, neglected. It was away from the small beach, ragged palms towering over it. The driver said to Evelyn, "Painters are poor," as though this explained the condition of the shack.

Fischer had gone ahead through the rough grass, an odd

figure in his linen suit, his Panama hat put exactly evenly on his head. The image of Fischer as a beachcomber wouldn't stick.

She joined him. "He died here," Fischer said, looking at the house where it was just possible to see the walls had once been blue, "one of the greatest painters of any age." The heat of the day pressed up from the sand and rough grass beneath their feet. "In poverty," Fischer added. "In poverty."

Out on the surface of the ocean a small boat sat almost still on the silver sea, a picture in itself. Fischer turned to follow Evelyn's gaze. "He saw this," Fischer said, and his voice was not that of the Fischer of decision, but of a younger man, perhaps the Fischer he might have been. "What courage he must have had."

"He ran away." Evelyn didn't mean it as an accusation but a simple statement of fact: Gauguin had fled his responsibilities.

But Fischer was shaking his head before she had stopped speaking. "No," he said, "not at all. This was his responsibility. This . . . the rest . . ." He stopped, searched his pocket for a handkerchief to wipe the heavy line of sweat that had broken out above his beard. Evelyn undid the clasp of her Hermès handbag, handed him her own lace handkerchief, woven by the nuns in the convent in Harbin. He wiped his face, refreshed by the eau de cologne. "Did you know he sold almost no paintings in his lifetime? He painted menus here for food."

Sensing that Fischer wanted to be alone with Gauguin's ghost, she walked down toward the black sand beach, took off her kid shoes, and stood watching the fishermen out on the reef. The waves lapped lazily near her feet, soothing her.

Behind her, the driver, who had finally left his car, said, "Soon many visitors come, many more ships." He sounded more resigned than pleased.

"I suppose so," Evelyn said.

Fischer walked back toward the car. "You want to see the island?" the driver offered. He seemed more interested in her than in the island.

"I'll have to ask my husband," Evelyn said, a lie she had never used before. She felt a thrill of the forbidden but also noticed how slyly the driver smiled at her, a seductive smile.

She walked back to Fischer, feeling ungracious, Western, too civilized. "Are you ready?" she asked. "The driver wants to know if we'd like to tour the island."

"No," Fischer said. "Let's go back to the boat. We'll come back later tonight."

In the early evening they bathed and changed like married people, moving silently around each other with consideration, touching as they leaned toward the mirrors in the bathroom, stepping aside as they chose clothes from the wardrobe. When they were done, they looked at each other ruefully, then laughed.

"What do you think?" Fischer asked. He wore the crushed white linen suit trousers he had worn earlier, a fresh shirt open at the neck, and canvas espadrilles that Evelyn had bought him in San Francisco but that he had never worn.

"Gauguin would be proud," she said. She had chosen a loose navy blue silk dress, low-heeled shoes. Beside Fischer she looked formal, almost overdressed; it was a reversal, one among many lately.

"I think perhaps not the shoes," Fischer said.

"What?"

"The Tahitians went barefoot." Fischer raised his eyebrows as though she were the formal, stuffy one.

"I can't go through the ship barefoot," she protested.

Fischer raised his shoulders. "Very well. If you cannot shed civilization . . ."

"Oh, Fischer," she said doubtfully.

"Come," he said. "Wear your shoes." He was bubbling with new laughter. "I've arranged a surprise."

They were up the companionway before she could make up her mind what to do about her shoes. There at the entrance to the gangway the ship steward was waiting with a hamper. "Sir," he said, offering it to Fischer.

The launch was below with other passengers waiting. Fischer helped Evelyn down, carrying the hamper himself.

The moon cut a gold path across the black water, and the launch headed for the lights of Papeete.

Evelyn saw the tall, shadowed outline of Moorea, looking much larger at night, almost threatening. She thought of the religious cult that had lived there once and how Tahiti must have looked to them across the water at night. Reaching down, she took off her shoes and threw them in an arc toward the white line of the surf.

"Bravo," Fischer cried, clapping his hands like a child.

Evelyn saw how the other passengers murmured among themselves. Strange, we are a scandal, she thought. In Shanghai they had never been a scandal, except to poor Alex. In San Francisco, people had been too busy to care much. But here, right on the edge of paradise, they had created a stir.

The music from the town reached fingers across the gently stirring waters of the lagoon. Laughter joined the music as they bumped against the side of the jetty. The driver was waiting for them as they came out of the launch. "I have arranged," he said with pride.

"Good man," Fischer told him.

"My friend takes you," the driver said, pointing down to where the small river that ran behind the corniche joined the sea. There was a canoe such as the original islanders must have used. "You are coming, too?" Fischer asked.

"Of course," the driver said, quite in the spirit of the night. "It is necessary for two men to row."

Fischer and Evelyn walked away from the passengers, who seemed rooted to the earth. The ground felt cool and damp beneath her silk-stockinged feet. She put her arm about Fischer's ample waist. We must look like fools, she thought, but she didn't care.

The driver's friend was naked except for a lava lava. He laughed, held up a dozen fragrant strings of flowers, and came forward to put them over Evelyn's head, then Fischer's. The driver put the hamper in the canoe, pushed it further into the shallow water, then turned to help Evelyn. But it was Fischer who, laughing, waved him away, stooped, and picked Evelyn up. Now they were truly absurd, she thought, but she was laughing with the driver and his friend as Fischer waded into the thigh-high water to deposit her roughly in the back of the canoe.

Soon they were out where the water was deeper. Dark shadows moved through the depths. The moonlight rippled with the tide. Ahead the island grew and grew until it blocked out the sky and the horizon. This time it was silence that came to draw them forward. Evelyn looked back involuntarily to where the ship was framed with lights in the bay, and further in, the town seemed to rise and fall as the tide lifted the canoe.

They ran aground. Fischer said, "You will have to fend for yourself."

"So much for chivalry," she said, hitching up the silk skirt and leaping after him into the water, which was deliciously warm. She felt abandoned, free as she had never been. While Fischer waded in she allowed herself the sensation of walking through the shadows, feeling the touch of the water. The driver and his friend were pulling the canoe up the beach.

Fischer was searching in the pale moonlight for a place to put the hamper. He explored the beach and the grass beneath the coconut palms that arched toward the water with the same meticulous care he applied to everything else. Evelyn followed him inland into the silence to where the vegetation was denser, the night darker. The palm trees were interspersed with rustling casuarinas. She could feel the hush wrap itself about them.

In a small clearing, Fischer said, "Here."

The trees pressed about them. Above, the night was black, sparkling with stars. The moon was unseen, a dim light above the rim of trees. They could hear the driver and his friend laughing in the distance.

Fischer knelt down, a child playing in the shadows. He took out a linen cloth with the ship's crest on it, two plates, two wine glasses, champagne. Evelyn found she was crying. He never spoke of his youth, but now she saw he must once have been a playful child. All his knowledge of the world that she admired, relied on, must have cost him dearly, bitterly.

When he was done, he asked, "Do you like it?"

"I would like anything you did," she heard herself say.

She thought she had spoiled the moment because his smile faded, but it quickly returned. When the chicken, fruit, and wine were all arranged, he said, "Sit with me."

She folded to the grass. The air was heavy with perfume. "I feel so sleepy," she said. "I could fall asleep again."

"An honorable Polynesian tradition," Fischer said, pouring wine into the glasses. He offered her one. "They had no understanding of work at all when the missionaries arrived, just play. They lived off the lagoon and the breadfruit trees. They danced and made love. . . ."

"It sounds wonderful," Evelyn said, sipping the sharp, tart champagne.

"And they slept at any time. The first missionaries were startled to find the natives would lie down beside the road and fall immediately into sleep for ten minutes or an hour, shaded by the bushes and trees. They thought it outrageous sloth."

"How foolish." She leaned back against Fischer. "And yet they allowed this life to be taken from them."

"They had no concept of war," Fischer said as he raised his own glass. "There had been wars, fierce ones, and there were other tribes on other islands who were warlike, but here they had come to an accommodation with nature and forgotten how to fight. They believed in the essential goodness of men. That was their downfall."

She loved him. "Fischer," she said, looking at him in the dim moonlight, "I think you do, too."

He was startled. "No," he said, but she continued to accuse him with her stare. "I believe," he said with a sigh, his eyes slipping away to where they could see the dance of the moonlight on the rougher surface of the ocean beyond the reef, "that there are still possibilities for goodness, but I think most people are corrupted young. The world is too complicated now," he finished thoughtfully. "Events move too fast."

"As they did here," Evelyn said.

"Yes. They were corrupted, destroyed, without ever understanding what was happening. Many of the natives slept themselves to death, did you know that? Oh, yes, that, too, was a tradition. A man who was tired of life could lie down beside the road, and his body would stop. There was no shame. It was a phenomenon of nature, the first westerners thought, but in fact it wasn't so peculiar. A thousand years before, these Polynesians had set off from the continent of Asia, fleeing God knows what, and crossed the Pacific in their canoes, going from island to island looking for their half-formed dreams. They must have brought with them the same impulses that elsewhere created Buddhism, yoga, all the eastern cults in which the mind controls the body, for here, hundreds of years later, they could will themselves to a gentle death."

Evelyn held Fischer's hand. "We could stay here, Fischer," she said harshly, and her desperation ruined the moment.

Fischer undid her grasp, purportedly to pour more wine, but she felt that he was abandoning her, and she reached for him again. "Fischer, we don't need all this money. We don't need to go on."

"I suppose not," Fischer said, watching as the yellow liquid bled from the bottle into the waiting glasses. "And your little house in China," he teased her, "the house you love so much. What would become of that?"

"We would build another blue house, like Gauguin's, here. You would fish for us."

"And you?" Fischer asked her, his eyes very bright near her face. "What would you do?"

"I would wait for you to come back from the lagoon to make love to me. Make love to me, Fischer, now, here. . . ."

Fischer took the glass from her hand. They could hear the voices of the driver and his friend. Nothing moved about them except the breeze in the casuarina trees, rustling dryly.

Fischer put his hand on her neck, raised her face to his, and kissed her slowly. She touched the hair of his chest, spilling out of his open shirt. Lying back on the grass, she could imagine what Fischer would look like if they stayed here. His beard would grow unkempt, his hair long, his body firmer, heavier like the Tahitians. He would wear less clothing and look more as he did now, taking off his shirt to reveal his barrel chest. He undressed himself first—unusual—and crouched naked above her, his sex dangling between his legs.

He began to make love to her, hungrily, without his old care and tenderness, making all of her body respond to him, first with his kisses that plunged deep into her mouth, then the heat of his breath as he ran his own mouth along the line of her chin, down her arching throat. As his hands slid into the silk dress a button tore, and he pulled the dress away to free her breast.

She felt an abandon she had never known, not even the first night that they had made love in the temple with the snow falling outside. That night had been silent, too, but with a silence that shut them in, whereas now they were becoming one with the grass about them, the wind, the trees, and the joyous noise of the two Tahitians who were playing in the water of the lagoon.

When she was naked, he touched every inch of her body with his mouth, as though he could take sustenance from her. She became quieter, the languor working like a drug within her. She watched how Fischer gained strength, how his eyes glittered, how his body loomed above her, blocking out a patch of the sky; and when she raised her legs for him to enter her she heard a voice that was not at all like hers say, "Fischer, Fischer, Fischer," an invocation broken as he entered her, and then they were making love, the love of two bodies that know everything there is to know of each other yet still find pleasure, ecstasy, need. . . .

Later, they held each other. Still later, when the natives were silent, they walked down to the beach. Choosing the ocean side of the island where the water was rougher, they swam like children, diving to the sand of the ocean floor and rising into the warm night air. Coming back naked hand in hand up the beach, they saw that their guides were asleep, wrapped around each other like children. In the clearing it seemed too much trouble to dress, and then they lay awake, watching the moon make its night's journey across the bowl of the stars.

Dawn was washing the sky pink as Fischer and the two Tahitians sleepily pushed the canoe back into the water. They heard the whistle of the steamer, and Evelyn, her blue dress a ruin, realized she didn't care if they missed the sailing. Premonition washed about her like the cool water of the sea as she waded out to the canoe. Fischer helped her in. The natives looked at her with happy eyes.

Smoke plumed out of the stacks of the ship as they headed inland. "To the ship," Fischer said. "Not the town."

The canoe changed direction. Evelyn sat back, watching as the sky became lavender, then mother-of-pearl. The shrill whistle screamed in the dawn. The propellers were churning the water as they came alongside. The gangway was gone, and from the bridge they saw the officers staring down at the canoe in outrage. After some minutes a cargo net was dropped down the side of the ship.

"My dear," Fischer said, laughing, "we climb or we stay."

She willed him to say "Let us stay," even if for a few days, a week. They could take another ship.

"I'm sorry," Fischer said, taking her hand to steady her as the net whipped against the metal plates of the ship.

After dinner, Evelyn and Fischer walked on deck. The breeze carried the smell of earth and the very faint fragrance of flowers. A small island clipper passed a hundred yards away, a ghostly shadow with a single white lantern on its mast. Fischer lit a cigar with the heavy gold lighter that Evelyn had given him on their second anniversary.

Fischer was blowing out smoke, a familiar odor that reminded Evelyn of the first night she had met him, the memory as powerful as though it had been yesterday. He spoke, breaking in on her thoughts; Evelyn recognized his melancholy tone. "One wonders whether it matters," Fischer said. "There will be another war. Some nations and people will survive, and some will not. When you listen to people you see that it doesn't matter much. The mandate of heaven . . ."

"What?"

"A Chinese belief, very ancient, that to rule you must have the mandate of heaven. When you lose it, power passes to other hands, as it did from Russia, and before that, Rome. America will rule a few years, maybe a century. . . ."

"Fischer," Evelyn said, because he seemed lost in his own reverie, "we don't need this money."

Then Fischer said without looking at her, the cigar in one hand, the other in the pocket of his dinner jacket, "Marry me."

The shock was such that she thought he might be joking, though Fischer was neither cruel nor stupid.

"Your wife . . ." she blurted.

Fischer turned. His eyes were serious, glowing like the cigar tip. "They don't need me. I'm an embarrassment. Cassandra, always prophesying doom. I saw that when I was there, but I had decided to ask you to marry me anyway." When she didn't speak, he said, "I'm not sure I understand much about love, my dear. I'm almost old now, and I'm cynical. But we are good for each other, we take care of each other. If that's enough, then please marry me."

He sounded so humble that tears came to Evelyn's eyes. "All right," she said, then she laughed. "Oh, Fischer," she said, "we're both fools, you know. All right!" she repeated, just to hear herself say such a silly thing again. "Fischer, I love you. Yes," she said. "I'll marry you. Yes, Fischer, I will."

"Good," Fischer said, smiling. He leaned forward to brush her lips with his own, the first time he had ever kissed her in public. "That's settled. I'll have my lawyers in Geneva make the arrangement for us. It may take a while."

"I can wait," Evelyn said. She kissed him hard, holding him about the shoulder. When they broke, she saw that once more they were the focus of all the eyes of the passengers taking their last stroll along the deck.

He threw his lighted cigar in an arc, high and distant, over the black water. The red tip burned all the way, a rainbow of a single color, then was extinguished in a flash as it hit the water. "Should I carry you to the cabin?" Fischer teased her as they went back into the brightly lighted interior of the ship.

"Until we're married," she said demurely, "I'll walk on my own two feet."

"A sensible woman. I like that."

In their cabin they took their time preparing for bed, both nervous. There had been an important change in their life. When Evelyn was in her own bed, Fischer came into the cabin in his white silk pajamas. The pink nightlight near the door to the bathroom was all he left burning. He came to her bed then and slipped under the sheets beside her. They were awkward together, almost embarrassed, and when the lovemaking was done they held to each other like children.

"Don't worry," Fischer whispered. "It gets better."

"I know," Evelyn whispered back.

"You have no sentiment," he said, and he moved to get out of bed.

"Fischer, stay with me tonight," Evelyn asked, holding his shoulder.

"You won't sleep."

"I will," she said, still whispering to him as though they might be overheard, "better than I ever have."

So they slept fitfully together for some hours, then more deeply. When Evelyn woke, Fischer lay half over her, and she found it hard to breathe. She touched his shoulder to move him gently, and his skin was cool. She turned him over, saw how his eyes stared at her. The tears came flowing steadily as she, too, became so cold that she might as well have taken that last journey with him. "Oh, Fischer, Fischer, how could you?" she whispered, holding him to her breast.

Fischer was dead.

BOOK

FOUR

Manila, 1937

14

Evelyn stood in the shade, her hand to her eyes, watching the Pan American Constellation come in low over the palm trees at the edge of the airfield. The vibration of the twin propellers obscured the silver plane, but the noise came roaring ahead, deafening the people gathered to meet the passengers, many of whom had come all the way from San Francisco with stops in Hawaii, Guam, and Hong Kong. She turned her head away, as though the plane might miss the runway and come crashing on toward the two-story terminal, built two years ago to celebrate the independence of the Philippines from United States rule.

With her back turned, she heard the plane touch down once with a scream of tires, bounce, and touch down again. Then the engine made the growling sound of a beast, and she turned back to see the plane turning very slowly on the steaming tarmac where the ramps waited.

The plane had looked small as it came in from the sea, a silver bird, then large as it came down to land. Now, taxiing to a stop, it looked vulnerable and small again. She thought then of how the planes that were bombing Nanking must look. She had read the reports of the Japanese invasion of China, both for their news value and because she couldn't stop herself.

She knew Agnelli would be the first off the Constellation, as always. The ramp was just at the silver tube, the door just open, when she saw him push his way into the sunlight, thick-bodied, bullish. He didn't blink but came down the ramp at a run, briefcase in hand. He'd gotten accustomed to

Manila in this last year; he wore a loose white suit, a cotton shirt, also white, and a pale tie. Two-tone shoes, brown and white brogues, added a new dash since his last visit.

She saw him search for her among the waiting Filipinos on the second-story deck of the terminal. He waved, and she lifted her hand slightly, then turned toward the ninety-degree sunshine with ninety-five percent humidity. Customs and immigration would take one look at his passport, read whatever secret codes defined him as a very important person, and wave him through. But while immigration might understand the difference between the common herd and the important travelers, the Filipino baggage handlers, moving now toward the plane at a leisurely pace in their multicolored see-through shirts, did not. All the luggage would be thrown out at the same time.

Since Fischer's death she had traveled the triangle from Shanghai to Manila to San Francisco enough times that to Pan American Airlines, at any rate, she herself was a very important person.

She had hoped—no, assumed—that Victoria would come here to Manila on leaving the convent in Marin. In preparation for Victoria's arrival she had rented the big house out at the Marquesa de Camellias, the house with so much shade that the grass beneath the banyan trees only grew in spots, but Victoria had gone to Shanghai. Thank God she had kept the blue house. Maybe she had known in some part of her that Victoria wouldn't come to Manila.

"I want to find my father," Victoria had announced when Evelyn met her off the boat in Shanghai. She had become astonishingly beautiful: gold-eyed after Alex, dark-haired like her mother, a mocha complexion that was probably Evelyn's own English complexion dusted by California sunlight. She had a lithe body, very tall, again like Alex, and carried herself defiantly.

"I don't know where he is," Evelyn had said.

"No, of course you wouldn't," Victoria told her.

Agnelli came right out of immigration. He kissed her on the cheek. "So," he said with no preamble, "problems."

"Yes."

"What the hell is going on in China? It doesn't make sense."

"The Chinese have declared war on the Japanese," Evelyn replied.

"Some little yellow men fighting each other—what's that got to do with us? The Japs have been in Manchuria for five years."

"This time they may have overstepped—they created an incident in a village outside Peking, then demanded reparation for a dead soldier."

"Never!" That he could understand. He ran his fat finger around the inside of his limp collar.

"Chiang can't give in this time. He'd lose all control. Even the communists, his old enemies, are with him."

"So they shoot each other up," Agnelli said irritably. "They've done it before."

"There's an army outside Shanghai," she told him sharply. "They're trying to cut off the road between Shanghai and Nanking, where the government is."

He listened, his eyes narrowing. "Tu can get our ships through, can't he?" he asked.

"As long as Chiang's president of China, Tu can do what he wants. Chiang was one of Tu's henchmen twenty years ago, you know that."

"So where's the problem? I haven't come this distance on a whim."

"You've come this distance, Guido, because you stand to make millions," she told him dryly. They had worked together since Fischer's death. They were conspirators, not lovers, as Agnelli had suggested at their first meeting in Shanghai, when he had come running to see what could be saved of his profits. Evelyn had read all Fischer's notes by then and hidden them in the Chartered Bank in Hong Kong, and she was prepared.

"You look well," Agnelli said, the sweat pouring from a line at his brow. "Christ, I hate this climate. I guess it doesn't affect you."

"I've learned to move slowly," she said with a smile. She had taken to wearing white in the day, sharkskin suits mostly, and black at night, silk or taffeta evening dresses that had become her trademark. She hadn't given it much thought, but when Agnelli agreed to her stepping in for Fischer, she had known that she would have to have some authority, and that clothes were the place to begin. She had put away Fischer's jewels with his detailed notes on the whole operation in the safe deposit box at the Chartered Bank. For jewelry she wore jade bracelets, earrings of jade with very small but blue-white diamonds, a single platinum band that implied a marriage somewhere back. She had bought the band for herself, but no one would know. The pure apple-green jade, however, that seemed inexpensive to westerners when she had to deal with them, was easily spotted by Asians as worth as much as diamonds. Once in a while she wore flowers in the long hair drawn back at the nape of her neck in a chignon. She was elegant, she knew, but she wasn't flamboyant. She was concerned only that her appearance serve her own more distant purpose of seeing this venture to its conclusion.

"Tell me about it," Agnelli said, mopping his face with an already-damp silk handkerchief.

"It's Queson," she told Agnelli as they moved away from the crowd of people. Among the Filipinos even Evelyn felt very tall, and Agnelli towered over them. He looked like an oaf among their smiles and laughter, and his white suit seemed to fade against the men's elaborate rice cloth shirts and patterned trousers, the traditional butterfly-shouldered, brightly colored dresses of the women.

"This guy Roosevelt's been made President."

"Yes."

"He wants money."

"Someone does. I think it must be Queson. It's very"—she searched for the word—"Asian. One of his wife's cousins has come to me with a suggestion that we use their docks."

"So?"

She looked at Agnelli evenly. "So they don't have any docks."

He was shocked, then amused, then annoyed, shaking his head. "We build them docks to unload one ship and load another. That's it?"

"Yes."

"And when this is over they get to keep the docks."

"That's more or less it," she admitted.

"They might as well hold a gun to us," Agnelli said.

"That wouldn't be their way. It all has to have the illusion of legality, of business, of friendliness."

"But they still get to keep the goods."

"Yes," she said.

They walked out of the terminal into the searing sunlight. Agnelli's heavy Abercrombie and Fitch bags came sliding across the rack. Two porters took them at Agnelli's gesture and carried them to the curb. At some unseen signal, Evelyn's dark gray Buick with the Filipino driver had slid out of the rank of chauffeured cars and was waiting for them.

They didn't speak again until they were moving away from the curb toward the avenue of royal palms leading to Admiral Dewey Boulevard. They passed through an area of shacks no taller than Agnelli's shoulder where a hundred thousand people squatted amid piles of garbage, lean dogs, half a dozen water taps, and rows and rows of ragged laundry. They headed for the center of the city, the cathedral and the new palace just visible. At the edge of the bay loomed the imposing white Manila Hotel, designed by Parson of New York, and, by the terms of the new constitution, incorporating a penthouse apartment in perpetuity for the American advisor to the Philippines.

"How is Rachel?" Evelyn asked.

"More religious than ever," Agnelli said. "If I didn't stop her, I would own a cathedral by now, or at least have paid for one. She's in Rome."

"I heard that you had been awarded the Order of Isabella," Evelyn said.

Agnelli beamed. "Franco gave it to me."

"For services rendered."

"He's been the savior of Spain," Agnelli said defensively. "The Marxists would have ruined it. Where did you read that?"

"In *Time* magazine."

"Luce is a good man. He understands power."

The palms along Admiral Dewey Boulevard stood still in the midafternoon heat. "He's behind Chiang, too," Evelyn said, thinking of how Shanghai had resembled an armed camp when she was there last month. The European settlement huddled behind its treaty line while the Japanese prowled like jackals at the city limits.

"Chiang's a Christian, isn't he?" Agnelli asked, looking out across the bay. "What's that?"

"Corregidor Island. The bigwigs all go there on holiday."

"Did you speak to Tu?"

"Of course, when I was in Shanghai. If we can sort this out, the ship will go through with no trouble."

"Good."

She could see the American flag hanging from MacArthur's suite at the hotel as they approached. "You're coming in?" Agnelli said.

"For a moment. MacArthur's giving a reception here tonight. I'm going. I thought you should come, too."

"All right."

The car swept around the curved entrance and pulled up under the portico. In the shade they were suddenly blind for a moment after the bright sunshine. They sat side by side while the door was opened and his bags taken in, and then got out when their eyes had adjusted to the shade. They moved with the care that the climate pressed on anyone who wanted to live there any length of time. Two U.S. Marine guards stood as unostentatiously as possible at the entrance to the public hotel.

"MacArthur," Evelyn noted, stepping into the cool, tiled lobby framed by long windows onto the gardens and driveway. Beyond, an interior lobby's square pillars held up a truly imposing roof carved of local wood. "He wants to make his presence felt." She gestured with her chin across the lobby. "One elevator is set aside for his own use."

"The man understands power," Agnelli said.

"Like Luce," Evelyn commented. Before Agnelli could reply, the American manager was upon them. "Madame Lezenski, we're honored."

She shook hands, smiled, introduced Agnelli yet again. Agnelli, like many self-made men, had an open contempt for people who served him.

"Everything's ready," the manager said. "The luggage will already be in your suite, Señor Agnelli."

"Mr. Agnelli."

"Mr. Agnelli." With just the smallest hint that "Mr." was an assumed title of some type.

In the elevator up, Agnelli snorted. "I think independence will be good for this place if it gets rid of fools like that."

"That won't be the only thing to go," Evelyn commented.

In his suite looking out at Corregidor rising like a fortress from the blue water, he asked, "What did you mean in the elevator?"

She dropped her black crocodile handbag on the rattan and linen couch and took off her jacket. The air this high up freshened the room. "I mean," she said, "that the American method of business, ethics, anything you want to call it, is going out the window with American rule. It's a casino now, with everything up for grabs. The president and his family are moving in everywhere, traditional Asian business as usual. It's just as well this will be our last shipment. They might as well take out guns and hold us up. The only consolation is that it isn't personal. They're holding up everyone in sight, anyone who wants to operate in the Phillipines."

"Why's nothing being done? You don't read about it."

The explanation was wearying. It was the same in China. On the ship up to Shanghai she had met the inevitable missionaries, thrilled that Chiang, married to the daughter of a bible college graduate, was now president. They didn't know, or wouldn't believe, that Soong, Chiang's father-in-law, was one of the most corrupt men in China. One daughter was robbing the Bank of China through her husband, Chiang himself had been a hired killer, Big-Eared

Tu was behind him, and the only one of the family who might have stood examination on her ethics was the widow of the man they vilified as having opened the door to the Bolsheviks.

She hadn't tried to convince any of the missionaries of this; not out of weariness alone, but because her own interests and life—to say nothing of Victoria's, whom she had come to meet—would be endangered. It was an open town, an open country. Nobody was safe.

"It wouldn't be any better with another man," she said to Agnelli, who was standing at the window with his arms out to cool off. "It's not even considered corruption. It's . . . it's their view of human nature. They don't blame Queson and his cronies for grabbing the spoils. They would have done the same thing. It's a matter of balance more than anything else; he can do what he wants as long as everyone gets something. I don't know if I can explain it any better. It's like politics in a big American city."

"Ah," said Agnelli, turning.

She sat down on the chair to the side of the brand new couch. The couch and the three chairs were all of highly lacquered rattan, woven, she had read somewhere in the local papers, on one of the thousands of small islands that made up the Philippine archipelago. The cloth, white with a green palm leaf pattern, had been woven elsewhere, as had the rush mat on the polished floor, which itself had been hauled as a tree trunk from a Filipino rain forest. "We're going to have to pay them," she said.

"How much?"

"It depends on how much they perceive is at stake."

"Christ," Agnelli said for the third time that morning. "It's just like the old country. I hate it."

Evelyn let him think about their problem for a while. She took out a cigarette case, the single gift from Fischer that she kept on her person. The silver case had her initials in diamonds on the cover. She lit a cigarette with a black cloisonné lighter she'd bought in Hong Kong and sat back.

"You think I should meet with them?"

"Yes."

"A man's country, huh?" he said, pushing her.

She drew in smoke and said nothing.

"I didn't mean that," he said. At first Agnelli had tried to find a man to take Fischer's place, but he couldn't find one he could trust, and certainly not one who knew as many details about the whole operation.

"It doesn't matter. That's not why I asked you to come out. They're scared of America. This is the big gold rush of nineteen thirty-seven. That's what it is. On paper, Queson makes a good president—local hero, church man, American-educated—which is why Roosevelt chose him. And though it's local knowledge he's got a girlfriend who used to be a taxi dancer in a fifty-cents-a-dance club, and a wife who hates him but will never divorce him because of her religion—that he owns houses and gambling halls, among his other more legitimate interests—he's still the president of the Philippines, because America says so. And he's not going to get anybody angry who could go home and point out his other side."

"What an idiot Roosevelt is," Agnelli said.

"He couldn't have found anyone different."

Agnelli looked out at the bay. "You mean there's not an honest man out there?"

"Not one whose name would ever reach Washington," she said, wondering at his outrage. His own ethics wouldn't have pushed him easily through the eye of a needle.

"All right. When?"

"Tonight, after the reception."

She stood and reached for her coat. "Anyway, you'll get to see the whole cast at the reception tonight. MacArthur makes it a command performance. It's worth seeing."

As she walked toward the door Agnelli asked, "How is Victoria?"

She turned with her hand on the crystal handle. "She's in Shanghai."

"I'm sorry," he said. He was a kind man beneath all his greed and bluster, Evelyn knew; even a decent family man.

"She wanted to see her father," she said, and she knew he could hear her own troubles in her voice. She had been very careful to ensure that no one, particularly not Agnelli, would think her a weak woman, susceptible to emotions. She had had no life of her own since Fischer, but then she hadn't missed one.

"Will she?"

"I don't know." She let a beat pass, then decided to tell him. "Her father's in Nanking."

"Christ!" Agnelli was shocked. "What's he doing there?"

"Teaching at Chiang's staff college." She drew breath because it was hard for her to talk about it. When she sat alone in the high, dark rooms of her rented house in the Marquesa de Camellias, smoking and trying to understand what had happened and what the future held, her breathing would get shorter and shorter until even in these airy rooms she thought she would suffocate.

"He was trained as an engineer. Did you know that?" she asked, "Though of course he never used it; it was just part of their training. Anyway, he's at the staff college in Nanking training cadets for Chiang."

"He'll be on the winning side for a change." With the light of midday blazing behind him, Agnelli looked like a dark prophet.

She was silent, thinking of how Victoria had looked when she stepped off the boat from Europe, so much the young Alex of London, Poland, Russia come to life again. Suddenly afraid for her daughter, she wanted this enterprise finished so she could go to China to keep her safe.

The ship had dropped anchor after midnight. Evelyn stood on the Bund, watching as the Chinese customs launches left to bring in their immigration officials. Most ships timed their arrival for midday, starting up the long yellow course of the Yangtze at dawn, but Chiang's gunboats were stopping even the liners from Europe like the P&O *Spirit of Asia* that was bringing Victoria back from England. They were looking for Japanese spies, they said, and those they caught were executed on the riverbank.

When the immigration launches had returned, the British-born Chinese customs officials, stiff and formal in their crisp brown uniforms with the Sam Browne belts and looming above their Chinese subordinates, had the shocked expression of men caught in something beyond their control. From the length of the delay, Evelyn thought that they had probably apprehended someone political, another of Chiang's enemies. Many English officials had returned to England to live on their pensions, but others, not yet due decent pensions, were staying on in hope.

Hoping for what? Evelyn wondered, watching the first passenger tender knock against the white hull out in the river. Behind it the docks of the Whangpoo area shone with lights arranged by Big-Eared Tu to unload ships for Chiang and the Japanese. And for herself, Evelyn thought. One ship they had chartered from a Panamanian-registered company was over there. It had taken the scrap metal out of an American-registered ship in Manila and loaded it into another to clear through China. Without Tu's help, those lights would be dim and the riverbank just a line of shadow.

Her heart began its uneasy acceleration as the tender swung away from the ship. Victoria might keep her waiting, as she had in Switzerland last year.

The decision to go from California to Switzerland to finishing school had been Evelyn's. She had thought then that Victoria would fight her, insist on returning to the East. But by that time she had come to realize that she didn't know her daughter, not at all. Two years ago she had been seventeen, very tall and slender like Alex, with the same expressionless face except for the eyes, which always seemed to have their own joke. Evelyn wondered if it was her own guilt that made her so afraid when she saw the glitter in the gold depths. She wondered if the same glitter, the same contempt, was there for others.

Victoria had accepted the suggestion easily, left the convent with the sisters' blessing, and, escorted by Evelyn, been enrolled in Switzerland's most prestigious school. She had a princess for a roommate, a future queen as a schoolmate, the children of dictators and the simply rich as companions. On the way into dinner each night they were lined up in order of rank and precedent. To Evelyn's satisfaction and Victoria's amazement, Victoria Lezenski, as a deposed Russian countess, was matched with the daughter of a grandee of Spain and ahead of many minor European nobles.

Two years had passed in uneasy truce, but Victoria had been adamant about returning when she graduated.

The tender slowed, churning the oily river, and Evelyn saw Victoria in the front. She was helped up the river-washed stone steps by the uniformed porter of the P&O Line, then was upon her mother before Evelyn could be afraid.

The shock was her beauty, of the type that made you realize all your standards had been wrong until this moment. "They shot some of the deck passengers," she said. The eyes glittered as always, and she didn't kiss her mother or offer her hand.

"Oh, my dear, I'm sorry," Evelyn said, leaning forward and standing on the toes of her handmade snakeskin shoes to touch her daughter's cool cheek. The girl's dress, she saw as she stepped back, was well-made, expensive. She had told her she could buy clothes in Paris and London before boarding the boat in Southampton for the trip through Suez. Evelyn had in mind some tropical clothes, a carefully planned wardrobe for an eight-week sea journey through three climates, but this long azure gown that clung to her at the bodice and hips and swung about her calves was impractical, and excessive. She wore it with the same disregard with which the Russian nobles had worn their uniforms and jewels long ago. Her hair was held back by a dark fedora, worn like an officer's cap over one eye. The striking similarity to her father moved Evelyn to look away.

"I've brought the car," she said. "I don't expect they'll have the luggage off tonight."

Victoria shrugged. "I'd like to take a rickshaw." She drew a deep breath of the rank river air. "God, that smells so good." She looked at her mother defiantly. "I'm glad I'm back. As soon as the boat turned into the river I felt better."

"I'm sorry your homecoming was marred by the . . ." She didn't want to say executions.

The broad, elegant shoulders shrugged again. "It was interesting, in a way," Victoria said, but her brow furrowed slightly. "They looked so . . . so ordinary."

"Perhaps there was a mistake," Evelyn said. "There have been some." The fear of the Japanese army camped outside the city had driven the Nationalist Chinese to extremes of their own, and many of the executions were for old scores that had little to do with China's present crisis.

"The passengers watched," Victoria said, scanning the long line of impressive buildings along the Bund. "I'd forgotten how much like Europe Shanghai is. It looks smaller, too. I suppose that happens when you grow up." A look at her mother then, to make sure she had understood. "The oddest part was when they took them off the ship and the ship went absolutely silent. I had gotten so used to music and bells and whistles and people all about that it was twice as strange when we were silent, just standing there along the rail. Some turned away at the last moment."

But you didn't, Evelyn thought. Alex wouldn't have, either. He would have felt he owed it to the condemned to stay with them to the last moment, even if just in spirit.

Evelyn told the chauffeur, Ah Foon's husband, that they would need a rickshaw, and he signaled one out of the thick stream of traffic heading down the late-night street. The man was skin and bones, his ribcage heaving. "He can't pull both of us," Victoria pointed out. "You'll have to follow."

Evelyn had a rush of emotion that she didn't identify until she was in the back of Fischer's old Packard following Victoria, sitting as stately as a mandarin, through the moving traffic. The emotion was rage, not loss. Also a rush of guilt: This was how the girl would have looked if she had had her birthright. A proud carriage would have taken her into St. Petersburg to the winter palace, let her ride like a noble across her own estates.

For a moment Evelyn slipped back years to that tiny room above the herbalist's where Alex pored over his maps, unable to understand that it was over, an empire lost.

A bus screamed across the line of traffic, filled with Chinese, blocking her view of Victoria. Evelyn was afraid.

Craning forward, she tapped the driver on the shoulder. "Don't lose her," she commanded.

"No, mem," he said, but no one could keep up with a rickshaw in the Shanghai night traffic heading for the brothels and the nightclubs, the gambling clubs, the political meetings in hidden rooms, the power brokering in private houses and public buildings. The city was an anthill of conspiracy. There was blood and money in the air.

The rickshaw driver was waiting to be paid as they drove up to the blue house in the French quarter. Evelyn blessed her own foresight in keeping the house. At the time she had thought it an extravagance. She was rich enough even then not to have worried, but Fischer had taught her that you could never be rich enough. Fischer had taught her his own type of frugality also. No amount of money was wasted on jewels or luxury for yourself, but the essentials—houses that you didn't need, servants, cars, chauffeurs—all of that you could acquire at any time.

"It's my banker father's background," Fischer had said. "You can spend any amount of money at one time, but a slow leak will ruin you. The overhead is the only thing you need to watch. Keep that in line with your ambitions, and you can give yourself anything you want at least once."

She had defied him, keeping the blue house out of the worst of motives: sentiment. Fischer had left her no more money, but to her surprise, he had willed her the temple in Harbin, a sentimental gesture of his own. The lawyer read the will in his dry British voice, clearly disapproving of an adventuress who was getting exactly what an adventuress deserved. Over his lawyer's half spectacles he had stopped his crisp reading to enjoy her tears, not knowing that it wasn't the loss of money that Evelyn cried for, but the loss of the Fischer she had just begun to know. Besides, Fischer had left her his careful notes, and she knew, because of all Fischer's hours of training, what to do.

She was back in San Francisco within a month, and then back here again to see Tu. That had been the time she decided to keep the house, rationalizing that she would need a place in Shanghai. She knew Fischer would have whispered that she could have the most expensive suite in the Cathay Hotel for what it would cost to keep the blue house, Ah Foon, the house servants, and Ah Foon's husband as a driver and gardener when she was away.

Victoria was standing in the long hall facing on the garden. She had pulled off the brown felt fedora, and her hair, thick and shining, lay on her shoulders. "You haven't changed anything," she said.

"No." Evelyn went into the small living room where Ah Foon had set a fire against the spring chill. There were candles burning on the red lacquer chow bench in front of the long divan. Evelyn snuffed them out and went about switching on the lights until the room was nakedly revealed: the red divan, the multicolored Persian carpet, the willow furniture that had been her prize years ago. When Fischer had bought this house she could remember agonizing over every item she put into it, but now she never thought about furniture—now just money.

"Why did you keep it?" Victoria asked her.

"I thought we might need a home someday," Evelyn answered. "Would you like something to eat?"

"I'd like something to drink," her daughter said.

Startled, Evelyn turned and rang the long bell pull by the fireplace. When Ah Foon came in, bowing nervously to Victoria as she was introduced, Evelyn said, "Bring the drinks tray, please."

They stood awkwardly, neither of them choosing either the red divan or the two formal carved wooden chairs that stood sentinel by the fireplace until Ah Foon rolled a cart of glass and bamboo into the room. There was ice and several bottles of liquor. "What do you drink?" she asked Victoria.

"Scotch will do," her daughter told her, walking around touching items: the small collection of jade and rose quartz birds on twin shelves flanking the fireplace, the Japanese scrolls of peach blossoms that accentuated the rose silk, the door handles on the long French doors that opened onto the garden.

"When did you learn to drink?" Evelyn asked her, bringing her the scotch. The door handles were carved crystal and worth as much as the rose quartz birds. Fischer had bought them, and she noted how Victoria appraised them. She had her aunt's look then—greed—except in Natasha it had been directed toward food.

"In the convent," Victoria answered, a gleam of defiance in her eyes. She took a long draw on it, then walked past her mother to top it up. "That's better."

Evelyn sat down in the chair by the fire. "I'm glad you're . . ." She had been about to say "home," but it occurred to her that this had never been Victoria's home. "Back."

"Do you know," Victoria said, standing by the open doors to the garden, "that I thought about Shanghai all the time I was in school?" She looked back over her shoulder. "I did." The girl sounded almost soft, the way Evelyn had thought she would be. "All those days and nights in California when other girls talked about their houses and families, I didn't envy them once. That surprises you, doesn't it?" Maybe a little defiance there, Evelyn thought. She saw how rigid Victoria's neck and shoulders were, a proud carriage, but filled with tension. "They talked about things that I didn't know anything about, and I didn't care. I wanted to be back here."

"Well, you're back now," Evelyn said weakly.

"Yes, I am," Victoria said, sipping her drink.

Evelyn drew breath. She had to return to Manila in three days to meet Agnelli. "I wish you would come with me to Manila," she began, "for a while, anyway."

"I have no reason to go to Manila."

The hurt struck. "No," her mother said quietly, "I suppose you don't. But I would feel better if you came with me for a little while. The East—"

"What would there be for me in Manila?" Victoria demanded.

A second arrow, this time less painful. "I have a house there where you could be comfortable. There's a nice social life among the young American officers. I thought after California you might enjoy yourself."

"No."

"Shanghai isn't a good place for a young girl alone," Evelyn said.

"I won't be alone."

"What do you mean?"

"My father's here, isn't he?" Victoria said, sending the next shot right to her mother's heart. "I won't be any more alone here than I would be in Manila."

Evelyn walked across the room and barely stopped herself from showing her own feelings by pouring a drink. Instead, she said, "I haven't heard from your father in years."

"Have you tried to get in touch with him?"

Of course she hadn't. "He wouldn't have wanted me to try to contact him," Evelyn said, rearranging the four glasses on the cart. She heard Victoria crossing the room.

"I suppose a man wouldn't want to be reminded that he'd been cuckolded," Victoria said, reaching for the decanter of scotch.

Before she understood what was happening, Evelyn turned and slapped Victoria across the face. The glass dropped from Victoria's hand, shattering the bamboo and glass cart. Bottles fell, glasses broke, liquor spilled across the multicolored pattern of the Persian rug.

The blood pounded in Evelyn's temples as she heard Ah Foon come into the room. She must have been listening, Evelyn thought. No matter. There could be no secrets from the servants.

Victoria hadn't moved. The pattern of her mother's hand appeared across the pale alabaster skin of her cheek. "Would you like me to leave?" she asked.

Ah Foon was on her knees cleaning up amid their feet. "Apologize to me," Evelyn said. The pain throbbed in her temples, and she could feel her nails tearing at the soft skin of her palms.

"You don't deny it, do you?"

"You are not my judge," her mother told her.

"Would you like me to leave?" Victoria asked her. It was a taunt. Where would a twenty-year-old girl go in Shanghai?

"No."

251

Victoria took the last unbroken glass out of Ah Foon's hands, stooped and picked up the unbroken decanter, which still held a few inches of scotch. She picked ice cubes off the Persian rug while Evelyn said to Ah Foon, "It's all right, leave us," and the amah scurried away.

"Don't you think you've had enough to drink?" Evelyn asked.

"If I did, I wouldn't pour another one," Victoria said.

"Why are you doing this?"

Victoria walked toward the window. "I don't know," she said without turning. "I should be grateful, shouldn't I? You've made my life better than it could have been."

"Your life is just beginning."

Victoria looked into the garden. "Look," she said in a voice that Evelyn recognized; it was the accepting voice of the refugee, wise in the ways of the world. "I don't hate you. I don't know what it is I hate . . . smugness, maybe. All those girls were so . . . smug."

"They don't know," Evelyn said. They didn't know what it was like to be poor or homeless, without papers or dreams. Victoria's childhood had been a place of ghosts, of a dead czar and czarina, of talk of castles that she would never see, ancestors that she would never honor. "You can't blame people for their ignorance."

"I'm glad to be back, anyway," Victoria offered finally.

From the garden they heard the sound of the trees rubbing their branches together in the fitful wind from the river. Evelyn said, "I have to go back to Manila in a few days. What will you do here?"

"I'll look for my father," Victoria answered. "That's what I've come back for." She turned, astonishingly beautiful. The glass was empty. She tossed her head, throwing the rich hair out of her face. Evelyn was afraid for her; beauty would protect or weaken a woman. Fischer had taught her that. For the first time she noticed the small brass brooch in the shape of a firefly pinned to Victoria's collar.

"What a pretty brooch," she commented, for lack of anything else to say.

Victoria touched it, covering the brooch as though to hide it from her mother's prying eyes. "It's a firefly," she said. "Did you know the Egyptians believe they carry the spirit of the dead?"

"No, I didn't."

"Uncle Morgan gave it to me."

Evelyn had tried to write Morgan once, but there had been no answer. She hadn't been surprised; Morgan would have moved on.

"When did you see him?" she asked carefully.

"He came aboard the ship in Alexandria."

So Victoria had kept in touch with Morgan. How had she managed to defy Evelyn's instructions at the convent? "What is Morgan doing in Egypt?" Evelyn asked, hoping that her worries were well hidden.

"What Uncle Morgan does everywhere," Victoria said, smiling for the first time since stepping off the tender. "He's being charming."

"I'd come to Suez with you," Morgan had said as he bade her farewell on the Alexandria dock, palms unmoving sentinels behind him in the Egyptian dusk. The baroque buildings of the Croisette were bathed in a buttercup sunset. "But there's been a bit of trouble." He looked abashed as he scuffed his white canvas shoes. His suit was bagged at the knees and worn through at the elbows.

"Come with me, Uncle Morgan," she said.

"Not 'Uncle.'" He begged her with his still-young eyes. "Not now, surely."

"Come with me," she repeated. The yellow was washing down the faces of the waterfront buildings. A quick sense of déjà vu passed as she held onto Morgan's sinewy arm. "Come to Shanghai," she said.

Morgan replied with only a smile, the smile that she had found in their two days together could go from humor to bitterness in a flash.

But he wouldn't be budged, so Victoria had boarded the ship herself. She understood that a change was coming over her, a change deeper than anything that had happened in Alexandria with Morgan. The warmth of the East had come to draw her forth as the ship moved along the narrow canal and through the Indian Ocean, where silver flying fish arched out of a steel-bright sea, through the archipelago of the Indies, through Rangoon, Singapore, and Hong Kong. As the ship turned in at the mouth of the Yangzte the sudden shock of recognition, the understanding of that sense of déjà vu six weeks before in Alexandria: She was home.

The smell came out to greet her first, blown on the wind: rotting vegetation, dankness, heat, and humanity. And then as they moved up the river at dawn, past the forts, a sense of excitement. She couldn't remember any of it, yet everything she saw—the long paddy fields, the distant line of hills, the white sky, the villagers plodding like animals with their baskets slung across their shoulders on poles—spoke to her with an immediacy she had never felt elsewhere.

The moment when the city came into sight the circle of recognition that had begun in Alexandria was complete; the Bund, after midnight, looked exactly like Alexandria.

In three days back none of this had changed. The sense of having awakened from a deathlike sleep coursed through her as the rickshaw driver padded through the Chinese section. She breathed in the smell of the noodle stalls, watched how the little rice birds sat patiently in their cages while their friends were grilled on hot coals below, saw a Chinese amah pushing two neatly dressed European children quickly past a leper, knew that the man with the small table and the line of pens crouched on the sidewalk was a professional letter writer waiting for an illiterate customer ready to pay a small fortune for a letter home to his village. The coolie pulling the rickshaw spat a glob of mucus at the feet of one of the noodle vendors, who waved his wooden ladle as the rickshaw passed.

The other girls had talked of their families, their homes, marriage prospects, a world she would never enter. She didn't miss it, and the girls at school had sensed her unspoken contempt. Their hatred had come slowly and in small ways. She couldn't make friends. They mocked her.

Any weakness was pursued to cruelty. Slowly she had withdrawn into herself, become haughty and disdainful.

When she had agreed to go to Switzerland the mother superior had taken her aside. "Victoria, do you know why I wish to speak to you?"

She denied it.

"I want to speak to you of pride," the mother superior had said in the cool room from which could be seen the sun-baked hills, the olive groves, the square-cut fields where the girls paraded each day, the sandstone walls of the convent.

"It is a sin," the mother superior informed Victoria. She was a small, intense woman, and Victoria considered her guilty of that very sin.

"Would you prefer that I despise myself?" Victoria asked.

She saw with satisfaction how the flush came to the old nun's cheeks. "I would prefer humility," the mother superior answered.

"And I would not," Victoria told her, knowing that she would leave this place of confinement tonight forever. She could speak her mind and not fear retribution, the disapproval that gave the other girls the signal to persecute her.

"I am sorry for you, Victoria," the nun said. "I will pray for you."

"Thank you," Victoria said. "I will pray for you, too." And she saw again how the flush reddened the thin, old neck.

She should have come back to Shanghai immediately, she thought as the dome of the Russian church appeared above the shacks of the Chinese section. Except that on his two long visits to San Francisco, Morgan had told her of Europe. The loneliness after her mother's departure had been more intense than she had expected. She had loved her grandmother, loved her so much that when she died, Victoria had wanted to be buried with her. But she hadn't loved her mother or her aunt Natasha. Her mother had bought her own child and then sent her away.

Year after year she had waited for her father to write. As time passed he had become a shadowy figure: tall, intense, proud, a figure to whom she attached her love. He couldn't write her, she told herself, because her mother had taken her away, but he loved her as she loved him.

Now she would find him, and together they would face the world. She saw now, however, that she had been foolish to think she would find him still in the two rooms. The herbalist was still there, but when she had inquired all she had gotten was a shrug and silence. She had gone then to the only place she could think of—the church—and been told by the shabby priest in the ragged white robes that he knew nothing of her father. It was only on leaving that she had thought to ask about her aunt. She owned a restaurant somewhere, he said reluctantly; she didn't come to church.

It had taken two more days to find the restaurant.

The rickshaw passed in front of the church, the doors shuttered against the cold afternoon. The coolie ran on into the international sector. They were passing the smaller European shops now, tailors and yard goods, luggage, a chemist. The streets widened; ahead was the square.

"Lezenskis" was written in Russian script above the narrow front of the restaurant. Victoria paid off the driver and pushed open the wooden door. The smell of rich cooking choked her. The room was long and narrow, tiny tables crowded together, all filled with diners. Half a dozen fair, buxom waitresses in Russian costumes moved about between the tables, their hands and forearms burdened with deep, thick plates, sweat running from their faces.

Victoria loosened the scarf at her neck, threw back the cashmere coat she had bought at her mother's expense in Paris. "Yes?" a waitress inquired, her arms still laden with dirty dishes. She looked Victoria up and down suspiciously.

"I want to see Natasha Lezenski," Victoria said.

"She's not here," the woman told her. Another waitress who could have been the sister of the first passed by. "Ignore her," she told Victoria with a leer. "She's jealous. Natasha's in the back at her table."

"Thank you."

Victoria felt self-conscious as she made her way through the overcrowded room to the back. Most of the diners were the poorer Europeans who lived here. Her aunt appeared as a mound of flesh bending over a bowl of thick noodles washed with cream and paprika. The hair was gray now, unwashed. Her arms were the size of legs of lamb, her face still familiar as it turned up, sullen and layered with fat. "What do you want?" she asked as she wiped the cream from her thick lips. She looked at Victoria's coat, her silk scarf, the plain leather shoes, the pearl earrings given to her by Evelyn on her eighteenth birthday. "Fallen on your luck, huh? You want a job." Victoria saw with disgust how Natasha examined her body quite openly. "You," she shouted at a passing waitress. "Take this away." She shoved her dish into the center of the table where neat lines of invoices told that she was doing her books. To Victoria she said, "Or perhaps you want something else, huh?"

"I'm Victoria Lezenski," her niece told her coldly.

The tiny eyes blinked. She didn't say anything, but her fat fingers moved the papers in front of her a fraction of an inch.

"I'm looking for my father."

Natasha wiped her fingers on the tablecloth. "So," she said indifferently.

"I thought you would help me," Victoria said. The room was stiflingly hot. She undid her coat further, but as her aunt's small eyes flicked back to take in the pale lavender silk dress she closed it again. Natasha smiled scornfully. "Why should I care?" She looked toward the kitchen doors as they opened for yet another blond Russian girl to push through, arms laden with plates of steaming food.

"He's your brother," Victoria said.

"He's a fool," Natasha retorted. She snapped her fingers loudly at a passing waitress. "Bring me tea," she commanded. Then, as though she felt obligated, she asked resentfully, "Do you want something?"

Victoria pulled out a chair. "Tea would be nice."

"Tea," Natasha told the waitress.

"Biscuits?" the waitress asked.

"No." The anger in Natasha's eyes was the anger of greed. She couldn't share so much as a biscuit.

"Do you know where he is?" Victoria asked.

Natasha shifted her enormous bulk, and a smell of dirt and woman came across the table. Victoria stopped herself from raising the handkerchief to her face. "He's gone."

"Where?"

Natasha made an effort at shrugging, but the effect was negligible under the layers of clothing. "To the north." Then, in a murmur, "With the government."

"Papa?"

Natasha laughed, a rough, mannish, grating sound. "Yes, 'Papa.'" She mocked Victoria's voice. "'Papa' has gone north to kill communists."

"Nanking?" Victoria asked.

The waitress came back with two small glasses of tea, each in a silver cradle. She put down a sugar bowl that Natasha held onto as though afraid Victoria would help herself to too much, then added a small pitcher of milk.

Victoria accepted the pale tea. "I want to see him," she insisted.

"It's impossible," Natasha said with satisfaction, tracking everything going on in her restaurant. "The Japanese will take the city soon."

Victoria sipped her tea, saying nothing, wondering what she would say when she returned to the blue house in the French quarter. She would never go to Manila.

As though she had read the girl's mind, Natasha said, "Is the whore back?"

This time it was Victoria who colored. "Is Papa well?" she asked.

Natasha made another effort at shrugging her dirty flesh. "Well?" she asked, as though the question confused her. "Who knows? He has food. He kills his enemies. It is enough, eh?"

"Very nice," Agnelli said with appreciation as she came into his suite.

"Thank you." She was wearing a black taffeta sheath with a bow at one shoulder holding it up. Fischer's diamond butterfly pin—her good luck charm—was the only jewelry other than Alex's plain wedding band she had taken to wearing after Fischer's death. It acted as a protection against the interest of men, an interest for which she had no time anymore.

"Each time I see you," Agnelli said, lighting a cigarette, "you look more beautiful." He looked powerful in his white dinner jacket, the collar of his evening shirt straining against the fleshy neck. The wedding ring was no protection. From the moment she had arrived in San Francisco to tell him of Fischer's death Agnelli had been stalking her.

"It's my healthy life," she said, dropping her beaded evening bag on the rattan table. "Everything in moderation."

"Including moderation," Agnelli said, touching her hand as she reached to accept a cigarette.

She took her hand away, accepted the light, and said, "Are you ready?"

"What should I do?" Agnelli asked philosophically, "Stick my hands in the air and tell the little monkeys that they can take my money?" Like many tall, powerful men, Agnelli found it difficult to accept power in shorter men. Evelyn walked toward the window, where Corregidor was a dark shadow against the moonlight-bright sea. "Don't let them think you consider them fools, Guido," she said. She turned to face him and was aware that he had been watching her closely. "We need them. The only other ports in the Pacific we could use would be Honolulu or Suva. Suva's too small, and Honolulu has too much close supervision."

"Have you ever known me not to be agreeable?" he asked, his palms wide in a gesture of fake submission. "Tell me what to do. I'll be a good little boy."

"MacArthur makes a big show of who's really in control here. He doesn't believe Roosevelt should have given the islands independence . . ."

"Neither do I," Agnelli interjected.

"MacArthur was raised here on the army base, at least part of his life," Evelyn went on. "He's a strange mixture— part American democrat, and a much bigger part Asian power broker. He throws these receptions once a month;

Queson hates it, but he comes. He'll be late, and when he does arrive it'll be a difficult moment. Someone will approach you then, and you can come up here and make whatever arrangements you can with them."

"You won't come?" Agnelli asked.

"No," she said, drawing on the cigarette and stubbing it out in the ashtray. "I'm a woman. They won't take me seriously; or if they did, the price would be higher, much higher. Make certain that payment isn't given until the ship is five miles out at the least. They'll try to make us pay twice if they can—once while it's here and then again when she sails. I've seen it happen with much less . . . shall we say, embarrassing cargos, so it's certain that they'll try it on you." She looked at him to make sure he was taking all of this in. She missed Fischer desperately at times like this, but she had come to realize that even the most powerful men were frequently not that bright. And they had their enormous vanity. Fischer had been many things, but not vain.

"We don't have to do this much longer," she reminded Agnelli. "We have to talk about that, too."

"Of course we'll continue," Agnelli said flatly. "We haven't scratched the surface. The profit's going to be enormous."

"It already has been," she reminded him.

"Don't speak like this," Agnelli ordered her. "I haven't gone to all this trouble to stop now."

She dropped the subject, picking up her handbag, and went to walk past him. He took her arm roughly, snapping, "We're not going to talk about this again."

"Let go of me." He did so, and she stood in the hall waiting for the elevator while he gathered his cigarette case and lighter. They rode down in silence, the door opening to a long line of men and women in evening clothes inching slowly toward the ballroom.

"Jesus Christ," Agnelli said.

"We could have a drink in the bar," Evelyn suggested, "but it won't get much shorter for a while. And the Filipinos haven't arrived yet," she pointed out. The few Filipinos who had already arrived—the men in the white dinner jackets and black trousers that were the nightly uniform, the women in elaborate wide-sleeved native costume—stood out among the taller Americans in their dress uniforms.

"No," said Agnelli, "let's get it over with."

They had only just joined the end of the line when Evelyn saw a tall, fair officer coming toward them from the door to the ballroom. He walked with a brisk, youthful stride, and when he was closer she saw that he was smiling as though they were old friends.

He spoke, however, to Agnelli. "Mr. Agnelli?"

"Yes." Agnelli bristled at the presence of the slim lieutenant in his crisp uniform.

"The general would like you to come forward," the lieutenant requested.

"Jump the line, huh?" Agnelli was mollified.

"And Countess Lezenski," the lieutenant added. "Lieutenant Miles Foster."

She offered her hand. "Thank you, Lieutenant. This is very good of you."

"Nothing to do with me, ma'am," he said, the same half smile playing about his lips. He had a boyish face, with wide-set pale green eyes, a narrow nose, and lips that opened and closed as though the smile threatened to break into outright laughter at any moment. He had very fine teeth, she thought, American teeth so bright and white they might have been false. "Someone sent the general a cable that there was a VIP in town."

He led them along the line of curious and resentful guests toward where MacArthur and his short, plain wife stood just inside the door. The general, parrot-faced, looked at Agnelli as though he saw the enemy himself. "You're a moneyman?"

"I'm a banker, General," Agnelli said.

Evelyn was conscious of the restless movement of the reception line behind them. Jean MacArthur, her ruddy neck festooned with cheap local bead necklaces that seemed a last-ditch attempt to pick up her drab batik evening gown, stared at Evelyn with the disdain of the plain wife of a powerful man.

"I've never gotten along with bankers," MacArthur said challengingly. "They look at the world differently than soldiers."

"How do soldiers look at the world, General?" Evelyn could see the tension in his jaw.

"As a potential battlefield."

"Then you should get along with bankers," Agnelli said smoothly. "They see the world the same way."

There was a fraction of a second's silence, until Miles Foster laughed. It was a young laugh, a laugh of astonished delight at seeing his commanding officer have his guns spiked, but it saved the moment. "Very good, Agnelli," the general said, looking the banker over as though he had misjudged him. Only Jean MacArthur stared furiously at Foster, her face a study in contained rage.

They moved on, Foster with them. "Shouldn't you be helping out somewhere, Lieutenant?" Agnelli asked him.

"I'm assigned to see you enjoy yourself, sir," Foster said. His eyes held mischief and no regret.

"I would stay away from the general's lady for a while," Agnelli suggested as they circled the large, mirrored ballroom. "She wasn't pleased."

"It's that way, I guess," Foster said easily, pushing his blond hair off his face, "when you tend a shrine."

This time Evelyn laughed. "Lieutenant," she said, "I fear you haven't much future in the military."

"Gee, you don't think so?" Lieutenant Foster said, standing stock still, as though struck by a new thought.

"Lieutenant," Agnelli said, "let an old man give you advice. . . ." He stopped, and Evelyn realized that Agnelli was waiting for the lieutenant to protest that Agnelli wasn't old. The lieutenant stood wide-eyed. "An older man." Agnelli corrected himself finally, a frown furrowing his wide, tanned brow. "Never cut off your lines of retreat, even if you don't think you'll need them. As a military man, you should understand that."

"Well, I do, sir," Lieutenant Foster said earnestly. "But if you don't allow yourself any roads of retreat, well, you just have to fight on that much more fiercely." He looked as serious as he could. "It builds character, that's the way I see it."

After a second's pause, Agnelli said, "The way I see it, Lieutenant, you should have been spanked hard and regularly as a child. That builds character, too."

"Orphans don't get spanked much. Too late now, I guess." The lieutenant's eyes slid insolently toward Evelyn, who, to her mortification, felt a blush begin to rise up the naked column of her neck. "Would you like some refreshment, sir? Madam? Something cool?"

In his absence Agnelli said, "That young man is going to get himself into trouble."

"He's just young," Evelyn said thoughtfully, following his uniformed back as he made his way through the crowd toward the buffet tables. When she turned, Agnelli was watching her; she began to blush again and turned away quickly, relieved to see a commotion at the entrance, where MacArthur was leaning forward to greet a very small, dark-haired Filipino dressed in a double-breasted dinner jacket and flanked by two aides, each draped with more gold braid than General MacArthur.

"Queson," Evelyn murmured. There was a momentary hush, and then the Marine band that had been lazily playing one American show tune after another struck up the new Philippine national anthem. Afterward there was a quick adjusting of attitudes and clothing, then the opening chords of "The Star-Spangled Banner" began. The room stood at attention for that, too. Then the band went back to show tunes, and the room became a kaleidoscope of moving colors, Americans and their allies moving like ocean currents passing over each other without mingling.

"Baby gangsters," Agnelli said dismissively.

Before Evelyn could reply she saw one of Queson's men coming toward them. "Here's Romolos," she murmured.

She introduced Agnelli to the neat, thin old man who was reputed to be one of the power brokers behind the new, more flamboyant president of the republic.

The little man smoothed his silver hair and asked, "We can talk somewhere?"

"In my suite," Agnelli suggested, heading for the ballroom door.

"No, no," the elder statesman said, turning toward the terrace. "We can leave this way, I think. Countess, will you walk out with us? It will look better."

Evelyn allowed herself to be moved forward between Agnelli, breathing heavily in the hot climate, and Romolos, cool and calm. On the terrace Agnelli nodded to Evelyn. "You'll wait?"

"Yes."

"Good night, Countess," the silver-haired Filipino said.

"Goodnight, Señor Romolos."

After they walked away, Evelyn stood looking at the sea. She had meant what she had said to Agnelli about ending their business. She had a suspicion that Fischer would not have allowed it to develop this long. There had been a change in Fischer at the end. She thought of how he had looked swimming in the lagoon, and her heart contracted with such sorrow that she had to calm herself and draw breath slowly. The cosmic joke of Fischer dying the very night he'd asked her to marry him brought bitterness like a taste of bile in her throat.

"Dumped, huh?" The lieutenant's voice spoke up behind her, and she started, very angry. She could understand why Jean MacArthur protected her vain and arrogant husband with such fierce devotion—love could be like that. You weren't blind to the weaknesses and foibles of the one you loved, but you felt that others had no right to their criticism or condescension.

"I'm sorry," he said, abashed. "I didn't mean to startle you." He held out a glass of champagne.

He was just a child, not much older than her daughter. She softened, sipped the champagne, said, "I was thinking . . ."

"You looked as though you were dreaming."

She looked more closely at the slight smile on the full lips. His eyes showed the seriousness of the precocious child. "Are you really an orphan?" she asked.

"Almost a lost breed now," he said. He drew a deep

breath of his own and looked at the sea that stretched away like an empty plain of battle. "Have you noticed how you never hear about orphans now?" His voice was brittle.

"I didn't mean to pry."

He shook his head, clearing it of cobwebs, a gesture she understood well. He put his hands deep into his pockets and looked at her levelly. "It doesn't hurt, though it did once. I didn't live in an orphanage or anything. I was raised in Massachusetts by my father's very proper sister." He smiled the tight, mischievous smile. "Not much spanking, but plenty of Bible reading. I can quote the Bible for almost any occasion."

"You must have been a very bad boy, then," Evelyn suggested, smiling herself.

"Yeah," he said cheerfully, "the worst. I got sent away to school at the first possible moment."

"How did you like that?"

"I was expelled," he said. "Three times, from three different schools. I finished high school in a military academy in Louisiana."

"Oh, dear," Evelyn said vaguely.

"Yeah," he agreed cheerfully. "'Oh dear' about covers it."

"And you stayed there?" she asked. She sipped the champagne, thinking how attractive he was, then caught herself and blushed a third time. This time the night was kind to her, and it covered her confusion.

"I was a prize student."

"You were?" He must have heard the surprise in her voice.

"I'm real good at war," he said, rocking back and forth on his heels. "Or I would be," he said with a sudden change of expression, "if there ever was one."

"I think there will be, don't you?" she asked.

He faced her. "I'm sure of it," he agreed soberly.

"You haven't touched your champagne," she pointed out, indicating the glass on the balcony along the terrace.

"Oh, I brought that for Mr. Agnelli. He's loaded, isn't he?" he asked with the simplicity of the young.

"He sure is," she agreed cheerfully.

"And up to no good, I expect," he said with a sudden return of the smile.

"I wouldn't know."

He kept rocking back and forth on his heels, the smile playing about his lips. The air between them was suddenly charged with a current that she was too old, too knowledgeable not to recognize. "You're a very naughty boy, Lieutenant Foster," she said mildly, but she was outrageously flattered.

"Yeah," he admitted happily. "I should have been spanked more, I guess."

"Well, it's too late for that," she said briskly, putting her own glass down by his, "so we'll just have to pray for your soul." She turned and started toward the windows of the ballroom. He called after her, "I don't think that would help."

She turned. "And why not?"

"Because I don't think I want to be saved," he answered, still rocking back and forth, back and forth. The moon, a silver sliver, hung in the sky just above his head. She had a momentary vision of him on a string hanging from the moon; then he rocked again, and the moon seemed to recede back to where it belonged.

"I'll pray for you anyway," she offered in parting, and she went in to where the dancing had begun. She was restless—something she hadn't been in a long time—and irritable now that she was alone again. She wondered when Agnelli would come down. Romolos would exert courtesy, delay, all the little tricks of business that meant so much out here and that Agnelli would find merely irritating. He was like so many Americans, absolutely convinced that their ways could be transplanted roughly into this more ancient soil. If she had had to take bets, she would have placed her own money on the East continuing as it had for a thousand or more years, but there was a rough self-confidence about the Americans that was attractive. You didn't want to disillusion them, as you didn't want to disillusion children when they started out in the world.

She wondered what would happen to the lieutenant when

he found himself in a war. He was little more than a child, really—twenty-five or twenty-six—and she could see from the occasional sullen cast of his fine features that he thought noncombatant life dull.

He would get a real war soon enough, she reflected as she decided that she had had enough of all this noise, the crush of uniforms and evening dresses, the dance of the chandeliers' light on medals and jewels. She pushed her way through the crowd at the edge of the dance floor, saw General MacArthur talking in a very patronizing manner to the new president, and had a sharp pang of loss for Fischer. It was all a little game to them: the general, the president, Agnelli, the boy lieutenant with his sullen longing for a real war. Only Fischer hadn't been a fool, and Fischer had lain down beside the road like the ancient Tahitians could and gone to sleep. Died, she reminded herself harshly as she walked through the wide lobby with its white tiled floors, the palms in pottery planters with golden carp cavorting around the rims, the tiny bellboys as young as the lieutenant must have been when he was sent away to military school dressed in white uniforms with smart little hats like Philip Morris cigarette pages.

One of these tiny dolls opened the main door for her, and she gave her license plate number to the concierge. She stood in the humid night air while the number was announced over the loudspeaker set in the distant parking lot. She should have told Agnelli she was going—left a message at the very least—but she didn't think she could stand to be here one moment more.

The Buick came creeping out of the dark, its golden headlights pushing the shadows back. The doorman opened the door for her, and she slipped into the gray flannel interior with relief. "Home," she said to the driver, and the car was rolling away from the vast bulk of the hotel. It wasn't until they were on Admiral Dewey Boulevard under the palms moving in the first breeze of the evening that she realized that she had misplaced her handbag somewhere. She craned back to see the hotel, now tiny like an architect's model, on the other edge of the bay. In Agnelli's suite, she thought, and she leaned forward to tap the driver on his white-coated shoulder—but she couldn't bring herself to go back . . . she couldn't. There wasn't anything of any importance in the handbag anyway, she thought, collapsing again against the deeply cushioned seats. There was some money, a cigarette case made of local tortoise shell, a handkerchief. Let them have it, whoever found it. She had stopped carrying anything of worth years ago when she understood that a woman alone in Shanghai could be robbed in broad daylight and expect very little help.

The car rolled past the stalls frying fish at the edge of the sand, past the open dance halls where the newly prosperous wheeled to the latest American tunes, into the darkened suburbs where the night was hushed with the reverence for money and property, good Catholic families and their dreams of future riches. At her own house, Carmella—the little maid Evelyn had imported from Luzon to take care of Victoria—was waiting inside the front door. The girl, no more than sixteen, stood up sleepily from where she had been asleep on a bench and followed Evelyn up to her bedroom. The house seemed very large tonight, much larger than Evelyn needed. But then she had taken the lease with the thought that here in these vast rooms she would introduce her daughter to what society there was. The living room was decorated in the heavy Spanish manner the higher-caste Filipinos admired, with fringed sofas and elaborately carved chests, the library full of books that Evelyn had discovered were all mildewed. In her room the bed was set almost in the center of the room with a canopy attached to the ceiling like a coronet.

"I won't need you," she said to the girl, who hesitated. "I'll undress myself," Evelyn assured her, knowing that the girl would think she had done something wrong and perhaps be sent back to her village. "It's all right. I'm just a little tired. I want to be alone."

"Yes, señora."

When the girl was gone, Evelyn stripped, letting the satin sheath fall on the red tiled floor. She undid her brassiere, then slipped out of her half slip. Naked, she walked toward the window onto the long silent garden. The stars were bright, and the same moon that had seemed to want to lift the lieutenant like a Christmas ornament shone brightly across the distant city and bay.

She ran her hands over her shoulders and cupped her breasts, feeling a need she hadn't had in a long time. She offered a small prayer, her talisman against disaster; Fischer would have laughed at her—very gently—dismissing her superstitions, but she saw that the prayer was different tonight. It was a prayer against a sadness that was pressing toward her.

She closed the windows and went into the deep darkness of her room. She slept fitfully, waking with her heart racing, dreaming of Fischer, of how he had wanted to marry her, of how much safer she would have felt if they had married. The fear was for the loss of Fischer and the dream that had seemed to dance just ahead out on those blue, blue seas before it vanished.

Then, with a shock, she understood that it wasn't Fischer she had been dreaming of. Her body was damp with desire, and she had woken from a dream where a stranger came for her, touched her, started to make love to her. She tried to leave the face of the stranger in the dream, but Fischer had taught her the importance of honesty, and in any case that mocking half smile came back to her even in the dark. Finally, to still her heart, she had to throw back the long, heavy drapes and let in the fresh air of morning. Watching the dawn, pink and green above the sleeping city, she wondered at herself.

"For you, señora." Carmella giggled as she held out the clear plastic box.

The room felt hot and stuffy. Evelyn had lain down for a moment after the dawn had whitened the sky. "What time is it?" she asked quickly.

"Nearly twelve," Carmella said. She looked disappointed that Evelyn wouldn't take the box of white orchids.

"No!" Evelyn sat up, threw back the silk sheets, and reached for her robe. "Why didn't you wake me? Has Señor Agnelli called?"

"No, señora," Carmella said sadly. She put the box of orchids on the dressing table, drew the curtains, and left the room.

"Wait," Evelyn called, feeling as though she had been in a deep, deep sleep that had lasted years. "Come back, Carmella. I'm sorry . . . I fell asleep again."

The maid stood with her hands folded across her stomach, her head low. When she had first arrived six weeks earlier she couldn't look at Evelyn. Now it was only when she was uncertain that she still stared at her feet in their tiny black slippers. "You came in late. I thought you would want to sleep."

"I'm sorry," Evelyn said again. The sleep had renewed her, and she was filled with enthusiasm for the day ahead. "You're right. If I had wanted to be woken I would have told you before I went to bed. Is there any tea?"

"Yes, señora. It is ready," the maid said, brightening. She glanced up and across the room. "The flowers arrived just now," she said. "I thought . . ."

Agnelli, Evelyn thought with relief. He'd managed his arrangements with Romolos. "Thank you, Carmella," she said. "I'll have my tea now."

The maid left reluctantly, and Evelyn went into her bathroom. She leaned toward the mirror, examining her neck and eyes, turning sideways to look at her chin. Today she held her skin between her thumb and forefinger, testing. Yes, she was still beautiful, but it was not the beauty of youth. There was a contrivance to the artful cut of her hair, her careful makeup, the simplicity that she achieved with such care.

She sighed, refusing to allow the knowledge to depress her. She had forgotten what it was to feel like this, hopeful. Was it because she had decided to tell Agnelli that she wanted to end this long business venture? Or possibly . . . but she put that other thought away with decision. A woman had no control over her dreams, but if she was sensible, she had firm control over her thoughts.

The maid had set the tea tray by the long turquoise silk chaise at the window. The sun fell across the tiled floor, shimmering like tropical waters over red sand. She sat down, all the while glancing at the headlines of the newspapers: MacArthur was there and Queson, Queson's wife in native dress, Jean MacArthur . . . She opened the paper out of habit, searching for the news of China, but it was relegated to the third page: The Japanese were advancing on Nanking.

The maid, still smiling as she looked at the white orchids, was pouring tea as the telephone on the table at the side rang. "I'll take it," Evelyn said, not waiting for a boy somewhere in the house to answer. It would be Agnelli.

"Hello."

"Did you get my flowers?"

Her heart missed a beat, something that hadn't happened in so long that she had forgotten the sensation. "Thank you, Lieutenant," she said, trying to keep her voice even. With one hand she was trying to tear at the white silk ribbon that wrapped the plastic box that she had dropped at the end of the chaise. She gestured frantically at Carmella, who, giggling, took the box away from her and carefully began to untie the ribbon.

"Am I forgiven?"

"For what?"

Carmella took the small white envelope out of the box and handed over the engraved card.

On the back was written, "I behaved like a brat. Forgive me." It was signed Miles Foster.

"For being a brat." It was the voice of a young man used to getting his own way, of charming his way past life's hurdles, she thought.

"You're forgiven, Lieutenant," she said primly. "The flowers are beautiful, but they weren't necessary. You behaved . . ." She wanted to say "charmingly," but a swift look in the mirror across the room made her think instead, What an old fool you are. She had seen the middle-aged women in Shanghai with their young escorts and thought them ridiculous. "You behaved refreshingly youthfully."

She wanted to put down the telephone immediately to stop the feelings of confusion and awkwardness that were rising in her. She hadn't flirted with anybody in years and years.

"I want to see you," he said finally.

She still didn't reply.

"Look," he went on. "I don't know what you think of me, but I've never done this before."

"Lieutenant," she said, finally finding her voice and proud of its calm, despite her shaking hands.

"Miles."

"Lieutenant, please make this easy for me," she managed in the same calm voice. "I enjoyed meeting you last night, but I don't think . . ." She didn't think what, she wondered.

"You ever take chances?" he interrupted.

She laughed. It seemed to her that her whole life had been one long risk. "Yes, Lieutenant—Miles—I've taken a chance or two."

"They work out?"

"Some of them," she said carefully.

"Take another," he said, his voice dropping an octave to throb along the line.

Again she let the silence draw on. As Carmella folded back the bed to air the sheets Evelyn saw the imprint of her head in the pink satin pillowcase, how the place where she had lain was outlined along one side of the bed. "I'm not sure, Lieutenant," she said quietly.

"I'll behave, I promise you," he said.

Another minute. "All right."

"I'll be around in an hour," he said, and he hung up.

"Miles," she called down the line. "Miles . . ." She looked at the heavy Bakelite receiver, the dial tone mocking her, and then up into Carmella's laughing eyes. They smiled conspiratorially.

The telephone rang again. She lifted it to her ear. "All right," she said, laughing. "I'll be ready."

Agnelli's voice said, "Where the hell did you get to last night?"

Evelyn closed her eyes and drew breath. "You were gone. I left."

"I got that," he said. "We have to talk."

"Yes, all right. Later."

"Later, nothing," Agnelli told her. "What the hell is wrong with you? You leave me at the hotel with that damn bandit. Have you forgotten what's at stake here? We have a ship out of Seattle right now."

He was right. "When?" she asked, feeling a great letdown threaten to overwhelm her. She stood up, undoing her robe.

"As soon as possible. We can't make a deal with these monkeys. You're going to have to go to Shanghai. We may have to cut Manila out."

"I'll come right over."

"Send the car. I'll come there."

"No," she said quickly. "That's not possible." She searched for an explanation and decided that she didn't owe him one. "I'll pick you up. We can drive out along the coast to lunch."

"Okay," he agreed. She could hear the anger in his voice. "I'm going to try to get on tonight's plane to Hong Kong. If I can get to Honolulu before the *Pacific Star* gets there, maybe we can reroute her."

And he hung up. She was already undressing as she moved toward the bathroom. "Call for the car, Carmella," she said. "I'm going out."

She turned at the door, naked. "Tell him . . ." The disappointment struck her then, twisting her heart as it hadn't since she was a child. She was a fool, she told herself. An old fool. "Tell Lieutenant Foster when he gets here that I had to go out."

"Yes, señora," the girl said sadly.

Agnelli opened the door before the doorman could reach it, slid into the car, and said, "Let's get the hell out of here." She had seen this foul, dark mood before when he hadn't gotten his way. Alex had been spoiled, too, but then he had been raised that way. Fischer, though, had been self-indulgent in his luxuries but relentlessly self-disciplined where money or work was concerned.

She gave the driver directions, and they slid out of the

shadow into the bright sunlight of high noon. Looking out the side window, she was dazzled, and she turned to see Agnelli scowling at her. "You shouldn't have left," he said.

"I was tired. I didn't think you would need me."

"They took me out to some shanty district. A dump—Cafe Tobasco. Christ, the girls had to be thirteen." His thick tongue ran over his lips. "It takes more than a few drinks and young—" He stopped. "Look," he said seriously, "they're going to make trouble."

"Tell me about it."

Agnelli looked at the driver. "It's okay," she told him. "Go ahead."

"They want fifty percent."

She was astonished. "Of what? Fifty percent of what?"

"Of what the shipment's worth. They know where it's going."

She didn't answer immediately. The car ran smoothly through the town, past the twin towers of the cathedral, pale pink in the heat, and on through the gardens of the suburbs. A white-uniformed nanny pushed a pram behind a high iron fence where bougainvillea trailed a bloody path between the spikes. "Their opening bid?" she suggested. Her mind was turning over the alternatives. There was Guam, but the island was almost entirely military. After one, maybe two shipments, someone would come down to investigate the traffic.

"So we go down to twenty-five percent," Agnelli said with asperity. "They might as well walk in the doors of one of my banks with a gun."

Twenty-five percent was much more than they should pay, she agreed. At this point their profits were already so high it didn't really matter to her, but she knew that Agnelli would claim there was a moral principle involved. As she imagined the wide sweep of yellow sand at Kuzo bay, palm trees arching toward the blue water, a native parang set against the white sky like a picture, all devastated by bombs, she wondered how he could invoke a moral principle, but she knew he would. Money was money.

"Perhaps this has gone on long enough," she murmured.

"Don't start that again," he ordered as the restaurant came into view. "They're not going to get away with this."

Inside the restaurant they were led to a table near two parangs piled up on the beach. The only customers, they ordered fried fish and beer. Evelyn sat back.

"How's Tu?" Agnelli asked abruptly.

Tu was so large, he had become a caricature of himself, sitting in one of his own teahouses. The layers of fat formed ridges above his cheeks so he seemed to be peeking over them from behind a barricade of flesh. "He has Chiang in his pocket, of course."

"I think you should go up there."

"I just got back."

"Go again," he snapped irritably. The circles under his eyes showed he had been up all night. "Find out if he can take delivery for us at another port further north. See our little yellow friends, too," he said, ignoring the waiter, who had arrived with a platter of fish. "If they have so much of China, there should be some way we can stop all this farting around and just send the ship directly there. Let *them* get it to Japan." The waiter had the impassive demeanor of a statue carved from the hard monkey wood of the northern islands. Agnelli picked up a fish with his thick fingers, laid it on the clean white plate, and tore the skeleton out of it in one deft move. He stuffed the rest of the fish in his mouth and chewed. "I'll see them in hell before I'll let these little brown monkeys take money off me. Let them think what they want. You go up to see Tu; I'll do something about the ship." As the waiter left, the tired eyes looked at her with spite. "The oldest couldn't have been more than thirteen."

"What did she call you?" Evelyn asked sweetly, pushing the carcass of a fish about her plate with a fork. " 'Papa'?"

He stopped his chewing for a long moment, then he laughed, spraying bits of fish onto the table. "That's funny." He snorted. "I've never heard you be funny." He looked at her curiously, his eyes narrowing. "Something new?"

She fought desperately for an answer, something to sidetrack him. The slightest hint and he would be after the scent. "Perhaps I'm a little jealous," she replied. "I'm not thirteen any longer."

He picked up another fish, tore the spine out, and this time cut the fish into pieces as though he'd remembered to mind his manners. "You're a good-looking woman, Evelyn," he told her. "I always told you that. You shouldn't sit out life on the sidelines." He shrugged as he waved his fork about with the fish on it. "There are lots of men who would be interested." The fork went still. "Like me."

"It's different for a man," she suggested quietly.

"Yeah," he agreed, finally putting the food into his mouth. "What the hell would you do with a thirteen-year-old boy, anyway?" he asked her, and he thought it a fine joke.

"What indeed?" She lowered her eyes.

Twilight turned the sky behind the cathedral mother-of-pearl as she rode home from the airport. Starlings played in the evening light, rising and falling in their game amid the twin towers. The bells summoned the faithful to the evening mass, and Evelyn felt a loneliness waiting for her she hadn't felt since Fischer's death. In those first months she had been to Samoa, to Shanghai for the reading of Fischer's will, to San Francisco to meet with Agnelli, and the blue house had seemed to mock her with its emptiness. At night she often stood under the banyan tree, unable to stay alone in the house without Fischer. She couldn't bring herself to throw away his clothes for a long time, indeed had kept a few silk robes and handkerchiefs on the pretense that she would use them herself one day. They were still in his long wardrobe.

As the car swept in between the twin gateposts, she remembered her plan to fill it with friends of Victoria's. Young girls from local society, young men attached to the American military. Young men like Lieutenant Miles Foster . . . She was startled to see his face passing like a ghost by the car window. She thought for a moment that she had conjured him up from her imagination, but then she craned about and saw him in the flesh.

Her own car came to a stop in front of her steps. She got out very slowly, nodding to the boy who had come out of the door at the sound of the car. "No come in," the boy whispered.

She walked slowly back down the driveway toward the bright red, very shiny sports car with a small metallic American flag attached to the door.

"Hello," she said, holding her handbag with both hands.

"I'm very stubborn," he told her without moving. He wore his uniform and drummed on the wooden steering wheel with one palm. He looked older tonight, and he did look stubborn. Angry, too.

"I was called away," she explained. "They must have told you."

"Yeah."

Once again silence stretched out between them. She heard the gardening boys talking to themselves as they watered the lawns in the cool of the evening. "I suppose I should invite you in," she said.

"It would be nice," he admitted. He wasn't smiling. He was like a spoiled child, determined to get his way.

"I really did have to go somewhere," she said to him, for he still hadn't gotten out of the car.

"With your millionaire banker."

She turned and walked back toward the house, where the boys were lighting the rooms for her arrival. The house actually looked inviting, and there were lights above too—one in the round window on the stairs and one in her bedroom, where Carmella would be waiting for her to bathe and change for the evening.

She heard him slam the door of his tiny car. There was a strong smell of frangipani perfume in the air tonight, steamed by the heat of the day from the white and pink trees that shaded the lawn beneath her bedroom window.

"I'm sorry," he said from behind her.

"For what?" she asked, turning on the steps. He was standing directly behind her, and she was very conscious of how tall he was, how solid. Not a boy at all, but a man.

"For being a pill," he said, and now the smile came out to play and he was a boy again. "I'm not used to being stood up. What are you smiling at?"

She hadn't known she was smiling. To cover her pleasure at his presence, she said, "I was thinking you must have very light duties to be able to wait out here all day."

"I was up till three o'clock last night," he said, "making sure all the general's guests had a good time. Your Mr. Agnelli seemed happy when he came back to the hotel."

"Really?" She walked into her house.

"Some place," he commented, standing in the hall.

"I rent it." She seemed to have a need to make sure he didn't misunderstand certain details of her life.

Carmella, stopped, wide-eyed at the sight of Lieutenant Foster. He is very handsome, Evelyn recognized again. Then, as an afterthought, she wondered, Why is he here? What does he want with me? She was angry at the thought that he must be playing with her.

"Don't think me rude, Lieutenant," she said as she led him into the living room, "but I'm very tired. I'll give you one drink."

"I guess you're sort of tired of this," he said after a moment.

"You like ice in your drinks, don't you?" she asked Foster as the downstairs houseboy came in.

"Americans do, don't they?" he said. "Every European always asks 'You want ice, don't you?' as though it was a sure sign of barbarity." He was smiling, but his face was sullen. She felt an aftershock of the wave of desire. The planes of his cheeks were so smooth, she could see the lines where his razor had passed.

"I like ice myself," she said. "I guess that makes me a barbarian."

"Look," he said, facing her across the faded red and yellow Persian rug, "could we stop sparring? I just want to know you. I don't meet many interesting people in my line of work."

"I'm sorry," she said, feeling a fool. She was making too much of all this. "I've really been very busy today," she explained again as the boy came back with a crystal bucket of ice. "I've just come from the airport. I was going to take a hot bath and have dinner on a tray and go to sleep." She looked at him quickly as she dropped the ice cubes into a heavy glass. "I'm glad you're here. I really am. I wasn't looking forward to coming back to the house. What do you drink?"

"Anything you're drinking," he said indifferently. "Light. I got drunk once and didn't like it."

"So you stopped?" she asked in quiet wonder. He was looking at the garden boys, and at the small flock of starlings that had come down from the frangipani trees for the worms that would now come to the surface. As she handed him his drink she felt something, but now she enjoyed it. Her body felt as though she had put it away like a good piece of clothing for another season, and now it had been brought out to air.

"I'm that sort of guy," he said, taking his light rum and holding her glance.

All younger men flirt with older women, she told herself, settling into the corner of the wide sofa. It's expected. That's the way he sees me, as a mysterious older woman.

To confirm her thoughts, he asked, "What's Agnelli out here for?"

"I don't know," she said evenly, a new suspicion entering her mind.

"And you wouldn't tell me if you did?" he suggested.

"I wouldn't think it was my place to do so." The suspicion was growing. "Why didn't you ask him?"

"He didn't strike me as the type of man who would want to be questioned by a lowly lieutenant."

"No, he wouldn't."

"He certainly created a stir," Foster told her, putting the drink aside after one sip. "Even the general has instructions to follow." She liked the irreverence in his voice.

"You don't show much respect."

"You're wrong there," he told her. "I respect him a lot. But he's a type I've studied."

"How old are you, Lieutenant?" she asked. She was

feeling pleasantly relaxed now. Agnelli was gone, and the rum had made her immediate problems in Shanghai fade somewhat.

"Why?" he asked truculently.

She teased him. "Only the very young and the old are afraid to tell their ages, Lieutenant."

"How old are you?" he asked her defiantly.

"Thirty-eight," she said evenly. She noticed how the tiny flame of fear rose in her heart and blazed away while she waited for his answer.

"Twenty-seven," he said.

"You look younger."

"So do you."

"What type is the general?" she asked, because the atmosphere in the room had changed once again. She thought she might be very slightly drunk, and she didn't want to make a fool of herself if she could avoid it—not publicly. Privately she had already done so, for her own amusement.

"He's a self-created myth," Foster answered. She recognized how his eyes narrowed as he folded his uniformed arms about his chest, how his wide lips set. He could be a serious man, she saw, and she wondered why he hid it. "You see it in many of the great leaders—Frederick the Great, Napoleon, even Roosevelt. Abe Lincoln did it brilliantly, because he managed to do it without anyone seeing him pull his own strings. If the general has a weakness—and mind you," he added with a disarming smile, a return to the naughty boy, "I'm not saying he does—but if he does, it is that he doesn't think anyone can see him create the myth. But he's a brilliant general, make no mistake. A very sound man, militarily. He'll be very good when the time comes."

"And you believe it's coming for Americans, too?" she asked curiously. Even Agnelli thought it would be a European and Pacific war in which America could sit on the sidelines. Only Fischer had believed that it would be larger.

"We'll be in," Miles Foster said, with a quick return to the serious cast of his face. "There isn't any other choice, if you understand Asia, and the general does."

"Do you?"

"I was born here," he told her.

"Here?" she asked, surprised. The Americans who had been born in the East or raised there for any length of time took on a different patina, and she thought she would have noticed it.

"In Formosa. Ever been there?"

"Once, with a friend." She decided suddenly that the room was too dark and walked about switching on more lights. She had been to Formosa with Fischer, stayed at the Grand Hotel overlooking the lake, and fed the monkeys that came right onto their balcony in the morning when they were having breakfast. "Did you grow up in Formosa? No, you told me you grew up in . . ."

"Massachusetts," he helped her. "No, my father was ambassador to Thailand. I was born in Formosa by accident."

"You didn't grow up in Thailand, either?" She began to pour herself another drink, then saw his untouched on the mantel.

"You can have another drink," he told her, as relaxed as though he was in his own home. She could see that what looked like insolence would be what her mother had once called breeding, and her poor father leadership. "I won't tell."

"I really am surprised you weren't smacked more," she said, laughing as she went ahead with her drink. "You're a very insolent young man. So tell me, then, where did you grow up before Massachusetts?"

"In Bangkok until I was three. Then in Rio for two years. My father wanted to come back here—to the East, that is—but he was sent to Argentina in one of those strange diplomatic postings that make no sense. Then he died."

"I see." She wanted to ask more—why his mother hadn't raised him, for instance.

"They died in an automobile accident in Rio," he told her flatly. She could tell he had been asked this question before, and this was the answer that he used. It was true, but it was washed clean of emotion.

"I'm sorry."

"Yeah, me, too," he answered. He picked up his drink, looked at it, and put it down, then smiled again. "But it was all a long time ago. I'm over it."

He had the self-containment of other men she had met who had never had enough love as children, she thought. They looked strong but were often weak. She didn't think he was weak, but she was fairly sure that there were strong currents running just beneath the surface of his character that could wreak havoc with his life if they were ever let out. She wondered if he knew how obvious his vulnerability was. Like MacArthur, he was creating his own myth. She found she was wondering if she was looking at a young man who would himself be famous one day. He had a look of destiny in the way he seemed to be so aware of himself in his surroundings. Or vanity, she decided, or vanity.

"Would you like to stay for dinner?" she asked without moving.

"Yes, I would."

As she got up she offered, "Make yourself at home."

Halfway up the stairs Evelyn turned to look back into the long living room. There he was, still with his back to the mantelpiece, still with his hands in his pockets, but no longer rocking. From here he didn't look so aggressively young, but all the male strength in his solid body was still there. As though he knew he was being watched, he looked up suddenly and smiled. He had caught her out.

She waved and continued up the stairs out of sight, but more quickly, laughing at herself for her foolishness. In the room Carmella was turning down the bedcover for the night. "Don't do that," Evelyn ordered her sharply, and she saw how the little maid looked shocked, hurt.

"But señora, I always do this," she protested.

"Yes, of course. But still, leave it for tonight. Go tell the cook there will be one more for dinner."

"Yes, señora," the girl said with a smile and a quick look at the bedside table. There beside the picture of Victoria were the white orchids in a crystal and silver vase.

When the girl was gone Evelyn went to the bed to look

more closely at the orchids, needing to touch their soft flesh. But her eyes moved to the picture of her scowling child at sixteen, resenting even this San Francisco studio photograph. She picked up the tortoiseshell frame and sighed. Going into her bathroom, she washed her face almost clean of makeup, repainted herself very slightly, and combed her hair. There she was as she was, she thought, staring at herself in the mirror.

She had meant to change her white suit but instead briskly returned to the living room, where Foster was looking through a stack of phonograph records. "Have you seen this stuff?" he asked her.

"There's a gramophone over there," she said, indicating an elaborate carved teak case and a junk with its sails as speakers sitting in a corner. She hadn't looked at the records, figuring Victoria would want to buy her own.

"You wouldn't want to hear this stuff," Foster told her, replacing them in the cabinet. What had he been doing in there, she wondered, turning away to hide her frown.

"They have 'Ave Maria' for the cocktail hour," he was saying, "the Air for the G String for light dinner music. These people must be a barrel of fun."

"I've never met them," she said. "They live in Europe most of the year. I took the house from an agent."

"I'll have to get you something livelier."

"That won't be necessary," she told him, now thoroughly angry. "I seldom listen to music." And she hadn't since Fischer's death.

"I bet you'd be a great dancer," Foster told her, unabashed at having been found snooping in closets.

"I don't dance," she told him, her anger rising still higher.

"Never?" with disbelief.

"Not anymore."

"That's a shame." He had come right across the room and now was so close that she had to look up at him. She had a desire to strike his handsome face, but years of reason saved her. At a movement across the room, she stepped away to see the boy standing in the door.

"What is it?" she demanded, and she knew that her voice

must sound strange, hoarse. She was furious that her own body would betray her like this after all this time.

"Dinner, señora."

She was going mad. Of course, dinner. "Dinner," she announced, as though Miles Foster might be deaf. Once again she walked away, almost running across the highly polished hall floor and into the long dining room. The servants, not used to guests, had made an extra effort. There were frangipani blossoms floating in a silver bowl, white candles in the two tall wooden candelabra, lace placemats at each end of the table, the Royal Crown Derby china that she had bought herself in Hong Kong to replace the shabby china that had come with the house, and fine Irish crystal glassware. For the first time the room looked warm and inviting, and she wanted to sweep it all off the table, all of it. But she took her place very properly at one end of the table, indicating with what she hoped was regained composure the other place for Foster.

As she was seating herself he pressed his fingertips to the lace placemat and pulled it down the shining table until it was in front of the seat to her right. "Do you mind?" he asked.

"No, of course not."

She was afraid that if she looked directly into his face he would know what troubles she was enduring with his presence. She kept her eyes on her meal as the servants brought each course—simple food, for she asked the servants to cook for her as they would for themselves.

"Do you eat Filipino food all the time?" he asked as he ate the fish and rice course.

"I like the food fresh," she admitted. "I think the local food is always best wherever you are. There is usually a reason they've settled on certain foods."

He seemed less threatening, and she asked, "You were raised by your aunt?"

"My father's sister. You'd like her." She felt a shot of something close to annoyance and then had the sense to think, of course, he's right. She's probably much closer to my age.

"She's an interesting woman," he continued as the fish course was taken away. "She'd like you, too. She's very independent."

"Yet you went away to school." The dessert was in front of her, and though she hadn't touched the silver serving spoons, a girlish panic assailed her. When he left here tonight she might never see him again. What reason would she ever have to call him or invite him here?

"My father had gone to Choate. I was sent in my time. That was about it. I hated it—all the regimentation."

"Yet you went into the military."

"Yes," he admitted, disbelief in his tone. "It's very hard to explain. Military school seemed more . . . more like real life."

"That seems astonishing," she said, and she began to ladle out the fruit.

"No," he countered, "no, I understood immediately that everything about war was more important than all the gentlemanly things I was being taught. Literature, all of that."

"You amaze me," she said. "I would have thought in a civilized society it was just the opposite."

"I think all the rest—art, literature, music—all of that comes after war, and only if you have a victory for the . . . the just." Now the smile came back, fleeing across his somber face. "I mean," he said, peering at her more closely through the shadows thrown across the table by the flickering candles, "there has to be such a thing as right and wrong, don't you think? And it's important who wins."

Her body betrayed her again, and she wanted to put her hand on his wrist, wanted to touch his cheek, wanted . . .

Instead she very carefully put the two silver spoons back into the silver fruit bowl and rose. "You'll excuse me, Lieutenant," she said carefully. She felt weak all over and for one brief moment thought she might actually do something as out-of-date as totter on her legs. "I don't feel well. Finish your meal, please."

He believed her, she saw, for he half rose to his feet. To stop him she reached out and put her hand on his shoulder.

285

The contact finished her, and she fled up the stairs to her room.

She closed the door behind her, ranting silently at herself for the fool she was. The door opened, and she turned to tell Carmella to leave the lights off, because now she was in tears.

He stood in the doorway. He came to her at his ease, and when he stood beside her he took her into his arms. She could smell his scent through the rough texture of the tunic and feel his strength as he held her. And when he released her enough to raise her face to his she found words, not good words, but what seemed to be uppermost in her mind.

"I have a daughter almost your age," she said.

"You're lucky," he said, leaning closer, his lips parting, his words brushing hers before his mouth closed over her own. "I have no one."

15

Morgan Valentine leaned forward on the rail, peering through the lashing late summer rain at the yellow stain spreading in the dark water below the bow. In the distance, dimly seen, the China coast was a fingerprint smudge against a gray sky.

"The river empties here," the Chinese in the ragged European suit who had traveled with Morgan up the coast from Hong Kong in second class said. "Soon the water will be as yellow as the imperial silk. Then we will be properly in China." The Chinese's accent was curiously English, clipped and precise. He carried a shabby black umbrella that he held absurdly above his head.

"You have a passport?" The Chinese inquired carefully. In his concern, the umbrella had moved, away from its spot above his head. His face ran with rain that looked very much like tears as it slipped over his thin young face. The shabby suit hung on his shoulders.

"A British passport."

The ascetic face beamed. "Very good. The customs is British. They will treat you with respect."

Morgan doubted that. He had left Egypt in a sudden flight from Suez to Aden, one step ahead of the authorities who wanted him "for assistance in their enigma" about some missing securities. He had only "borrowed" the securities from the safe of his fat American employer for a pledge against a small loan at the racetrack in Cairo. If his luck had improved, they'd have been back before anyone knew they were gone, but only the sudden warning of his loan shark had saved him from a stiff jail sentence. That, in a way—the warning—might be looked upon as luck. "My sister lives here," he said, more to himself than to the Chinese.

"She will meet you?"

"She doesn't know I'm coming."

The ship began to turn then, the water much lighter as the silt pushed toward the open sea. The sky had cleared slightly, and just visible ahead was a break in the land.

"You surprise her?"

"Yes," Morgan said.

"She will be happy to see you," the Chinese said. "A family reunion is a happy time."

The rainclouds tumbled out from the darkening line of the shore. The ship rolled on the waves. The Chinese man said, "Perhaps we should go inside. I could buy you a drink."

"You most certainly could," Morgan told him. The rain had almost stopped. They walked back across the wet deck, threading their way among the huddled deck passengers and into the corridor that led to the second class lounge. Morgan was one of just a few Europeans, all of them carrying with them the unmistakable look of poverty in their discrete patches, out-of-date suits, proud, bitter carriages.

At the bar the Chinese said, "Order what you wish."

"A beer," Morgan said to the Chinese waiter.

"You wouldn't prefer a whiskey?" the Chinese asked him.

Morgan looked at the Chinese's own shabby dark suit, the rolled umbrella, the cracked shoes. "A double whiskey," he said.

The Chinese spoke to the waiter. "You aren't what you seem, are you?" Morgan asked him.

"Who is?" the Chinese replied with a broad spreading of his long, thin fingers. He might be thirty, Morgan calculated, seeing the one or two strands of gray hair, the almost imperceptible squint lines at the corners of the eyes, but he could just as easily be forty. The thin body could be any age.

He was probably thirty or less, Morgan decided, aged by his troubles.

"You can quit, you know," Morgan told him as the whiskey was moved in front of him. "I don't care who you are."

The eyes narrowed to slits again, then opened clear and calm. "My name is Wei Kuen," he said.

"Morgan Valentine," Morgan said. He picked up the double whiskey, tipped half of it down his throat, and enjoyed the warmth that flowed deep into him and then exploded with a comfortable, familiar flame in his belly.

They heard the ship's engines slow almost to a stop, then shouting on the deck as the pilot came aboard. Then the engines gained speed, and they began to move more smoothly forward toward the entrance to the estuary.

"Mr. Valentine," Wei Kuen said as he watched Morgan relax under the anticipated influence of the whiskey, "you have very little money."

"Very little," Morgan confirmed. There was something comforting in standing here at the bar at the very edge of a foreign continent, waiting for the proposition that he was sure was coming. Morgan took his time with the small glass of whiskey, watching the woman with the neatly parted gray hair try to adjust her skirt to cover the hole in her stockings.

"There will be difficulties with your debarkation," Mr. Wei was saying as Morgan watched the two Indians who had boarded the steamer in Hong Kong arguing in quiet whispers, heads low. The argument had continued unbroken for twenty-four hours. Neither side seemed close to winning, nor to backing off.

Morgan looked at Mr. Wei over the rim of his glass. "My sister will come to the dock if I call her." Victoria would. But Victoria had told him in Alexandria that she was determined to find her father. He had had no idea he would be following her to Shanghai.

"It is much better to arrive at a relative's house with money in your pocket," Mr. Wei pointed out.

"Old Chinese proverb?" Morgan asked.

"Universal truth," Mr. Wei countered.

Morgan laughed. He put his empty glass down on the bar, signaled the waiter himself, and, as he saw the pilot passing along the deck, said, "Perhaps you should be direct, Mr. Wei."

Mr. Wei considered. Looking evenly at Morgan, he said, "I need you to carry some papers for me."

"Why don't you take them in?" The waiter brought Morgan another double whiskey.

"I do not wish to draw attention to myself."

Morgan touched the whiskey to his lips. He was considering what this could be worth. "Political?" he asked.

"You don't need to know anything about the papers," Mr. Wei said. "They are not dangerous for you."

Political, then. "How much?" Morgan asked. The gray-haired woman was examining her passport nervously.

"One hundred pounds."

"Sterling?"

"Yes."

Morgan drew on the whiskey, not taking his eyes off Wei's worn clothes. Despite them, there was more money here, he was sure of it. But this was a new country where a contact like Wei might be useful. "Very good," he said.

Mr. Wei looked surprised. His face was as smooth as glass for a half second, then he smiled. "I will give you the papers when you finish your whiskey. You will take them through customs, and that is all."

"You'll have someone waiting to accept them."

"We will contact you," Mr. Wei explained. "You will not be in any danger."

Morgan drained his glass. The two double whiskeys had made him lightheaded, delighted by this good omen for his arrival in China. His luck had been abysmal in the last few years. "All right."

Mr. Wei led him out of the lounge to a small, cramped stateroom with six bunks, smelling of sweat and garlic.

Two figures lay with their faces to the wall, groaning pitifully. "You wait, please," Mr. Wei said, gesturing to the corridor.

Morgan lit a cigarette to cover the smell of vomit. Mr. Wei came out of the cabin and closed the door. "Not good travelers," he said. He held two sheets of paper. He looked down the corridor to where a coolie was hauling along a cart of unwashed glasses. "Come," he ordered.

Out on the deck, the rain had stopped to reveal coastline, a long, low horizon of pale green. A junk with ribbed sails pressed out of the mouth of the river. Mr. Wei handed over the sheets of paper, carefully folded. Morgan put them in his breast pocket without looking at them.

"You will wait at the dock?" Mr. Wei suggested.

"Wherever you want, sport," said Morgan, smelling vegetation on the wind.

Mr. Wei made to leave.

"Haven't you forgotten something?" Morgan asked.

"We pay you when you deliver."

"Then it won't be of much help to me if the immigration officers ask to see my money, will it?"

Mr. Wei scowled. He took a small black purse out of the pocket of his jacket, counted out fifty English pounds from a tightly rolled bundle, and handed them over.

"Thanks." Morgan threw the stub of his cigarette over the rail. He strolled off without a word, wondering which of the many political factions Mr. Wei represented.

The day was much warmer by the time the customs and immigration launch, flying its yellow quarantine flag, appeared at a bend in the river, and the pilot directed the captain to slow the ship. The officials came up the gangplank looking crisp and officious in their navy blue uniforms. The ship gathered speed again, traversing the long, leisurely curves in the river as the passengers were called to have their documents checked before the ship reached the city.

Going inside just as the night was closing over a jade-green landscape, Morgan saw Mr. Wei in a row of Chinese waiting to have their documents stamped by a European customs officer and a Chinese official. The Chinese did the questioning while the bored European inspected each piece of paper.

At a second table, the gray-haired woman from the lounge was arguing volubly with a red-faced second official. Her ragged passport lay untouched between them on the table. Morgan took his place behind her in line.

"I cannot accept this, madam," the customs official was saying. "Your passport is out of date."

The woman protested in accented English, "It is valid, it is valid."

"The document is out of date, madam." The official snapped it shut and threw it across the table. "When the ship docks you will not be allowed to land. Sir!" He was talking past her shoulder to Morgan, who handed over his passport.

The woman was crying now, refusing to pick up the abandoned passport. "My husband will be waiting for me."

"Your first trip to China, sir?" the red-faced Englishman asked, ignoring the crying woman. He had hardly glanced at the passport beyond noticing the British crest on the cover.

"Yes."

The woman stood between Morgan and the officer, but still he craned to look at Morgan's wet jacket.

"I was out in the rain," Morgan explained, trying to look slightly shamefaced at his condition. "I wanted to see the coastline."

The customs officer smiled. He stamped the passport, handed it over, and said, "You'll have customs on the dock. Welcome to China. Next!"

On the deck Morgan threaded his way through the bundles and suitcases of the deck passengers. A wide brown stain marked where the Yangtze met the Whangpoo. The landscape faded to gray on either side of the river, then went black, with single, very small lights gleaming here and there in the night. The sight of his one well-scuffed brown leather suitcase on his bunk yielded a moment of severe loneliness, and he sat down on the bunk as the unaccustomed feeling flowed through him. He wasn't a man to examine his interior feelings. He had stopped that long ago, somewhere in the trenches of France where the men under his command died one by one for decisions that Morgan had heard made back in the command tent, decisions that he already knew were doomed to failure.

Searching in his pockets, he found a packet of Players cigarettes, lighting one with the stamped gold lighter already acquainted with the pawnshops of three continents. Blowing out the smoke, he looked at the fading gold letters on the suitcase. His father had given it to him when he had gotten his commission.

"You have to have a decent case to keep your civilian kit" had been his words as he presented the shining leather luggage to Morgan. They had never been close, but at that moment Morgan had known with a flash of intense loss that there was another, unknown side to his father. He had stammered out his thanks, standing proudly and a little foolishly in his new infantry officer's uniform. Driving away to meet his regiment, he had vowed that he would take time later to know his father. There had been no time and then too much time, years and years of it.

Morgan stood at the rail as the steamer took a long, slow swing around a bend in the river, and there, rising from the night, was Shanghai, Babylonian skyscrapers flushed with light. Morgan peered forward, his heart hammering with the most intense feeling of belonging that he could ever remember. "Hello," Morgan whispered to the lights. "Hello." His excitement grew, and he yearned to be off the ship, moving through those milling people, walking among the imposing buildings with their crowns of light high in the sky.

The immigration authorities were still at their tables in the lounge. He saw no sign of Mr. Wei. The launches were already by the ship. Morgan pushed to the front of the crowd waiting to disembark and was in the second tender as it moved away from the rust-stained steamer.

The customs shed was lit by the white flare lamps high overhead. As he stepped ashore he was asked, "Will you have any other luggage, sir?"

"No," Morgan told the khaki-uniformed Britisher.

"Nothing from the hold?"

"Just this," Morgan said, indicating the leather case. He registered the disapproving look that had swept over his filthy suit, the cracked shoes, the suitcase.

"Will you be staying long?"

"I'm not sure."

The customs inspector gestured at a Chinese, who stepped forward and lifted Morgan's suitcase. Morgan put his hand on the case. "What are you looking for?" he asked.

"This is an official inspection, sir," the man replied frostily.

Morgan lifted his hand, silent as the locks were unsnapped to reveal a tumble of dirty clothes. He could sense the Englishman's distaste and turned away with the thought that he didn't give a damn what a man such as this thought. He had seen a thousand of them throughout the empire, little men from middle-class schools swollen with their own authority away from England. When he looked back, his clothes had been stirred about, but there was nothing to find. He wondered if they would have the nerve to search him, and, if they did, what they would make of Mr. Wei's list.

"Thank you, sir," the inspector told him without looking him in the eye.

Morgan was left to close his own case. He waved away the coolies who swarmed forward to take it from him and walked with a broad stride through the customs shed and out into the night.

Morgan strolled away from the pier, looking down into the black water where formless shapes moved on the sluggish tide. Beggars approached him, looked up into his cold eyes, and moved away, murmuring to themselves. He waited, smoking yet another cigarette, his throat asking for a drink. He recognized some of the passengers from the ship as they came out of the shed, but there was no sign of Mr. Wei or a deputy.

After an hour, Morgan impatiently turned back his frayed shirt cuff. He made the gesture automatically and once again saw his bare, thick wrist where his watch had been before he'd sold it in Calcutta for the passage to Shanghai. He watched the Packards, and the Rolls limousines, the Pierce-Arrows and the old but articulate Hispano Suiza, pulling up at the hotel across the boulevard. Finally he gestured to a rickshaw coolie who had been eyeing him for a quarter of an hour.

"You got money?"

"I got money," Morgan said.

"Must see."

Smiling, Morgan pulled out Mr. Wei's fifty pounds. He could have used the other half. At the same time he took out the scrap of paper and read off the address Vicky had given him.

"Okay," the coolie said.

Morgan put his case in the rickshaw and stepped in, rocking the light cart. He sat back as the coolie pulled into the moving traffic without looking back. As a bus filled with Chinese faces drew abreast, he waved, but not an expression changed.

He wondered now what he would say if Evelyn was there. They hadn't exchanged a word in five years, yet he had always known somehow that he was heading toward Shanghai. He had long ago stopped worrying about the future. It took care of itself—not as well as you hoped, but well enough as long as you kept moving.

He found, in any case, that he wasn't worried. The sense of recognition he had experienced at the first sight of the city rising on the riverbank had stayed with him, getting stronger now as he watched the teak-colored Sikh police on their stands in the middle of the road. He could operate in this atmosphere. He knew that. He had felt himself a stranger everywhere since the war, most of all in England. For a while in Africa he had thought he had found his place: a hut on a distant river, room enough to lose himself to drink and dark women, to do whatever it was that displaced men were meant to do. There was a long tradition for men like him; Conrad and Melville, Maugham, had books full of them.

But the restlessness had never gone. He could get drunk enough but never lose his own sense of cool control. The missionaries with their earnest, meddling good works had amused him for the first year, and the swarming tribes that appeared at the post to trade skins for whatever he had been sent to get rid of had had some interest for him. But he found the anger at the senseless waste of the war had never left, and the dreams that had seemed common enough after the war had stayed, becoming strangely frightening as the years went by and events from beyond his own stretch of an African river reached him.

The smell of the river became more pungent as the rickshaw slowed to cross a small, arched bridge over a tributary creek. The houses here were smaller, set further back and lighted like homes. The evening air was cool, and soon, as they pushed further away from the water, Morgan smelled the faint perfume of summer flowers.

The rickshaw coolie stopped abruptly, dropping his handles. Morgan slid forward in the seat. "Here," the coolie said, pointing at a high, closed gate. Morgan stepped onto the road, seeing that there was a house beyond the gate, the long veranda around its second story just visible from where he stood. "Wait," he said.

"Pay," the man demanded, holding out his thin arm, palm upwards.

Ignoring him, Morgan made to ring the brass bell attached to the gatepost, but the clawlike hand grabbed his sleeve. Morgan shook his clasp off gently, but the claw grabbed him for a second time. He shoved the man on his heaving, ribbed chest, sending him sprawling. "Wait," he ordered the coolie, who looked at him with naked hatred. He had the now-familiar sensation of feeling two emotions at once: pity for the man in the road and the knowledge that if he showed any weakness, he would be the victim of a lifetime of grievances, anger, and revenge.

He heard the bell reverberate in the night. The coolie got up out of the dust, his face clean of expression, and stood by his rickshaw. Presently the wooden gate opened slightly to reveal a long driveway that curved before the stone steps of a pleasant blue house with the lights in windows on both stories.

A man much taller than any Chinese Morgan had ever seen outside of China called out, "Who is it?"

"Is this the house of Countess Evelyn Lezenski?"

"Who?" This time the demand came out in a suspicious hiss.

The coolie shifted closer to Morgan in the dark street. "Countess Evelyn Lezenski," he said more loudly.

The tall Chinese looked him up and down. "Who wants?"

"Her brother," Morgan replied evenly. He saw the disbelief in the face of the Chinese and the gate began to close. Morgan put his hand on it. He said in a voice that he had learned to use, low, but with its own menace, "Answer me."

"You wait," the Chinese told him, staring until Morgan dropped his arm.

The gate closed, and then Morgan and the coolie heard the bar going back across the gate. They listened to footsteps disappear back up the curving drive, to the distant sounds of Chinese voices working behind the house. They, too, stopped suddenly, and then the only sound was the soughing of the wind through the tall trees that washed into the street from the hidden garden beyond the wall.

"You pay," the coolie demanded softly, but with new menace.

Turning his back so he was protected by the gate, Morgan said, "Give me my case."

The coolie took the case off the floor of the rickshaw and dropped it in the dirt at his bare, filthy feet.

Taking Mr. Wei's money from within his jacket, Morgan peeled off a single pound—much too much, he knew, but all he had except for a few Hong Kong dollars that would be useless to the man.

The coolie examined the note in the dim light of the half moon. He picked up the shafts of the rickshaw and turned slowly, bending his thin shoulders as he gathered speed, disappearing into the dark.

Morgan had felt no fear of the coolie, but now that he was alone in the street a sense of danger seemed to seep out of the shuttered gardens. He turned up the collar of his jacket, wondering if the tall Chinese would return or if he would have to pick up his leather case and walk back toward the river. His well-developed instinct for foreign cities warned him that his chances of walking without harm along the dark streets to where the lights burned more brightly were slim.

He reached up and rang the bell hard. A cat screamed as though struck, and then there was silence. Time passed. A sudden rush of sound filled the night, footsteps coming down the drive. The bar was thrown back, the gate began to move slowly wider than before, and the tall Chinese stood before Morgan again.

"Morgan?"

He hadn't seen her, for the tall Chinese blocked all view of the garden. He stepped in, stooping to pass beneath the arm of the Chinese.

Disbelief this time. "Morgan?"

He couldn't make her out. The road to the house seemed as deserted as before, and then she called to him a third time. "Morgan!" Happiness changed the husky, unfamiliar voice, that of a much older woman. He looked up and saw her at the corner of the veranda on the second floor, standing just beyond the light from the room beyond.

Walking on, he registered spreading lawns and even flower beds, trees all along the perimeter, and, near the house, creepers that rose to envelope the building like lace. They surrounded the long windows of the first floor and trailed along the balcony, twisting about the columns that supported the roof and smothering the house with leaves and flowers.

He stood halfway up the drive and said, his voice quite steady, "I was passing, so I thought I'd drop in."

She disappeared within the room above. Morgan heard the gate close, and the tall Chinese came up carrying his suitcase. "Thank you," Morgan said.

The Chinese ignored him, walking up the drive toward the steps where Victoria appeared, running. She came down the steps and along the drive, stumbling, arms wide, calling, "Morgan, Morgan, Morgan." And for a flash of a second Morgan was transported back to the days when he had been away at boarding school and would come home to a greeting of flying arms and legs—to this child's mother.

Then she was in his arms, holding him tight, her face buried in his sweat-soaked shirt.

He put his arms about her, feeling the soft waves of her hair against his face, smelling the expensive perfume and, through her silk dress, the full body of a grown woman.

"Vicky," he murmured, overcome by an emotion that had taken him unprepared.

She stood back finally without letting him go. "Oh, Morgan, look at you," she said in shock.

His memory had protected him against her beauty. Even in his most feverish dreams, tossing in dirty, sweat-soaked sheets of some filthy Alexandria rooming house.

"Your poor suit" was all she said, but he knew that he had shocked her by his appearance in quite a different way.

"It's my best," he told her, shrugging.

"I wouldn't want to see your second-best," she said, smiling. As though she was afraid he might disappear if she let him go, she threaded her arm through his, hugging him to her as she led him toward the house. He saw two Chinese women, servants, peering at him through the open door.

"My God, Morgan, you smell," she said.

"I haven't had a bath in four days. I came steerage, second class on the *China Star* from Hong Kong."

As they neared the light he had a better look at her. She was slimmer than when he'd last seen her, in a plain gray silk dress whose cowl neck showed off her smooth shoulders and slim, straight neck, giving her an elegance that somehow he had never foreseen.

"You're lovely, Vicky," he told her.

The wide eyes brimmed with sudden tears. "Oh, Morgan. You're going to stay, aren't you?" she begged as they stepped up onto a small porch in front of the door.

The house took definition: polished walls, a floor that shone like a mirror, a very good rug in muted purple and turquoise that had to be a hundred or more years old, a delicately carved teak table facing the staircase. The table held a rose quartz statue of Kwan Ying, the goddess of mercy, worth a month's living anyplace you wanted to name in the world.

Victoria seemed to know what he was thinking. She didn't let go of his arm, but she looked down at her feet. The light came from a chandelier of beaten silver twisted into curling vines holding up tiny lamplit candles.

"Mother's, of course," she muttered. "The whole house."

"Is she here?" Morgan asked. He wasn't often nervous, but now his palms were sweating, his face damp. He smelled his own rankness, the sweat of fear.

"No," said Vicky, holding her head defiantly high for her mother's servants. For a moment Morgan had a flash of Alex as Morgan had last seen him twenty years ago, boarding the boat there at Paddington with this child's mother, a child herself then. Morgan took Victoria's chin in his hand, staring into her golden eyes, and winked.

"Are you hungry?" she asked but her blush only deepened.

"A drink would be nice."

He heard running water—more like falling water—and when Victoria dropped his arm and rushed down the hall, he strolled into the living room. This room was as lovely as the hall, with its rose carpet picked out with apple blossoms, stately, uncomfortable-looking chairs of white birch covered with red silk cushions, low tables with many, many delicate silver boxes all very highly polished, and at the end tall windows framed with rose silk that stood open to a garden where a lawn smoothed away to a tiny waterfall. He went out onto the lawn and stood in the pearl-white moonlight, looking at the blue shadows of the trees that arched overhead, hung with delicate bamboo birdcages. The sleeping rice birds shifted at the sight of him but didn't make a sound. All the way around the second story more floor-length windows stood open, showing golden light from within.

He had a sharp pang of what might have been envy. He'd put aside his own dreams a long time ago, but this tranquil house brought back his years of flight with a rush, turning the sense of adventure that he allowed to nurture him in the lowest moments of his fortunes into what he knew it to be in the darkest moments of the night: fear and emptiness. Failure.

Victoria came out of the living room, searching for him. "I thought you had gone," she said fearfully.

"Not a chance."

She stood where the lawn began, the house rising all about and the garden flowing from the tips of her shoes. She was lovely, a lovely child. Yet he knew other things about her, so that when she moved slightly and the light threw shadows across her face he saw the pain of her long, confused childhood, the complexity of a woman much older than her years.

One of the Chinese women servants appeared in the living room with a silver tray and two glasses. "Your drink is ready," she called.

Victoria turned back, but Morgan put out his hand and took her wrist. "I like it out here."

They each took a glass off the offered tray. He had never seen her drink whiskey. There must be a thousand things—natural acts, part of her life—that he had never seen her do.

"Why are you here?" she asked.

He sat down on the stoop of the house, elbows on his knees, drink held between his hands. It was the move of a young man, the young man he had once been, and Victoria watched him from above with the familiar feeling that she was the older one.

"I lost some money," he said.

"Oh." She sounded disappointed.

He looked up. "And to see you," he admitted. She had moved further into the darkness.

"How is your mother?" he asked.

"Driven." The word hung in the spring air. Clouds came to draw a thin cover before the moon, making the garden very dark, then, as they passed, unnaturally brilliant. Uncle and niece were revealed to each other, man and woman, aware of all they were avoiding.

"And your father?"

She shifted in an awkward movement, and he saw her mother in her, too. "Driven," she had said of Evelyn, but it was herself she described, he thought. He was struck again by how often our own elusive qualities enrage us in others.

"He's not in Shanghai." She sounded more angry than disappointed. "He's in Nanking. Teaching." She sounded almost scornful, but whether it was at her father or the circumstances that had reduced him to teaching was unclear. The young, he thought, rushed to judgment at every turn. Perhaps *he* still did; perhaps that's why nothing had ever worked out quite right for him.

"Will you see him?"

"I can't!" she retorted, brilliant moonlight reflecting off her wide eyes and teeth, making her look half-demented, a case for Bedlam. She tossed down the rest of her drink. "There's this damn war on with Japan. Nanking's almost cut off. You can't get in or out unless you have some sort of priority," she added as an afterthought.

He watched her closely, feeling sad for her, and old, too. She was fighting her own battles, battles in an old war best forgotten.

"I'm glad you're here," she said abruptly, looking at him with the same burning eyes. He shivered inadvertently and was shocked by the reflex.

She cocked her head. "We can help each other."

"Oh?" he said blandly, raising his eyebrows.

"Don't be horrible," she begged, "please. I need you."

"I need a bath."

She went back into her mother's beautiful house. He sat listening to the soft night sounds. From here you could be unaware that there was a city out there. He thought Evelyn must have chosen this house very carefully. It was as though he had arrived home after a long, long journey. Perhaps he had, he thought, as a Chinese servant came softly up behind him and whispered, "Bath ready."

He followed the Chinese woman through the house, already familiar with the luxury, not out of place or scornful. He had to get used to the idea that Evelyn fitted into this house, with its long silk draperies and ancestor portraits such as he had seen in museums in England. He knew the long carpet on the second floor, this one almost the color of dried blood on the lacquered floor, and the celadon bowls filled with floating gardenia blossoms were all worth a great deal of money.

Two thoughts coalesced: that the only way a woman could achieve such wealth was through a man; and that since he'd entered the house he had been resenting that she had been living this well while he drifted from port to port.

The servant left him in the plain, handsome room over the street, a room with a single bed made up in soft white linen, a bare floor, a tall chest with a man's mirror, and a double-faced closet of black lacquer. Curious, he opened the lacquered closet doors. Taking out a silk robe, he held it against him and saw that it fit a short, heavy man. Fischer? But Victoria had told him Fischer was dead. Fischer must have left Evelyn a very great deal of money for her to live like this. But she lived in Manila, he reminded himself as he loosened the greasy knot of his tie. Curious.

He put the robe back just as there was a knock, and Victoria opened the door. He wondered if the almost imperceptible change in her expression meant she knew that he had opened the closet. Probably, yet she had offered him this room.

"I've sent for some clothes for you," she said.

"At this hour?"

"You can get anything here at any time if you can pay for it." She turned to hide the color that rose again into her face. "It won't be much, anyway. Just some pajamas and a robe."

"I have some clothes in the suitcase."

"The servants are deciding now whether to burn them or wash them," she informed him tartly. As she came across the room her eyes were alight with a long-remembered mischief as she put her hand on his chest. "When you come downstairs there'll be a meal ready."

He must have stared at her for a moment longer than intended, because she took on a wary, defensive look.

"It's wrong," he whispered. "You know that, don't you?"

The color deepened, and she started to look away, but this time he held her. When she looked back it was to say, "I don't want to think about it."

He touched her lips with one dirty finger the way he had that first time, when she was fifteen, swearing her to secrecy. In those days it had always been he who had broken the rules. This time, it seemed it was to be her. "Oath."

A shudder passed through her whole body. "Oh, Morgan, I'm so glad you're back."

"Oath?"

"Oath," she repeated, her eyes brimming with tears.

"I won't tell if you won't," he said.

She moved away from his loose embrace. "No one really cares out here," she said, "unless you've done something terrible." She stopped and looked over her shoulder. "You haven't killed anyone, have you?"

"No."

She shrugged, an indifferent movement of her shoulders while her eyebrows came together very slightly, like those of a petulant child. "Then nothing will matter. There are different rules out here. Look at Mother."

"I haven't killed anyone," he repeated.

"Even that wouldn't matter here," she said, not facing him, "as long as you didn't kill the wrong person. People die all the time. . . ." Her voice had trailed off, dropping away, lost in memory for a second. She turned, and her eyes were afire with the memory. "Life is very cheap here."

"It is everywhere." He had seen a lot more of the world than she had, whatever she thought.

She blinked and was quiet as the memory faded from her eyes. "I'll be waiting for you downstairs," she said, going past him quickly. "The clothes will be here soon. The bath is through that door."

He would have to teach her, he thought as he stripped off his dirty clothes, how to tell a lie with a straight face by first making yourself believe it. How to steal from the pantry and make a mess so it was blamed on a cat; how to play one adult against another. Tossing the clothes on the floor and crossing the room he pushed open the door she'd indicated and came face to face with his unfamiliar naked reflection in a long mirror. Much thinner, his ribs stood out, yet his shoulders were still strongly muscled, and his neck, though sinewy, was thick. His hips and thighs still testified to a youth spent on boarding school athletic fields, and his calves were handsome and strong.

"The playing fields of Eton," he murmured to his image, peering forward through the fragrant steam to see what others would make of his face. He seemed to be frozen at the age he had finally reached some years ago. Five years ago he had looked worn and lined, and before that—in the first few years after the war—he had looked dissipated. Now he had grown into his face; the eyes were clear and bright, framed by crow's-feet from squinting at the equatorial sun. As he moved his full lips into a smile he saw they made him look good-natured, wise, experienced. His nose, always straight, had somehow gathered the very slightest curve to it. His nostrils had narrowed, and his chin had set. He knew that this was the result of anger and tension, a fury that had forced him to clench his jaw and breathe deeply so as not to strike out, but he saw a handsome, predatory face that would be useful.

He stepped into the bath, sinking deep into the scalding water, feeling the whiskey pump through his blood, and he lay back feeling that he had arrived after a long journey at an exciting destination. He would teach Evelyn, he thought drowsily, how to handle memory. It was the same lesson he had taught her as a child about lies: You denied it.

Victoria found the bathroom door closed and unwrapped the package on the bed. The pajamas had come from a tailor catering to the European trade, and like many Chinese copies, they were somehow not right—the collar too small, the jacket enormous, the pants billowing out large enough for two men. She giggled at Morgan's probable reaction, but then, Boon had found them on an hour's notice.

The Chinese robe was better: larger, and made of royal blue silk with a white peony on the breast pocket. She laid it beside the pajamas and picked up the clothes Morgan had dropped on the floor. Emptying the pockets onto the lacquer chest, she closed the door behind her.

Morgan's clean hair was golden. In the dim light of the living room, he seemed a young man.

"Very glamorous," she commented.

He came forward, and the lines in his face revealed not a boy but a strong man. Women in Shanghai would fall for him.

"I put your gold lighter on the chest," she said mischievously.

He took it from the pocket of the robe and held it up. "My capital!"

"Dinner's ready." She took him into the square room, hand-painted gold swallows swooping near the ceiling. Two places had been set facing across a rose bowl of floating petals. They were halfway through their meal of fish baked with ginger and vegetables before Victoria put down her fork. "I've got to get to Nanking. Will you help me?"

He moved his fork helplessly over the plate. "How? I've just arrived myself."

"A man can always manage these things better," she said testily.

He sighed. "Could you write?" She hadn't seen her father in years, and as Morgan knew, a man could create a whole new life in much less time. He might not want this evidence of another life unbidden on his doorstep. Men didn't always want to be saved.

"I have to see him!" The redness returned to her eyes.

"All right," he said quietly. "Whatever I can do, I will."

"Thank you."

After the meal he was tired. They had a brandy—Evelyn's brandy—in the living room, and Morgan had a cigar from a camphorwood humidor. Whose? he wondered. He kissed Victoria lightly and went up to his narrow bed.

He lay in the dark, feeling confidence in the future that he had thought had left him forever.

When the moon had passed beyond the garden, he was awakened by her in the narrow bed with him. His body was alert, his member erect before consciousness had fully come to him. They made furious love, as passionate as the first time in California when he had come to see her on a Sunday afternoon, as passionate as later in Paris, in Alexandria.

His eyes widened with some thought that had broken his sleep. She was gone. He couldn't recall the dream. He tried to sleep again, then got up to search among his few belongings for Mr. Wei's list. Finding the two sheets of paper folded in his passport, he examined them by the dawn light that paled the sky above the unseen city. He had a strong, overwhelming conviction that the incomprehensible Chinese characters were important.

Morgan checked the cuffs of his new jacket, shooting his hand-tailored silk shirt out of the sleeve, nodding with satisfaction. "Yes, that'll do very nicely."

Ly Sam, the fat Chinese tailor, bowed happily. "Very good suit."

"Very good six suits," Morgan reminded him.

"Much best," Ly Sam agreed.

"What about the dinner jacket?" Morgan reminded him. "I need it tonight."

"Ready soon."

"Tonight."

"You see, have jacket soon."

"All right," Morgan said, slipping out of the gray silk suit jacket. He handed it to the tailor, letting his eyes run over the other fabrics. The black would be in keeping with the conservative profile he wanted to cut in Shanghai. The darker gray and the two white suits would be useful at the Shanghai Club, which Victoria had pointed out to him as a bastion of power. In his two weeks here he'd made a point of having the driver, Ng Ho, regularly drive along the Bund past the club.

Vicky had insisted on giving him five hundred pounds,

drawn, he knew, from her mother's account. He took the money, resolved to cut a good figure in Shanghai. He'd pay Evelyn back eventually.

"You will send the evening clothes to my room," he ordered Ly Sam. "To the new address."

"Will do, will do," Ly Sam assured him, taking away the jacket with loving care.

The bachelor's rooms in the Chinese city had troubled Vicky. "You could stay here. Mother lives in Manila," she insisted. "It's wasteful to have another home."

He touched her chin. "And where would we meet when she's in Shanghai?"

He could have added that he also wanted privacy to follow his own path. He had learned to separate business and passions of the flesh, even flesh like hers, whose touch took control of his mind. "I intend to make a lot of money," he told Vicky.

Well dressed in European clothes, she had the aristocrat's disregard of whose money he spent—Alex's blood, no doubt. "You promised you would help me find Papa," she reminded him.

He felt a flash of annoyance at being lectured by her. Their positions had been reversed; she was more experienced in local ways. He couldn't think why that annoyed him so much except that in all his travels he had kept somewhere in his mind the picture of her as a young girl and himself as the seducer. He wasn't so sure anymore that his memory had been accurate.

As he left the tailor shop he saw an old man squatting carefully, reproducing Chinese lettering on a paper. A letter writer.

"Wait," Morgan ordered Ng Ho, who held the open door of the Packard. He pushed his way through the crowd and stood over the old letter writer.

The man looked up, his brush raised over the paper of the woman squatting near him. She would dictate a thought, and he would phrase it, often formally and not completely accurately. He would read it back to her and wait while she considered what to say next.

"Can you speak English?"

The old man looked at Morgan without moving. The woman turned toward the crowded street. This was an important and expensive moment for her.

"Here," Morgan said, thrusting Mr. Wei's list at the letter writer. "I want this copied."

The old man put his brush down with care, read the list carefully, then looked back at Morgan without expression.

"Copy," Morgan said, pantomiming writing.

The old man affected not to have understood, but then slowly he raised his brush again and began to copy Mr. Wei's list onto a fresh paper.

Morgan took a tin of Players Navy Cut from his suit pocket and leaned against the rickshaw. The noodle vendors stoked the fires under their stalls; a man carried a dozen live ducks, their eyes glazed with pure terror, strung upside down to a pole; a coolie spat at his feet, just missing the polished toe of his new boots. Morgan breathed in the sweat and stink of daily life, and he loved it. He threw his cigarette at the bare feet of the rickshaw coolie, ground it out with the heel of his boot, and turned back for his list.

The woman who had been dictating her letter sat as still as a stone, her face turned away. The old man blew sand across the characters, shook the paper, and held it up to Morgan. They looked the same, Morgan thought, but he couldn't be sure. The old man's eyes had a gleam of malice. Morgan paid, shoved his way back to the car, and folded both lists away in the pocket of his jacket. Ng Ho shouted at the crowd as he walked around the hood of the car.

They traveled out of the Chinese city with its low roofs, the strings of laundry strung like garlands between the buildings, the smell of poverty, spices, humanity pressed together. Soon they were in the international settlement, passing the townhouses of the great taipans.

A spring breeze came from the river, fetid with the smell of decomposing corpses, with rank river mud. At the French concession the driver headed north, gathering speed on the broader avenues. They heard the sound of the crowd long before they reached the place of execution near the railroad station. Morgan peered ahead to where a wall of backs blocked his view of the killing ground. He wondered who they were today—thieves, pirates, more likely communists. In league with the local gangsters, Chiang had rounded up a cell of communists last week.

"Stop," Morgan ordered, craning forward over the heads of the crowd. The five prisoners were lined up on their knees, each head forward for the executioner's sword. At the flash of the sword, the crowd gasped, then jeered as the blood spouted into the dirt. The other four prisoners waited without protest, without a sigh or plea for mercy.

Morgan sat back, ashamed of himself, and Ng Ho drove on. They had passed beyond the station when the second sigh came to them like a breeze in the budding willow trees that lined the river bank near the Soochow Creek.

At the river bridge, where the European jurisdiction ended, they were stopped by Chinese troops. Beyond this point was China. "What do they want?" Morgan asked the coolie.

"Papers."

Morgan handed his passport to the Nationalist soldier, who scanned it without understanding and returned it surlily. As Ng Ho moved the car forward Morgan observed a Japanese staff car approaching from the other direction and thought how strange it was that a country at war with China could have a large presence on the continent. But Shanghai was an international settlement, and therefore not part of China. That fine Chinese distinction suited him.

They moved through the suburbs, a curious mixture of bourgeois European architecture and Chinese shanties. Nothing Morgan had encountered in the two weeks he had been here had changed his mind that this was the place he was meant to be. He saw another Japanese car approaching fast, and the driver swung the Packard heavily off the road onto the mud shoulder as the khaki green swept past. He allowed himself to turn and utter a string of curses at the disappearing car.

Soon they were passing through open countryside. The great houses of the various Shanghai taipans sat back from the road amid splendid gardens just now fading into late autumn colors. They passed houses owned by opium millionaires, British trading house partners, Austrian bankers, and then were once more amid the shacks. Soon the nightclubs and dance halls appeared, clustered together at the very outskirts of the city, and it was here that Morgan had found the rooms he wanted.

Ng Ho pulled the Packard up, in silent disapproval, before a pale pink villa of two stories, its paint neither new nor fresh. Behind it a sign, "New World Dance Hall," rose like a warning of the future, but now the lights that circled it after dark were off.

As the car pulled away, Morgan stepped over a muddy ditch and along a path laid through the runoff of last night's rain. He let himself into his rooms on the lower floor, the upper floor being his landlady's, a florid Chinese woman who spoke only through an interpreter. The long living room held two low couches, some tables, some cheap fringed lamps. The living room gave onto a walled garden where a chipped Buddha sat in a lichen-covered niche just beneath the New World sign rising beyond the garden. There was a dining room and a bedroom in the same style, and a smaller room beyond the kitchen for one servant. At night you could hear the music, which was why the rooms were so cheap. They were intended for a dance-hall girl, and the agent who had brought him here had done everything he could to discourage Morgan.

When he saw them he had thought that they might have been waiting for him. He liked to be hidden away from the glare of respectable society, and out here amid the nightclubs and houses of prostitution, he was sure to find his way to the fortune that was waiting for him.

He poured himself a drink now and watched as night fell and the signs came on. The music wouldn't begin until after midnight. Elsewhere in rooms like this the girls would be waking, stretching from a night of dance and paid-for love.

Morgan liked the sense of a city that never slept, of one army leaving the streets to sleep as another took possession. A man could be anything he wanted here, even himself.

Coming down the staircase of the blue house in a clingy silver dress, Victoria said, "I don't know why you had to choose to live out in the red-light district."

"It's not all whorehouses," he told her. She looked completely self-possessed, he thought, like a woman of the world, and for a moment he was sad for her. But then he dismissed that thought, knowing that you took whatever life was offered.

She stopped at the foot of the steps and put her hand on the shoulder of his new jacket. "You look very handsome," she said, and she kissed him on the mouth as Lye Choy went by with an armful of linen without looking at them.

"You shouldn't do that," Morgan cautioned Victoria.

"Why not? It's the truth, isn't it?" she asked him. Only then did a flash of child appear, a defiance of convention.

"You embarrass them."

She laughed. "Oh, Morgan," she said, "deep in your soul, you really are very bourgeois, aren't you?"

"As opposed to the uncaring aristocracy?" he shot back.

"Impoverished, uncaring aristocracy," she said, adjusting the two silver and diamond earrings that dangled from the lobes of her ears. Every single part of her seemed to have been created perfectly, Morgan reflected. He had seen that in other misfits; they were complete, self-made, and lost. He feared for her, but he had abandoned concern for others years and years ago, and he couldn't hold the feeling long.

"This aristocrat seems to have recovered her fortune," he observed, putting her silver lamé stole about her shoulders.

"Someone did," she said, looking at him shyly. "It does help to have a clever mother."

"Are those real?" Morgan asked, looking at the earrings.

"I think so," she laughed. "I found a tiny little safe in Mother's room, not hard to open. It must be her getaway fund or something. There were these and that money I gave you." She taunted him with the knowledge that he was her partner in crime as they went out the front door to the waiting car. "I could have sent Ng Ho back for you," she told him.

"There are lots of taxis out there," he said, sliding in beside her. "That was one of the reasons I chose the rooms."

"One of them."

The car took them downtown to where the night was bright with lights. At the Palace Hotel they walked through the lobby toward the elevators, and Morgan saw how the eyes of both men and women followed Victoria. Taking it as her right, she stood with her arm through his until the elevator cage descended to the lobby; then they rode to the top floor, where the doors slid open to the dining room and nightclub. The forty-piece orchestra was already playing, and a path seemed to part for them as they walked through the dancers toward their raised table.

She's going to be a very famous woman, Morgan thought. He was more reflective now that he was used to the strange transformation that was coming over her since he'd seen her last. We're the same type, he thought, watching as she slid into the banquette, throwing the lamé stole in such a way that her throat, the tops of her breasts, her shoulders were revealed all at once. A nearby dancer stumbled.

Alex's tiger eyes swept about the room. "Do you think they know they're outdated?" she asked Morgan as he ordered champagne. "Champagne?"

"To celebrate our mutual debut in Shanghai," he suggested. "Are they out of date?"

"Of course they are," she said, watching as the dancers moved smoothly past the table. "You see the Japanese everywhere."

"You think that they'll take over in China?" he asked scornfully.

"I think we're not here for long." She looked thoughtful. "Or these people aren't."

"You don't consider yourself part of them?"

"No," she said, shocked. "You don't, either."

"No, I don't," he agreed.

"What will you do now?" she asked him as the waiter popped the cork. She ignored people's stares.

"Seek my fortune," he suggested, tasting the wine and nodding without looking at the waiter. "A good imperial trait. What about you? You can't just hang about, can you?"

She laughed, taking her glass. "Hang about?" she said. "It sounds like a death sentence. No," she said, raising her glass. "I'm going to find Alex first."

He had never heard her refer to her father as Alex. The sullen schoolgirl had gained confidence, defiance, strength. She was home, he saw. "In Nanking?"

"Yes," she said, sipping the champagne. Her eyes got angry, then empty of expression. "I have to see him." She sighed. "He's my father," she said, as though she was trying to convince herself of something.

"To our mutual success, then," Morgan said, raising his glass in a toast. They clinked glasses, then they got up and danced, clinging to each other amid the dancers. The feel of her body along his brought back stronger desires than he had ever felt, and he knew he should take her away from the watching eyes. But one dance became another, then another. When they finally left the dance floor they were both breathless.

"I want to see your rooms," she said.

"Now?"

"Yes—I'm tired of this," she said with the irritability of a child easily bored. "Let's go."

Morgan said, "We're making a scandal of ourselves."

She shrugged indifferently. "That would be a novelty in Shanghai. There's only one real scandal, and that's financial ruin."

Seeing the huge New World sign flick on and off imperiously, she commented, "I can see why you like this."

"What do you want?" Morgan asked her, moving into the dark living room. "I haven't hired anyone to look after me."

"You," she said, and he turned to find her naked, her dress at her feet. The diamond pendant earrings swung as she came to him, her breasts very full, her waist as narrow as a child's, but her hips those of a woman. She put her arms about him and leaned against him, kissing him hard. "Treat me like a whore," she begged him.

"Why not?" he whispered to her in the dark. "You are one."

Her gasp was real, but then she smiled. "Yes," she said with a sigh that might have been relief. "It's better that way. Mother's right there, anyway."

He kissed her, then pushed her away so he could undress. She went into his bedroom and lay on the bed, the lights from the sign bringing her into focus, then banishing her to darkness, second after second. He was angry as he tore at his new jacket, threw it on the floor amid the sparkling threads of her gown. When he went into her, he pushed her back as she reached for him, climbed above her and entered her with such force that she screamed out. She clawed at his shoulders, fighting him for a moment, then calming, finding his rhythm. They climbed a mountain together, collapsing at the top amid Morgan's groans and her high cries.

In the silence afterward, the light went on and off, on and off. "Is that how you treat whores?" she asked.

"Shut up, Vic," he told her. "Don't play that on me."

She said nothing. Then, "All right." Then, later, "I have to get to Nanking, you know that, don't you?"

He sighed, rolled away from her.

"What's wrong?" she asked him as he closed the heavy, lined curtains and they became invisible to each other.

"Every whore I ever knew had a sentimental depth somewhere," he said. "It's the secret to them—a child, a past, some man . . . even a father, I suppose."

He could hear her breathe in the dark. "You're a bastard, aren't you?"

"Yes," he said. "We're alike there, anyway. It's what attracts you to me."

"You'll help me get to Nanking?"

He came back to the bed. "I don't know how, but I will. You shouldn't go there, you know. The Japanese are right outside the city."

They made love in the dark, then fell asleep and made love again, and then fell asleep once more, until the room smelled of their lovemaking and they both fell away into a deep sleep. In Morgan's dreams he was back in England, touching Victoria, who sat with her back to him, the diamond earrings dancing in the light from a pale English moon. As he leaned down to bite her shoulder she turned, and it wasn't Victoria but Evelyn. He was stunned, his heart racing so fast that it awakened him.

The other room was still gray with night. The sign went out as he pulled on the trousers to his dinner suit. Then he started, for sitting on the sofa was Mr. Wei.

"Jesus!" Morgan exclaimed, wondering how he had gotten in and how long he had been there.

"Good morning, Mr. Valentine," Mr. Wei said quietly. "You have prospered since last we met, I see."

Morgan crossed to the open bedroom door and closed it. "You scared me."

Mr. Wei glanced at the closed door. "Mr. Valentine, I do not think much would scare you."

16

The red sports car shuddered as they took the sweep of the bay at seventy-five miles an hour. Evelyn reached out to touch Miles's bare arm. He had left his uniform behind today, and she found it difficult to accustom herself to this fair-haired, white-shirted man. He wore white duck pants and no socks, light shoes with no laces, and she thought he should have been playing cricket or baseball, writing poetry in the shade of chestnut trees with green lawns and parkland stretching away for as far as the eye could see.

His green parklands, *his* shade, *his* trees. He had the petulant look of a young heir; yet as he swung the car back onto the center of the road she saw the familiar clenching in his jaw and reached up to trace a path along the line of his chin. "Open your mouth."

"What?" His eyes were impatient at being interrupted in his thoughts.

"You're going to bite your tongue in two one of these days," she said, putting her hand under his open collar to massage the tension at the nape of his neck. He was a deceptive man—boyish, callow at first meeting—but the current ran strong in him. She had the impression that Miles Foster was always fighting some battle within himself and would be for all his days.

"I just get so damn frustrated," he explained.

"Leave all that behind today," she asked him.

"I will if you will," he said, and the smile flashed like lightning across the dark shadows of his eyes.

"All right." She thought she had learned her lessons well, but in the ten days they had known each other Miles Foster had startled her more than once by cutting through her deceptions. Agnelli's cables were becoming more peremptory and he was quite capable of getting back on a plane and turning up in Manila. Yet she couldn't bring herself to return to Shanghai, to do anything about the ship that by now was steaming relentlessly toward Manila.

The clouds coming down from the distant ridge of green hills cast a rash across the sea's dark surface. She watched a fishing boat rising and falling on a strong tide and thought about that other ship out there on the Pacific, its hold filled with a fortune in junk metal, coming closer. The news from China was very bad. The Japanese army was encamped between Shanghai and Nanking, where the government was now making a brave show of defending the old capital. Peking had been abandoned.

With no word from Tu, she knew she had to return soon. She couldn't conceive a fall into Japanese hands. Chiang had been practicing the ancient Chinese art of retreat in war, withdrawing further and further into the vast, empty countryside. The Russians had done that also for centuries, she thought as Miles turned off the coast road, slowing for a bus loaded with marketgoers, the pigs and chickens strapped, terrified, to the roof. Perhaps Alex had more in common with the Chinese than she had at first thought. When she thought of Alex, she thought of Victoria alone in Shanghai in the blue house. She was afraid of facing Victoria. Her weekly letters went unanswered, though a considerable sum had been withdrawn from the Hong Kong Shanghai bank in the last month.

There wasn't any way Victoria could get to Nanking, she reassured herself. And Alex would have to leave if the Japanese took the city, would have to go back to Shanghai, protected by international treaty.

"You promised," Miles Foster said, another perceptive shot.

"I've been known to break promises," she said, trying to shift her mood.

"Not to me," he said, and his eyes were solemn, the needy

eyes of an unloved boy. When he looked like that she wanted to reach for him and tell him she would love him forever. But just as strongly she wished she'd never met him—not here, at least. He had too many needs, and she wasn't sure she could meet them. He was a surprisingly virile lover, however; not a boy at all, but a man, selfish, hungry, who made her feel desired in a way she never had before. She wasn't sure she could ever give that up.

"You promised," he said more firmly.

"I know."

"You're thinking about Shanghai again."

"The news is so bad."

"But Shanghai will be fine. Tell her to come here."

She knew he thought she was too embarrassed by his own presence to send for Victoria and she would have been, that was true. But Victoria wouldn't have come anyway. And she couldn't explain about Fischer. All Miles Foster knew was that she had been married to Victoria's father—was *still* married to him, she reminded herself. When Fischer died, she hadn't gone through with the divorce that she had planned. She knew Miles suspected that there had been someone else, but he never pried. He had good instincts, she thought, and she knew that she could be happy in a world of their own creation.

She reached for his knee to reassure herself. Alex had felt powerful, and Fischer had been intelligent. But with Miles, she had only to touch his body to feel she didn't care much what happened anywhere.

"Now, that's better," he said, still laughing as he swung the car about around a sharp corner and then shot up the long stretch of road as though in a race. "I like a woman who makes the first move."

Rain began as they started up into the higher hills. "I hadn't planned on this," Miles said. The loose plastic window blinds were blowing against the framework of the car. "There's a lodge sort of thing by the falls," he said. "We'll stop there if it's still raining."

The lodge, perched on stilts, sat to one side of the road with the dark jungle growing up the mountain behind. He parked the car, and they ran hand in hand through the already impressive mud and into the windy building.

There wasn't a soul in sight. "I'll see if we can get some service," Miles said, and he went off through the wide front room with its low rattan couches and plain wooden tables. Evelyn leaned against the railing and looked down into the jade-green pool where the waterfall met the jungle. The rain, sleeting across the surface, looked like bullets.

Miles reported with wonder, "We're alone."

Evelyn leaned her head against his chest. "The rain will stop after a while."

He put his arms about her. "Maybe it won't. Maybe we'll be here for days."

"That'd be nice."

As the rain fell in an unbroken sheet past the window, she lay against Miles's chest, feeling wrapped in warmth and safety. She thought back on the night he'd arrived in his little car shortly after midnight. He came through the front door as though he had lived there for years. Waiting up for him in the long living room—the servants asleep—she had seen there were lines in his face that she couldn't remember.

"Would you like a drink?"

"I want a bath and oblivion," he told her, and she thought she saw how his father must have looked. "God, I'm tired."

"You should have gone home and slept," she told him. "I would have understood." Yet she knew that this was a lie.

"I wouldn't have slept anyway," he said, and he pulled her against him and kissed her on the mouth.

The sense of familiarity, of a routine picked up as naturally as picking up a man's towel dropped on the floor, was very strong. She had forgotten how powerful familiarity could be, and she was afraid to speak in case she was making more of this than she should.

They went into the kitchen, and she made him scrambled eggs. She had little idea where anything was, and they made a game of finding things, making so much noise that the cook arrived, sweat-stained T-shirt over his bulk. They sent him away and played like young lovers, eating scrambled eggs from plates held up to their mouths, drinking milk, and then going off to bed too tired to make love, too aroused to fall off.

"I need a bath," he said, pulling his shirt out of the band of his trousers.

"Just get in bed," she ordered.

"I stink," he said.

"Get in bed."

He sat on the edge of the bed and undressed, kicking his shoes across the floor, throwing his clothes all about, and then dragging the sheets down. He rolled into the cool cotton of them with a sigh. "Marry me," he said. "You're perfect."

"And you're not quite right in the head." She had changed in the bathroom, not wanting him to see her. Stretched out on the bed like a naked beast—the hair on his chest matted, his thighs heavier than she remembered them—he looked overpoweringly male. "You should never ask a woman to marry you after knowing her one day."

"I've never cared much what I should do," he told her. "Come here."

She slipped into the sheets with him, inhaling his pungent smell, and he leaned over her, his face again looking much older. He kissed her, and she could feel her arousal but she whispered, "You're tired."

"Bitch of a day."

They lay together in the bed in the center of the room, the mosquito net shimmering above their heads. Through the milky netting the moon shone more gold than silver. After a while they fell into a sleep, Miles on his back, snoring, and Evelyn fretful. She was awakened while the room was still dark by the insistent pushing of his body against hers. "I want you now," he murmured in a voice still groggy with sleep.

He was very hard and savage as he entered her, thrusting

at her greedily until he exploded into her before she could come to a climax. As he kept pushing at her more gently, rhythmically, trying to bring her satisfaction, she murmured, "Don't. It doesn't matter."

"Shut up," he said, his face just above hers in the dark, his breath sweet and known, welcome. His voice was still half asleep, but his shoulders pressed against her neck and his chest rubbed up and down against her breasts, brushing them with chest hair like tight wool. She let herself go and reached for her own satisfaction as she would never have dared with Fischer or Alex. She didn't care what he thought of her as she called out and moaned and held him to her, as she bucked beneath him. Then the wave struck her, broke over her, made her cry and cry and cry.

He lay over her, half smothering her, and she felt safe, safe, safe to be someone she had never allowed herself to be before. A door had been opened, and she could walk through it . . . into where? What mysteries and dangers lay beyond the garden wall?

He rolled off her, his lips brushing over hers. She went to get out of the bed, but his hand closed over her wrist. Letting the languor take her, she let herself be carried off until she felt the heat of the morning sun on her bare arm and looked up to find the mosquito net pulled away from the bed and Miles sitting there naked, watching her from the chaise.

She loved Miles Foster. There was no doubt about it. The thought frightened her, but as with a loaded gun, she felt compelled to touch it, bring the thought back when they were walking, talking, dining, talking on the telephone. The feeling was strongest when he was above her, their bodies entwined like two vines planted so close they had grown together as they reached for the air and sunlight. As they made love she wanted to cry out aloud, "I love you, I love you, I love." But she hadn't.

He played with the words himself, but his moods could change so swiftly. She was afraid to make a fool of herself . . . and afraid of losing him. For when he was absent she thought of him all the time, and when he was there it was all she could do not to reach out every second of the hour and touch his hair, his skin, any part of him.

They'd stayed away from public places. They were safer, happier alone. She was happy waiting for him, though he was gone long hours. She was happy when she heard his car coming into the driveway, when he appeared before her like some miracle come into her life to revive her. The future was never addressed.

"My father loved the rain," he said, looking out at the falls. "He loved Formosa because it rained. Did it rain when you were there?"

"I don't remember." The years with Fischer seemed like a time of family, to have nothing to do with passion. She didn't want to think about them.

"My mother liked the sun," he went on. "My mother loved Rio. Perhaps she managed to pull that posting for them; I never thought of that. My father wanted to come back to the East, but my mother was very happy in Rio. It would have been like her to do something very subtle."

"You don't talk about her much."

"No." He put both arms about Evelyn, cradled his head against hers. "It's nothing mysterious. I loved her, but I was closer to my father. He was a serious man. You don't see so many of those, and I was lucky; I recognized right off how special he was."

"Most children love their fathers." Her own mood changed as she thought of Victoria. The rain seemed much louder for a moment or two, and the humidity in the open lodge oppressive. She shifted in his arms, but he held on.

"Yeah, but this was different. He didn't have to create any legends about himself. People just saw it. He loved everything about the East, too, took it seriously, which not many do, you know. We think we do, but we really know very little about this place. We think of it as "Asia," yet it's more complex and interesting than Europe, if you know what you're looking at. MacArthur takes it seriously, whatever his other problems; knows a lot about the place, too. My mother . . ." he considered. "My mother was a spoiled woman. But nicely spoiled. She supported my father's career very nicely, but she had a strong mind of her own, and she was capable of making her own private decisions and then working behind the scenes to make sure they came true."

"Knowing what's best for everyone."

"Womanly wiles," he suggested. "And she had a lot of money, which helps if you're trying to get something in the foreign service. Or anywhere, I guess."

So he was rich. She hadn't given much thought to that, but his recklessness about his career would only make sense if he had alternatives. Miles Foster was a composite of the serious father and the flirtatious, rich mother.

"In the end, it didn't matter," he said thoughtfully. "They were killed in a taxi crash in Rio. Really crazy drivers there."

She held his hands where they were crossed over her chest. "Anyway, you remember them well," she said. It was inadequate, but it was the truth. Perhaps because they were taken from him so young, they remained shining figures in his mind.

"The best," he admitted, and she could feel the tension in his arms. "Pretty soon after that I decided to follow my father's interests."

"As a diplomat?"

"I thought so. It just turned out differently. I began to read the military histories, and I liked school. Then I saw the maps of Asia, and somehow all of it just came together for me. My father's interests, war, Asia, all of it."

"So here you are," she said as lightly as she could. The room seemed to be closing in on them, the rain thunderously loud, the sky darker. She unclasped his hands and stood up.

"Here I am," his voice said behind her, but it was strange, a whisper almost, and she turned to find him assessing her.

"Think we'll be able to get back tonight?" she asked.

"I don't know. And I don't care," he said, stretching out

on the rattan sofa that was too short for him, his legs over the arm, a young gladiator at rest. "I don't want to go to that damn party at the club anyway, do you?"

She shivered violently. It was more than the damp and rain. It was the thought of the women waiting for her. "No."

"So it could be a blessing in disguise," he said.

As though to defy him, the rain stopped instantly. One moment they could barely see or hear each other, the next it was as silent as the dead. The sun broke through immediately, and the waterfall, stronger with the rainfall but still bright green, dropped pleasantly into the jade pool. A macaw flew by, calling his happiness at the sunlight, and Evelyn watched the natives, almost naked, appear at the jungle's edge all about the pool.

"Look," she said, pointing.

Miles put both hands on the rail and leaned out into the cool air. "Indians," he said, "the original native tribes."

"I didn't expect them to be so primitive," she said, staring down at the line of dark-skinned warriors who looked up at them, many with mud designs on their skin, most in loincloths. "What do they want?"

"Our money," Miles said. "Imperialism at its most basic. They used to live in the jungle quite happily, but we—well, the Spanish, actually—came along, and now they compete for tourists. They'd carry us up the falls like beasts of burden so we don't exhaust ourselves. But there are two of us, you see," he said, looking at the men facing the lodge so intently that they might have been worshipping an idol. "And there are a dozen of them."

"Do you want to see the falls?" she asked.

"That's why I brought you here."

So they left the deserted lodge and went down the slippery mud path to the edge of the pool. Down here, close to the water, the pool was the color of green apples. The waterfall was loud and threw a fine mist all over them so they were soon as wet as if they had stayed out in the rain. Miles bargained with the small warriors until a satisfactory price was arranged, and two dugout canoes appeared from within the jungle. A warrior took the end of each one, and Miles instructed, "You have to climb in."

Once they were each seated in a canoe, four warriors lifted them, and they began a swaying ascent up the steep mountainside. The remainder of the warriors simply disappeared back into the jungle without a word. They kept to the edge of the stream, and Evelyn found herself level with the thick underbrush. High above, other trees, bare trunks below, fanned out into deep green cover so that they seemed to be almost swimming through a quiet green sea. She found herself staring at monkeys who faced her back, outraged to be disturbed in their private life, and once she saw the last foot or so of a snake as it made its silent departure before the advancing party.

She was sorry she had come. Everything was very wrong suddenly, and she wanted to cry out that they should go back. She calmed herself, amused at the thought that she must look like some captive princess out of one of the old boys' adventure stories that Morgan had loved so much as a child. The canoe with Miles in it had gone ahead, and she realized with a shock that she was alone.

"Miles!" she cried out. "Miles!" She heard the panic in her voice as it echoed off across the long sweep of jungle, the stream visible as a scar in the mountainside. A scattering of birds flew like confetti out of the jungle, mocking her with their own cries as they planed away across the green.

The natives went on, ignoring her. The canoe rocked back and forth, and the fear grew. Then they came around a bend in the river to the first of the pools that spread across a short plateau. At the other end she saw another, smaller waterfall, and above that another climb to the next pool.

Miles was floating in his canoe. The water here was murkier, the banks clogged by some sort of water lily, and as the natives lowered her canoe, she saw a ripple of movement across its surface. "Let's go back," she said to Miles, who was paddling toward her.

"Don't you want to see it through to the end?" He watched her closely, and she saw something new in his eyes:

cruelty. A second later it had changed to concern. "All right," he agreed. "I thought you'd like this, seeing what the islands were like before any of us arrived."

The four natives stood impassively while Miles pushed Evelyn's canoe into the shallows. He spoke to them in a guttural tongue, and they came forward to help her out. On the bank she said, "Could we walk down?" Then, because she had to admit it, "I'm frightened."

He was staring at her as though at a stranger, and now she was frightened of him as well. He paid off the natives and held out his hand. "Come on."

His warm touch reassured her, her fears suddenly seeming very stupid. "What were you speaking?" she asked.

"One of the dialects."

"Where did you learn it?"

On the path, the mud was deep, the footprints of the men who had carried them up showing clearly. "I thought it might be useful," he said.

"When?"

"Sometime," he said irritably. His brow cleared as the sky above the falls had an hour earlier. "Now. It was useful now, wasn't it?"

"You're very strange," she told him.

"You think so?" The way he slid a glance at her, half smiling, she thought he was pleased. She had thought him a private person, but now she saw he might be one of those men who liked secrets. They kept him his own man.

"Look," he said, pointing. There, a very great distance away across the plain of jungle, was a bay and a village.

"It's lovely."

"It's more than that," he told her. "It's a perfect landing place for an invasion. See how the two arms of the bay give cover for any landing craft? All you have to do is control the two peninsulas, and you have a perfect harbor and a good, gentle beach on which to bring your troops ashore."

"Except for aircraft."

He turned so quickly to look at her that she stepped back. "Yes," he agreed, "the war in the air. That's the way it's going to be, isn't it?"

She had a flash of the fear she'd felt coursing through her on the higher falls. "I don't know."

"It is in China. China is the Spain of Asia. You know that, don't you?"

She felt she was being interrogated. "I don't know," she said, trying to press on, but he held her.

"Well, it is," he said quietly. Then, shrugging, he started down the path again, and not another word was said. The fear receded like a tide as they came down the roaring side of the steepest waterfall to the lodge. There below them was the thatched roof, and beside it the wet oilskin top of the red car. The pool looked innocent enough, and there were people in the lodge, apparently its owners, who came out smiling, apologizing extravagantly for their absence. They offered food and drink, but Evelyn wanted to be away, so Miles refused the hospitality. They got back into the little car and started down toward the bay that appeared and disappeared as they went around the slopes of the hills.

She began to relax as the city appeared in the distance, a tiny scattered settlement of lights that grew and spread across the landscape until they were passing through the first shacks on the outskirts. "I'm sorry about today," she said to him.

He looked at her after a long silence. "That's all right. Sometimes things take all of us strangely."

"Yes."

"Would you mind if we met at the club?" he asked as he turned in at her driveway. "I have some things to check on."

"What time?"

"Nine."

"All right." She was relieved, yet as he stopped the little car under the portico she was reluctant to get out. He looked at her as though they were parting for a long time, his eyes distant. Then, as he leaned over and snapped open the door, she felt a wave of anger and rejection.

As she went to get out he touched her arm. "Aren't you forgetting something?"

She was going crazy, she decided, didn't understand at all what had happened today.

"Kiss me," he demanded.

The relief was as great as the feeling of rejection had been. She allowed him to put his arms about her, wrapped her own about him, and kissed him, feeling safe again.

"Nine."

"Nine, at the club. If you're going to be late, please call."

"I promise."

At the club a message was waiting for her. "I missed you. I'm sorry. I'll be half an hour late. Miles Foster." But she felt happy again and didn't care that she was alone. The club steward suggested she might like a drink on the terrace near the pool and said that he would put it on Miles's account. She strolled out to the terrace, startled by the sight of so many people—many, many more than she had expected—and so many of them civilians. There were more women than men, too, which was unusual in the European set. She had thought Victoria would like being here for just that reason. Many young girls came out to Manila from the States, known as "the fishing fleet"—the daughters and cousins of military personnel, looking for a husband. The laughter all about her seemed louder than normal. Nervous, she thought, accepting the drink.

At a table in the corner of the terrace she could watch the arrivals undetected. She heard the band begin to play in the larger room behind her and watched the colored lights sway above the pool, reflected like strings of Christmas ornaments in the water's surface as it was stirred by a breeze.

"God, do you suppose it's going to be like this from now on?" a woman's voice barked from the room behind her.

"It's the women from the *President Cleveland*," a second woman offered. "They were turned away at Hong Kong, if you can believe the nerve of the British."

Then the unmistakable tones of the dreaded Mrs. Kornworth, the colonel's wife, already slightly drunk. "It's those damned Japs. They've shelled Shanghai. My husband told me, and he should know. The British are evacuating all their own people—unofficially, of course—and the Chinese are running like rats for Hong Kong. I think it was very wise of the *President Cleveland* to head straight here. We'll be seeing a lot more of this, you mark my words, before this China incident is over."

"Well, it might be fun," suggested the first woman, new blood and all."

"Speaking of new blood, I suppose you saw that Lezenski woman. You know who she's here for, I suppose."

"Hardly new blood," suggested Kornworth, and then there was a laugh, the sound of glasses. "Steward, another round."

"The Chinese are so awfully stupid," the second voice said. "You wonder if they'll be able to run the country themselves."

"They're not the only stupid ones," the first woman said. "Look at Miles Foster. He must be insane. She's old enough to be—"

"There may be more there than meets the eye," interrupted Mrs. Kornworth.

"What do you mean?"

"I can't say. Sworn to secrecy, you know."

Evelyn was cold now, her hands clutching the chair, feeling undone in ways she hadn't since her childhood. She thought she might cry but knew that she wouldn't. She wanted to leave, but that meant passing right in front of the window. She cringed, praying that they would go, or at least change the subject.

"You mean . . ."

"I can't say," said Mrs. Kornworth with satisfaction.

"Of course, his job . . ."

"That's hush-hush, too."

"I see."

"Yes, of course. It makes sense now." There was relief in the voice.

"You didn't hear it from me," said Mrs. Kornworth.

"What will they do to her?"

"A woman of her age," said Mrs. Kornworth. "You'd think she would see through him, wouldn't you?"

"No fool like an old fool."

"Exactly."

"Sad, really."

"Pathetic."

17

Flames licked the night above the Chapei district as Morgan, looking very dashing in his new uniform of a major in the Shanghai Volunteers, piloted Vicky through the river of Chinese refugees pushing into the international settlement. "Listen," he shouted above the noise. "I think we should go back."

"No. He's going tonight. You know that," she said.

The street cleared as the Chinese pushed against the walls of the houses on either side. The shell passed over with a soft sigh, exploding with a deafening explosion only blocks away. The air vibrated around them, and then a long wail of pain and terror broke the silence. Vicky took the chance to move ahead. Morgan ran after her padded blue Chinese coat, her black pants and white stockings with padded Chinese boots, a straw hat low over her face.

At Bubbling Well Road they could hear the fire engines coming from a long distance away. The refugees thronged the street again, men and women, families, carts with all their belongings, pigs and chickens, ducks and geese, bags of rice carried on bent shoulders, all pushing out of Chapei toward the safety of the settlement.

"Look," he said, grabbing hold of her coat roughly and spinning her about in the center of the street, "if you're determined to go to Nanking, we'll find another way."

Facing him, fury written large across her slavic features, he thought that she might just pass as a Chinese, perhaps a Mongol. The straight bangs, the hacked-off hair, left on the floor of the bedroom in the French quarter, gave her features an Asian cast. Only her height and the tiger eyes hinted at her true heritage. "I can find the house without you," she retorted.

"I'll come." He took hold of her arm, pushing into the crowd, throwing aside the refugees that threatened to press them back. They made their way through the Bubbling Well Road and off into the side streets where the crowd was thinner. At irregular intervals they heard shells pass overhead, pressed against the walls with the others, their hearts in their mouths until they heard the explosions. By now they could smell the burning houses of the Chapei sector. Soot fell from the night air, and the sky had a gray cast where the smoke clouded the moon.

The house where Mr. Wei had said he would wait until eight o'clock was in Three Bamboo Street. Morgan thought they must be lost as the streets they passed through had fewer and fewer people, the houses shuttered, and he was not sorry. But Victoria moved quickly, following some inner map from her childhood. He had tried to talk Victoria out of her idea of traveling to Nanking by boat.

As they pushed deeper into Chapei the fires worsened. The streets were filled with police and frightened Nationalist soldiers, Japanese from just beyond the city. The soldiers shouted orders, pushing at the crowds fighting to save their houses. The flames burned in a golden ridge above the low roofs of the narrow streets. Smoke stung their eyes, and they coughed in the thin air.

Victoria turned into yet another, narrower street, searching for the door she wanted. "Here."

At the end of the street two Nationalist soldiers were stopping all passers to demand their documents. Morgan said, "He won't be here."

But the door opened immediately on the face of a young woman, no older than Victoria. "Come," she whispered. "He is waiting."

The dark hall was less than two feet wide. They followed her shadow through the house until they came to a plain room in the back. Mr. Wei was dressed in the black trousers and thin black tunic of a coolie, his ankles bare above his thin shoes. Looking at Morgan's splendid new uniform, he commented, "So, you will defend the city."

"If it comes to that," Morgan said easily. Still, there was a sense of unease beneath his casual words.

Mr. Wei looked at Victoria silently. "We must be gone before the curfew," he said to Morgan.

"How will I know if you make it?" Morgan asked.

Mr. Wei smiled slightly, raised his shoulders beneath the thin tunic. "You will not." He looked at Victoria. "You will only know if we make it back."

Morgan faced Victoria. "Change your mind."

"Please," she begged him. "I have to."

From the moment she had come out of the bedroom and seen Mr. Wei waiting for his list, she had been determined. From what she had heard behind the door as Mr. Wei and Morgan sparred for advantage, she knew enough to press her own case. It had been pure luck that Mr. Wei wished to go to Nanking for reasons of his own.

There was a brief silence, recalled by Morgan as that of people parting who know that they may not see each other again. He put his hand out to touch Victoria's arm. He couldn't take her into his embrace with Mr. Wei and the girl, who was sitting cross-legged on a low couch in the corner, watching. But Victoria was already distant. She had been that way in the few days while the arrangements were made, as though she had started out already on some journey of her own.

She hugged him suddenly, pressed her face against the dark leather Sam Browne belt across his chest. "Goodbye," she whispered. "Don't worry about me."

Mr. Wei gathered up his belongings already wrapped in a faded blue scarf. The girl on the couch turned her face away as he spoke to her. He went to sit beside her, touching her wrist, but she shook her head angrily and spat out a string of Chinese invective at Victoria.

"She does not understand," Mr. Wei explained. "She thinks I am going to Nanking for you."

Morgan understood that they were putting Mr. Wei in severe danger. He took out the list and said, "Here."

Mr. Wei took the list, turned it over. "And the copy?" he asked.

"I could have made yet another copy," Morgan said.

"I think not," Mr. Wei said. "I think you are a peculiar man, honorable in your own way."

Morgan unbuttoned the pocket of his tunic. "If I give it to you, you could refuse to take my niece to her father."

"Yes, I could," Mr. Wei said.

Morgan looked at Victoria. "Give it to him," she said.

Morgan handed over the second list. "I will take your niece to Nanking," Mr. Wei said. "It will be important when the city falls that some representatives of . . . other views can observe for later."

"Later?" Morgan asked.

"In China we understand that there is always later," Mr. Wei said. The lists in his hands were like white petals as he turned them over, looking at the lines of Chinese characters. "However," he added as he handed them to the girl, "we have learned much from the West, too. We have learned impatience. That can be a virtue, a modern one."

They heard the girl go down the dark corridor, followed by a gust of warm air redolent of burning wood.

"We must go now," Mr. Wei repeated.

As they heard the door to the street close Morgan reached out his hand. "Goodbye, Mr. Wei."

Mr. Wei hesitated, then took it. His thin hand felt dry. "Mr. Valentine. We will meet again, it is my hope."

Looking in the Chinese's eyes, Morgan searched for the fear he had seen in other men and saw anger. "God willing."

"I think China will have to put its faith in men," Mr. Wei said.

Victoria made a movement of impatience. "Goodbye," she said to Morgan, and she walked down the hall. Mr. Wei watched until she had gone, then turned. "This is very dangerous."

"I thank you for it," Morgan said.

"No, no," Mr. Wei said, shaking his head. "I have accepted the danger. But for your niece . . ." He shook his head. "If Nanking is taken, there is a Japanese tradition that the men are allowed to do as they wish for three days."

"I have heard stories," Morgan said evenly. "There will always be exceptions in war. But the Japanese army is a disciplined army."

"They are peasants," Mr. Wei snapped. "The men are not officers. They are very simple people, very frightened, and if they conquer a city, they are given this time as a reward. It will not be different in Nanking."

"Chiang would never let Nanking fall," Morgan said angrily. "It's only the journey that's the danger. You should have gone by river."

"It is impossible. There are Japanese gunboats in the river."

It was true. The Japanese flagship, the *Idzumo*, was at anchor off the Bund. "Bluff," Morgan said.

"You Europeans do not understand," Mr. Wei said, abandoning his last arguments. "Not yet."

Victoria was waiting by the door. Mr. Wei opened it, and the wave of smoke and cinders that washed into the small hall forced them back. Drawing breath, they went out into the street. The fires were more general now, the sky above the houses an orange wash.

Morgan said, "Vic . . ."

But she was heading away from him with Mr. Wei toward the end of the street, where an unbroken crowd of refugees moved away from the fires toward the safety of the settlement.

Mr. Wei turned as they reached the end of the street, half raised his hand, and, as Morgan was about to call one last farewell, blended with Victoria into the river of refugees.

18

The Clipper banked over the city, and through her first-class window Evelyn saw the gray smoke rising. At an angle she saw the park beyond her house in the French quarter, then the bridge over the Soochow Creek, the facades of the Chartered Bank and the Cathay Hotel, and then they were coming down the long stretch of river that was kept clear for the Pan American Clipper.

"Ladies and gentlemen, Pan American World Airways is happy to announce our arrival in Shanghai. Please have your documents ready."

Gathering together her alligator handbag, her passport, and the briefcase of documents that she had gathered quickly in Manila for her dawn departure two days earlier, Evelyn felt the fear pass through her, then die away again in the face of the numbness that had overcome her ten days before.

"No fool like an old fool."

"Countess?" Evelyn looked up to see the young American stewardess in her gray and white tailored uniform leaning forward. "Countess, the other passengers are in the launch."

"Oh, yes, of course."

As she stepped gingerly into the bobbing launch she smelled the smoke. The river looked strangely congested. There were two Canadian Pacific liners, the *Empress of Asia* just getting up steam for the run to the mouth of the river and the *Empress of Canada* just arriving. There were more freighters than was normal, and there was the pristine white hull of the *Idzumu*, challengingly at anchor right off the Bund.

Dohira, she thought as she stepped into the launch. Getting a passage on the clipper out of Manila up to Hong Kong had been difficult. Arriving home half hysterical from the Army-Navy Club, determined to leave immediately, she had phoned the Pan American agent.

"I don't think it's possible, Countess. All this trouble in China . . ."

But she had prevailed. When the phone rang late that night she was steeled.

"Hey," had said Miles's slow drawl. "Did I miss something?"

"I'm sorry," she said, thinking the words would choke her. "I just couldn't stand the club one second more. Don't hate me."

"Don't hate me." What did he really think of her, she wondered. But by then the very worst of the first pain had left her thankfully numb. At first all she felt was the sudden shock, almost as though she had been struck hard. "His job, of course." "The woman is . . ." But she knew the words were engraved in her heart as on a tombstone. Then, in the Peninsula Hotel in Kowloon, holding the apple-green silk spread of the bed, she had felt she couldn't breathe. She had choked on her agony until much later the tears came, wracking sobs, the first since Fischer's death.

Only much, much later, when the hotel corridors were finally quiet and she lay awake in the huge room staring at the ceiling that had come to be familiar in its rosette pattern, did Fischer's voice come eerily into her memory. "Be careful of the young, they'll tear your heart out and laugh."

Soon after, the hatred came.

The corniche along the Bund was thronged with people staring at the bright Japanese flagship in ominous silence. A thousand people, maybe more, faced silently across the dirty water of the river where the crew of the *Idzumu* went about their business.

At first she thought the cannon was thunder, but the October sky was gray with smoke alone. The second cannon shot sent a ripple of movement through the silent mass of people, who turned as one to search the empty sky for some sign.

Evelyn was through immigration when the first planes came overhead. "Very bad trouble," Ng Ho said as he loaded her suitcase into the Packard.

The Zeros cruised across the quiet city and headed out into the countryside. In the car, Evelyn sat back and listened to the distant rhythm of the Japanese bombardment.

The feelings came in rushes: despair, anger, humiliation, and every now and then, unbidden, the recollection of Miles Foster's touch. She hated him less for how he had thought to use her than for awakening her body and leaving her with her fires smoldering.

"Is Miss Victoria at the house?"

Ng Ho glanced at her in the mirror, then back to the road, where silent crowds still moved through the international settlement looking for a space to rest. "No."

"Do you know when she'll be back?"

Ng Ho drove on silently, and she thought he hadn't heard. "Ng Ho, do you know . . ."

"Missy go Nanking."

The impossibility of the news flooded her. "No," she said, the panic rising, "no, Missy can't go Nanking."

Ng Ho shook his head. "Gone."

Terror hit her. "When?" she whispered.

"Before."

"Before when?" she demanded. "Before when did Miss Victoria go?"

"Before yesterday."

She slumped back into the corner of the seat. Nanking was besieged, the Japanese army at its gates. She could remember every news story of the Japanese advance. Her pulse calmed slowly as she tried to sort out what to do.

"How, Ng Ho, how did Miss Victoria go?"

"Not know," Ng Ho said. They were in the French quarter now. Shutters were closed, and many gates were chained shut, their gardens already looking rakish and abandoned. "Tuan Morgan come. Miss Victoria go."

"Tuan Morgan?" It was not possible. Yet even as she spoke, she began to see the possibility. "He's at the house?"

"He live in Kwangshei district."

"Not to the house," Evelyn ordered Ng Ho as they approached the gates. She saw her beloved little house sitting back from the road, the shutters still open to the long garden. "Colonel Dohira."

She turned and craned to see it disappear as they turned the corner on Admiral Joffe. As they came out of the French quarter the refugees pressed close on either side, and they slowed to the pace of the rickshaws, hand carts, and bicycles loaded with the belongings of the poor. Whole families were working as beasts of burden, all heading away from the perimeter of the Chinese city. The bombardment seemed closer, a distant, constant thudding beyond the city limits.

At Bubbling Well Road, where a burned tram sat forlornly in the center of the road, workers replaced the tracks that had been torn up the night before by a stray bomb. In front of the Japanese consulate Evelyn saw a deep, silent crowd facing the sentries in their ill-fitting uniforms and oversized rifles. The guard came forward, newly defiant. "Nobody allowed," he told her as she gave her name.

"Call Colonel Dohira."

"Nobody allowed," he shouted, so close she could smell the fish and garlic on his breath. He turned, satisfied at his performance in front of the crowd, and sauntered back to his post.

"Drive through," Evelyn told Ng Ho.

The gates to the drive stood defiantly open. She could see Japanese staff cars and the consul's diplomatic Rolls Royce parked in front of the stately two-story house.

Ng Ho looked back at her over his shoulder, then, shaking his head, put the car in gear. The swaggering guard shouted and jumped out of the way as the Packard plunged into the Japanese compound. The house was thirty yards ahead, the red and white flag of the rising sun hanging crisp as fresh laundry in the cold early winter air.

The first shot ricochetted off the road behind. Evelyn looked back to see both guards on their knees taking aim.

Ng Ho swerved onto the lawn as the second shot careened off the fender. He spun the wheel, and the heavy limousine bumped back off the lawn, tearing a six-foot gash in the perfectly tailored green. The third shot smashed the back window, showering Evelyn with glass as she lay on the seat with her face pressed to the gray velour.

Angry shouts from the rest of the guards filled the air as Ng Ho was dragged from the car and flung to the road. Evelyn was taken by the arm and roughly hauled out to the center of the circle of guards. The guard from the gate was running toward them, screaming at Ng Ho.

An officer appeared on the steps. He shouted an order, and there was silence. Ignoring Evelyn, he walked past the prone form of Ng Ho and slapped the guard from the gate hard twice before dismissing him. The guard saluted and marched off across the lawn toward the barracks.

"So," the officer said, turning to Evelyn. "You are on Imperial Japanese territory."

"I wish to see Colonel Dohira," she told him. "I am Countess Lezenski."

The officer, small and thin, as tense as a cat, looked at her. "You can be shot," he told her.

"You would be well advised to talk to Colonel Dohira first," she said. Her anger, a pool of rage as deep as her newly awakened passion, gave her courage. "Let my driver up. I ordered him to drive through."

The Japanese saw the circle of men watching him and shook his head. "You stay here."

"Let my driver up."

Her overpowering rage was matched by the hatred that blasted in his eyes as he faced her again. "On Japanese Imperial territory, you will not speak like that."

"I will speak softly if you will let my driver up."

More members of the legation had come to stand on the steps. Pocked by the bullets, the rear window gone, the Packard looked like a beached ship half on the lawn. A man in a gray cutaway coat called to the guard, who answered him angrily. The cutaway spoke again, very quietly.

Turning to Evelyn, the officer said, "He will wait here with the car. You come."

"All right." She stepped forward to help Ng Ho to his feet but was pulled roughly back. When the big Chinese man got up, he was pale, the nearness of his death there to be seen in the expressionless eyes. "Stay with the car," Evelyn instructed. "Don't allow them to take you away."

On other visits she had been ushered past the severe receptionist in her neatly tailored suits, but today she was ordered to a seat on the French-style settee that sat in the wide hall far from the delicate receptionist's desk. She could remember when the first guards appeared here—not the usual legation guards, but a whole platoon of regular Japanese army—and could remember when the wrought-iron bars were fixed to the lower windows. Now she realized that she had ignored the signs for years.

The consulate was alive with activity, a conquering army preparing for one last advance. She knew now that Fischer had been right. On many counts. The war would come, sweep over all of them, and leave what? A new world? The last war had swept away all of Alex's world and given what in return?

But then she thought of Victoria between Shanghai and Nanking and approached the neat little woman behind the French desk. "Would you tell Colonel Dohira I have been waiting two hours now?"

The woman didn't look up. "He knows."

Defeated, Evelyn returned to her seat for another hour. Finally, an aide in full uniform appeared. "Now."

The colonel received her seated. He was short, with a very broad neck and close-cropped gray hair. He looked, Evelyn thought, like a frog, a satisfied frog.

His eyes were cold. "What do you want, Contessa?"

"I want to talk about my daughter." He hadn't asked her to sit down, but she had been sitting for three hours now, and five before that on the flight from Hong Kong.

"So, you have a daughter," the colonel said, flicking at the dossier in front of him. "She is a child?"

"She is grown."

"Ah." He made a note on the dossier, the frown still on his face.

"She is here," Evelyn said.

The colonel pushed the dossier away. "You have broken into Japanese territory at a time like this to trouble me about your daughter?" he asked quietly, his eyes tiny in his face.

"She may be in trouble."

"So." It was a statement. She could feel his contempt.

"She has gone to Nanking," Evelyn said.

He continued to stare at her. Beyond the door behind her she could hear continued activity, though the afternoon was waning. "I am afraid for her," Evelyn said.

Dohira drew breath and stood up, revealing himself to be shorter than even the average Japanese, his stature that of a wrestler. They had been doing business for years now, but she had never considered Dohira's ambitions.

"And our own business?" he asked as he looked into the garden. "How is that?"

"I must speak to you of that also," she admitted.

He turned very slowly, his face alert. "Ah, so," he said. "And why is that?"

"I think there may be some trouble."

He picked up her dossier again from his desk, studied the cover, and said, "I do not think so."

"It is not something we can control."

"Tell me."

She told him of the problems in Manila, of the demands for bribes, of the hope that the ship could be rerouted. And at the end, she said very quietly, "I think that this business is near its end."

"No!"

"It may be impossible to make deliveries soon," she explained.

"The imperial army has need of the metal. There will be no changes."

"But we cannot unload the ships in Manila," she protested.

He slapped the table hard with both palms, leaning

forward to speak each word clearly. "You come here to ask my assistance for your daughter?"

"Yes," she admitted.

He stared at her with each palm pressed to the desk. As she waited, a few early snowflakes fell past the window, and she thought of winter with a sudden hope. In winter the Chinese could retreat again, as they always did, into the vast empty interior. Then she saw the snowflakes were gray. The bombardment of the Chinese city had become so much of the background noise that she had forgotten what the fire brought.

"Then you will arrange for the ships to arrive here. You can speak to your Chinese partner, can you not?" His contempt for Tu was even greater than his contempt for Evelyn. The Japanese hated the Chinese business class.

"He may not be able to do anything." She chose her words carefully. "Your imperial army may make it impossible for him to . . . make arrangements in China as he has in the past."

Dohira shrugged his heavy shoulders. "You will speak to him, make arrangements for the shipments to continue." He stood up, dismissing her.

"And my daughter?" she begged.

She thought he wasn't going to reply. The anger came back in a wave, and with it, desperation. Then he spoke. "If she has not reached the city," he said carefully, "there may be hope. If she is in Nanking . . ." He opened his hand in futility. "It will be a captured city soon. I will not be able to help you if she is in the city when it is taken."

"But she's not involved," Evelyn cried. "This is not our war. This is your war."

His face burned with his own indignation. "As long as you Europeans are in Asia, it is your war," he shouted, the veins in his neck swelling like worms. "Until you understand that, you are at risk." He steadied himself, perhaps unnerved by his own outburst. "You will make arrangements."

"And if I cannot?"

His cold eyes had the slightest smile. "Then you will be of

no further use to the imperial Japanese army, Countess Lezenski."

"I will see Tu," she conceded, unable to conceive of any other reply.

He nodded. "Excellent."

"And my daughter?"

"I shall think on the matter," he said, wrapping one hand in the other. "Perhaps if I think enough, I may help you."

Jeers and shouts followed the shattered Packard as Ng Ho piloted it out of the consulate. The autumn evening was already upon the city. The bombardment, now more sporadic, as though gathering strength for the night's attack, was muted by the sounds of the city's workers trying to reach their homes through streets clogged by refugees. The sign on the Select Department Store flashed into brilliant light as the Packard made its way slowly down the Bund.

The *Idzuko* was lit up again, the only ship in the river carrying lights. The Clipper was gone. She saw the crowd entering the Cathay Hotel, the women well-dressed, the men in evening clothes or the comic uniforms of the Volunteers. It seemed that several cities were living side by side, unaware of one another.

"I have to see Tu," she told Ng Ho. "Later."

Ng Ho nodded. He had the stunned look of a large, powerful man who had been humiliated. "Curfew," he reminded her.

"I have to change my clothes," she said. "It won't take long. Could we send a message first?"

"Can do. More better send coolie first. Very hard to drive, I think."

"I'll have a message ready as soon as we get to the house. Send it to his office. Find a reliable coolie."

"Pay only when answer come," Ng Ho said.

"You arrange it."

Her mind now was recovering from the fear. Her pain had become anger. Fischer would have thought them innocents—and innocents were the victims, she thought now, watching how the refugees had accustomed themselves so easily to their condition. She saw the tiny shelters erected from packing cases, the fires, the way the children played among the crowd that huddled all along the side of the road. She could remember how it had been to flee Russia with the last of the White armies. The shock had soon passed. Humans could accustom themselves to almost anything, she thought as she watched a mother bathe her child under a garden tap in a deserted house. You forgot what you had lost because you had to fight to stay alive to survive. It was a blessing of sorts.

At the blue house the refugees had climbed over the wall to camp under the trees. "Get coolies. Make them go away," Ng Ho said as they passed in the car.

"No," Evelyn told him, seeing their fear. "Leave them."

"Soon they come to house."

"Leave them, Ng Ho," she ordered.

Ng Ho had closed the shutters over all the windows, but light showed through the cracks. A crouched child scampered away like a crab from where he had been peering into the house through the shutters.

The door opened at her touch. "Ng Ho . . ." she began, then stopped.

"Hello, Evvy," Morgan said, standing there so close he seemed to overpower her. "Long time no see."

"You know this place?" Victoria asked.

"Yes." Mr. Wei's voice was thoughtful. "I lived here for some years when I was young." He looked at her. "My own father was killed during the Young Marshals revolt. I was sent to my uncle's house because my brother became the head of my own and I was not so welcome."

They walked for a long time then, and she saw his strength begin to fail. "My father will come down from Nanking eventually. I can see him then. Please," she begged. "I don't want to be responsible for your health."

"We are all responsible for one another," he said in the moonlight. "I have followed that teaching. And I must go to Nanking for my own reasons."

Irrationally she felt betrayed, lessened in importance. They crouched, waiting in a ditch near the side of the road.

"Do not feel that my life is so important," Mr. Wei said, not looking at her. "My deeds may be, but my life is not." He faced her, his young face ascetic and serious with the round silver moon behind him. "As yours is not."

She was rebuked, but before she could form a reply, they saw the headlights. "We must be careful now," he warned. "There will be an escort. We must choose the last truck."

The convoy rumbled out of the night, dark beasts with their headlights dimmed against a night attack. As they passed Victoria saw the Nationalist guards in the first and second trucks. But then several passed filled with bleating livestock. As the final truck approached Mr. Wei took hold of her wrist. "Do not run," he cautioned. "The guards are far enough away that if we do not make quick movements, they will think we are part of the bamboo."

The driver, forewarned, slowed his truck as they left the bamboo grove and walked as steadily as they could into the road. Victoria expected the click of a rifle, the sound of a shot, but nothing came. From the back of the truck, a young boy from the village leaned out to assist Mr. Wei. Victoria was dragged in a second later, and then, whispered commands passing through the cab wall, the truck gathered enough speed to catch up with the others.

"We must rest now," Mr. Wei told Victoria as the convoy continued on toward the Nationalist camp. "During the day we'll have to climb toward the hills."

He lay back and was soon in a fitful sleep. Despite the village boy's accusing glance, Victoria adjusted Mr. Wei's tunic against the cold, but in his sleep he brushed her hand angrily away. She sat back to watch the moonlit Chinese landscape pass beyond the open rear of the truck and was still awake some hours later when the boy indicated that dawn was coming again and they would have to resume their journey on foot.

Standing in her living room for the first time in months, Evelyn felt that somehow time had become confused. There before her, gold cigarette case in hand, was Morgan. The fall of his blond hair across his brow and the beautifully tailored uniform of the Shanghai Volunteers created an illusion of having been transported back to the last war.

As he looked up she said nervously, "You'll have to forgive me. I'm . . . upset."

"About Victoria."

Why did she feel that he was guilty of something? Years and years ago, when they had been children—several lifetimes away, she thought, she had been able to tell when Morgan was lying when no one else could. When the child from next door began to sicken and cry, it had been Evelyn who knew somehow that Morgan was involved. When it was discovered that he'd been offering to take the baby for a ride in the park while the nurse visited with her friends, and that then, out of sight, he'd been drinking the baby's bottle himself, she had been the only one in the house who had not been scandalized with shock. All that had been a long time ago, she reminded herself now. They were both different people.

Just then he headed toward the bar, now set up in the living room. Victoria must have arranged that.

"Drink?" he asked. The way he cocked his head, half-taunting, made her wonder for a second if he, too, was remembering the past.

"No, I may have to go out soon. I have to change." Then she heard herself and said, "I'm sorry. I don't sound very welcoming."

"You look well enough, however," he said appraisingly. He had always been able to read in her things that others couldn't, and she wondered if he could see now that she had been the object of a young man's love. But that thought brought a rush of such fierce desire that she turned away so as not to be discovered. And then, very soon, came a terrible sense of loss, forcing her to focus on what had to be done in the next hours.

"You saw Victoria?" she asked. Then, realizing that he must have, "Of course you did."

"I stayed here," he said, pouring himself a drink. Behind

him in the garden she saw the movement of shadows as the refugees settled for the night.

"Here?" Perhaps she sounded outraged, because he put the top back on the crystal decanter very deliberately and looked at her. "Wouldn't you have wanted me to?" The challenge this time was direct.

What could she say? "Then you know that she's in Nanking?"

"I would doubt they're even halfway yet," he said, sipping the whiskey.

The flash of rage was so strong that she had crossed the floor to him before she had any recollection of moving. He was lifting the glass again when she grasped his wrist. "What do you mean?"

He shook her off, and this time she recognized the fury in his own eyes, the fury that as a child had made him beat dogs, the rage that had destroyed rooms where he'd been locked up. At that moment she couldn't see what she had loved in him, but what she did feel was a terrible fear for her daughter. "What have you done now?" she hissed.

He put his large hand on her chest above her breasts, just as he had when they were children, and pushed her back, gently but threateningly all the same. "Careful, little Evvy," he said evenly. "You may need me. These are perilous times."

What mattered was what he knew, she thought, trying again to sort out what she herself had to do. "I'm upset," she apologized, and she saw a flash of the old charm. But superimposed on it for one moment was Miles Foster's handsome face. I am going mad, she thought.

"Tell me, please. I need to know. She could be in grave danger."

"She's on her way to Nanking," Morgan said.

"How did you arrange it? How long have you been here?" She looked at his uniform. "This is recent, isn't it?"

Something in her tone must have warned him, for he moved away. "I've been here almost a month."

"The uniform becomes you."

"That was rather an accident," he said. "It embarrassed

me at first." He pulled on his Sam Browne belt, touched the heavy revolver. "Now I think it might be the wisest thing I've done in a long time." He looked at her across her own rug, looking out of place in this delicate house furnished for herself and Fischer. "Except for coming to Shanghai," he added, looking about. "You should have told me how . . . welcoming Shanghai could be for a man of spirit."

"If my child is hurt," she said evenly, "I will see you in hell."

There! She saw it, the fury at being crossed, at being called to account for himself. And with this insight she was suddenly not afraid of him. He had been stuck as the same person for so long that he seemed sad.

"I think that is more than she would do for you," he said.

When she just stood her ground, with a quick return to petulance, he offered, "I met a man. He . . . offered to take her to Nanking." Then, looking defiant, "Nothing would have stopped her. She's like you in that."

"And when did they go?"

"Two nights ago."

She calculated quickly. "She may not be there yet?"

Morgan became serious for a moment, and again she had the sensation of looking back many, many years. He looked briefly repentant, as he often had when he'd come into her London room. After a particularly bad action, he would lie there and ask, "Evvy, why am I like this?" He was truly repentant, but sometimes it seemed his behavior only became worse. She had never known why. Now, she asked, "This guide, is he political?"

"Yes. I don't think there's much to worry about, though. All these politics out here seem to be a bit muddled, don't you think?"

"Death isn't," she answered angrily. "They kill politicals." She looked at the door to the living room. "Perhaps she won't get there," she said, more to herself than him.

"I don't think that would make much difference," he said quietly.

"Why not?"

"Because they say the road will be cut between here and Nanking soon. She wouldn't be able to get back."

In the moment of sheer terror that struck her then, she said nothing. Ng Ho appeared in the door. "The coolie is back, mem," he said.

"You've found Tu?"

Ng Ho nodded.

"Where is he?"

The old Chinese looked uneasily at Morgan, who stared him down. "He is with the Red Sands tonight." "Very big meeting. Very bad joss."

They could feel the wind coming in the shattered back window of the Packard as they drove up Avenue Joffre toward the water bridge. Morgan smoked his cigarette moodily, staring at the refugee camps that now made an unbroken line of humanity on either side of the boulevard. The bare winter trees stood spectral sentry over the small fires, the makeshift tents. "God," he said, "at least if the Japs come in, this will be cleared away."

Evelyn was too tired now to remonstrate. She hadn't wanted him with her on her journey to Tu's house, where she'd never been. All their dealings had been in one of his tea shops or the godowns near where the ships from Manila were unloaded. But he had said, "Don't you think it would be better to have an officer of the Volunteers along? You may be out later than the curfew."

"All right," she'd conceded.

"Who is this man Tu?" Morgan asked as they came to the bridge. The Nationalist soldiers shouted, rifles poised, for the car to stop. They circled it, examining the gunshots from the Japanese legation, talking among themselves, and pointing to the shattered rear window.

"They're frightened," Morgan said quietly to Ng Ho. "Don't do anything to startle them." At just that moment the Japanese bombardment started, an enormous explosion of gunfire from beyond the Chinese city that shook the remaining glass in the car and made all conversation futile.

When the first bombardment, several minutes long, had

stopped as suddenly as it had begun, Morgan said, "Have you any cash?"

"Yes, I think so," Evelyn said.

"Give it to me," he ordered her. "And for God's sake, take off those rings."

She fumbled in her handbag, handed him the roll of folded bills—American dollars from the Philippines, Hong Kong dollars, and Shanghai dollars—the cash she had needed for her journey.

"Good God," he said. "How much is here?"

"About ten thousand sterling."

He looked at her with frank admiration. As the soldiers came out of their sandbagged positions, he separated the Hong Kong dollars, then thoughtfully peeled off half the American dollars. Stepping out of the car authoritatively, he started to shout at the soldiers in English. Still gesturing at the smashed windows and the bullet holes, he pressed the cash into the hand of the man who appeared the most senior. There was one uneasy moment when the Nationalist officer weighed his hatred for the Japanese terrorizing him from behind the city against that for the Europeans with their money. Then he shouted at his own troops, and Morgan quickly got back in.

"Get moving," he ordered Ng Ho. They rolled off just as the second bombardment began lighting the night sky with rosettes of war, orange and gold, red and white. The first of the fires blazed up in the old city, sending plumes of dark smoke against the sky.

In the next silence Morgan asked, "Who's Tu?"

"A Chinese millionaire. A very important man, a backer of Chiang's."

"What do you want from him?"

She didn't want to tell him anything, but apprehension faded at the thought of Victoria between Nanking and Shanghai. "He's been a business partner of a sort," she said carefully. "I need him to allow some ships to be unloaded here without questions."

She was saved from more questions by the steady roar of the battle. The planes cruised low over the city, and she found that she was praying. But Joss Road, past the vast mansions of the rich, stayed clear, so they made steady time, and she began to feel hopeful.

"And the destination?" he asked in a sudden silence as frightening as the battle.

"Japan," she whispered.

"Ah," he said. It was a sigh of satisfaction. The houses on either side, set far back behind their walls, were all dark, cracks of the thinnest light showing where here and there the curtains had not quite met.

"A profiteer," he said. He took out his cigarette case, offered one, lit both. As the flame played beneath his eyes he was smiling. "My, my, my."

"We're not at war," she reminded him.

"No," he said, still smiling. The flame went out. "Not yet, we're not."

The gates to Tu's house stood open, and they were waved through. Way down the driveway she could see the stone Tudor mansion, warped by Chinese craftsmen so that, though as large as a small European palace, it was strangely lonely, neither Western nor Chinese. The bombardment had begun again, and now the sky was one long streak of blood-red fire.

In front stood several Rolls Royces, an American Cadillac, a Bentley, a Hispano Suiza. "Impressive," Morgan murmured. There was not a driver in sight. The house, monstrous in its darkness, stood as though deserted.

Evelyn approached the door, once again certain that she would be stopped. No one answered the bell set in the door frame to the right. Morgan pushed; two startled servants, their arms laden with boxes, looked up from a wide, carved staircase. The pictures were gone from the walls, the museum-style display cases emptied of their priceless collection of art, the carpets lifted from the floors.

"Doing a bunk, are we?" Morgan asked lightly.

"Mr. Tu?" Evelyn asked. "Where is he?" When they didn't seem to understand, she called, "Tu, Tu," and looked about.

"This is like a children's party." Morgan had finished his

cigarette, and stubbed it out on the marble floor. "Do you suppose they're all hiding, and we'll have to search them out?"

The servants pointed down the length of the hall. In these unfamiliar corridors Evelyn tried to calculate where Tu could be.

"You take the high road and I'll take the low?" Morgan suggested. More servants came back silently, carrying more of Tu's collection.

"He has to be in one of the big rooms," she said. "He has got the whole Red Sands with him."

Morgan laughed. "Of course, the Red Sands."

Evelyn looked over. "Be serious, Morgan," she warned him. "These men may be just as frightened as the soldiers at the bridge and less accustomed to fear. They are used to great power."

"And they call themselves the Red Sands?" he asked skeptically.

"It's a society of priests," she explained. From the night came a low roar of men's voices. She reached up as though to knock, but the voices died to silence, and instead she pushed the door open on the Society of the Red Sands.

Once the ballroom, the room was now empty except for a high table that on closer inspection was revealed to be a deep box filled with blood-red sand. Twenty or thirty Chinese, most in European costume, stood about it. Tu, enormous, sat in a raised chair at the head of the box while at the side a small, black-clad priest stared down into the patterns that he had formed in the sand.

Tu's eyes fastened on Evelyn, who put her hand on Morgan's arm to warn him. They closed the door and stood watching as the priest erased the design he had made in the sand and, standing back, nodded to Tu.

Tu was helped out of his chair by two members of the society. Breathing heavily, he plunged his hands into the red sand. The priest began to murmur while Tu stirred the sands, his face turned away from his fate toward the sparkling diadems of the Czechoslovakian chandelier. He seemed to be in pain as his hands moved through the sands like serpents, leaving a mounded path of red dirt behind them.

He took his hands reluctantly from the sand, the red grains filtering through his fingers. Seeing the pattern, he made as if to touch the sands again, but the priest gave out a short, sharp exclamation like a gunshot, and he recoiled. In the silence that followed, the priest leaned over, looking at Tu's fortune. The other members of the society, their faces impassive, stood guardian while Tu, in an agony of indecision, gasped for breath. From afar could be heard the irregular explosions of the assault on the city like a heartbeat pulsing its last strength into a body.

Finally the priest spoke in short sharp sentences, gesturing to the patterns as the society leaned forward. Then, with one last explanation, he stood back.

Tu spoke in Cantonese.

The priest shook his head.

Tu screamed. He ranted at the priest and had to be held back by the society. He looked in appeal to Evelyn by the door, to the heavens, to the curtains that fell across the windows of the room. When he was calm, his guardians released his arms, and he struggled back into his chair, his folds of fat settling into a new pattern of their own as they flowed together beneath his long Chinese gown. The society members bowed to the priest as he walked toward the door without another word. As Evelyn stood back for Morgan to open the door, they followed the priest out of the room.

His hands coiled about the arms of his chair, Tu looked murderous. He stared at the sand in hatred, then at the unseen war beyond the windows. "You violate my house," he stated without looking up.

"These are difficult times," she began.

"This is unforgivable."

"Mr. Tu—"

"No," he shrieked. "You never come here! My family are in my house. You"—he let his thick features twist themselves into disgust—"you are . . . business."

"Steady on, old fellow," Morgan said easily. He walked toward the sand.

355

"Who are you?" Tu demanded.

"Your defender," Morgan replied, just as lightly. The bombardment was steady now, an unbroken roar. "I expect you'll be coming into the settlement, won't you?"

Tu's eyes flicked at the pattern that was still drawn boldly in the sand.

"Bad news, is it?" said Morgan, following his reasoning. "It happens that way sometimes. A man can't roll a good toss of the dice every time."

"I must speak to you, sir," Evelyn interrupted.

She had never called Tu "sir" before, and she noted his satisfaction. "The ships—"

"Ships!" screamed Tu. "I cannot talk of ships."

"You must," she said, hearing the desperation in her voice. "I must ask that you arrange with the generalissimo for the ships to come here directly before continuing to Japan."

Tu's face was swollen like a ripe plum left too long in the grass beneath the tree. "Japan," he said in a voice that was ominously quiet. His eyes furtively sought hers once again. "You have given them power."

"Oh, come on, old chap," Morgan said, but Evelyn saw he understood the danger, for he had casually undone the flap of his holster. "You knew all this."

But Tu was swallowing as though he was choking on his words. "I will do nothing," he returned. "Nothing."

Feeling her knees begin to buckle, Evelyn would have fallen at Tu's knees, but Morgan reached out quickly and stirred the sand into a whirlpool of confusion. Tu screamed and lunged at the box, falling to his knees. He clutched at the edge of the table, which broke, spilling the sand down his chest, running across him and onto the floor of the ballroom.

His cries were screams of terror. He scrambled like a baby, gathering the sand together into piles. Morgan had his gun out as the doors flew open on Tu's guards, still holding his treasures.

Tu screamed at them and pointed at Morgan. But Morgan fired directly into the chandelier, a sound so startling as the glass shattered and fell like stars on the fallen millionaire's head that no one moved.

"Tell them to go away," Morgan said.

Uncertainty showing in the depths of his fat-enfolded eyes, Tu hesitated, then spoke.

"Good," said Morgan. "Help me, Evelyn," he ordered, putting his gun away and fastening the flap, "help me get Mr. Tu on his feet."

Together they heaved the fallen Tu back into his chair. "There, now," said Morgan brushing the sand off his ornate tunic, "much better. You mustn't worry about all this," he said, stirring the sand with the toe of his boot. "It's superstitious. A modern man like yourself would be beyond this, I'd think."

Still panting, Tu had recovered some of his self-possession. "I can do nothing," he repeated. "The generalissimo would not allow it."

For a moment Evelyn had thought Morgan had saved the day, but now despair came back. Taking hold of Tu's hand as though they were friends, she begged him. "Then I must go to Nanking," she said. "My daughter is there."

Tu's breathing was now under control. He took his hand away, looked at the spilled sand, and seemed to be thinking. "It is difficult."

"But not impossible," she said, hope flowing.

He listened to the bombardment of the city. "And it would cost much money."

"How much?"

He named a sum so enormous that Morgan laughed.

"All right," Evelyn agreed before Morgan could interrupt. She was ruined. She didn't care. Her eyes sought the spilled sand, and she wondered what the priest would have prophesied for her.

"You must go tomorrow," Tu said.

Morgan stood back in frank amazement, still thinking of the enormous sum of money. He lit a cigarette, his eyes never leaving his sister's face.

"How?"

"Generalissimo's plane will leave the Bund at dawn. I

cannot guarantee more." His eyes looked at her from up close, and they were filled with the old Tu's greed. "I want the money first."

"I can't get it tonight."

He raised his shoulders indifferently. "I will be gone tomorrow."

Evelyn looked at Morgan. "I could give my brother power of attorney tonight," she proposed. "He could draw it out for you tomorrow." A distant memory surfaced. "You will have to go to the bank yourself," she ventured in one last hope. "You've boxes there."

Tu stared at her for a long moment. "You remember?"

"Yes."

"Such a long time ago." He sighed, with something close to friendship there for a second. It was gone in a moment, and he looked instead at Morgan. "In China," he said to Morgan, "family is important. You will be my hostage."

"A hostage to fortune," Morgan said, blowing out smoke as casually as though he were at the Cathay bar. He tapped his foot in the sands of Tu's future. "To all our fortunes."

"So," said Tu, clapping his hands. The doors opened. "I have much to do tonight. I will arrange that you can go to Nanking with the generalissimo's plane. You must be ready on the Bund before dawn. You understand?"

"Thank you."

To Morgan, Tu said, "And tomorrow you give me money."

"Couldn't be clearer." Morgan dropped the butt of his cigarette on the floor and crushed it out in the red sand.

They left Tu giving instructions for his house to be stripped. The driveway was deserted except for Ng Ho and the battered Packard. As they rode away from the darkened mansion the city was outlined by the reflected flames of the fires against the rising columns of smoke. When they were closer and the air coming through the shattered rear window was acrid, Morgan said, "He strikes an expensive bargain."

"He's dangerous," she warned, "don't think he isn't."

Morgan didn't answer. He watched as they crossed over the same bridge, the officers and sentries gone. "Not much of a future, though," he commented, "not if the sands are right."

She couldn't tell if he was being funny. The curfew was already upon the city, all the settlement buildings dark, the only movement the stirring of the refugees who camped where the beggars and rats of Shanghai usually lingered along the sidewalks.

"You don't believe that?" she asked Morgan's shadow.

"It doesn't matter what I believe. It's what a man himself believes that defines his fate."

She reached across the seat and took his large, strong hand in hers, the first time since his unexpected appearance that she had touched him. "But you'll do as you promised?"

He took his hand away. "Yes."

359

19

Returning from Tu's, Evelyn had cried out that they needed a lawyer for a power of attorney, but Morgan had surprised her. He was efficient, withdrawn into some private world, in his Volunteers uniform able to travel about the city. He had found a lawyer, the small English man who had helped him rent his rooms in the red-light district. He brought a witness also, a young subaltern who was in reality a junior clerk out from England assigned to the great trading house of Jardine Matheson.

She had almost balked at signing the document when it was on her desk in Fischer's room. She felt surrounded by Morgan and his subaltern, the gray little Englishman, and by Fischer's ghost warning her against this. But she signed.

After that there was just the matter of waiting for the dawn. Tu had sent a coolie to say that the generalissimo's plane would leave the river at first light.

She bathed, and lay on the bed that she had shared with Fischer, thought about Victoria. She had given everything she had for this flight—years of fear, years of work. But she couldn't go on, because Fischer's presence was so powerful here in the room where they had loved.

She rose while the curfew was still over the city, the windows still darkened with black cloth, the bombardment ongoing. Morgan was sitting in the living room, a glass and decanter at his elbow. But his eyes were focused, his speech clear.

"I can't sleep."

"You should try."

But there were things she had to tell him. "If I don't

return . . ." she began. Then, after a second's hesitation, "But if Victoria somehow does, I want you to tell her this."

There were still a few things, not much, that she had saved from Tu. Some jewelry, this house, some cash in San Francisco—not enough to last a lifetime, as Fischer had warned she would need, but enough for the young. "And there are earrings, as well as some money in a safe upstairs," she told him.

"I don't think so."

"Why not?"

"Vic's taken them," he told her evenly. He knew more about this, she realized, but she didn't care. "Then she has it already."

So she herself had nothing, or almost nothing. Fischer might have enjoyed the joke. It was on herself alone.

She did laugh, and Morgan raised his eyebrows. "I was thinking I am ruined," she explained.

"I've been ruined most of my life. You get used to it. It's not unpleasant except in parts."

"You're not a woman," she pointed out.

He got her through the night, letting her talk. In a sense it was a relief, so she told him about Fischer, almost everything. She kept out the parts that might have made Fischer sound weak, sentimental. She kept out the parts about Samoa, of his death, except to say he died on the ship.

She didn't tell Morgan that Fischer had asked her to marry him. That, too, seemed like a bitterly cruel joke. There was some comfort in it, though; seeing life as a long string of misfortunes that, viewed properly, were merely funny, not tragic.

"We're irrelevant," she said to Morgan as she saw that the night beyond the blackout curtains was darker than it had been an hour ago. The full moon was fading from the sky, and with it the cruel light that had revealed the helpless city to its attackers. The stars had already disappeared.

"Not just us. We know it, that's all," Morgan said. He had started on another decanter, yet he still looked as crisp as though he'd had a full night's sleep.

"Not knowing might be better." Fischer would never have

agreed to that. Fischer insisted on intelligence, in himself, in her, in others. Knowledge was everything. "I think I'd rather not understand," she said mildly.

"Maybe in your next life," he said, and his voice sounded almost kind.

"I don't think I want one," she said. "I don't think I could cope again."

"You handle what you must," Morgan said without sympathy. "You have no choice. Though," he added more lightly, "I doubt there's anything beyond. Do you?"

She had prayed off and on, in pieces and in long-forgotten prayers, for Victoria. "I still pray," she said.

"For yourself."

"No."

"Then for something that connects to your life."

"Yes."

"That's still self-interest," he said.

The crack of sky out the window was now almost clear. "It's dawn," she said.

"Yes." He put the top on the decanter very deliberately, and stood up. "You'd better dress. I'll call Ng Ho."

They drove through a quiet city stirring uneasily after a sleepless night. At the Bund they could see the generalissimo's flying boat in its military drab colors crouched for a takeoff near the enemy's flagship. She thought how stupid this all was; they sat side by side in neutral waters, while not ten miles away they battled for territory.

"Thank you," she said to Morgan as he handed her over to the waiting official, who stared in quick, furtive glances at the white battleship, as though it might fire on the Bund at any moment. That was impossible, though; this was Europe, this was territory set aside to make the world free for trade, inviolate.

"You'll go to Tu," she said.

Morgan patted his breast pocket where he had her power of attorney and bank withdrawal, as well as a letter. Tu would be at the bank taking out his own deposits, the ones—probably much greater now—that he had put in the vaults all those years ago when Sebowski had been manager.

"I'll go right there."

"Then . . . goodbye," she said. She was going to kiss him but stopped.

He looked at her oddly, almost guiltily, then leaned forward and kissed her on the neck, then the cheek. He drew back. "We were friends, weren't we?"

Tears that might have been brought by the cold, late autumn wind off the river came, but she knew that if she cried now she might not be able to face what she had ahead of her. Older now, she couldn't walk into the future with hope. She had to go blindly.

"My only friend," he said, and he sighed, looking out at the four propellers making a corrugated corridor of the water below the wings.

He dropped her hands and she left quickly, getting into the small launch that took her out to the plane. The doors to the plane were hardly shut when it began to move down the cleared section of the river, past the *Idzuko,* past Tu's one-hundred-foot private yacht still taking on cargo across the river, past the impressive, indifferent buildings of the Bund, so out of place in China with their European facades, their unshakable self-confidence, and then, with a shuddering of the whole machine, they bounced twice on the water and were airborne, heading north.

In the highest part of the hills, Mr. Wei's breathing had become short. Stopping, Victoria urged, "We have to rest."

"No," he insisted, pressing on up the steep path along the side of the cliff. "It is important that we be there soon."

A full moon hung over the landscape, turning the distant paddy fields into squares of bright, dark glass. The roads were winding serpents through the still countryside.

Victoria sat down. "I'm not going on."

Mr. Wei's thin face was impatient. "We will have to cross the river to the city at the right moment," he said. "We must be at Nanking by the light."

"You will not reach Nanking at all if you die," Victoria said.

He sat down reluctantly, his head against the cliffside.

The wind coming off the plain whistled about them. Victoria took off her coat and went to him to wrap it about his shoulders. "No," he protested, "you will freeze."

"And if you don't accept it, you will."

Amusement passed through Mr. Wei's pained eyes. "A truly Confucion dilemma."

"We could share it," she suggested.

He smiled now. "With a Marxist solution."

Irritated by his sardonic humor, she put the coat about her own shoulders as a cloak, sat beside him, and tried to shelter him. They were awkward with each other, aware of where their bodies brushed against each other. "We have to survive," she pointed out.

Feeling him shivering beneath his tunic, she touched his forehead and felt fever. "Why did you come out like this?" she demanded.

"The peasants wear these clothes," he said, looking with interest as a column of trucks appeared as a dark, eyeless snake below.

"That does not mean you have to," Victoria snapped irritably. Too aware of him, she shifted out of his close embrace but was pulled back by the cloak. "That's simply foolish."

"I meant," he said softly, "that I would blend in more with the peasants on the road."

Swallowing the rebuke, she asked, "Do you really think something will change?" The column was moving through the moonlit landscape with an almost processional precision.

"It must."

"Nothing changes," she said.

"China does. Slowly, but she changes. You have to take a historical view; we have endured a dozen invasions and absorbed each into China. Now we have another, except it did not come on horses, but in words."

Victoria watched the moon move slowly across the dark dome of night as Mr. Wei slept. She put her arm carefully about him to keep him warm. He spoke in Chinese in his sleep, and she raised the collar of the coat against the wind.

He woke to see her watching the long sweep of hills that towered around them in every direction. "There are stories for every inch of China's soil. Did you know that?" he asked, as quietly as a child.

She looked down into his eyes. "It's a large country."

"Yes, but it has been civilized for three thousand years. These mountains were spoken of by philosophers, priests, and storytellers."

"How can there be anything new, then?" she asked.

"Because a country and a people are their history," he replied, his eyes feverishly bright. "We will still be China when the new rule comes."

"You sound very confident." She mocked him.

"Yes," he agreed, looking at her with the light of fever in his eyes. "Because it is right. It is important to be just. Nobody can rule forever without justice."

He slept again while the sky paled. Cold, she held him tightly, and then a new emotion came to her: regret. She envied Mr. Wei's simplistic beliefs. She wanted to believe in more than her father had—a return to their former status— more than the mother superior's credo—a long acceptance of God's will its reward in another life. Now, today.

She looked at Mr. Wei more closely as the light of dawn gilded the country like pale green moss on old brass. He was very pale, and as her heart started, she shook him.

His eyes opened wide. "What?"

"I thought you were dead," she admitted, feeling her heart race.

They were close to the entrance that lovers find. He, too, could feel the movement of her heart. "I cannot die," he said, smiling. "I have to take you to Nanking."

"Yes," she said more loudly than she intended. She moved away from him, embarrassed by their nearness. The sun was on the face of the cliff, warming them.

"There is an old temple nearby," he said. "There will be water there and, if there is still a priest, some food."

"You know this path, then?" she asked suspiciously.

"Every foot of China is known," he reminded her. He stood up and stretched. The beauty of the scene below him seemed to restore him, and he stared for a long time at the fields, at the stands of trees so small they looked like models, at the hills and the bright river far away.

Then they heard the sound of a plane coming up the river, saw a flying boat come out of the sun and follow the river's path northward toward Nanking. Mr. Wei turned away. "Come," he said. "We have a long journey ahead of us."

20

Rosettes of fire exploded beyond the windows of the flying boat as it came out of the clouds, following the river toward Nanking. As the aircraft shuddered, Evelyn could see the formation of the Japanese army on the plain beyond the city. Its sheer size—battalions stretching as far as the distant hills, troops moving like insects across the landscape, tanks, trucks, lines of transport—brought the taste of death into her mouth.

The guns hammered at the plane as it came toward the city that rose in pyramids of ancient architecture in the curve of the valley. She saw the blockade of Nationalist gunboats on the river, and as they flew closer faces turned up in fear. Then they were below the range of the Japanese guns and coming in for an awkward landing.

The plane taxied toward the dock, where she could see the Chinese troops standing guard as a transport was unloaded. When the four propellers went silent the noise rushed at them, the incessant thudding of the Japanese guns, and then, as she was helped from the plane, the shock as the incoming shells exploded further into the city, throwing shards of houses, fire, the fine dust of destruction that hung everywhere in the air.

Beyond the throng of troops supervising the unloading of the transports she saw a crowd several thousand strong trying to push through the frightened soldiers to make their escape by river. She hadn't thought how she would get to Alex. Morgan had told her that Victoria had made inquiries, and that he would be at the military academy, but now she saw she might never find the academy.

"Please," she said to the Chinese official who stood rigid with fear in the face of the terrified crowd.

Before she could continue, the high, whining scream of the air raid sirens began, and the crowd miraculously melted away, running in every direction for shelter. The shadow of the incoming planes started at the very edge of the city—five, then ten, then many more—all in formation coming in across the ancient city.

She stood fascinated as the day became dark with sky predators, and then before her eyes the first bombs fell like the deadly droppings of prehistoric birds, specks against the sun that became larger, screaming down at an angle, hundreds of them. The explosions started singly, then blended into one long roar of destruction as the buildings flew apart, the very air vibrating in her ears.

She was dead. The thought passed through her mind with absolute clarity. No one could survive this.

The squadron passed over toward the hills on the other side of the bowl of the city. The noise of their engines dragged like a train of sound behind them. The sound of fear followed the screaming of terror, a child's cry, the roar of the soldiers fighting for control of the dock. She saw a man thrown to the ground and watched as the first of the soldiers brought his rifle butt down on the fallen man's skull, splitting it like a winter melon.

She ran after the Chinese official moving along the docks. "Where is the military academy?"

He shook her away, mute with terror. She grabbed the sleeve of his coat and was thrown back herself, tumbling into the dirt. "There!" he pointed. "There."

She followed the direction of his arm, saw the almost manic pleasure he took in showing her the highest building deep within the city. "There!" he said, then turned, was lost in the thick cloud of dust still falling from the sky.

The only vehicles were the long lines of khaki green transports passing slowly along the river road, each with a Chinese soldier on the hood. As she watched they shot at the crowd ahead, scattering them, the dead and wounded lying untended in the road. The trucks moved forward without slowing, leaving behind a trail of crushed bodies. A howling wail of anger and pain rose out of the narrow streets, but the guns were sending in their second bombardment now, rhythmic, almost welcome for the curtain of brute noise it dropped over the human pain.

She pushed her way through the line of soldiers and into the first street leading from the river. She could see there had once been a line of stately houses facing on a broad boulevard, now pockmarked with bomb craters. The houses stood in stunned, irregular lines, some perfectly preserved, glass windows facing out of their elegant facades, while others had had their faces torn away brutally, the interiors there to be seen by any passersby. The interiors of some were stripped as clean as though carrion birds had passed, while others had been ravaged with a halfhearted effort, as though the looters understood that they could keep none of it.

The trees along the center of the boulevard were charred hands clawing at the sky. The troops patrolled in squads of a dozen men, peasants all, in ill-fitting uniforms, a look of silent despair on their faces.

She stood in the center of the boulevard, searching for the landmark of the academy, when she heard the sudden silence as the bombardment stopped, then the distant humming of the deadly bees now coming toward the city from the other side. The bombs fell first on the walls of the ancient city and moved forward, a curtain of death. This time she ran with the rest, a screaming, milling mass of humanity running for the nearest shelter. She had heard in Shanghai that a doorway was the safest place, but the first one she found was filled with crouching bodies, faces pressed into one another's clothes. She ran on, but the next and then the next were all filled with people. The bombs were falling into the boulevard, stretching a path down the length of the road. A barricade of sandbags exploded a hundred yards away. The ground underfoot shuddered, and the wall to which she pressed her face vibrated beneath her skin. She ran on, clawing to get into the shelter of the next doorway, but was pushed back, flung into the street by the Chinese.

Now the sky was dark with the steady, even overpass of the bombers, the deadly capsules falling as evenly as winter rain. She saw the Chinese gun supplement at the end of the boulevard begin its retaliatory firing, dark puffs spewing from the muzzle of the heavy cannon. The world was all the noise of the darkened sky and the uneven explosion of the bombs. She felt the fire of nearby houses and then saw the bomb fall directly toward the Chinese cannon. The explosion—awaited for a long few seconds—was perfectly choreographed: the rising of the dust of the immediate impact, the cannon itself lifting from its mount, rising up into the dust-choked air intact, to explode into several pieces thirty feet above the ground, the soldiers thrown like dolls, splayed like crucified icons as they rose into the air after their relic. And then, in a sudden shifting of the sequence, all of it falling back to earth—the pieces of the gun, the bodies, the sandbags—and throughout it all the steady movement of the bombers overhead, the roar, the falling bombs, and on every side a musical cacophony of destruction.

As the squadron passed over, the screaming rose like a chant. The Chinese soldiers came down the boulevard, half-crazed with fear and frustration. The cowering populace ran on to wherever they had been going when death appeared in the morning sky.

Evelyn joined the people who turned off the boulevard. The older streets were narrow, the sky at best just a white streak between the overhangs of the sandstone houses. Here, where the houses were old and more traditional, there were no windows on the streets. Moving as quickly as she could in the melee of fleeing people, she passed entire streets that stood untouched, their walls facing serenely on the river of panic, then, abruptly, entire streets that stood as wastelands of rubble.

From a deserted gun emplacement in a square she could

see the imposing military academy, and she ran on, aware that the squadron would be back. From somewhere near the river the Chinese gunners had taken up a reply, and far to the right, where the old walls of the city faced out across the encamped army, another battery of guns spoke up.

Bodies lay abandoned, open-eyed in terror. Children lay in death in piles, as though they had clung together in one last futile struggle with life. She ran on toward the open gates of the academy across the square, and as she passed she heard the third squadron come across the wall, raining vengeance.

Within the thick walls of the academy the sound of the battle was muted. In the deserted parade ground the flag of China hung in tatters from the flagpole. The shadows that darkened the day reached her as she ran into the main building. Here, a lone cadet looked at her with eyes dead with the knowledge of real war. "Lezenski," Evelyn said as he stood at attention by the door. "Lezenski. Can you tell me where he is?"

Then the roar was upon them, louder, and the bombs began to fall without, and the cadet stared wide-eyed at the door, watching as though he would see the bomb that would come to kill him. He was so young, she thought, a boy, and felt her own fear begin to ebb. She reached for him and took his shoulders under her arm, but he reacted angrily, silently shouting at her to stand back, gesturing with the rifle. She stepped away, pressed against the wall, and waited as the bombs fell, row after row. As the sound receded the boy sobbed once before he choked back his fear.

"Lezenski?" she asked quietly.

He gestured toward the broad staircase that led out of the impressive main hall. As his companions returned from their shelters below the building he stood at attention again. Evelyn hurried up and around the wide corner onto the second floor.

An officer in a dark blue tunic and trousers with gold braid at the shoulders and down the seam of his pants came crisply up the stairs, each booted foot snapping on the marble. He looked at Evelyn with surprise. "Lezenski," she said. "Alexander Lezenski. I must find him."

She could see the suspicion in his eyes, the suspicion of fear held back.

"Please." She pulled her coat tightly around her, hoping that she looked respectable, not alarming. Other officers were coming up the stairs, moving with the look of men with little time and much to do. The cadets ran in all directions.

"Upstairs," the Chinese in the dark uniform said to Evelyn in perfect English. "He will be in his office up there." He pointed to the other staircase at the end of the hall. Evelyn followed his directions, knowing that he was still watching her as she fled down the wide hall. At any moment she expected to hear the order to stop. She could pretend she didn't understand, pretend she didn't hear, for now the sound of Chinese voices barking orders, shouting over the turmoil, rose all about her.

Her heart was in her throat as she reached for the door at the top of the stairs. She was about to knock, but then she stepped into the room, ready to answer him, shout at him, beg him.

The perfectly square room held a table and a chair. Wide windows separated by thin columns were set in each wall. As fear left her, so did hope. She had come this far, and he was gone. The table was strewn with maps. Maps. Maps. Her mind went back to the room above the herbalist. All the maps of Russia, all the campaigns Alex had fought across those maps. These maps were of China, and as she stood there, numb with the knowledge that she had lost, she touched the river on the map, and thought of how it sparkled, beyond the narrow windows, in the dust-clogged air, where particles of the city floated slowly downward from the empty sky.

"I could have you shot as a spy," he said from behind her.

She was startled by the memory of his voice, unchanged. She thought her mind had played a game with her; this voice was that of the man who spoke to her so many years ago on a sunlit green in England.

She turned, still touching the table with her fingertips, very, very frightened, but not sure anymore of what. Her life was like the particles of dust that moments ago had been formed into houses, streets, trees, people, falling now to earth after one cataclysmic moment. His appearance shocked her. Thin, stooped, he seemed to have shrunk. His hair was white. The eyes, however, were the same tiger eyes.

For what seemed a long time, they could hear nothing from within the academy, but from without came the sounds of battle. "I would have recognized you anywhere," he said finally, his voice soft, bemused. "I've sometimes wondered if I would. Memory can be so treacherous.

"So," he said, looking at her more closely, "you've come."

"Yes." She paused, uncertain as to how to continue. As he came closer she saw that he had the same intensity that she remembered. His restless eyes looked at her hand on the maps.

"I still play with maps, you see." He sounded more amused than anything else. "I have just been up on the roof." He pointed to the ceiling. "Observing the war. We could never do that in Russia, do you remember?" His voice was distant, nostalgic. "We were too busy squabbling among ourselves for the eventual victory." He sighed. "You didn't come to see me," he stated.

She could see sorrow in his eyes, perhaps some small amusement. "I've come for Victoria."

He seemed not to understand.

"She was coming to find you," Evelyn said.

He seemed to shrink before her eyes, the already thin shoulders to bend. His eyes blinked several times, and he looked quickly toward the window. "My dear," he said softly. "Not here."

"Yes."

"And you didn't stop her?" There was the sudden burning fury that she also remembered from twenty years ago.

"She wouldn't . . . listen to me," Evelyn said, unsure how to continue. She felt very strange to be standing here after all these years talking like this, as naturally as though nothing out of the ordinary had happened. This close, she found it hard to believe that he had been her first lover, that they had had a child together a long, long time ago in another land that existed no longer—not the Russia that they had known. "It is you she wants to see," Evelyn told him, and the words stung the walls of her heart.

He walked away from her. "She hasn't come here," he said, looking from his narrow tower window upon the ruined city. His shoulders rose as he took a long breath. "When did she leave?"

"Two days ago."

"From Shanghai?"

"Yes."

He turned. "And you?"

"I came on the generalissimo's plane." She hesitated; then, to her confusion, a blush began along her neck and colored her cheeks. "A business associate arranged a passage," she said.

"A business associate. Yes, of course," he said.

Out of her confusion came anger. "I won't allow you to speak to me like that," she retorted.

As he looked at her from under his heavy brows his eyes were filled with their own anger. "You won't allow me?" he asked her, his lips beginning to smile.

She closed her eyes, and suddenly she was back in the herbalist's shop. The past was a trap, a tiger trap ready to open beneath her feet. "Alex," she said, "we have a child." Behind the darkness of her eyelids she saw small motes of bright light. She opened her eyes. "You and I are not important any longer."

"I thought for years about you. Did you know that?"

"Don't do this to yourself, Alex, please," she begged him.

"Yes, for years. For a long time my hatred sustained me, all I had in those days. It burned like the fires out in the city, fierce, bright. I would wake up at night filled with hatred for you."

Evelyn moved away, feeling faint. The loneliness of her life chilled her heart. She knew the tears would begin to flow and wrapped her arms about herself beneath her coat, hoping to keep away the worst of his assault.

His voice was quiet, mesmeric as he traveled back in his own memory. "Sometimes when I was out in the city I would think I saw you. I wasn't raised to be afraid, yet I began to fear the sight of you. My heart would literally stop at the movement of a head, a glimpse of a woman coming toward me, hidden in the crowd. I expected it at every moment, and I became afraid."

She sat down in the single chair.

"Once I even did see you," he said in the same distant voice. "Yes, not in the Chinese city, of course, but on the Bund. I was dressed in the overcoat of an old uniform, another shabby Russian refugee, and you . . ." It became too much for him for a few seconds, and Evelyn had time to fight her tears.

"You looked beautiful," he said finally. He seemed to find the thought as troubling now as on that long-ago day. "I was almost proud of you. You were getting out of a car to enter a hotel. . . . You looked"—he faced her again coldly—"well loved."

She coughed it back, turned away from his cruelty, but the tears came, as she knew they would.

"And then I hated you," his words said behind her. "Because then I saw him." Without looking she heard his confusion, his pain, summoned from the past. "A Jew. A Jew. Yes, a Jew."

"He was a good man," she said, the need to defend Fischer as strong as her pain.

He grabbed her from behind, spun her about. "He was a *rich* man," he shouted at her.

They were inches apart, hatred written large across his thin, strong face. "Yes," she whispered, "he was a rich man . . . but a good man, too."

She was sure he would strike her then as he had years ago, when he sent her into the streets penniless. But then he had had nothing to give her, either, she reasoned. "You didn't want me," she told him.

"I may have needed you," he answered, holding her shoulder in a painful grasp. He undid his fingers, brushed the fur contemptuously.

"I was there for you." She walked away, calmed herself.

"All is lost here, did you know that?"

"Yes."

"The Chinese don't know it," he said, bemused. "Sometimes I'm so struck by the similarity to the past, I think that I must be wrong. I was raised to believe that I would lead men, because through generations of breeding I had gained wisdom with my mother's milk. Then later, I saw that I had been living in a fool's paradise."

"You were never a fool."

"You are . . . kind to say so," he said without looking at her, but the anger was gone, replaced by memory. "But a man is not what he believes about himself. That is merely a romantic's view. A man is only a man insofar as he can affect his own fate." He faced her. "I was powerless that day I saw you on the Bund. That was why I hated you. I was just another dirty refugee clinging to a foolish pride, if I were to tell the truth, and"—he smiled, a smile that was almost friendly, almost nostalgic—"and why should I not be cheerful now, eh? The planes will be back soon. They are efficient, the Japanese, if nothing else. If I were to tell the truth, then perhaps you helped me that day. I could deny my position no longer. Seeing you there, I finally understood that what I believed was of no consequence, that my world was gone, and a new one—yours—had arrived."

"Not mine."

He looked at the coat. "Yours," he said. He raised his head to listen. "They are coming back soon."

"If she is not here," Evelyn said to his back, "then she's out there somewhere."

"She's safer there." He faced her again, considering. "And you," he said, "you'd be safer to take advantage of your . . . business associates . . . and fly away again."

"The plane will be here for a while yet," she said.

"I'm not sure. If she comes to me, I could send her to join you at the river."

"I'll stay with you," she said.

He watched her, searching for something he had to know. Then, losing interest and looking down at his maps, he said, "As you wish. I don't go to the shelters. I like to watch the battle."

Unable to look at each other, they waited in silence for the planes to return.

In the highest part of the hills, the air was cold enough to see their breath. Victoria touched Mr. Wei's red face. A fever made his eyes unnaturally bright, as though he was drugged.

"You're dying." The thought had been with her for some hours as they climbed the narrow path away from the small monastery where a single priest still lived to tend the flame.

"I cannot die," he said. "We are not at Nanking." He had become giddy as his sickness grew, childlike at times.

"We must stop," she insisted. "You must rest."

To her surprise, he agreed and sat down where the path made an oval around a stunted pine tree, reaching like hands of prayer out into nothingness. He lay back against the cliff. She took off her coat and put it about his chest and shoulders, and if she needed proof that Mr. Wei was ill, she found it in his lack of protest.

Feeling the cold, she tried not to shiver so he would not insist on giving back her coat.

"Superstition," he said finally. The temple was lost to view a long way behind, but he looked in that direction anyway.

"He was kind."

"Yes. But it is not enough."

"What would be?"

"Hope," he answered, moving to face her with his bright eyes. Then, without warning, "Do you love your uncle?"

It wasn't fever that made her own face burn. "One should love one's family," she said angrily, looking away to where the path led further up the steep mountainside.

When he said nothing, she turned to see that he was still

watching her. "You needn't be ashamed," he told her. "I was educated in the West."

She laughed at the absurdity. "So you think we are decadent, is that it?" But the words struck too close to home, so she added, "Why would it matter to you? You Chinese don't value girl children anyway, you sell them in the markets. I have seen it."

"Only the poorest of us," he said, more seriously.

"Not only the poorest. The rich may not sell their children, but they do not value the girls."

"It will be different later," he told her.

They had nothing further to say, it seemed. They rested, but not for long. They had to cross the ridge before the sun was gone. The world was very quiet, and Victoria found this a new feeling, a sense of peace. She had heard of peace, she thought with wonder, but had not been able to understand what it could mean.

"I think," she said, watching how the shadows played across the steep slope, "that I can understand why each place has a story."

"It's a false understanding," he said shortly without opening his eyes. "Nothing can remain exactly as it was, year after year. It is not modern."

"But it could be peaceful."

He opened his eyes, looking at her curiously. "Are you so disturbed?"

"No."

"I think you are."

"I think we should walk," she said in vengeance.

Then they heard the planes, and he turned to face the sun. Unlike the earlier sounds, this was far away, very soft, and then it grew very slowly, like a wave, until the horizon was shadowed, as though the great storm was rising. Even under that assault of sound, she heard Mr. Wei take in his breath very sharply. Without thinking, she reached out to take his hand as the first row of bombers came out of the sun—ten of them, followed at exactly even places by another ten, then another, row after row of them moving slowly across the sky until it was black with the dark crosses of their shapes, crucifix after crucifix of destruction passing inland. They stood like worshippers, hand in hand, as the machines of prey passed over them—at least a hundred, possibly more—and then they were alone on the side of the Chinese mountain, and the silence that the planes left behind was not the silence of serenity but that of fear.

"So many," said Mr. Wei, his brow furrowed. "Something has happened."

"Why?" She could feel the strong, dry texture of his skin as he held her hand.

"I have never heard so many planes at the Nanking airfields," he said. "The Japanese are bringing them from somewhere else."

"You watch their planes?"

"Of course," Mr. Wei said, looking at her. "We are not entirely dreamers." Aware that he still held her hand, he opened his fingers, letting her hand drop away like that of a corpse. He turned. "We must hurry," he said. "There may be less time than we thought."

When the planes came, Alex said, "You must go to the shelters. I will send you with a cadet."

"No."

He looked more sad than angry. "Don't be foolish," he said to her, and already the reprise of the advancing squadron of bombers was such that he was shouting, as though he was indeed angry. "This is not a time for heroics."

"I will stay."

"No," he said, as though she was behaving like a child. "I will find someone to take you to the shelters."

"I am not a child, Alex."

He shrugged. "As you wish."

He went to look across the walls of the old city toward the south. Presently he saw the first thin line of planes as it topped the horizon and watched, unmoving, while they inched across the pale blue dome of the winter sky. The air raid sirens wailed below, and Evelyn could hear that the building was emptying by the thud of boots on the stairs below.

She was first very frightened, then not at all. The moment was upon her before she could consider the consequences. The first of the planes came across the distant wall, heading toward the river very low. Then she could no longer hear the Chinese antiaircraft bombardment because the explosions of the bombs began, sudden, almost musical as they played their song of death, point and counterpoint. The tower shuddered, and Alex turned very slowly to look at her. Whatever fear she might have felt was numbed by the relentless noise, the sense of danger muted by the inescapability of the planes as they cruised in wave after wave, raining death.

Finally they were gone, the Chinese guns hammering futilely at the last of the bombers. Dogs barked with fear as at a retreating thief, and then they, too, were silent. From beyond the walls the Japanese artillery began again, small coughing sounds that seemed irrelevant after the bombardment. She realized she was partially deaf from the bombing but was filled suddenly with the most extraordinary feeling of happiness. She was alive.

Alex turned from the window. "Come," he said, and he disappeared through the narrower door. The walls of the stairwell brushed her shoulders as she followed him up into the cold air of the roof of the tower.

Alex was standing at the edge, the toes of his boots almost in the air as he looked down on the destruction. She went almost as close to the verge and saw that the academy had taken a bomb in the roof of one wing. A gaping hole, as though someone had thrown a large rock, stared at them from below, and through it she could see the twisted form of a bed.

"Unexploded," Alex said, following her gaze. "It may go off later. Don't be frightened."

Instead she was almost exhilarated. The numbing pain of

her betrayal by the American was overwhelmed by her sudden gratitude at being still alive. From here she saw how the old city was spread around a central cone, how the municipal buildings were all to the right, facing out toward the river from where the barges of the emperors must once have arrived. She saw the narrow streets and the geometric courtyards of the old Chinese houses, many now smashed, as though a destructive giant had walked upon a model of serene design. She saw where the parks—now burning—had once been, and she saw beyond the city walls the roads that led toward what had once been the country homes of the nobles.

Below, every street was filled with people, so small from here that they, too, might have been toys. They moved in rivers of terror, eddying about the still-standing buildings, flowing hopelessly one into another.

The Japanese planes were now small specks just passing over the hills. "Why do the Chinese planes not follow them?" she asked Alex. She saw how the rivers of people blended together far below.

He smiled. "They don't exist except on paper."

"But I saw reports," she exclaimed. "I read of the air force."

He shrugged, his voice coming to her through the smoke. "Oh, yes. But this is an ancient country," he said to her, a shadow standing nearby, "a *noble* country. The cadets can buy their degrees."

She stood stunned, looking into the darkness, hearing the cry of the ambulances, the sharp, barely heard screams that rose for just a fraction of a second and then were lost in the greater terror.

"If you fail a cadet from a good family, then there is strong protest. The theory is that good breeding makes the finest men. Therefore, of course, the children of good families . . ." He stopped. "Oh, my dear," he said wearily, "do I need to tell you this? We saw this once before together." He looked at her out of the darkness of noon and she thought his eyes were more than sad, more than tired.

She thought she saw despair such as she hadn't seen even when his own cause looked hopeless all those years ago. He had still believed—bitterly, with fury and hatred, but he had believed. "The air force," he said, "is only on paper. Less than a quarter of the planes could be put in the air, and those"—now the bitterness rose again in him—"those, of course, must be saved in case there is a final, last need to defend . . ." He couldn't think of what it was they would defend.

The smoke had thinned. He turned to face away from the river. "This was once the ancient capital of the empire, did you know that?" He pointed out across the battlements toward the blue hills. "There are the Ming tombs. A thousand years of history lies buried there."

She could remember the long climb toward the western hills outside Peking to bury the corpses of the grand duke and his duchess, bodies carried as sacred relics across Siberia. The shabby column of refugees had believed that they would one day take them home to Russia. They must still be there, she thought, still waiting.

"History can be a burden," he said, as though he, too, was remembering. "We tell ourselves it is an inspiration, but we are wrong."

As they watched there was movement across the plain. At first it seemed like passing clouds, but then, as the fires below were brought under control, they saw it was the distant movement of a great army. The Japanese artillery had fallen quiet. The city lay all about, waiting.

"Perhaps she won't come," he said finally.

"She will come," Evelyn told him. "She is your child."

"Our child," he said without turning.

"Yes," she said softly. If she cried now, she wouldn't be able to stop. "Perhaps she won't be able to reach here," she said, seeing how the shadow on the plain grew darker, denser, closer.

"No, she is your child, too," he said.

As though to underscore his words, the sky over the city

exploded in a thousand-shell burst, the sound echoing through the ruins of the tallest buildings. The screams below rose like a chorus of the damned but were lost as the hills threw back the echoes.

"Come," Alex said to Evelyn as the very sky seemed to become noise and fury. "Let us go below."

21

"Poor bloody Chinks," Murchison said to Morgan as they met on the steps toward the Cathay. The Chinese had capitulated during the night, and by morning the side streets in the city were filled with sullen resignation, the stores open, the noodle vendors once again working over their open fires. The two gentlemen turned away from the sight of the victorious Japanese army parading through the city, and looked to the harbor. In a moment of panic, Morgan saw Tu's yacht pulling out, steaming away from the city. Had he made a mistake? But as he focused again on Tu's departing boat, he breathed a sigh of relief.

"You'll be giving up your uniform, I expect." The Australian newspaperman's voice broke in on Morgan's thoughts.

"Yes, I'd think so. Things will settle down to normal," he answered. He saw a few motes of dusty ash float from the gray sky and wondered vaguely if there was still a fire. The cease-fire had come suddenly at midnight, and the last of the fires, according to the reports he had read at the Volunteer headquarters on Joss Road, had been put out. The city was safe, had been the gist of the report. It was over.

"Look," he said, lifting his hand to try to catch the scattered snowflakes. "Snow."

"Hip, hip, bloody hooray," Murchison said sourly.

Morgan felt a sense of melancholy settle over him at the thought of Victoria and Evelyn in the north. "They'll capitulate, won't they?" he said to Murchison. "There's not much point, is there?"

"Survival," Murchison said. "If the Japs get hold of

Chiang and his crew, it's a long drop off a short platform. They'll fight on.

"Where are you headed?"

Until that moment Morgan hadn't decided. "The Russian-Asiatic bank."

Murchison looked at him. "Got business?"

Morgan ignored him. "I'll drop you on the Bund," he said as they walked to the street and hired a rickshaw coolie.

When they reached the Bund they saw the *Idzuko* had raised a head of steam and turned north, ready to sail upriver. "Nanking," muttered Murchison. "Blow the bloody Chinks out of the water, I should think."

Morgan let him off and gave directions to the bank. He could feel Evelyn's power of attorney pressed against his chest and was thinking coolly now. At the bank he walked stiffly through the marble hall, and demanded to see the manager. He went up the staircase to the second floor, waited very briefly, and presented his credentials.

He saw how the uniform helped, how the manager—middle-aged, uncertain of himself in the silence that seemed to press in on the tall, gilded room—took notice. "You want to close this account out?" he asked.

"Yes, in a draft."

"May I ask why?"

"It's a private matter," Morgan answered tartly.

Twenty minutes later he was on the sidewalk outside. The same coolie squatted, hawking into the gutter. Morgan got back into the rickshaw and gave directions to the Chartered Bank. The day was very cold now, and Morgan reflected that soon he'd have to buy a car. Evelyn's Packard would be useless, and he couldn't travel about the city in rickshaws in this weather. He put aside a brief feeling of guilt. As far as Evelyn was concerned, he had given the money to Tu. Tu was gone, and he wouldn't be back for a long time, if ever, while the Japs were here to stay. Morgan dismissed Murchison's gloomy predictions; China would keep them busy for a good long time. In Morgan's experience, it didn't do to worry too much about the future. The future tended to surprise you, and nothing was better for dealing with surprises than a good-sized piece of change.

At the Chartered Bank he told the coolie to wait, went in, and asked to open an account. Sir Ernest Cunningham, the bank's president, came out to see him while he was filling out the forms.

Morgan finished signing the last document with a flourish. Sir Ernest waved his passport away. "No need for that, old chap," he said, picking up the documents himself. His eyes, long out of practice, scanned the size of the deposit, and his eyebrows went up. "We're very happy to have your business, Major Valentine," he said, handing over the papers. To the Chinese clerk he said, "Immediate credit.

"We Europeans must stick together," he said, walking Morgan out. "Though I must say I'll be glad when all this nonsense is finally settled. My wife's talking about going home."

"Many people are," Morgan said.

"I'm against it," Sir Ernest said forcefully. "It gives the impression we're frightened."

"Everything will be back to normal soon. Perhaps if Lady Cunningham waits a few weeks . . ." Morgan suggested.

"Not married, are you?"

"No," Morgan admitted.

"Thought not," Sir Ernest said, slapping him jovially on the back at the door. The tailcoated Chinese doormen stood ready to open the door for Morgan. "If you were, you would know the impossibility of telling anything to the woman you're married to. I tell you what. Maybe if you came out to the house for tiffin one night, you could talk to her."

"I'd be delighted," Morgan said. His plans were falling together just as he had wished.

"Tomorrow?"

"Certainly."

"Strike while the iron's hot, before she gets herself involved in a lot of plans and things. Can't get her on a boat right now anyway. There seems to be a rush on them."

"People scare easily," Morgan suggested.

"Not the right type of people," Sir Ernest said approvingly. "Eight o'clock, then."

"Right."

Morgan went out into a gentle snowfall. The coolie was wrapping his feet in rags. Morgan lit a cigarette, looking up at the white, snowy sky. The lights were coming on in all the buildings, windows sparkling gold in the dim midafternoon light. The Japanese battleship was far upriver, a white shadow moving through the falling snow.

"The right type." Morgan had been the right type of boy, then later the right type of officer. They were called on to fight the battles for such fat fools as Sir Ernest and his panting, frightened lady. They would want him now at their dinner table, but later, when they were less afraid, when the memory of the uncomfortable weeks had passed, he would be forgotten unless he made himself essential in other ways.

The plan had come to him quite simply as he'd gotten steadily drunk in his own rooms in Kwangshei. He could still smell Victoria's heavy scent on the bedclothes, and his well-practiced indifference had seemed to desert him. He'd taken the bottle of whiskey to bed and lain there watching the dance hall sign flick on and off, advertising life and excitement, the pleasures of the flesh, all the things he knew could be relied on. Whereas love, the friendship of the great, none of that came to anything when you most needed them. Murchison was right, the Nips were here to stay. And so was Morgan. There was a new wind blowing through Asia, as cold as the wind coming down the Bund, and he would be with it.

When the coolie was ready, he got back into the rickshaw. "The Japanese legation," he ordered.

The coolie turned, and Morgan stared him down. They started off along the boulevard as the snow gathered along the sidewalks, turning to slush as it landed among the cars and rickshaws, the trams and pedestrians hurrying through the gloom of the day, anxious to catch up on business that had been delayed by the Japanese assault.

Vic, he thought, Vic, keeping his mind deliberately blank.

It had been her decision to leave the safety of Shanghai for a father she hadn't seen in years. He wasn't responsible for her. If you squinted, you could be in Paris or Beirut—any elegant city built for trade. The rickshaw left two knife-edge tracks behind as the coolie pulled his burden through the falling snow. Morgan had a terrible sense of loss, as though something unusual had been there within reach, something worth having, and he had somehow missed the moment.

There wasn't anything worth having, he reminded himself, except money and power. He'd learned that years ago himself, but they had eluded him until now. The gates to the Japanese legation stood open, proud guards on duty outside. Out of the past came a snatch of poetry, painfully learned a long time ago in a chilly boarding school.

"There is a tide in the affairs of men, which, taken at the flood, leads on to fortune . . ."

He couldn't remember any more than that. Something about disaster if you missed the moment. Well, he wouldn't, not this time. He had a sense that he was one of the few who wouldn't. Because he had nothing to defend, no entrenched self-image like Sir Ernest, no land like the Chinese, no little gangster routines like Tu. He was a free man, and he could see the future more clearly for all that. And as he saw it, the future included the rising sun hanging crisply in the cold day above the gates of the legation.

At times he had doubted himself, thought that perhaps the others, the boys he had despised who later were transformed into men of power and money, were in some way he couldn't comprehend more worthy than himself. He felt vindicated, and as the coolie slowed to allow Morgan to speak to the Japanese guards who approached the rickshaw, he felt himself flush with the knowledge that there was a new order coming, and that he, Morgan Valentine, would be part of it.

The moon was a silver dollar above the stricken city as Victoria and Mr. Wei crossed the ridge. Mr. Wei stopped, his breath leaving his body in a long hiss. There below on the plain the fires of the Japanese stood in perfect golden rows.

The city was a carpet of fire, flames licking at the winter sky. From here the guns were faint, muffled tongues of tiny paintbrush flames erupting from the artillery set about the ancient walls.

Below them was the dark western bank of the river, and then the bright ribbon of water that ringed the exposed flank of the city. Before, Victoria had been frightened of the planes, had prayed when the bullets stitched the rice paddies. She had thought of what she would say if they were stopped on the road. But now she was struck with true fear: the fear that if she entered this cauldron of death, she would live no more days.

"It is not long," Mr. Wei said. He sat on the ground as the wind came over the hills, and if she had not known that it was impossible, she would have thought that Mr. Wei was crying.

"We can't go down there," she said to him.

He looked up at her, his eyes filmed with light. "I must."

"My father . . ." She turned away in despair and frustration. Now, seeing how she had insisted, how she had defied her mother and Morgan, how she had pressured Mr. Wei, she felt a weak and afraid. All her demands and confidence were revealed for what they were: the petulance of a child. Her flesh crawled with the sense of her own mortality; her breath was rank with her own fear. "I'm afraid," she whispered.

"Your father would not want you to do this," Mr. Wei reprimanded her.

"We can turn back now," she responded. He never complained about the cold, and only when they stopped would he allow her to share her padded coat. The sense of his body leaning against her had come to feel familiar, though he would never have made such a gesture himself.

"I must go on," Mr. Wei said.

"You can't," she cried out, her voice thin and filled with fear. "The city is burning."

He closed his eyes, opening them again as though he might have been hallucinating, the city untouched below. "It was the ancient capital."

The planes moved away over the river and their noise filled the night for many minutes. In the ensuing silence, Victoria found that she had crouched beside Mr. Wei, as though the planes might press down upon her. He looked at her. "If you are careful and do as I tell you, you can return, and I think you will be safe."

He was abandoning her, and she knew that there would be no reasoning with him. "You'll die," she said.

"Yes, I think so," he agreed.

The play of the fires in the night mesmerized her. Where the new bombs had fallen the flames rose as high as a tall building, the red and gold filled with the darker shadows of rising ash. The fires lit up the sky above the city so the full moon seemed to fade and the stars were lost to sight. She saw the tents of the sleeping army and thought, They will come into the city there, through the wide ancient gate that had stood guard against all other invaders, and there will be nothing but death when they are done.

"I will go with you," she said to Mr. Wei.

"Then you will die also."

The reality of her death showed itself in the way her heart wished to break from her chest, in her inability to breathe. "No," she said when she could finally form words. "This is something I must do." It wasn't her father who forced her to continue, but the sense that if she did not, she would have to return to the life she had had, to the woman she had been. She wanted something else.

"Yes," he agreed, searching her face. "I think that is so."

"We should rest for a while," Victoria said, undoing her padded coat.

"Not for long," he said. "We must be at the riverbank before daylight. We can cross with the sampans that bring food."

They found a place where they could watch the burning city, and there he settled against her. The flames rose higher still, trying, it seemed, to burn the very fabric of the sky before, defeated, they ebbed. The exhaustion of the climb across the blue hills brought sleep in small pieces. In her dreams she saw another fire, long ago, when she was a child, another city burning, and she woke with a sense of pursuit, of the enemy close by, of salvation lost. It was the bombers back, coming again, refueled, over the ridge behind them, and she saw how the bellies of the planes opened to bring new destruction to the dying city.

Mr. Wei said near her face, "We have no more time."

Before the fear could betray her, she rose, seeming, impossibly, to feel the heat of the flames on her face. She searched for words of hope, but the planes came. She thought it strange that the fire looked so beautiful in the moonlight as the sky became lighter with the approaching dawn.

Morgan watched the little nightclub owner as he bowed low to the Japanese officers. You could tell the victors in any war, Morgan thought; they got the best tables. The alcohol that he'd consumed at Sir Ernest's table was thinning in his veins. Fearing sobriety, he pushed through the manic dancers toward the bar at the back.

Sir Ernest had said, "I have it on very good authority that this whole matter will be concluded in the next day or so." He spoke as though he was talking of a loan, but outside on the Nanking Road the stream of refugees continued unbroken into the city.

His wife, a woman almost as imposing as he, said, "I think it folly to expect me to stay."

"Show the flag," he said from the end of his imitation-Sheraton table. Everything about his mansion was meant to recall scenes from "home," as Lady Cunningham kept referring to her destination. It was her desire to leave on the first possible ship heading for England.

"It should never have been allowed to develop this far," his wife sniffed, in a dress suitable for a hunt ball in some very shabby county. "You mark my words: There's going to be no end of trouble now that the Japanese think they can push the Europeans around."

"They haven't pushed us around, my dear," her husband pointed out. "It's the Chinese they've shoved a bit."

The sheer stupidity of the night had made Morgan watch

himself carefully. Faced with their massive self-congratulation, the unbroken whining of the Europeans over their inconvenience, he knew he might easily become drunk and speak his mind. He'd made his excuses as soon as he could and headed for his own rooms, but the dance hall lights had held his attention, and he couldn't sleep. His old fears, the ones that woke him in the middle of the night dead sober, had returned. Outside the dance hall run by the little Russian who had no eyelids were the staff cars of the Japanese army that now held the Chinese city.

At the bar he ordered a double brandy and turned to watch the tiny Japanese piloting the Russian hostesses about the small floor. The Japanese looked like schoolboys, he thought, as they stared almost unbelievingly at the women that could be theirs. The women had the glazed look of people who were afraid not to look as though they were having a good time. The American dance music went on and on, unbroken, and the dancers moved around and around the floor until Morgan thought he was getting dizzy.

He went back out into the cold night. The snow had begun to fall again in heavier flakes, early for this part of the continent, according to Lady Cunningham, who was dismayed that she would have to return to her summer house yet again to make sure it was shut up tight for the winter. The Japanese advance on the city had made a mess of all her plans, and she wasn't at all sure she could catch up in time to put on a good show for Christmas.

At the Japanese legation he had eventually been brought before a Colonel Dohira. Evelyn had mentioned Dohira, and it had been very little trouble to sketch out for the colonel the new arrangement. He wondered what Evelyn would have made of his arrangement with Dohira, but when she turned up he would simply tell her that he had taken over her business. From the way she had spoken that last night, he had seen that she was about to abandon the venture.

He signaled to a taxi that stood waiting outside the club, ordered it back into the city. The Japanese presence here made him uneasy. His meeting with Dohira had been everything he had wanted. The colonel had understood about the shipment, and with Shanghai in their hands, there was no need for Tu at all now. Anyway, the word was that Tu would head for Macao, where the priest from the Red Sands had said they should sit out the conflict. He would come back one day, of course, but by then Morgan would have the support of the Japanese.

As the taxi came to the outskirts of the city he decided that he didn't want to go to the Cathay bar. He couldn't stand Murchison's cynicism, or his dire predictions. He would go instead to the house in the French quarter to wait for Evelyn. The silence of the night after the relentless bombardment made him uneasy. She would come back, he told himself; both of them would.

As he approached the house a figure moved out of the shadows and he thought it was a thief or looter. He reached for where his holster had been a day earlier and remembered that he was in evening clothes. By then the figure stood in the full moonlight at the top of the steps. "Hello," he said in a soft accent. American, Morgan thought. Yes, definitely; he could see the uniform under the long coat.

"What is it you want?" Morgan asked. The house seemed to be shut up. Where were the servants?

"I was looking for Evelyn Lezenski," the man said. Taller than Morgan, with blue eyes and fair hair, he carried his cap under his arm like a schoolboy.

"Who are you?" Morgan demanded.

"My name is Miles Foster."

Morgan was trying to understand where this American army officer could connect with Evelyn. As a shot in the dark he said, "You're from Manila."

There was a hesitation, then "Yes, that's right."

"What do you want with my sister?" Morgan asked.

"Oh." The officer looked surprised. "I didn't know she had a brother."

"We have been . . . apart for some years," Morgan said easily. The servants must have abandoned the house and grounds, he thought. They weren't expecting her back, then. He kept the knowledge of what that would mean on the horizon of his mind. "I'm taking care of her affairs now, though," he said. He walked up past the American and stood by the door, making a point of not inviting him in. "Could you tell me the nature of your business with her?"

"It was private," the American said finally. His eyes, seen close up in the full moonlight, were the eyes of a very young man, his face unlined. Morgan had the uncomfortable sensation of thinking that he might have been looking at himself twenty years ago.

"Then I'm afraid I can't help you," Morgan told him. He looked at the dark house. "She's gone, as you can see."

What he saw was what might have been pain in the young officer's eyes. "Yes," he said, "I see." He looked back into the garden, where the refugees had left a carpet of debris on the moonlit lawn. "Would you know where I can find her?"

"Traveling," Morgan said.

"To where?"

"She hadn't decided. A lot of civilians have left the city in the last days."

The man seemed reluctant to leave the porch. Morgan offered, "I'll tell her you were here if I see her."

The officer looked at him, now clearly in pain. "Yes," he said, "do that." He stepped off the stair and stood in the cold garden. He seemed to be searching for the right words.

"Is there any message?" Morgan asked, thinking that a message might clarify the officer's role, since the metal shipments came from America. The ships had already been rerouted by cable, and there wouldn't be any need to go to Manila anymore.

"No, no message," he said finally. He stood taller, braced himself, and said, "Goodbye, then."

"Goodbye," Morgan said.

He watched until the officer had reached the gate without turning, then went into the empty house. The looters had already gone through the place; the carpets and furniture were gone, the fixtures torn from the ceilings. The house was stripped to its shell.

He walked through and stood looking out at the banyan

tree in the back garden. The bird cages that had hung in the boughs of the tree had been opened; the birds were gone. Not set free, but for food, he thought. Well, they would have frozen tonight anyway.

"Traveling," he said to himself, thinking of the American officer. "Traveling."

They crossed the river before light. The city on the other bank was engulfed in flames. The light of the dawning day fought with the firelight reflecting off gathering clouds that came over the tops of the hills, higher than the squadrons of bombers that now came in wave after unbroken wave.

Crouched in the bottom of the sampan, Victoria saw how the water of the river ran as red as blood with the reflections of the fires. The Chinese gunboats stood guard downriver, but there in the distance was the white form of the *Idzuko*.

She held tight to Mr. Wei's hand as the fishermen poled them through the clogged river traffic, some boats burning, some already sunk by bombs gone astray.

The cries reached them through the booming of the guns and the loud steady roar of burning houses. There would be no true dawn today, she thought as Mr. Wei helped her wade through the icy shallows. The fisherman had set back again, fleeing civilians who stood on the bank imploring him. He disappeared into the smoke that clung like thick fog about the river.

The heat burned her flesh as she followed Mr. Wei away from the river. The fires stretched up two stories into the sky, firetrucks, long abandoned, standing amid the ruins.

"They are abandoning the city," Mr. Wei said, indicating the advancing column of Chinese trucks. The guards rode on the roof, shooting into the crowd that tried to cling to them as they fought their way through the debris toward the rear walls of the city.

As they listened they heard another sound, turned, and saw the flying boat that had sat in the river begin its run through the fire and smoke, straining to lift off across the flotilla of sunken boats. At the last moment the heavy plane lifted, tearing away the mast of the nearest boat. It seemed to hesitate, to turn slightly and drop, but then it gathered momentum and was gone, lost in the smoke and cinders that shrouded the other bank. The Japanese artillery stitched a pattern of explosions in the sky around it until it had vanished across the plain, headed north again.

"The generalissimo has gone. I cannot help you anymore," he told Victoria through the smoke. He looked a shadowy figure in his thin tunic.

The fear was steady now, as constant as the pumping of her heart.

"You will find your father at the academy," he said.

"Please . . ." she called, but he was gone into the burning city. She was alone. The column had passed, trailing a line of wailing civilian refugees who clutched at their children and their last belongings, running to be near the protection of the trucks as they crawled through the ruins.

Victoria headed up the bomb-pocked boulevards, coming upon a platoon of drunken Nationalist soldiers, sitting within a restaurant where ceiling and walls were gone, everything except a table and six chairs and the bar, untouched in the center of the room. She passed a bullock lying on its side, its throat torn out, the blood seeping away. The dead were everywhere, bodies in pieces and bodies in sweet repose that might have been sleep.

The planes came back as she neared the golden sandstone edifice of the academy. In lieu of sirens, the people fled the streets in every direction, screaming with silent, open mouths as the new wave of fire fell upon them. Victoria's eyes stung, and she thought that the city had been gassed, but then her tears flowed and her eyes cleared. She moved on, the tears still falling, making pale streaks on her face in the soot and dirt of the journey.

When she reached the academy she saw how the hospital wing was torn away, the façade fallen so that the five floors stood like an open doll's house hammered by a giant fist. The dead lay in their beds, exposed to the view of any who passed. She could see the operating rooms, the wards with their beds thrown all about by the force of the bomb that made the direct hit. She could hear screams of pain, but she pushed on into the courtyard, where the sentry boxes stood abandoned.

More trucks were drawn up in the courtyard. The Chinese soldiers were wide-eyed with the knowledge of their impending deaths as they loaded the trucks with the last of the supplies. The interior of the building was in chaos. She fought her way through the panic toward the stairs.

He was here, she thought, he was here. Taking hold of the first cadet who passed, she screamed her questions into his face. The boy, no more than sixteen, slapped her hard, throwing her to the floor as he ran for the door. She pulled herself to her feet, pressing against the wall as the cadets poured from the shelters below the building, the knowledge of the retreat spreading as fast as the fires outside. Now the bombing was steady again, an unbroken assault that shook the ground beneath the building.

She clutched an officer as he passed, refusing to be shaken loose as she screamed her questions. He pointed wildly upward at the stairs and then shoved her against the wall and fled out of the building that seemed to be rocking on its foundations. The floor was undulating beneath her feet, the steps rising and falling like waves underneath her.

On the second floor, the rooms stood open, already deserted. Where the wall was gone she could see the whole of the city spread out below, a garden of gold and red burning in the bright day just rising beyond the city. The building shook again, and she saw a new wave of bombers just coming over the ancient walls. She turned, fearful that the floor would give out beneath her and she would fall into the rubble of the courtyard below.

The figure was a hallucination, something from her dreams, striding through the smoke and fire with the fallen city burning behind him. She could remember how she had screamed in her nightmares as a child, and how he would come to her just as he came now, enormous, shadowy, comforting. She was going to die, here with the city all about her in flames and the death raining from the clouds, and she would never see him, never be able to tell him that she had loved him, never be able to . . .

"Victoria?"

The voice was the cruelest part of the dream, older but unchanged, deep, the voice of her father remembered through so many nights of loneliness and fear. Then he was before her, taking her against the filthy tunic of his Chinese uniform.

"Papa?"

"Yes, Papa," he said. "Papa."

"Papa," she said. "I've come for you."

"Oh, my dear, my dear," he said, kissing her head, stroking her so that she trembled less. "Oh, my darling child. It's too late for us. Come. Your mother is waiting for you."

Epilogue

A stranger came to her in her dreams, not every night, but on those nights when Victoria twisted on her cot, cried out, waking her mother, and then fell back into her tortured sleep.

The stranger would come to Evelyn as she tossed in her own half-waking sleep. Sometimes she thought he was Alex, and sometimes Fischer; but always, as he was about to be revealed, she woke with the memory of the terror to choke back her cries.

On one of these mornings, as the window in the shack showed her that it was almost light, she got up quietly so as not to wake Victoria and, taking a light cotton dressing gown, went out onto the broken porch. Here she thought that her mind had played another trick on her, like the tricks that it had played when they were taken from the hospital the month after the fall of Nanking, when reality and fantasy had mercifully blended and she no longer knew what was real and what was not.

At that time she had thought that the Red Cross workers who had found them had come to kill them; she had begged them to. It wasn't until much later, coming out of what then seemed merely a long, drugged sleep in Shanghai, that she understood. She and Victoria had survived, though Alex was dead.

"I was going to wait until light," Miles Foster said.

So he wasn't some fragment of memory called up by her treacherous mind. She couldn't answer.

"I didn't know where you were," he said. "I went to your house once, and your brother told me you were gone."

She never thought about Morgan. She stayed sane that way. "I was," she said then, her voice sounding harsh. "To Nanking."

She drew breath and watched while the large yellow butterflies came out of the fringe of banana trees about the compound. She liked to watch them play in the sunlight, dance among themselves with the joy of living. She would point them out to the silent Victoria and wonder what Fischer would have said if they had stopped here as she had begged him, if he had lived.

"I read the reports," he said softly.

She wanted to shout at him that nothing could be put into words to match what had happened there. You couldn't speak of half a million dead, of three hundred thousand women raped, of children dying in the streets, of what man's heart could conceive to torture others, of what his mind would allow, his hands and body do.

Instead she said, as quietly as she could because it was important that Victoria not wake, "We survived."

Yet as she said it she saw in her mind how Alex had died, hopelessly defending his wife and child, fallen with his maps scattered all about, the slash of the saber half severing his face from his skull.

She looked at him. "That's what's important, isn't it?"

It might have been a challenge, or it might have been confession.

"It's important who wins," he said, looking down at his brightly polished shoes. "We talked about that once, I remember. At Pasanjang Falls."

The cruelty of her own heart was that, at the memory his words recalled, she wanted to touch him again, to have him hold her, to erase everything that had happened since then.

She shuddered and looked at where the path from the compound vanished into the lush green jungle that sloped from the volcano's dormant ridge. Sometimes, when Victoria was calm, she would walk up the path to where Stevenson was buried and sit there trying to understand her life.

"We're going to win, you know," he said. "We will."

She heard the planes at night as they passed over the island on their way to the bases in Australia. At first Victoria would wake, whimpering at the sound, but eventually even she had come to understand that these planes wouldn't hurt them.

The warm sun was above the island now, the butterflies motes of gold rising and falling in the light. A brightly colored parrot flew quietly over the thatched hut and was gone down the length of the unseen valley.

"I'm sorry," he said. "I wanted you to know that."

She turned her back on him, unable to look at his fair hair, his clear brow, the eyes that at any moment might change before her gaze, a smile that might finally bring too much pain.

When she said nothing, he walked down the uneven steps to the grass, then hesitated, his cap in his hand, looking very young and strong. She would have cried then, tears for herself. And perhaps spoken words of accusation, of pain, of feelings that still startled her, of how she still dreamed of his touch, of how he had looked at her when they had first made love. . . .

He turned. "I wanted you to know," he said. "I only heard a week ago that you were here."

Then he walked away toward where the path led through the banana trees, and as the shadows of the trees wrapped themselves about him, making him less distinct, she saw that it was he who came to her in her dreams. He was the stranger. She saw how he turned his head exactly so, how his shoulders looked with the light behind them, how his head was cocked just as it always was when he was watching, thinking, considering. This was God's last cruel joke, that she could survive everything and then be undone by the memory of this man.

Just as she thought that she, too, would cry out as Victoria did in the darkness of the night, he turned to face her from across the ragged grass and started back. The light was behind him, and he seemed to grow larger before her eyes. She would have nothing to do with this, as she had vowed that, except for bringing Victoria back to health, she would have nothing more to do with any form of feeling, flesh, anything that could bridge the last seeds of humanity buried deep in her heart with the worst painful memories.

He stopped at the foot of the steps. Then, putting the cap of his uniform on the peeling rail, he put his arms about her again and held her gently close.

She could hate him. She could send him away. She could find bitter words to try to wound him. Instead, as he leaned down to kiss her, she began to cry. His lips touched hers, and life itself flowed through her limbs again as they clung together. The worst of the pain began its long slow ebb when he murmured close above her, "Forgive me."

THE MOST FABULOUS WOMEN'S FICTION COMES FROM POCKET BOOKS

___ **WIDEACRE** Philipa Gregory 64903/$4.95

___ **GARDEN OF SHADOWS** V.C. Andrews 64257/$4.95

___ **LUCKY** Jackie Collins 52496/$4.95

___ **HOLLYWOOD HUSBANDS** Jackie Collins 52501/$4.95

___ **HOLLYWOOD WIVES** Jackie Collins 62425/$4.95

___ **SOMETHING WONDERFUL** Judith McNaught 63779/$3.95

___ **LACE** Shirley Conran 54755/$4.50

___ **LACE II** Shirley Conran 54603/$3.95

___ **SMART WOMEN** Judy Blume 64990/$4.50

___ **FOREVER** Judy Blume 53225/$3.50

___ **WIFEY** Judy Blume 50189/$3.95

___ **ONCE AND ALWAYS** Judith McNaught 60633/$3.95

___ **TENDER TRIUMPH** Judith McNaught 66825/$3.95

___ **WHITNEY, MY LOVE** Judith McNaught 52808/$3.95

___ **DOUBLE STANDARDS** Judith McNaught 61455/$3.50

___ **DECEPTIONS** Judith Michael 63671/$4.95

___ **POSSESSIONS** Judith Michael 63672/$4.95

___ **PRIVATE AFFAIRS** Judith Michael 61968/$4.95

___ **SAVAGES** Shirley Conran 66320/$4.95

Simon & Schuster, Mail Order Dept. FWF
200 Old Tappan Rd., Old Tappan, N.J. 07675

POCKET BOOKS

Please send me the books I have checked above. I am enclosing $_____ (please add 75¢ to cover postage and handling for each order. N.Y.S. and N.Y.C. residents please add appropriate sales tax). Send check or money order—no cash or C.O.D.'s please. Allow up to six weeks for delivery. For purchases over $10.00 you may use VISA: card number, expiration date and customer signature must be included.

Name _____

Address _____

City _____ State/Zip _____

VISA Card No. _____ Exp. Date _____

Signature _____ 288-02

Judith Michael

America's New Sensational Novelist

Judith Michael knows what you want to read. She burst on to the scene with her bestselling novel DECEPTIONS, bringing us every woman's ultimate fantasy...to live another woman's life for just a little while. She swept us away with POSSESSIONS, a sophisticated, poignant novel of love and illusion, loyalty and betrayal, society and family. And now Judith Michael brings us into the seductive, secretive world of PRIVATE AFFAIRS.

___ **PRIVATE AFFAIRS**
61968/$4.95

___ **DECEPTIONS**
63671/$4.95

___ **POSSESSIONS**
63672/$4.95

POCKET BOOKS

Simon & Schuster, Mail Order Dept. JMP
200 Old Tappan Rd., Old Tappan, N.J. 07675

Please send me the books I have checked above. I am enclosing $_____ (please add 75¢ to cover postage and handling for each order. N.Y.S. and N.Y.C. residents please add appropriate sales tax). Send check or money order—no cash or C.O.D.'s please. Allow up to six weeks for delivery. For purchases over $10.00 you may use VISA: card number, expiration date and customer signature must be included.

Name _____

Address _____

City _____ State/Zip _____

VISA Card No. _____ Exp. Date _____

Signature _____ 755

Outstanding Bestsellers!

____ 62324	**LONESOME DOVE** Larry McMurtry	$4.95
____ 65764	**TEXASVILLE** Larry McMurtry	$4.95
____ 66320	**SAVAGES** Shirley Conran	$4.95
____ 64012	**FLIGHT OF THE INTRUDER** Stephen Coonts	$4.95
____ 66492	**SATISFACTION** Rae Lawrence	$4.95
____ 66159	**VEIL** Bob Woodward	$4.95
____ 43422	**CONTACT** Carl Sagan	$4.95
____ 64541	**WOMEN WHO LOVE TOO MUCH** Robin Norwood	$4.95
____ 52501	**HOLLYWOOD HUSBANDS** Jackie Collins	$4.95
____ 64445	**THE AWAKENING** Jude Deveraux	$4.50
____ 64745	**THE COLOR PURPLE** Alice Walker	$4.95
____ 64256	**FALLEN HEARTS** V. C. Andrews	$4.95
____ 63184	**CYCLOPS** Clive Cussler	$4.95
____ 64159	**A MATTER OF HONOR** Jeffrey Archer	$4.95
____ 64314	**FIRST AMONG EQUALS** Jeffrey Archer	$4.95
____ 64804	**DEEP SIX** Clive Cussler	$4.95
____ 63672	**POSSESSIONS** Judith Michael	$4.95
____ 63671	**DECEPTIONS** Judith Michael	$4.95
____ 55181	**WHEN ALL YOU EVER WANTED ISN'T ENOUGH** Harold S. Kushner	$4.50
____ 61963	**PRIVATE AFFAIRS** Judith Michael	$4.95
____ 64257	**GARDEN OF SHADOWS** V. C. Andrews	$4.95
____ 67386	**PRINCESS** Jude Deveraux	$4.50
____ 66218	**POSTCARDS FROM THE EDGE** Carrie Fisher	$4.50
____ 62412	**STINGER** Robert R. McCammon	$4.95
____ 66063	**DIRK GENTLY'S HOLISTIC DECTECTIVE AGENCY** Douglas Adams	$4.50

Simon & Schuster, Mail Order Dept. OBB
200 Old Tappan Rd., Old Tappan, N.J. 07675

POCKET BOOKS

Please send me the books I have checked above. I am enclosing $_____ (please add 75¢ to cover postage and handling for each order. N.Y.S. and N.Y.C. residents please add appropriate sales tax). Send check or money order--no cash or C.O.D.'s please. Allow up to six weeks for delivery. For purchases over $10.00 you may use VISA: card number, expiration date and customer signature must be included.

Name _____

Address _____

City _____ State/Zip _____

VISA Card No. _____ Exp. Date _____

Signature _____ 296-07